MIRROR IMAGE

Tom Clancy's Op-Center

MIRROR IMAGE

Created by Tom Clancy and Steve Pieczenik

Thorndike Press • Chivers Press
Thorndike, Maine USA   Bath, Avon, England

This Large Print edition is published by Thorndike Press, USA and by Chivers Press, England.

Published in 1996 in the U.S. by arrangement with The Berkley Publishing Group.

Published in 1996 in the U.K. by arrangement with HarperCollins Publishers.

U.S.   Hardcover   0-7862-0617-9 (Basic Series Edition)
U.S.   Softcover   0-7862-0618-7
U.K.   Hardcover   0-7451-7990-8 (Windsor Large Print)
U.K.   Softcover   0-7451-3791-1 (Paragon Large Print)

Thorndike Large Print ® Basic Series.

The text of this Large Print edition is unabridged.
Other aspects of the book may vary from the original edition.

Set in 16 pt. News Plantin by Minnie B. Raven.

Printed in the United States on permanent paper.

British Library Cataloguing in Publication Data available

Library of Congress Cataloging in Publication Data

Clancy, Tom, 1947–
    Tom Clancy's op-center : mirror image / created by
Tom Clancy and Steve Pieczenik.
        p.   cm.
    ISBN 0-7862-0617-9 (lg. print : hc)
    ISBN 0-7862-0618-7 (lg. print : sc)
    1. Large type books. I. Pieczenik, Steve R.   II. Title.
[PS3553.L245T66   1996]
813'.54—dc20   95-48825

Acknowledgments

We would like to thank Jeff Rovin for his creative ideas and his invaluable contribution to the preparation of the manuscript. We would also like to acknowledge the assistance of Martin H. Greenberg, Larry Segriff, Robert Youdelman, Esq., and the wonderful people at The Putnam Berkley Group, including Phyllis Grann, David Shanks, and Elizabeth Beier. As always, we would like to thank Robert Gottlieb of The William Morris Agency, our agent and friend, without whom this book would never have been conceived. But most importantly, it is for you, our readers, to determine how successful our collective endeavor has been.

— Tom Clancy and Steve Pieczenik

PROLOGUE

Friday, 5:50 P.M., St. Petersburg

"Pavel," said Piotr Volodya, "I don't understand."

Pavel Odina squeezed the steering wheel tightly. He looked unpleasantly at the man sitting next to him in the passenger's seat of the van. "You don't understand *what*, Piotr?"

"You forgive the French," Piotr replied, scratching a woolly sideburn, "so why not the Germans? Both of them have invaded Mother Russia."

Pavel frowned. "If you can't see the difference, Piotr, you're a fool."

"That's not an answer," said Ivan, one of four men seated in the back.

"It happens to be *true*," grinned Eduard, who was seated beside him, "but Ivan is right. It isn't an answer."

Pavel shifted gears. This was the part of the nightly, half-hour commute to the Nepokorennykh Prospekt apartments that he hated most. Just two minutes out from the Hermitage, they had to slow as they neared the bottleneck at the Neva River. They were mired in traffic while his political nemeses were proceeding at full speed.

Pavel pulled a neatly rolled cigarette from his shirt pocket and Piotr lit it for him.

"Thanks, Piotr."

"You still haven't answered me," Piotr said.

"I will," Pavel insisted, "when we've gotten onto the bridge. I can't think and curse at the same time."

Pavel swung the van suddenly from the center lane to the left lane, jolting the men to the other side. Having fallen asleep when they left the Hermitage, both Oleg and Konstantin awoke with a jolt.

"You're too impatient, Pavel," Ivan said. "What are you in such a rush to get home to, your wife? Since when?"

"Very funny," Pavel said. The truth was, he wasn't hurrying to get *to* anything. He was in a rush to get away from the pressure, away from the deadline that had consumed them for months on end. Now that it was nearly over, he couldn't wait to go back to designing computer animation software for Mosfilm.

Shifting gears again, Pavel zigzagged between the rows of small Zaporozhets-968s, with their sputtering forty-three-horsepower engines, and the larger, five-seat Volga M-124s. There was also a smattering of foreign cars, though only government officials and black marketeers drove them; no one else could afford to. He and his comrades wouldn't even be driving this van if the TV studio hadn't provided it. The powerful Swiss-made vehicle was the only thing he would miss.

No, that isn't true, he thought as he glanced west. He savored the sight of the Peter and Paul Fortress on the opposite banks of the Neva as the setting sun glinted off its tall, graceful spires.

He would also miss St. Petersburg. He would miss the beauty of these blazing orange sunsets on the Gulf of Finland, the calming flow of the blue waters of the Neva, the Fontanka, and the Yekateringofki rivers, and the simple splendor of the many canals. Though the waters were still somewhat dirty from years of Communist neglect, they were no longer thick with foul-smelling industrial waste as they wound through the heart of the ancient city, Russia's Venice. He would miss the majesty of the ruby-red Belozersky Palace, the gilt interiors of the Alexander Nevsky Chapel, where he sometimes went to pray, the towering golden onion domes

9

of Catherine the Great's palace, and the peaceful gardens and cascading fountains of Peter the Great's palace, Petrodvorets. He would miss the sleek, white hydrofoils that skimmed along the Neva looking like something from a science fiction novel by Stanislaw Lem — and he would miss the magnificent battleships that dwarfed them, coming and going to the Nakhimov Naval School on Aptekarsky Island in the Neva.

And, of course, he would miss the incomparable Hermitage. Though they weren't supposed to wander in the museum, he always took time to do just that when Colonel Rossky was occupied. Even if someone did see him day after day, he was supposed to be an employee there. No one would give it a thought. Besides, a religious man can't be put among the likes of Rembrandt's *Descent from the Cross*, or Carracci's *Lamentation of Christ*, or his favorite, the School of Ribalta's *St. Vincent in a Dungeon*, and not be expected to look. Especially when he felt such a kinship to the trapped but resolute St. Vincent.

But he would be happy to get away from the work itself, from the stress and the seven-day workweeks and especially the watchful eyes of Colonel Rossky. He had served under the bastard in Afghanistan, and cursed the fate that had brought them back together for the past eighteen months.

As he always did when he reached the bridge of the Kirovsky Prospekt, Pavel made his way to the outside lane, with its low concrete barricade and more intrepid motorists. He breathed easier as he settled in among the faster-moving vehicles.

"You want an answer?" Pavel asked, drawing hard on his cigarette.

"To which question?" Ivan joked. "The one about your wife?"

Pavel scowled. "I'll tell you the difference between the Germans and the French. The French followed Napoleon because they were hungry. They've always put comfort before decency."

"What about the Resistance?" Piotr asked.

"A freak. A reflexive twitch of the corpse. If the Resistance in France had been as strong as the Russian Resistance in Stalingrad, Paris would never have fallen."

Pavel applied pressure to the pedal to keep a Volkswagen from cutting right and getting in front of him. *Black marketeer,* he guessed from the surly look of the woman. Pavel glanced in the mirror as a truck pulled behind him from the center lane.

"The French are not evil," Pavel continued, "but the Germans followed Hitler because they're still Vandals at heart. Give

11

them time. Their factories will once again be turning out tanks and bombers, I guarantee it."

Piotr shook his head. "What about Japan?"

"Also bastards," said Pavel. "If Dogin wins the election, he'll watch them too."

"And is paranoia a sensible reason to vote for any man for president?"

"It's not paranoia to fear old enemies. It's caution."

"It's provocation!" Piotr said. "You don't get behind a man because he's vowed to strike the Germans at the first sign of re-militarization."

"That was only one reason." The road ahead cleared and Pavel sped up as he crossed the wide, dark river. The men shut the windows against the sharp wind. "Dogin promised to revitalize the space program, which will strengthen the economy. He'll build more studios like ours, and constructing new factories along the Trans-Siberian Railroad will provide cheap goods and new housing."

"And where will the money come from to achieve these wonders?" Piotr asked. "Our little nest back there cost twenty-five *billion* rubles! Do you really believe that if Dogin wins he can cut enough fat from the government and from foreign adventures?"

Pavel blew out smoke and nodded.

Piotr frowned. He cocked a thumb over his shoulder. "That isn't what I overheard back there. Number Two was talking to an aide about the thieves-in-law. *That's* where he plans to get the money, and it's a dangerous association to — "

Pavel reacted instinctively as the Volkswagen suddenly angled in front of him. He pushed down hard on the brake and spun the wheel to the right. As he did so, he heard a *pop* and thick green smoke began pouring from under the dashboard.

"*What is it — ?*" Piotr coughed.

"*Open a window!*" one of the men yelled from the back as they all began to gag.

But Pavel had already fallen against the wheel, barely conscious. There was no one steering as the truck struck them from behind.

The Volkswagen was partly in the right lane as the truck drove the van into it. The left side of the van's front fender struck the car, skidding and sparking along its right side. Pointed toward the side of the bridge, the van hit the low concrete barrier and rode up and over, propelled by the truck. The right tire exploded, the axle hooked over the top of the barricade, and the van plunged nose-first into the choppy river.

There was a hiss as it struck the water,

the van standing upright for a long moment before falling over on its back. Steam and air bubbles rose from the sides, mixing with the dissipating green smoke as the van bobbed belly-up on the surface of the river. The rest of the van was entirely submerged.

The burly trucker and the young blonde woman who had been driving the Volkswagen were the first ones to reach the shattered railing. They were joined by other motorists who scurried from their cars.

Neither the man nor the woman said a word to each other. They just watched as the van drifted to the southwest, twisting slowly in the current, the air bubbles dwindling and the smoke now just a faint wisp. The vehicle was already too far away for anyone to dive in and attempt to look for survivors.

The two drivers assured those who asked that they were all right. Then they made their way back to their vehicles to await the police.

No one had seen the truck driver drop a small, rectangular box in the river as he turned away.

ONE

Saturday, 10:00 A.M., Moscow

Tall, powerfully built Minister of the Interior Nikolai Dogin sat behind the centuries-old oak desk in his office in the Kremlin. There was a computer in the center of the heavy, age-toned desk. To his right was a black telephone and a small, framed photograph of his parents sat on his left. The snapshot had a horizontal crease in the center. It had been folded by his father so he could carry it in his shirt pocket during the War.

Dogin's silver-gray hair was brushed straight back. His cheeks were sunken and his dark eyes looked tired. His plain, brown GUM department store suit was wrinkled, and his light brown shoes were scuffed — a careful, studied rumpledness that had worked so well for so many years.

But not this week, he thought bitterly.

For the first time in thirty years of public service, his man-of-the-people image had failed him. With his characteristic intensity, he had given his people the nationalism they had said they wanted. He voiced renewed pride in the military, and fanned suspicion of old enemies. Yet the people had turned on him.

Dogin knew why, of course. His rival, Kiril Zhanin, had cast out a tattered net one last, glorious time to try and snare the flounder of Old Peter's fairy tale, the fish-of-the-sea that would make every wish come true.

Capitalism.

While Dogin waited for his assistant, he looked past the seven men seated before him. His dark eyes were focused on the walls, on a history of the success of totalitarianism.

Like his desk, the walls reeked of history. They were covered with ornately framed maps, some of them centuries old, maps of Russia under different Czars going back to the reign of Ivan. Dogin's tired eyes took them all in, from a faded vellum map painted, it was said, with the blood of captured Teutonic Knights, to a cloth map of the Kremlin which had been sewn inside the pant leg of a murdered German assassin.

The world as it was, he thought as his eyes settled upon a map of the Soviet Union that Gherman S. Titov had carried into space in 1961. *The world as it will be again.*

The seven men sitting on sofas and arm-

16

chairs were also drawn with age. Most of them were fifty or older, some of them were over sixty. Most wore suits, some had on uniforms. None spoke. The silence was broken only by the hum of the fan in the back of the computer — and then, finally, by a knock on the door.

"Come in."

Dogin felt his heart sink as the door opened and a fresh-faced young man stepped in. There was a profound sadness in the youth's eyes, and Dogin knew what that meant.

"Well?" Dogin demanded.

"I'm sorry," the young man said softly, "but it's official. I reviewed the figures myself."

Dogin nodded. "Thank you."

"Shall I make the arrangements?"

Dogin nodded again and the young man backed from the office. He shut the door quietly as he left.

Now Dogin looked at the men. Like him, their expressions hadn't changed. "This was not unexpected," said the Minister of the Interior. He moved the photograph of his parents closer, running the back of his fingers down the glass. He seemed to be speaking to them. "Foreign Minister Zhanin has won the election. It's the time, you know. Everyone's giddy with liberty, but it's liberty without responsibility, freedom without sanity, experimentation without caution. Russia has elected a president who wants to create a new currency, make our economy a slave to what we can sell abroad. Eliminate the black market by making the rubles and goods it holds utterly worthless. Eliminate political rivals by making it impossible to oust him lest it upset foreign markets. Eliminate the military as an adversary by paying the Generals more money to serve his policies than to protect Mother Russia. 'Like Germany and Japan,' he tells us, 'an economically strong Russia needs fear no enemy.' " Dogin's eyes narrowed as he looked at his father's image. "For seventy years we feared no enemy. Your hero Stalin did not rule Russia, he ruled the world! His name itself came from *stal* — steel. Our people were made of it then. And they responded to power. Today, they seek comfort and respond to audacity and empty promises."

"Welcome to democracy, my dear Nikolai," said General Viktor Mavik, a barrel-chested man with a booming voice. "Welcome to a world in which NATO courts the Czech Republic, Hungary, Poland, nations of the former Warsaw Pact, to join the Western alliance without so much as consulting us."

Deputy Finance Minister Yevgeny Grovlev

leaned forward, his sharp chin resting on his thumbs, his slender fingers steepled under his hooked nose. "We must be careful not to overreact," he said. "Zhanin's reforms won't happen fast enough. The people will turn on him faster than they did on Gorbachev and Yeltsin."

"My adversary is young but not stupid," Dogin replied. "He wouldn't have made promises without agreements being in place. And when he pulls them off, the Germans and Japanese will have what they failed to obtain in World War II. The United States will own what it failed to get during the Cold War. In one way or another, they will all possess Mother Russia."

Dogin turned his eyes to one more map: the map of Russia and Eastern Europe on his computer screen. He pressed a key and Eastern Europe grew larger. Russia vanished.

"A keystroke of history and we're gone," he said.

"Only by our inactivity," said lanky Grovlev.

"Yes," Dogin agreed. "By our inactivity." The room was growing stuffy and he dabbed the moisture on his upper lip with a tissue. "The people have thrown off their mistrust of foreigners for the promise of wealth. But we'll show them that isn't the way." He looked out at the men in the room. "The fact that you or your candidates lost the election shows how confused our people have become. But the fact that you are here this morning indicates that you want to do something about it."

"We do," General Mavik said, running a finger inside his collar. "And we trust your abilities. You were a strong mayor in Moscow and a loyal Communist in the Politburo. But in our first meeting you told us very little of what you planned if the old guard failed to retake the Kremlin. Well, the old guard has failed. Now I would like some details."

"So would I," said Air Force General Dhaka. His gray eyes glared from beneath a heavy brow. "Any one of us would make a formidable opposition leader. Why should we back you? You promised us a cooperative action with Ukraine. So far, we've only seen a few Russian infantry maneuvers near the border which Zhanin himself quickly approved. Even if joint maneuvers take place, what does that accomplish? Old Soviet brothers are reunited, and the West trembles a little. How will that help us to rebuild Russia? If we're to join you we must have specifics."

Dogin looked at the General. Dhaka's full cheeks were flushed, his pendulous chin raw where it met his tightly knotted tie. The

20

Minister knew that the specifics would send most of them rallying behind Mavik or even running to Zhanin.

He looked at each of the men in turn. In most faces he saw conviction and strength, while in others — Mavik and Grovlev in particular — he saw interest but wariness. Their hesitation angered him because he was the only one who offered Russia salvation. Yet he remained calm.

"You want specifics?" Dogin asked. He typed a command on the computer keyboard then swung the monitor so it faced the seven men. As the hard disk hummed, the Interior Minister looked at his father's picture. The elder Dogin had been a decorated soldier during the War, and one of Stalin's most trusted bodyguards afterward. He once told his son that during the War he had learned to carry only one thing with him: the country's flag. Wherever he was, in any circumstance, in any danger, it would always find him a friend or ally.

When the disk drive fell silent, Dogin and five men rose at once. Mavik and Grovlev exchanged suspicious looks, then slowly got to their feet. Both men saluted.

"This is how I plan to rebuild Russia," Dogin said. He came around the desk and pointed to the image that filled the computer monitor, a yellow star, hammer, and sickle on a red field — the old Soviet flag. "By reminding people of their duty. Patriots will not hesitate to do whatever is necessary, whatever the plan and regardless of the cost."

The men sat down, save for Grovlev.

"We're all patriots," said the Finance Minister, "and I resent the theatrics. If I'm to put my resources in your hands, I want to know how they'll be used. For a coup? A second revolution? Or don't you trust us with this information, Mr. Minister?"

Dogin looked at Grovlev. He couldn't tell him everything. He couldn't tell him about his plans for the military or his involvement with the Russian mafia. Most Russians thought that they were still a provincial peasant people without a worldview. Upon hearing his plans, Grovlev might back down or decide to support Zhanin.

Dogin said, "Mr. Minister, I don't trust you."

Grovlev stiffened.

"And from your questions," Dogin continued, "it's obvious you don't trust me either. I intend to earn that trust through deeds, and you must do the same. Zhanin knows who his enemies are, and now he has the power of the presidency. He may offer you a post or an appointment you may be tempted to take. And you might then be required to work against me. For the next seventy-two hours, I must ask you to be patient."

"Why seventy-two hours?" asked the young, blue-eyed Ministry of Security Assistant Director Skule.

"That's how long it will take for my command center to become operational."

Skule froze. "Seventy-two hours? You can't mean St. Petersburg."

Dogin nodded once.

"You control *that?*"

He nodded again.

Skule exhaled and the other men looked at him. "My most sincere compliments, Minister. That puts the entire world in your hands."

"Quite literally," Dogin grinned. "Just like General Secretary Stalin."

"Excuse me," said Grovlev, "but once again I'm on the outside looking in. Minister Dogin, what exactly is this 'thing' you control?"

"The St. Petersburg Operations Center," Dogin replied, "the most sophisticated reconnaissance and communications facility in Russia. With it, we can access everything from satellite views of the world to electronic communications. The Center also has its own field personnel for 'surgical strike' operations."

Grovlev seemed confused. "Are you talking about the television station at the Hermitage?"

"Yes," Dogin said. "It's a front, Minister Grovlev. Your ministry approved the finances for an operational facade, a working TV studio. But the money for the underground complex came from my department. And the funding continues to come from the Interior Ministry." Dogin thumbed his chest. "From me."

Grovlev sat back down. "You've been planning this operation for quite some time."

"For over two years," Dogin replied. "We go on-line Monday night."

"And this Center," said Dhaka. "It's your command post for more than simply spying on Zhanin during these seventy-two hours."

"Very much more than spying," said Dogin.

"But you won't tell us what!" Grovlev huffed. "You want our cooperation but *you* won't cooperate!"

Dogin said ominously, "You want me to confide in you, Mr. Minister? Fair enough. For the past six months, my man in the Operations Center has been using personnel as well as the electronics that were already installed to watch all of my potential allies as well as my rivals. We've collected a great deal of information about graft, liaisons, and" — he glared at Grovlev — "unusual personal interests. I'll be happy to share this information with you collectively or individually, now or later."

Some of the men moved uneasily in their chairs. Grovlev sat rock-still.

"You bastard," Grovlev growled.

"Yes," said Dogin, "I am that. A bastard who will get the job done." The Interior Minister looked at his watch, then walked over to Grovlev and stared down into his narrow eyes. "I must leave now, Minister. I have a meeting with the new President. There are congratulations to tender, some papers for him to sign. But within twelve hours, you'll be able to judge for yourself whether I'm working for vanity, or" — he pointed to the flag on the monitor — "for this."

With a nod to the silent assembly, Minister Dogin left the office. His aide in tow, he hurried to a car that would take him to Zhanin and then back here. And alone, with the door closed, he would place the call that would set events in motion that would change the world.

TWO

Saturday, 10:30 A.M., Moscow

Keith Fields-Hutton burst into his room in the newly renovated Rossiya Hotel, tossed his key on the dresser, and ran into the bathroom. On the way, he stooped and grabbed two curled pieces of fax paper that had fallen from the dresser-top machine he'd brought with him.

This was the part of his job he hated the most. Not the danger, which was at times considerable; not the protracted hours of sitting in airports waiting for Aeroflot flights that never came, which was typical; and not the long weeks of being away from Peggy, which were most frustrating of all.

What he hated most were all those goddamn cups of tea he had to drink.

When he came to Moscow once a month, Fields-Hutton always stayed at the Rossiya, just east of the Kremlin, and took long breakfasts in their elegant café. It gave him time to read the newspapers from front to back.

More importantly, constantly draining his teacup gave Andrei, the waiter, a reason to come over with refills and three, four, or sometimes five fresh tea bags. Attached to the string of every bag was a label that bore the name *Chashka Chai* on the outside. Inside each tag was a circular spot of microfilm which Fields-Hutton pocketed when no one was looking. Most of the time, the maître d' *was* looking, so Fields-Hutton had to re-cover the film when other patrons came into the restaurant, distracting him.

Andrei was one of Peggy's finds. His name came from a list of former soldiers, and she later learned that he had originally intended to make money working in a West Siberian oil settlement. But he was wounded in Af-ghanistan and, after back surgery, he could no longer lift heavy gear. After Gorbachev, he could no longer afford to live. He was the perfect man to shuttle data between deeply buried operatives whose names he didn't know, whose faces he never saw, and Fields-Hutton. If Andrei was ever caught, only Fields-Hutton was at risk . . . and that came with the territory.

Despite what many people outside the in-telligence community believed, the KGB hadn't collapsed with the fall of Communism. To the contrary, as the new Ministry of

Security, it was more pervasive than ever. The agency had simply changed from an army of professionals into an even larger force of civilian freelancers. These operatives were paid for each solid lead they turned in. As a result, veterans and amateurs alike were looking everywhere for spies. Peggy called it a Russian version of *Entertainment Tonight*, with stringers everywhere. And she was right. The quarry was foreigners instead of celebrities, but the goal was the same: to report on furtive or suspicious activities. And because so many businesspeople assumed there was no longer a threat, they stumbled into trouble by helping Russian associates exchange rubles for dollars or marks, by bringing in jewelry or expensive clothes for the black market, or by spying on rival foreign companies doing business here. Instead of being prosecuted, foreign prisoners were typically allowed to buy their way out of trouble. Fields-Hutton joked that the ministry spent less time protecting national security than it did overseeing commerce. Japanese manufacturers alone paid Russian agents hundreds of millions of rubles a year to watch for competitors who might be keeping too close an eye on their activities in Russia. It was even rumored that the Japanese had put over 50 million rubles into the failed presidential bid of Interior Minister Nikolai Dogin to help protect the country from an influx of foreign investors.

The spy business was alive and well, and after seven years British agent Fields-Hutton was still in the thick of it.

Fields-Hutton had graduated from Cambridge with an advanced degree in Russian literature and a desire to become a novelist. The Sunday after his graduation, he was sitting in a coffeehouse in Kensington — reading Dostoevsky's *Notes from the Underground,* as it happened — when a woman in an adjoining booth turned around and asked, "How would you like to learn more about Russia?" She laughed, then said, "A great deal more?"

That was his introduction to British Intelligence, and to Peggy. Later, he learned that DI6 has a long association with Cambridge, going back to World War II and Ultra, the top-secret project to decipher the legendary German Enigma code.

Fields-Hutton went for a walk with Peggy and agreed to a meeting with her superiors. Within a year, DI6 had set him up as a comic book publisher who was buying stories and art from Russian cartoonists for publication in Europe. That gave him a reason to make constant trips with large, well-stocked portfolios and stacks of magazines, as well as videocassettes and toys featuring characters the Russians had designed. From the start, Fields-Hutton was amazed at how the gift of a superhero mug or bath towel or sweatshirt won him favors from airline employees, hotel workers, and even the police. Whether they turned around and sold the items on the black market or gave them to their kids, barter was a powerful tool in Russia.

With all the magazines and toys he carried, it was easy to hide the microfilm — sometimes wrapped around the staple of a comic book, other times rolled inside a hollow claw on the hand of a Tigerman action figure. Ironically, the comic book operation had taken on a life of its own, and British Intelligence was actually collecting a handsome royalty from the licenses. The organization's charter prohibited money-making ventures — "This is, after all, the government," Winston Churchill once told an agent who wanted to sell a code-breaking toy. However, then-Prime Minister John Major and the Parliament agreed to let the comic book profits go to social programs to help the families of slain or disabled British operatives.

Though he had come to love the comic book business, and decided he would become a novelist when he retired — with more than enough material for realistic thrillers — Fields-Hutton's real job with British Intelligence was to keep an eye on both foreign and domestic construction projects in Eastern Russia. Secret rooms, hidden bugs, and sub-subbasements were still being built and, when found and eavesdropped on, they provided a wealth of intelligence. His present contacts — Andrei and Leon, an illustrator who lived in an apartment in St. Petersburg — provided him with blueprints and on-site photographs of all the new buildings going up and renovations taking place on old ones within his territory.

After leaving the bathroom, Fields-Hutton sat on the edge of the bed, took the tea-bag tags from his pocket, and tore them open. Carefully, he removed each circular piece of microfilm and slipped them in turn into a high-powered magnifier — which, he told customs, he brought to look at transparencies of paintings for cover art. *("Yes, sir, I have many more Grim Ghost baseball caps than I need. Of course you can have one for your son. Why don't you take some for his friends as well?")*

What he saw in one of the photographs could be related to a small article he'd noticed in today's newspaper. The picture showed tarpaulins being rolled into a service elevator at the Hermitage. Pictures taken on successive days showed large crates of artwork being brought in as well.

That shouldn't have aroused any suspicion. Construction was taking place throughout the museum to modernize and expand it in honor of the city's tercentenary in 2003. Moreover, the art museum was right on the Neva River. It was possible the walls were being lined with tarpaulin to protect the artwork from moisture.

But Leon had faxed him two sheets, and according to the entirely symbolic Captain Legend comic strip on the first sheet, the superhero had flown to Hermes' World — that is, Leon had gone to the Hermitage — a week after the photos were taken. He reported that no construction using tarpaulin was taking place on any of the three floors in any of the three buildings. As for the crates, though artwork was always being loaned to the museum, no new pieces had gone on display, nor had any new exhibits been announced: with sections closed off for the modernization, exhibit space was at a premium. Fields-Hutton would have DI6 check to see if any museums or private collectors had shipped anything to the Hermitage recently, though he doubted they'd find anything.

Then there were the hours of the workers who brought the tarpaulins and crates to the elevators. According to Leon's strip, the men — the Hera's World slaves who brought the weapons and food to a secret base — went downstairs in the morning and didn't come back until early in the evening. He had been watching two in particular, who came there day after day and whom he would follow if DI6 thought it might help. Though they could very well be working on reno- vations, it was also possible they were simply using those to mask secret activity taking place underground.

All of which dovetailed with the accident reported in this morning's newspaper, and also described in Leon's second fax page. Yesterday, six museum employees heading home from work had skidded off the Kirovsky Prospekt into the Neva River, where all of them drowned. Leon had gone to the crash site, and his rough cover sketch for Captain Legend told him more than the two-inch article had reported. It showed the hero help- ing slaves from a rocket that had crash-landed in a pool of quicksand. The color notation for the smoke rising from the quicksand said "Green." *Chlorine.*

Were the men gassed? Was the truck that hit them off the bridge sent to do just that to cover the fact that the men were mur- dered?

The accident might be a coincidence, but intelligence work couldn't afford to overlook any possibility. The signs pointed to something unusual going on in St. Petersburg, and Fields-Hutton wanted to find out what it was.

Faxing Leon's artwork to his office in London, Fields-Hutton included a note that ordered them to advance him twenty-seven pounds — meaning they were to look at page seven of today's *Dyen* — and that he was going to St. Petersburg to meet with the artist about this cover design.

"I think we're onto something here," he wrote. "My feeling is, if the writer can come up with a connection between the pool of quicksand and the underground mines of Hera's World, we'll have ourselves a fascinating story line. I'll let you know what Leon thinks."

After receiving an okay from London, Fields-Hutton packed his camera, slender vanity kit, Walkman, and artwork and toys into a shoulder bag, hurried to the lobby, and took a taxicab two miles to the northeast. At the St. Petersburg Station on Krasnoprudnaya he bought his ticket for the four-hundred-mile ride, then settled in on a hard bench to await the next train leaving for the ancient city on the Gulf of Finland.

THREE

Saturday, 12:20 P.M., Washington, D.C.

During the Cold War, the nondescript, two-story building located near the Naval Reserve flight line at Andrews Air Force Base was a ready room, a staging area for crack flight crews. In the event of a nuclear attack, it would have been their job to evacuate key officials from Washington, D.C.

But the ivory-colored building was not an obsolete monument to the Cold War. The lawns were a little neater now, and there were gardens in the dirt patches where soldiers used to drill. Concrete flower pots had been erected on all sides to prevent anyone from getting too close with a car bomb. And the people who worked here didn't arrive in jeeps and Hughes Defenders, but in station wagons, Volvos, and the occasional Saab and BMW.

The seventy-eight full-time employees who worked here now were employed by the National Crisis Management Center. They were handpicked tacticians, generals, diplomats, intelligence analysts, computer specialists, psychologists, reconnaissance experts, environmentalists, attorneys, and even media manipulators, or spin doctors. The NCMC shared another forty-two support personnel with the Department of Defense and the CIA, and commanded a twelve-person tactical strike team known as Striker, which was based at the nearby Quantico FBI Academy.

The charter of the NCMC was unlike any other in the history of the United States. Over a two year period, the group had spent more than $100 million on equipment and hi-tech modifications, turning the former ready room into an operations center designed to interface with the Central Intelligence Agency, National Security Agency, White House, State Department, Department of Defense, Defense Intelligence Agency, National Reconnaissance Office, and Intelligence and Threat Analysis Center. But after a shakedown period of six months, in which they handled both domestic and international crises, "Op-Center," as it was familiarly called, now had parity with those agencies — and then some. Director Paul Hood reported to President Michael Lawrence himself, and what had started as an information clearinghouse with SWAT capabilities now had the singular capacity to monitor, initiate, and manage operations worldwide.

They were a unique mix of old professionals who took a methodical, hands-on, agents-in-the-field approach to intelligence, and fair-haired boys who reveled in hi-tech and bold strokes. And on top of the patchwork tapestry was Paul Hood. Though Hood was not quite a saint, his selflessness had caused his jaded coworkers to dub him "Pope" Paul. He was scrupulously honest, despite having been a hotshot banker during the Reagan terms. He was also exceedingly low-key even though he'd served as the Mayor of Los Angeles for two years. Hood was constantly schooling his team in the new art of crisis management. He saw this as an alternative to the traditional Washingtonian responses that leaned toward inactivity or all-out war. In Los Angeles he had pioneered the art of slicing problems into manageable segments and handing each to professionals who worked closely with one another. It had worked effectively in Los Angeles and it was also working here, though it went against the prevailing "I'm in charge here" mind-set of Washington. His number two man, Mike Rodgers, once told him that they'd probably find more adversaries in the nation's capital than anywhere else in the world, since bureau chiefs, agency directors, and elected officials would view Op-Center's management style as a threat to their fiefdoms. And many of them wouldn't stop at trying to undermine Op-Center's effectiveness.

"Washingtonians are like zombies," Rodgers had said, *"able to rise from the politically dead as times and moods change — look at Nixon, at Jimmy Carter. As a result, rivals don't just try to destroy careers, they try to ruin lives. And if that's not enough, they turn on families and friends as well."*

But Hood didn't care. Their charter was to look after the security of the United States, not to advance the reputation of Op-Center or its employees, and he took that mission very seriously indeed. He also believed that if they did the job they were supposed to do, their "rivals" couldn't lay a glove on them.

At the moment, Ann Farris didn't see the hotshot or the politician or the "Pope" sitting in the Director's chair. Her dark rust eyes saw the awkward young boy in the man. Despite the strong jaw, wavy black hair, and steely dark hazel eyes, Hood looked like a kid who wished he could stay here in Washington and play with his friends and spy satellites and field operatives rather than go on vacation with his family. If the kids didn't miss their old friends, and the move east hadn't put such a strain on his marriage, Ann knew that Paul wouldn't be going.

The forty-three-year-old Director of Op-Center was sitting in his large office at the high-security facility. Deputy Director General Mike Rodgers was seated in an armchair to the left of the desk, and Press Officer Farris was sitting on the sofa to the right. Hood's itinerary for his trip to Southern California was on the computer.

"Sharon wrests a week off from her boss, Andy McDonnell, who says his cable show can't live without her cooking-healthy segment," Hood said, "and we end up at Bloopers, the antithesis of healthy eating. Anyway, that's where we'll be the first night. The kids saw it on MTV, and if you page me there I probably won't hear it."

Ann leaned forward and patted the back of his hand, her dazzling white smile even brighter than the yellow designer kerchief she wore in her long brown hair.

"I bet if you let your hair down you'll have a blast," she said. "I read about Bloopers in *Spin*. Order a pickledog and French-fried pie. You'll love them."

Hood snickered. "How about putting that on our agency seal? 'Op-Center — making the world safe for pickle-flavored hot dogs.'"

39

"I'll have to ask Lowell what that would be in Latin," Ann smiled. "We'd want it to at least *sound* lofty."

Rodgers sighed and both Hood and Ann glanced over. The two-star General was sitting with his leg across a knee, shaking it briskly.

"Sorry, Mike," Hood said. "I'm letting my hair down a little too early."

"It's not that," Rodgers said. "You're just not talking my language."

As a press director, Ann was accustomed to listening for the truth behind soft-pedaled words. She detected both criticism and envy in Rodgers's voice.

"It's not my language either," Hood admitted. "But one thing you learn with kids — and Ann will back me up — is that you've got to adapt. Hell, I find myself wanting to say the same things about rap music and heavy metal that my parents said about the Young Rascals. You've got to roll with these things."

Rodgers's expression was dubious. "Do you know what George Bernard Shaw said about adaptation?"

"Can't say that I do," Hood admitted.

"He said, 'The reasonable man adapts himself to the world: the unreasonable one persists in trying to adapt the world to himself. Therefore all progress depends on the unreasonable man.' I don't like rap and never will. More than that, I won't ever pretend to."

Hood said, "What do you do when Lieutenant Colonel Squires listens to it?"

Rodgers said, "I order him to shut it off. He tells me I'm being unreasonable — "

"And you quote Shaw," Ann said.

Rodgers looked at her and nodded.

Hood raised his eyebrows. "Interesting. Well, let's see if we can all agree on what has to be done over the next few days, anyway. First, my schedule."

Hood shucked his boyish smile and was all business as he looked back at the computer screen. Ann tried to wink a smile out of the Deputy Director, but didn't get it. The truth was he rarely smiled, and only seemed genuinely happy when he'd been out hunting boar, totalitarians, or anyone who put their careers before the safety of fighting men and women.

"I'll be doing the Magna Studio tour on Monday," Hood continued, "and Wallace World Amusement Park on Tuesday. The kids want to surf, so Wednesday's a beach day — and so on. If you need me, I'll have the cellular with me. It won't be a problem getting to the nearest police station or FBI

41

office in case you need me on a secure line in a hurry."

"It should be a quiet week," Ann said. She had dumped Intelligence Officer Bob Herbert's morning update into her power-book before coming to the meeting, and now she flipped up the lid. "The borders in Eastern Europe and the Middle East are relatively cool. The CIA was able to help Mexican authorities close down the rebel base in Jalapa without incident. Things are calm in Asia after the near war in Korea. And the Ukrainians and Russians are at least talking again about who owns what in the Crimea."

"Mike, will the outcome of the Russian elections affect that?" Hood asked.

"We don't think so," Rodgers said. "The new Russian President, Kiril Zhanin, has crossed swords with Ukrainian leader Vesnik in the past, but Zhanin's a pro. He'll extend an olive branch. In any case, our projection is for no Code Reds during the coming week."

Hood nodded. Ann knew he put little faith in what he called the three Ps — projections, polls, and psychobabble — but at least he was pretending to listen to them now. When he first came to Op-Center, Paul and staff psychologist Liz Gordon got along like Clarence Darrow and William Jennings Bryan.

"I hope you're right," Hood said, "but if Op-Center is called in on anything over a Code Blue, I want to be the one who signs off on our activities."

Rodgers's leg stopped moving. The light brown eyes that usually seemed golden appeared dark. "I can handle it, Paul."

"Never said you couldn't. You showed everyone what you could do when you stopped those missiles in North Korea."

"So what's the problem?"

"None," said Hood. "This isn't about ability, Mike. It's about accountability."

"I understand," Rodgers insisted in his courtly way. "But the regulations allow for this. The Deputy Director is allowed to okay operations when the Director is away."

"The word is 'indisposed,' not 'away,' " Hood pointed out. "I won't be indisposed, and you know how Congress gets about foreign adventures. If anything goes wrong, I'm the one who'll be hauled in front of a Senate committee and asked to explain why. I want to be able to tell them because I was there, not because I read about it in your report."

Rodgers's high-ridged nose, broken four times in college basketball, dropped slightly. "I understand."

"But you still don't agree," said Hood.

"No. Frankly, I'd *welcome* the chance to

take on Congress. I'd give those seat-warmers a lesson in government by action, not consensus."

Hood said, "That's why I'd like to be the one to handle them, Mike. They still pay the bills around here."

"Which is the reason men like Ollie North do what they do," Rodgers said. "To get around all the Deputy Directors' Coordinating Committees. The milksops who take proposals under advisement and sit on them for months and finally give them back too diluted and too late to matter worth a damn."

Hood looked like he wanted to say something and Rodgers looked like he wanted to hear it and lob it right back. Instead, both men regarded each other in silence.

"Well," Ann said jauntily, "that gives *us* control over those tense, single-hostage Code Greens and multiple-domestic-hostage Blues, and puts the easy, overseas-hostage Yellows, and state-of-war Reds on *your* shoulders." She closed the lid of her powerbook, looked at her watch, and rose. "Paul, you'll send your schedule to our computers?"

Hood looked at the computer. He touched Alt/F6 on his keyboard, then hit PB/Enter and MR/Enter. "Done," he said.

"Great. Will you try to have a wonderful and relaxing trip?"

Hood nodded. Then he regarded Rodgers again. "Thanks for your help," he said, rising and shaking Rodgers's hand across the desk. "If I knew how to make this better for you, Mike, I would."

"See you in a week," Rodgers said, then turned and walked past Ann.

"I'll see you too," Ann said to Hood, giving him a little goodbye wave and an encouraging smile. "Don't forget to write . . . and relax."

"I'll send you a postcard from Bloopers," he said.

Ann shut the door and followed Rodgers down the hall. She elbowed around coworkers and hurried past the open office doors and the closed doors of Op-Center's intelligence-gathering departments.

"Are you all right?" she asked when she fell in beside him.

Rodgers nodded.

"You don't look all right."

"I still can't strike the right note with him."

"I know," Ann said. "Sometimes you think he's really got a handle on some kind of larger worldview. The rest of the time you feel like he's trying to keep you in line, like a smarty-pants school monitor."

Rodgers looked at her. "That's a fair assessment, Ann. You've obviously given this

45

— him — a lot of thought."

She flushed. "I tend to reduce everybody to sound bites. It's a bad habit."

To change the course of the conversation, Ann made a point of emphasizing the "everybody." She knew at once that that had been a mistake.

"What's *my* sound bite?" Rodgers asked.

Ann looked at him squarely. "You're a frank, decisive man in a world that has grown too complex for those qualities."

They stopped beside his office. "And is that good or bad?" he asked.

"It's troublesome," Ann replied. "With a little bit of give, you could probably get a lot more."

Without taking his eyes off Ann, Rodgers entered his code in the keypad on the jamb. "But if something isn't what you want, is it worth having?" he asked.

"I've always felt that half is better than none," she replied.

"I see. I just don't agree." Rodgers smiled now. "And Ann? Next time, if you mean to say I'm stubborn, just come out and say it."

Rodgers flipped her a little salute, walked into his office, and shut the door behind him.

Ann stood there for a moment before turning and walking slowly toward her office. She felt bad for Mike. He was a good man, and a bright one. But he was fatally flawed by his desire for action over diplomacy, even when that action disregarded little things like national sovereignty and congressional approval. It was his reputation as a fire-eater that had caused him to be passed over as Assistant Secretary of Defense, landing him here as a consolation prize. He accepted the post because he was first and foremost a good soldier, but he was never happy about it . . . or about reporting to a nonmilitary superior.

But then, she thought, *everyone's got problems of some kind.* Like her, for example. The problem to which Rodgers had indiscreetly alluded.

She was going to miss Paul, her good and honorable cavalier, the knight who wouldn't leave his wife however much she took him for granted. Worse than that, Ann couldn't help but fantasize about how she would make Paul relax if it were she and her son going with him to Southern California instead of Sharon and the kids. . . .

FOUR

Saturday, 2:00 P.M., Brighton Beach

Since being smuggled in from Russia to America in 1989, handsome, dark-haired Herman Josef had worked at the Bestonia Bagel Shop in the Brighton Beach section of Brooklyn. Here, he was responsible for covering the still-warm dough with salt, sesame seeds, garlic, onions, poppy seeds, and various combinations thereof. Working near the ovens was miserable in the summer, delightful in the winter, and pleasantly unchallenging throughout the year. Most of the time, working here was nothing like working in Moscow.

Owner Arnold Belnick buzzed him on the intercom. "Herman, come to the office," he said. "I have a special order."

Whenever he heard that, the slender, thirty-seven-year-old Muscovite was no longer unchallenged. Old instincts and feelings came to life. The need to survive, to succeed, to serve his country. They were skills honed in ten years of working for the KGB before it was transformed.

Throwing his apron on the counter and turning the bagel-finishing process over to Belnick's young son, Herman ran up the groaning old stairs two at a time. He walked right into the office, which was lit by a fluorescent desk lamp and the light coming through a dirty skylight. He shut the door, locked it, then stood beside the old man at the desk.

Belnick looked back at him through a cloud of cigarette smoke. "Here," he said, handing Herman a paper.

Herman looked at it, then gave the paper back to Belnick. The round, balding man put it in the ashtray, touched the glowing tip of his cigarette to it, and set the note afire. Then he dumped the ashes on the floor and ground them to powder.

"Any questions?"

"Yes. Will I be going to the safe house?"

"No," said Belnick. "Even if you're being watched, there's no reason anyone should connect you with the event."

Herman nodded. He had been to the place on Forest Road in Valley Stream before, after killing a Chechnyan rebel who had come to raise funds for the secession. It was a safe house operated by the Russian mafia for its operatives. From there, it was just a fifteen-minute ride to JFK International Airport, or a twenty-minute ride to Jamaica Bay. Either way, it was easy enough to get operatives out of the country if things got too hot. Otherwise, when the trail got cold, he could return to Brighton Beach and the Bestonia.

Herman went to a locker in a corner of the room, removed the false back, and reached in. And as casually as if he were gathering salt or poppy seeds, he began removing the things he'd need.

FIVE

Sunday, 12:00 P.M., St. Petersburg

His trusty old Bolsey 35mm camera slung around his neck, Keith Fields-Hutton purchased a ticket in a kiosk outside the Hermitage, near the Neva, then walked the short distance to the sprawling, gold-domed museum. As always, he felt humbled as he walked through the white marble columns on the ground floor. He experienced that every time he entered one of the most historic buildings in the world.

The State Hermitage Museum is the largest museum in Russia. It was established in 1764 by Catherine the Great as a separate area of the two-year-old Winter Palace. It quickly grew from the 225 pieces of art she bought for it to the current collection of 3 million pieces. The museum houses works by Leonardo da Vinci, Van Gogh, Rembrandt, El Greco, Monet, and countless masters, as well as ancient artifacts from the Paleolithic, Mesolithic, Neolithic, Bronze, and Iron ages.

Today, the museum consists of three buildings side by side: the Winter Palace; the Little Hermitage, located directly to the northeast; and the Large Hermitage, situated northeast of that. Until 1917, the Hermitage was closed to all but the royal family, their friends, and aristocrats. Only after the Revolution was it opened to the public.

As Fields-Hutton entered the great main hall, with its ticket takers and souvenir stands, he considered how sad it was that he was here. When Catherine established the museum, she'd posted some very sensible rules of conduct for her guests. The first and most important was Article One: *"On entering, the title and rank must be put off, as well as the hat and sword."*

She was right. The experience of art should ease personal and political squabbles, not conceal them. But both Fields-Hutton and Leon believed the Russians had broken that compact. In addition to the death of the six workers and the shipments of material, there were increased levels of microwave radiation. Leon had come over before his employer's arrival and used a cellular phone in different areas around the museum. The closer he got to the river, the more the reception broke up. That might explain the tarpaulins. If the Russians had established some kind of communications center here, below the waterline, the electronic components would have to be insulated from the moisture.

The fact that they may have set up a communications center in the museum made strategic sense. Art was as negotiable as gold, and museums were rarely bombed in wartime. Only Hitler had violated the sanctity of this museum by bombing it. However, the citizens of what was then Leningrad had taken the precaution of evacuating their treasures to Sverdlovsk in the Urals.

Did the Russians build a center here because they were anticipating a war? Fields-Hutton wondered.

Fields-Hutton consulted the layout of the museum in his *Blue Guide*. He had memorized it on the train but didn't want to arouse the suspicion of guards by appearing to know where he needed to go. Each guard was a potential Ministry of Security freelancer.

After glancing at the map Fields-Hutton turned to the left, to the long, columned Rastrelli Gallery. Every inch of floor space was exposed, leaving no place to hide a secret room aboveground or a hidden staircase that could lead underground. Strolling around the wall that separated the Rastrelli Gallery from the East Wing, he stopped when he spotted what had once apparently been a custodial closet. There was a keypad beside the door, and he smiled when he read the printed sign on an easel to the left. It said, in Cyrillic letters:

> *This is the future home of Arts for Children, a television service that will broadcast the treasures of the Hermitage to students in schools throughout the nation.*

Maybe, thought Fields-Hutton, *and maybe not.*

Pretending to read his *Blue Guide* while he watched the guard, Fields-Hutton waited until the man turned away, then hurried over to the door. There was a security camera above it, so he made sure not to look up from his book or show his face. He pretended to sneeze, covering his face with his hand and stealing a look at the lens. It was short, under twenty millimeters. It had to be a wide-angle lens, covering the door as well as the area well to the left and to the right, but not on the bottom.

Fields-Hutton reached into his pants pocket and removed his handkerchief. Inside was a Mexican peso, one of the few coins which had no value in Russia. At worst, if it were found, it would be picked up and kept as a souvenir — hopefully, by a high-ranking official who had something useful to say in private.

Sneezing again and bending hard as he did, Fields-Hutton slid the peso under the door. He was relatively certain that there would be a motion detector on the other side of the door, but that it wouldn't be sensitive enough to notice the coin. Otherwise, every cockroach and mouse in the museum would set it off. Rising quickly, he walked away, his nose buried in the handkerchief.

Meandering back toward the main entrance, he allowed a guard to search his shoulder bag and then went outside, found a spot under a tree by the river, and slipped his CD Walkman from the bag. He jumped the machine to different tracks on the disc—the numbers describing, in code, just what he'd seen in the museum. These numbers were recorded on the writable disc. Later, when he was away from any receivers that might be based in the museum, he would order the Walkman to transmit the signal to the British Consulate in Helsinki, where it would be relayed to London.

When he finished telling them about the TV studio, Fields-Hutton sat back to listen to what he hoped were the sounds of espionage taking place around his small peso.

SIX

Sunday, 12:50 P.M., St. Petersburg

When the coin slid under the door of the reception area, it passed through an electromagnetic CIS. The counterimpulse screen was designed to be disrupted by any signal that passed beneath it, down to the cadmium batteries that powered digital watches.

The disruption sounded a beep that overrode other information coming into the earphones of Operations Center Security Director Glinka. Though he wasn't an alarmist, Colonel Rossky was — especially with zero hour a little over a day away and a rumor that someone from the outside had been watching what was going on for the past few days.

He checked with the receptionist, who said that no one had come or gone. Thanking her, the short, muscular man slid his headset off, handed it to his aide, got up from his seat, and walked down the narrow corridor to the Colonel's cubicle.

He looked for any excuse to stretch his legs, having spent nine hours doing nothing but test open bugs in dozens of embassies around the world. This, after having spent four hours of running two of the Operations Center phone lines through a battery of tests for on-and-off hook voltages, on-line listen, tone sweep, high-voltage pulse test, and all-wire listen tests.

The central hallway was about the length and width of two bus aisles strung end-to-end. It was lit by three twenty-five-watt bulbs set in black fixtures and suspended from the ceiling. It was so thoroughly sound-proof that nothing less than a cannon or jackhammer could be heard or felt by someone on the outside. Both interior and exterior walls were made of brick covered with a liquid foam coating and six alternating layers of spun fiberglass and inch-thick sheets of hard, black rubber. These were topped with tarpaulin to insulate the facility from moisture and then by a layer of pasteboard. A coat of matte-black paint absorbed the light which might otherwise leak through cracks in the floors above them.

Like a tree trunk, the corridor had several branches, each leading to several areas: computers, audio surveillance, aerial reconnaissance, communications, library, exit, and more. General Orlov's office was on one end and Colonel Rossky's on the other.

Glinka reached the Colonel's office and pressed the red button on the speaker beside the door.

"Yes?" the high voice crackled through the speaker.

"Colonel, it's Glinka. I've picked up a .98-second disturbance in the reception area. That isn't long enough for someone to have walked through, but you wanted me to tell you if there were any — "

"Where is the janitor?"

Glinka said, "He's working in the Kurgan wings — "

"Thank you," Rossky said. "I'll look into it myself."

"Sir, I can go and — "

"That will be all," Rossky snapped.

Glinka ran a hand across his blond crewcut. "Yes, sir," he said as he turned from the door and headed back to his post.

So much for a short walk up the stairs, he thought. But it was better to be miserable than to cross the unforgiving Colonel Rossky, which is what poor Pavel Odina had done when he stole equipment from the facility. Glinka had only mentioned the theft to the Colonel because he didn't want to be blamed for it himself. He never thought the computer software designer would meet with such a horrible fate, which everyone here knew that Rossky had orchestrated.

Shambling back to his seat, he retrieved his earphones and settled in for what he was sure would be another unbroken shift of five hours or more.

He quietly considered all the ways he would love to derail the strutting son of a bitch if he had the courage. . . .

Tucked into his old, crisply pressed black uniform, with its distinctive red lapel flashes and freshly blocked hat, short, lean Colonel Leonid Rossky left his office and strode toward the fireproof door that led to the staircase. Like all soldiers of the spetsnaz — a word formed from *spetsialnoye nazhacheniye,* "special purpose" — he had both nerves and character of granite. It showed in his hard expression. His dark eyebrows dipped severely above his long, straight nose, and his thin lips turned down at the edges where they blended with the deep, hard lines from his nose. He wore a thick mustache, which was unusual for the breed. But his gait was typical of the special forces: fast and assured, as though only an invisible leash kept him from racing toward a goal only he could see.

Opening the door and shutting it firmly

behind him, Rossky pressed the keypad code to lock it, then hit a button on the intercom beside it.

"Raisa, lock the outside door."

"Yes, sir," she said.

Then he hurried along a dark corridor, up another flight of stairs, and through another keypad-controlled door to a TV studio. Ordinarily, he would have changed into civilian clothes before coming out here, but there wasn't time.

Workers in the studio were setting up permanent lights, monitors, and TV cameras. They ignored Rossky as he made his way through the cables, crates, and equipment. Beyond the glass-enclosed control booth was a steep, brightly lit stairwell. Rossky climbed and entered a small reception area at the top. Raisa rose from her desk and greeted him with a nod. She went to say something, but he put a finger to his lips to silence her and looked around.

Rossky saw the peso at once, lying innocuously under the receptionist's desk on the right side of the room. The two employees who were unpacking equipment stopped to look at him. He motioned them to keep talking. They continued discussing a soccer match as Rossky studied the coin. He circled it like a snake girdling its prey, never touching it and afraid to breathe on it. A glitch might have triggered the alarm in Glinka's headset, and the peso might be exactly what it seemed to be. But he hadn't survived twenty years in the special forces by taking anything for granted.

He saw that the peso was well-worn, as though it had been in circulation for years. The 1982 date seemed appropriate to its condition. He looked at the sides of the coin, at the faded ridges, at the dirt wedged between them. It all seemed very authentic. But the eye could be fooled. Pulling a long black hair from the back of his head, he held it near the coin. The hair dipped like a divining rod. Touching his index finger to the tip of his tongue, he gently dabbed the top of the coin with saliva. He looked closely at his finger and saw traces of dust; where he'd touched the coin, it was clean.

Static electricity had attracted both dust and the hair, which meant that something inside the coin was generating an electrostatic field. His lips tight with anger, Rossky stood and returned to the Operations Center. The transmitter in the peso wasn't very powerful. Whoever was listening through it had to be within a few hundred yards of the museum. The security cameras would tell Rossky who that might be, and then the spy would be dealt with.

SEVEN

Sunday, 9:00 A.M., Washington, D.C.

Mike Rodgers passed buoyantly through the keypad entry on the ground floor of Op-Center. After greeting the armed guards seated behind the lexan, who provided him with the day's password, Rodgers hurried through the first-floor administrative level, where the top officials had offices in the old evacuation-team headquarters. Like Paul Hood, Rodgers preferred to be downstairs, in the new underground area where the real business of Op-Center was conducted.

Another armed guard was stationed by the elevator, and after giving her the password Rodgers was admitted to the elevator. The anachronistic and less expensive "Who goes there?" sentry system had been chosen for Op-Center instead of the more elaborate hi-tech systems used at the other agencies, where fingerprint IDs had been compromised by computer-printed, laser-etched gloves, and voice identification systems had been fooled by synthesizers. Though Rodgers had seen the guard nearly every day for six months, and knew the names of her husband and children, he wouldn't have been admitted if he didn't have the password. If he'd tried to enter, he would have been arrested. If he resisted, he might have been shot. In Op-Center, precision, competency, and patriotism came before friendship.

Emerging in the heart of Op-Center called the "bullpen," Rodgers made his way through a maze of cubicles to the action offices ringing the hub. Unlike the offices above, the rooms here could tap into intelligence resources that ranged from satellite imagery to communicating directly with operatives around the world to accessing computers and databases that could accurately predict the rice harvest in Rangoon five years hence.

Rodgers was using Hood's office while the chief was away. The office was situated next to the conference room affectionately known as "the Tank." The Tank was surrounded by a wall of electromagnetic waves that prevented electronic surveillance. Rumor had it that the microwaves could also cause sterility and insanity. Staff psychologist Liz Gordon half-jokingly said that the waves explained a lot of the behavior that took place within these walls.

Alert and energized despite a late Saturday night on the town, Rodgers entered the code on the keypad beside Hood's office door. The door popped open, the lights came on, and for the first time in six months Rodgers smiled with contentment. At last he was in charge of Op-Center.

Even so, he knew he wasn't being entirely fair to Hood. He had his den-mother side, as Ann had said. But the Director was a good man. He was well intentioned and, more important, he was a highly capable manager. And it was efficient to delegate authority internally to a group of relatively autonomous experts like Martha Mackall and Lowell Coffey II, Matt Stoll and Ann Farris. But more and more, Rodgers felt that Op-Center needed to be run by one man's will, like Hoover's FBI. It had to be run by someone who didn't consult with the CIA or the National Security Council before acting, but let other organizations know what he was doing after the fact. After defusing a war in Korea and the potential bombing of Japan, he had come to believe that Op-Center needed to be more aggressive on the world stage, rather than reactive.

Which is one reason it can't continue being anonymous, Rodgers thought. But there was time enough to do something about that . . .

something passive, like leaking information to the press, or something dramatic, like sending Striker on the kinds of missions that had made Israeli commandos so feared and respected. Missions that didn't have to be attributed to others' operatives, the way their recent attack on the missile site in North Korea was attributed to the South Koreans.

Rodgers and Hood had had this discussion many times, and the Director invariably pointed to their charter, which forbade adventurism. They were supposed to act like police, he said, not fifth columnists. But to Rodgers, a charter was like sheet music. You could play the notes as written and follow the composer's instructions, yet there was still a great deal of latitude for interpretation. In Vietnam he'd read and reread Edward Gibbons's *The History of the Decline and Fall of the Roman Empire*, and something the author had written became Rodgers's credo that the first of earthly blessings is independence.

Fired up by Gibbons and by a dog-eared copy of George Patton's *War As I Knew It* that his father had given him, Rodgers served two tours of duty in Vietnam. He returned to the States and got his Ph.D. in world history from Temple University, after which he was stationed in Germany, then in Japan.

He commanded a mechanized brigade in the Persian Gulf and spent time in Saudi Arabia before returning to the U.S. to try for a job at the Department of State. Instead, the President offered him the post of Deputy Director at Op-Center. He wasn't sorry he took the job. It was exhilarating to be involved in crises around the world. He still savored the aftertaste of his recent, successful incursion into North Korea. But he didn't like being anyone's sidekick, let alone Paul Hood's.

The computer beeped. Rodgers walked toward the desk. He punched Control/A to receive. Bob Herbert's round face filled the screen, transmitted by a fiber optic camera on top of the monitor. The thirty-eight-year-old National Intelligence Officer looked tired.

"Good morning, Mike."

"Hi, Bob," Rodgers said. "What are you doing here on a Sunday?"

"Been here since last night. Stephen Viens at NRO called me at home and I came in. Didn't you read my memo?"

"Not yet," Mike said. "What's up?"

"Why don't you check the E-mailbox and beep me back," Herbert said. "The memo has all the times and exact spellings, and the satellite recon — "

"Why don't you just brief me?" Mike said, dragging a hand across his face. *E-mail. Beeps.*

66

Fiber-optic conferencing. How the hell did spy work go from Nathan Hale unbowed to Matt Stoll's screensavers of Derek Flint dancing Swan Lake? Intelligence work should be physically exhausting, like lovemaking, not electronic voyeurism.

"Sure, Mike. I'll give you a rundown," Herbert replied, somewhat concerned. "Are you okay?"

"Yeah," Rodgers said. "Just a little out of sync with the late twentieth century."

"Whatever you say," Herbert responded.

Rodgers didn't bother to explain. The Intelligence Officer was a good man, someone who had paid the price for what he did. He lost his wife and the use of his legs in the Beirut Embassy bombing in 1983. But after a great deal of initial reluctance, even Herbert was beginning to be seduced by the computers, satellites, and fiber-optic cables. He called this technological triad a "God's-eye view of the world."

"What we've got," Herbert said, "are two things, maybe related, maybe not. You know we've been picking up microwave radiation from the Neva as it passes near the Hermitage in St. Petersburg."

"Yes," Rodgers responded.

"At first we figured the radiation was from the TV studio the Russians are building at the Hermitage to broadcast artwork to schools. But my TV specialist has been watching their test broadcasts, and they're all in the 153 to 11950 kilohertz range. That's not what we're getting from the Neva."

"So the TV studio's a front for some other kind of operation," Rodgers said.

"Most likely. We thought it might be a new security setup to handle the extra tourists the Russians are expecting for the city's three hundredth anniversary, but that doesn't compute."

"How so?"

"Martha Mackall called a friend at Treasury to get me the budgets for the Russian Ministries of Culture and Education," Herbert said. "There isn't a ruble in either of them for what should be a five-to-seven-million-dollar facility. So we hacked around and found funds for the studio in the budget of the Ministry of the Interior."

"That doesn't mean anything," Rodgers said. "Our government transfers money all the time."

"Yes," said Herbert, "but the ministry earmarked *twenty* million dollars for the project."

"Interior's run by Dogin, the hard-line Minister who just lost the election over there," Rodgers said. "Some of that money may have gone to his presidential campaign."

"That's a possibility," Herbert agreed. "But there's something else which indicates that the TV studio may be more than that. At one-thirty yesterday afternoon, we intercepted a communication from the northern sector of St. Petersburg to New York. An order for bagels."

"Come again?" Rodgers said.

"It was a brunch order faxed from St. Petersburg to the Bestonia Bagel Shop in Brighton Beach. They asked for an onion bagel with cream cheese, a salt bagel with butter, an everything bagel plain, and two garlic bagels with lox."

"A take-out order from half a world away," Rodgers said. "And it wasn't a joke."

"No," said Herbert. "Bestonia sent back a confirmation. Definitely spooks."

"Right," Rodgers agreed. "Any idea what it means?"

"We sent it over to cryptology," Herbert continued, "and they're stumped. Lynne Dominick says the different bagels could represent sectors of the city or of the world. Or they could be agents. The different kinds of spreads could stand for different targets. She said she'll keep working on it, but she called Bestonia and they've got a dozen kinds of bagels with twenty different 'shmears.'

It'll take a while."

"What about that shop, the Bestonia?" Rodgers asked.

"Clean until now. Owned by the Belnicks, a family that came from Kiev via Montreal in 1961."

"So they're a deep plant," said Rodgers.

"Very," Herbert agreed. "Darrell informed the FBI and they put a stakeout team on the shop. Nothing's happened so far except for bagel deliveries."

Darrell McCaskey was Op-Center's FBI and Interpol liaison. By coordinating efforts between the agencies, he allowed each to benefit from the other's resources.

Rodgers asked, "You're sure they're bagels?"

"We videotaped the open bags from a rooftop, examined the footage," Herbert said. "They look like bagels all right. And the deliveryman seems to get the right amount of money for the size of each order. Nobody that gets a delivery goes out for lunch, so they must be eating what's in the bags."

Rogers nodded. "So that brings us back to something brewing in St. Petersburg. What's DI6 doing about it?"

"They've got a man on-site," said Herbert. "Commander Hubbard has promised to keep us informed."

"Good," Rodgers said. "And what do you think about all this?"

"I feel like I just took a short *Twilight Zone* hop back into the 1960s," Herbert said. "When the Russians spend big money on something these days, I worry."

Rodgers nodded as the intelligence chief signed off. Herbert was right. Russians weren't gracious losers, and they were faced with the possibility of the loser in an election having access to a secret operation with agents in the U.S.

Rodgers was worried too.

EIGHT

Sunday, 4:35 P.M., St. Petersburg

Whatever the season, the heat of the day leaves St. Petersburg almost immediately, chased away by the wind that rises from the gulf in the late afternoon. The cool air is carried to every corner of the city by the webwork of rivers and canals, which is why the warm glow of indoor lights appears earlier in the day. It's also the reason why pedestrians, who brave the often brutal winds and knifing cold, feel a special kinship after sundown.

The effect of sundown was almost supernatural, thought Fields-Hutton. For nearly two hours he had been sitting beneath a tree on the banks of the Neva, reading manuscripts stored in his Toshiba laptop. At the same time he was listening to his Walkman that was actually a radio receiver tuned to the frequency of the peso behind the door. Now, as he watched the sun drop lower in the sky and the streets begin to empty and the riverside promenade become virtually deserted, he felt as though people had to be indoors before the vampires and ghosts came out to prey.

Either that, he reflected, *or I've been editing horror and science-fiction comic books for far too long.*

He was getting cold. He felt colder than even his London-hardened flesh was accustomed to. What was worse, he was beginning to think that the afternoon had been wasted. All he had heard since he tuned in to the bug was trivial chatter about sports, women, whip-cracking bosses, crowbars ripping up crates, and the comings and goings of people working on the TV facility. Not exactly the kind of surveillance that made the pulses race back at DI6.

He looked out across the river, then gazed back toward the Hermitage. The museum was striking, its dozens of white columns now ruddy with sunset and the ribbed dome gleaming. The tour buses were beginning to carry their groups away. The day shift started to leave. The night shift was just arriving. The local citizens who had spent their Sunday at the museum were filing out to meet trolleybuses or to take the fifteen-minute walk to the nearest Metro stop, the Nevsky Prospekt Station. Soon, like the streets themselves, even the great museum would be deserted.

Fields-Hutton hoped that Leon had been able to get him a hotel room: he was going to have to come back in the morning and continue his surveillance. He was convinced that if anything untoward was going on here, the TV studio was the place.

The Englishman decided to go back inside and stake out the room for a few minutes, to watch and see if someone other than the work crew used the room near closing time. Someone he might be able to describe to the photo division at DI6 — a military person in civvies, a government official, a foreign agent. What's more, there was always confusion and pressure in the days before and immediately after the start of any new operation. Moreover, a worker leaving the place might say or do something that would tell him what was really happening here.

Closing up his computer and rising on bones that an American agent once described as belonging to Arthur Fiedler — he stood with a symphony of pops — Fields-Hutton brushed off his pants and left the Walkman on as he walked briskly toward the museum.

To the right, he saw a couple that had just left the museum strolling hand in hand along the river. He thought of Peggy, not

74

of the first fateful walk they took, the one where she brought him into the spy business, but of the walk just five days before along the banks of the Thames. They had talked about marriage for the first time, and Peggy admitted that she was leaning toward it. Of course, Peggy had the constitution of the Leaning Tower of Pisa, and it might take her an eternity to fall — but he was willing to run the risk. She wasn't quite the demure creature he had always envisioned himself ending up with, but he enjoyed her pluck. She had the face of an angel. And, most important, she was well worth waiting for.

He smiled as a young woman jogged toward the river with her Jack Russell terrier. He didn't think they had the English breed in Russia, though the black market was smuggling anything and everything these days, including dogs that were fashionable in the West.

The woman was dressed in sweat clothes and a baseball cap and carried a small plastic water bottle. As she approached, he noticed she wasn't perspiring. That seemed strange, since the nearest apartments were at least a half mile away and a runner should have worked up a sweat by now. She smiled at him. He smiled back. Suddenly, the dog broke free of its leash. It darted toward him and took a bite from the inside of his shin before the jogger was able to pull it away.

"I'm so sorry!" she said as she thrust the yipping dog under her arm.

"It's all right," he said, wincing as he dropped down on his right knee and examined the painful wound. He set his computer aside, took out his handkerchief, and wiped away the blood from the two semicircular rows of teeth marks.

The woman knelt beside him, her face a mask of concern. With her right arm clasped tightly around the frenzied terrier she held out her left arm, offering him the water bottle.

"This will help," she said.

"Thank you, no," Fields-Hutton said as the teeth marks filled anew with blood. Something wasn't right about this. She was too concerned, too attentive. Russians weren't like that. He had to get out of here.

Before Fields-Hutton could stop her, the woman poured water on his wound. Rivulets of blood streamed down his leg into his sock as Fields-Hutton reached out to stop her.

"What are you doing?" he demanded as she emptied the bottle on his wound. "Miss, please — "

He rose. Then she did, backing away as she stood. Her expression was no longer concerned but devoid of emotion. Even the dog was silent. Fields-Hutton's suspicions turned horribly real as the stinging in his leg began to fade — along with sensation in his feet.

"Who are you?" he demanded as numbness spread up his leg and he began to feel dizzy. "What did you do to me?"

The woman didn't answer. She didn't have to. Fields-Hutton suspected he'd been poisoned with a fast-acting chemical agent. As the world began to spin, he thought about Leon and bent to retrieve his computer. He fell, grabbed the handle, and dragged the laptop along as he crawled toward the river. When his legs became completely numb he tried to claw ahead, to remain conscious. He wanted to stay alive long enough to throw the computer into the Neva. But then his shoulders began to lose all sensation. His upper arms became dead weight and he fell forward.

The last thing Keith Fields-Hutton saw was the golden river flowing just a few meters away. The last thing he heard was the woman behind him say, "Goodbye." And the last thing he thought was how Peggy would cry when Commander Hubbard informed her that her lover had been killed on a mission in St. Petersburg.

His head rolled slowly to the side as the VX nerve agent stopped Fields-Hutton's heart.

NINE

Sunday, 9:00 P.M., Belgorod, the Russia/Ukraine border

The Kamov Ka-26 radial-engined helicopter landed on the floodlit patch of earth, its twin rotors kicking up dirt and swirling it into inverted sea horse patterns. While soldiers ran over and began unloading crates of communications equipment from the bay aft of the pilot's cabin, Interior Minister Dogin stepped out. Holding his fedora with one hand and the front of his greatcoat with another, he ducked low and walked briskly from the landing area.

Dogin had always loved temporary bases like this one — empty fields transformed overnight into pulsing centers of power, bootprints on the windswept soil, the dusty air ripe with the smell of diesel fuel.

The base was set up for mountain warfare, using a configuration designed in the closing days of the war in Afghanistan. To his right, one hundred yards away, was row after row of large tents, each housing a dozen soldiers.

There were twenty tents in a row, and they reached far beyond the glare of the flood-lights, nearly to the distant foothills. Beyond them, at the north and south corners of the camp, were firing pits for riflemen and dug-outs with overhead covers. In the event of a war, these positions would be used to protect the base from guerrilla attacks. To the left, where there were no hills, were rows of tanks, armored vehicles, and helicopters, the mess area and canvas shower stalls, garbage pit, medical tents, and supply de-pots. Even at night, there was life here — mechanized, electric, and invigorating.

Off in the distance, straight ahead, Dogin saw the immaculate, vintage PS-89 twin-engine monoplane that belonged to Dmitri Shovich. Two men stood guard, each carrying Avtomat assault rifles; the pilot sat in his seat, ready to depart at a moment's notice.

Looking at the plane, the Interior Minister felt a chill. What had only been talk until now was about to become a reality. The men and matériel here, and the equipment en route, would take them only so far. To get the money he needed to help undo the disastrous results of the election, he was about to make a pact with the devil. He only hoped that Kosigan was right, that the escape clause would work when the time came.

Beyond the supply depot were three more tents: the weather station, with its sensors outside, on tripods, hooked to computers inside; the communications center, with one satellite dish pointing northwest, another southeast; and the command tent.

General Mikhail Kosigan was standing outside the last of these, his legs spread wide, hands locked behind his back, head held stiffly erect. An orderly stood behind him, to his right, also holding onto his hat.

Though the hem of the General's jacket, his pant legs, and the flaps of the tent kicked wildly in the wash, Kosigan didn't seem to notice. From the iron-black eyes to the deeply cleft chin to the ruddy scar that ran diagonally between them, the six-foot-four-inch General was the quintessence of his strong, confident Cossack stock.

"Welcome, Nikolai!" the General said. "It's good to see you!" Kosigan wasn't speaking loudly, but his voice carried over the din of the helicopter.

Dogin shook Kosigan's hand. "It's good to see you too, Mikhail."

"Oh? Then why do you look so grim?"

"I'm not grim," Dogin said defensively. "I'm preoccupied."

"Ah, the great mind always working. Like Trotsky in exile."

Dogin shot him a look. "I can't say I like the metaphor. I would never have opposed Stalin, and I hope that being hacked to death is not in my future."

Dogin's eyes held Kosigan's. The General was a man of charm and incredible poise. He was twice world champion and an Olympic competitor in pistol shooting, the result of a youth spent in the paramilitary DOSAAF — the Voluntary Society for Cooperation with Army, Air Force, and Fleet, which trains young people in sports that have a military application. From there, his rise in the military was rapid and brilliant — though never quite fast enough to satisfy his towering ego. Dogin was sure that he could trust the General now. Kosigan needed the Minister to help him leapfrog over his superiors in the coming order. But what about later? Later was always a problem with people like Kosigan.

Kosigan smiled. "Don't worry. There are no assassins here. Only allies. Allies who are getting tired of maneuvers, who are eager to do something . . . but" — the smile broadened — "allies who are as ready as ever to serve the Minister."

"And his General," Dogin said.

"But of course." Kosigan smiled as he turned and extended a hand toward his tent.

Entering, Dogin saw the third member of

the strange triumvirate: Dmitri Shovich. The mobster was seated in one of three folding chairs set around a small, green metal table.

Shovich rose as Dogin entered. "My good friend," Shovich said softly.

Dogin couldn't bring himself to call the fiend "friend." "Dmitri," he nodded, bowing slightly as he looked into the slight man's hazel eyes. They were cold, those eyes, and seemed more so because of the close-cropped, peroxide-white hair and eyebrows. Shovich's long face was impassive and his skin unnaturally smooth. Dogin had read that Shovich had endured a therapeutic process of chemical peeling to remove the hard, cracked skin he'd suffered during nine years in a Siberian prison.

Shovich sat back down, his eyes never leaving the newcomer. "You're not happy, Minister."

"You see, Nikolai?" General Kosigan said. "Everyone notices it." He turned a chair around, straddled it, and pointed at Dogin, his index finger extended, thumb upraised as though his hand were a gun. "If you'd been less serious than you are, perhaps we wouldn't be here now. The new Russia likes leaders who can laugh and drink with them, not someone who seems to carry the weight of the world on his shoulders."

Dogin unbuttoned his coat and sat in the last chair. There was a tray with cups, a teapot, and a bottle of vodka. He poured himself tea. "The new Russia has followed a piper who will lead them laughing and drinking to destruction."

"It sounds like fun," Kosigan admitted. "But Russians have never known what's best for them — and, fortunately, we are here to show them. What a noble bunch we are."

Shovich folded his hands on the table. "General, I'm not noble, nor am I interested in saving Russia. Russia sent me to hell for nine years before Gorbachev's general amnesty freed me. I am only interested in the terms we discussed previously. Are they still acceptable to you both?"

"They are," said the General.

The gangster's cold eyes shifted to Dogin. "Does he speak for you, Minister?"

The Interior Minister stirred a lump of sugar into his tea. In the five years since his release, Shovich had gone from being a convicted robber to the leader of a global crime network that was comprised of an army of 100,000 men in Russia, Europe, the United States, Japan, and elsewhere — most of whom had been admitted to the ancient order of the thieves' world after proving their loyalty by murdering a friend or relative.

Am I mad to be joining forces with this man? Dogin asked himself. Shovich would be loyal only as long as they gave him twenty percent of the total assets of the former Soviet republics, which included the largest petroleum reserves on earth, double the timber found in the Amazon, nearly a quarter of the planet's unmined diamonds and gold, and some of the world's largest deposits of uranium, plutonium, lead, iron, coal, copper, nickel, silver, and platinum. The man wasn't a patriot. He wanted to exploit the natural resources of a rebuilt Soviet Union and use their legitimacy to launder drug money.

It made Dogin sick to contemplate, but Kosigan maintained that as long as he and his colleagues controlled the world's largest standing army, and Dogin ran the secret new surveillance operation in St. Petersburg, they would have nothing to fear from Shovich. He could be forced out at some later date, exiled to one of his residences in New York, London, Mexico City, Hong Kong, or Buenos Aires. Or he could be shot from the sky if he refused to go.

Dogin wasn't so sure of that, but there didn't seem to be any other option. He needed a lot of money to buy politicians and military officials, to wage an aggressive war without Kremlin assent. Unlike Afghanistan, this would be a war the Russians could win. But money was the key. How Marx would have bristled.

"I speak for myself," Dogin said to Shovich. "Your terms are acceptable to me. On the day Zhanin's government is ousted and I am named President, the man you select will become the new Minister of the Interior."

Shovich smiled a cold, chilling smile. "What if I select myself?"

Dogin felt a flash of horror, though he was too seasoned a politician to show it. "As I said, the choice is yours."

The tension of mutual distrust was thick when Kosigan broke it with a blustery, "What about the Ukraine? What about Vesnik?"

Dogin looked away from Shovich. "The President of Ukraine is with us."

"Why?" asked Shovich. "The Ukrainians have the independence they sought for decades."

"Vesnik has more social and ethnic problems than he or his military will be able to manage," Dogin said. "He wants to tamp them down before they get out of hand. We will help him do that. He also longs for the glory days, as Kosigan and I do." Dogin regarded the cold monster beside him. "My allies in Poland are planning to stage an

86

event there on Tuesday, 12:30 A.M. local time."

"What kind of event?" Shovich asked.

"My spetsnaz assistant in St. Petersburg has already sent a secret team to the border town of Przemysl, Poland," Dogin said. "They'll arrange for an explosion at the Polish Communist Party office there. The Communists won't tolerate the attack, and my people there will make sure the protest turns violent. Polish troops will be sent in, and the struggle will spread toward the Ukrainian border six miles away. At night, in the confusion, Vesnik's troops will fire on the Polish forces."

"When that happens," Kosigan jumped in, "Vesnik will contact me to request military support. Zhanin will already have learned that he is outside the real circle of power. Now he will scramble to find out which generals are on his side, just like Yeltsin when his officers elected to pound Chechnya. He will have very few allies, and the politicians we're buying won't support him either. Poles of Ukrainian and Belorussian descent will also be persecuted. When the Ukrainians and I counterattack, White Russia will join us, bringing the front to within one hundred miles of Warsaw. Russians will be caught up in nationalistic frenzy while Zhanin's foreign bankers and businessmen desert him. He'll be finished."

"A key to our success," said Dogin, "is keeping the United States and Europe from becoming involved militarily." He looked at Shovich. "We will work on that diplomatically, claiming that this was not imperialism but an attack on the Federation. But if that doesn't work, the General has talked to you about threatening key officials — "

"I did," Kosigan said, "but Dmitri told me he has a better idea. Why don't you tell him, Dmitri?"

Dogin regarded Shovich as the mobster adjusted himself in his chair. Dogin sensed that Shovich did it just to make him wait. He settled back, crossed his leg, brushed mud from the side of his black boot.

"My people in America tell me that the FBI has gotten very good at 'counterpunching,' " Shovich said. "If we run gambling or drug operations, they merely try to contain us. But if we hit their people, they strike back hard. It keeps the streets from becoming a war zone. Since most of the mobsters are in this for the money, not for politics, they refuse to attack government targets."

"Then what do you propose?" Dogin asked.

"An object lesson against a civilian target," Shovich said.

"To what end?" Dogin asked.

Kosigan answered, "To get America's undivided attention. When we have it, we tell them that if they leave us alone in Eastern Europe, there will be no further acts of terrorism. And we'll even turn over the terrorist, so that President Lawrence can look swift and decisive."

"Of course," Shovich said, "you will have to reimburse my colleagues in America for the loss of a man. But that will come out of your little treasure trove."

"Of course," Kosigan agreed. He reached for the bottle of vodka and regarded Dogin. "As we've said all along, Minister, all we need do is hold the U.S. off until the nightly news shows videos of soldiers who have been maimed or killed. The people of the United States will not tolerate American casualties. With the election just months away, President Lawrence will not intervene."

Dogin looked at Shovich. "What kind of civilian target will you strike?"

"I wouldn't know," he said with disinterest. "My people live there. Some of them are mercenaries and some of them are patriots. But whoever is picked will know how to strike at the American soul. I've left it entirely in their hands." He smiled humorlessly. "By this time tomorrow, we'll have

89

seen it on the news."

"Tomorrow!" Kosigan said. "We are men of action!" He poured vodka in his and Shovich's cups. "Our friend Nikolai does not drink, so we'll allow him to toast us with tea." He raised his cup. "To our alliance."

As the men touched the rims of their cups together, Dogin felt a burning in his belly. This was a coup, a second Revolution. It was empire building, and people were going to die. But while he accepted that, he found it difficult to accept Shovich's casualness. The mobster had moved from the concept of kidnaping to killing as though there was no difference.

Dogin sipped his tea and reminded himself that this unholy marriage was necessary. Every leader made compromises to move forward. Peter the Great changed Russian art and industry with ideas he brought from Europe. German cooperation enabled Lenin to overthrow the Czar and withdraw from World War I. Stalin consolidated his power by murdering Trotsky as well as hundreds of thousands of others. Yeltsin forged alliances with the black marketeers to keep his economy from collapsing entirely.

Now *he* was collaborating with a gangster. At least Shovich was a Russian. Better that than going to the United States with hat in hand, begging for money and moral support as Gorbachev and now Zhanin had done.

As the others emptied their cups, Dogin avoided Shovich's eyes. He tried not to think of the means, only the ends. Instead, he envisioned a map on the wall of his office. A map of a grand new Soviet Union.

TEN

Sunday, 8:00 P.M., New York City

After receiving the bagel order from St. Petersburg, Herman Josef had put ten pounds of plastique in a shopping bag. He placed bagels on top of them. Then he walked three blocks to Everything Russian, a shop that sold books, videotapes, and other goods from the homeland. Sixty minutes later, he'd taken another ten pounds of explosives to Mickey's Pawn Shop of Brighton Beach.

During the day Herman had made fifteen deliveries, bringing a total of 150 pounds of explosives to different locations. He didn't know if he was being followed, but he assumed that he was. So at each stop he took payment for the deliveries, even bitching audibly on the way back if his tip wasn't big enough.

When Herman left each site, the explosives were carried by another messenger to the Nicholas Senior Citizens Home, where they were packed into a body bag, taken to the

Cherkassov Funeral Home in the St. Marks section of New York City, and loaded into a coffin. The Chaikov family left the procuring of weapons and explosives to the Belnicks. Their expertise was in planning and executing operations.

The Queens-Midtown Tunnel stretches under the East River in New York, from 36th Street between Second and Third avenues. It connects Manhattan Island to the Long Island Expressway in the borough of Queens. The fifty-year-old tunnel is one of the principal arteries from the city, and at any given time its 6,000-foot length is filled with traffic.

At this time on a warm Sunday evening, the tunnel was not being used by commuters. The bright orange lights lit the way for families returning from a day in the city or travelers heading to JFK International or La Guardia Airport.

Tall, white-haired, white-bearded Eival Ekdol rolled down the window of the hearse. He breathed in the oil-thick air, air which reminded him of Moscow. He didn't think about who the people around him were or what they were doing. It didn't matter. Their deaths were the price of fighting for a new world order.

As he neared the tunnel exit, the Russian

native pushed in the cigarette lighter. His left front tire blew, and he guided the swerving hearse to the wall. He ignored the curses of drivers who had to change lanes to avoid hitting him. Americans were always swearing, as though bad things had no right to happen and, moreover, were directed at each of them personally.

Ekdol put on his emergency lights, got out of the hearse, and walked to the tunnel exit. Upon emerging, he took a cellular phone from his pocket and pretended to speak. He continued to speak as he walked toward the tollbooths.

He passed a transit officer, who was sitting in a police car by the booths. The young man asked if he needed help.

"Thank you, no," said Ekdol in thickly accented English. "I've phoned for help."

"Is it just the tire?" asked the officer.

"No," Ekdol told him. "The axle."

"Well, it's dark in there," the officer said. "Someone's gonna hit you. You got flares?"

"No, sir."

He popped the trunk. "We'd better go put some out."

"Thank you," said Ekdol. "I'll join you in a moment. I must phone the bereaved."

"Yeah," the officer grinned. "Helluva thing to have a funeral with no body."

94

"Exactly, sir," Ekdol said.

The officer got out of the car and went to the trunk. Removing a box of flares, he headed toward the tunnel, whistling.

Still pretending to talk into the phone, Ekdol walked around the tollbooth. Moments later, a Cutlass came through one of the token gates and pulled up beside him. Before getting in, Ekdol pressed the pound sign on the numeric keypad.

As the Cutlass sped off, a yellow fireball erupted from the mouth of the tunnel, sending smoke, chunks of stone, and shards of metal in every direction. Cars just emerging from the tunnel were blown end over end. One cartwheeled over the transit officer and smashed into a van at the tollbooth. Both vehicles blew apart, engulfing the toll booth in flame. Other cars were pounded flat at the entranceway by falling debris, while inside the tunnel there were the muffled sounds of secondary blasts as burning cars exploded. Within moments, the toll plaza was covered with rolling white smoke and a thick, horrific silence.

After several seconds, the silence was broken by the bass-fiddle groan of bending girders and the crack of concrete. A moment later, a quarter mile of expressway and the buildings along it shook as the roof of the tunnel collapsed. The roar of the water was like an ocean gone mad as it poured into the breach. The walls of the tunnel were battered down under the pressure, and shattered pieces were washed through the mouth of the tunnel as the river pushed the cars and fallen stone out of the way. The hiss of extinguished fires was drowned by the surging water as the river flowed outward, along the highway, taking down the few cars and streetlamps that still stood. Steam poured from the broken mouth of the tunnel, rising skyward to mingle with the darker smoke.

As the waters settled and the debris came to a rest, sirens sounded in the distance. Within minutes, police helicopters were racing low along the expressway, videotaping traffic leaving the scene.

But Ekdol wasn't worried. In less than a half hour, he'd have reached the safe house. The car would be dismantled in the garage and he would have burned the false beard, mustache, sunglasses, and baseball cap he was wearing.

For now, his job was finished. Arnold Belnick and his mercenary "bagel brigade" would be paid handsomely for their role in this and then it would be up to other soldiers in the *Grozny* cell to continue what he had begun.

Though his own life was about to be for-feited, he was honored to surrender it in the name of the new Soviet Union.

ELEVEN

Sunday, 9:05 P.M., Washington, D.C.

Mike Rodgers loved *Khartoum*.

It wasn't soft and warm like Elizabeth or Linda or Kate or Ruthie, but he didn't have to go out in the middle of the night to take it home. The movie was right there in his laser disc library, along with other favorites like *El Cid*, *Lawrence of Arabia*, *The Man Who Would Be King*, and virtually everything John Wayne ever made. What's more, he didn't have to be sociable. The movie didn't require him to do anything except put it in the player, sit back, and enjoy himself.

Rodgers had been looking forward to watching *Khartoum* all day, which is why he should have known that something would come between him and his film.

He'd begun his Sunday by jogging his daily five miles. Then he made coffee — black, no sugar — sat at the dining room table with his laptap, and brought himself up to speed on Paul Hood's schedule — now *his*

98

schedule — for the coming week. There were meetings with the heads of the other U.S. intelligence groups about sharing information more efficiently, a preliminary budget hearing, and lunch with the head of the French *Gendarmerie Nationale,* Benjamin. Just the thought of all that talk made his mouth dry. But there were some real challenges ahead as well. He'd be sitting down with Bob Herbert and Matt Stoll, their computer genius, to work out programs for coverage from the new ED satellite, the Electronic Disruptor. The ED satellite was being tested over Japan and could disrupt electronic impulses in objects as small as a desktop computer. He would also be receiving data from personnel on the ground in the Middle East, South America, and elsewhere. And then there were reports from U.S. agents in the Russian Army. He was looking forward to news of the Petroleum, Oil, and Lubricants Distribution overhaul, and he was curious to see how the new Russian President planned to compensate for personnel cutbacks in both the troop rear and operational rear.

Most of all, he was looking forward to the first conceptual sit-downs with Op-Center engineers for the proposed Regional Op-Center. After Korea, it had occurred to him that they should have mobile facilities which could be shuttled anywhere in the world. If it was feasible, one or more ROCs could make them an even more effective intelligence unit.

After lunch, Rodgers had gone to the shooting range at Andrews. There were days when he could dance around a bull's-eye with a .45-caliber M3 grease gun and miss it every time. Then there were days when he could pick his teeth with a .22-caliber Colt Woodsman. Today had been one of those good days. After two hours of marksmanship that left Air Force personnel stunned, Rodgers visited his mother in the Van Gelder Nursing Home. She was no more lucid than she'd been since her stroke two years before. But he read to her, as he always did, her favorite Walt Whitman poems, then sat and held her hand. After he left, he met an old Vietnam buddy for dinner. Andrew Porter owned a chain of comedy clubs up and down the East Coast, and he made Rodgers laugh like no one else.

While they were drinking coffee and getting ready to pay the check, Rodgers's pager beeped. It was Assistant National Security Director Tobey Grumet. He used his cellular phone to call her back.

Tobey informed him of the New York bombing and of an emergency Oval Office meeting called by the President. Rodgers apologized to Porter and left at once.

As he raced along the highway, Rodgers's thoughts went to General Charles "Chinese" Gordon. Gordon's efforts to protect indefensible Khartoum from the fanatical hordes of the Mahdi were at once among the boldest and most insane military adventures in history. Gordon paid for his heroism with his life, taking a spear in the chest and having his head paraded around on a pike. But Rodgers knew that that was how Gordon had wanted to die. The Englishman had traded his life for the chance to tell a tyrant, *"No. You can't have this place without a fight."*

Rodgers felt the same way. No one was going to do something like this to his country. Not without a fight.

He listened to the news on the radio and spoke on the phone as he drove to the White House. He was glad he had something to do: it kept him from dwelling on the horror. There were over two hundred deaths. The East River was shut down to traffic, and the FDR Drive on Manhattan's east side would be closed for days while it was examined for structural damage. Other transit points were being checked for explosives — bridges, railroads, airports, highways, subways — meaning that the hub of the world's economy would be effectively shut down on

Monday morning.

Op-Center's staff FBI liaison, Darrell McCaskey, phoned Rodgers and told him that the FBI had taken charge of the investigation and that Director Egenes would be at the meeting. McCaskey told Rodgers that the usual list of extremists had called to take credit for the bombing. But no one believed that the real perpetrator had come forward, and McCaskey had no opinion as to who the terrorist might be.

Rodgers also received a call from Assistant Deputy Director Karen Wong, who ran Op-Center on weekend evenings.

"General," she said, "I understand you've been called to a meeting."

"Yes, I have."

"Then here's some information you should take with you. As soon as Lynne Dominick in cryptology heard about the explosion, she took a fresh look at that bagel order from overseas. The timing and receiver location made it seem like a good fit."

"What did she find?"

"Knowing the outcome has allowed her to work backward," Wong said, "albeit very quickly. And it seems like a match. Assuming the last bagel represents the tunnel, she created a map. The rest of the order seems to be points in Manhattan — for example, places to deliver components of the bomb."

Then we'd be up against the Russians, he thought with dread. And if they were behind this, it would not be regarded as terrorism. It would be considered an act of war.

"Tell Lynne that was heads-up work," Rodgers said. "Memo her findings and secure-fax it to the Oval Office."

"Right away. There's something else, though, that's happened in St. Petersburg," she said. "We've just learned from Commander Harry Hubbard at DI6 in London that he lost two people there. The first one was yesterday afternoon, a veteran named Keith Fields-Hutton. He was outside the Hermitage, by the Neva, and suffered what the Russians say was a heart attack."

"A euphemism for 'We killed him,' " Rodgers said. "Was he checking on the studio?"

"Yes," Wong said. "He never got to phone a single report, though. That's how fast he was spotted and terminated."

"Thanks," Rodgers said. "Has Paul been briefed?"

"Yes," said Wong. "He called after he heard about the explosion. He asked to talk to you after the meeting."

"I'll phone him," Rodgers said as he pulled up to the sentry at the gate which led to the winding White House driveway.

TWELVE

Monday, 6:00 A.M., St. Petersburg

When he was a boy growing up in the early 1950s, in the small town of Naryan-Mar on the Arctic Ocean, Sergei Orlov thought he would never treasure a sight more than he did the orange glow of the hearth in his parents' home as he trudged through the snow carrying two or three fish tucked in his canvas sack, caught in the small lake near his home. For Orlov, the glowing fireplace wasn't just a beacon in the cold, dark night. It was a bright and hopeful sign of life in a cold and barren wasteland.

Circling the earth in the late 1970s, flying five *Soyuz* missions that ranged from eight to eighteen days and commanding the last three, General Sergei Orlov saw something even more memorable. It was not something new. Dozens of cosmonauts had seen the earth from space. But whether they had described our world as a blue bubble, a beautiful marble, or a Christmas-tree ornament, they all agreed that seeing it gave them a new outlook on life. Political ideologies were no match for the power of that fragile globe. Space travelers realized that if humans had a destiny, it was not to fight for control of their home but to cherish its peace and warmth as they journeyed to the stars.

And then you return to earth, Orlov thought as he stepped from the number 44 bus on Nevsky Prospekt. The resolve and inspiration weaken as you're asked to do things in the name of country which you can't refuse. Russians *don't* refuse. Orlov's grandfather was a Czarist, yet he fought the White Russians during the Revolution. His father didn't refuse when he fought in the Second Ukrainian Front during the Second World War. It was for them, and not for Brezhnev, that he had trained a new generation of cosmonauts to spy on the United States and NATO forces from space as well as to work on new chemical poisons in zero gravity. He was trained to see the world not as the home of all humans but as a thing to be peeled and cut up and devoured in the name of a man called Lenin.

Then there are the parts coveted by men like Minister Dogin, he thought as he walked briskly along the boulevard. Though it was still early, workers were already arriving at the Hermitage to prepare it for the daily crush of tourists.

Though the Minister was affable enough, and seemed consumed by an almost narcotic contentedness when discussing Russian history, particularly the Stalin years, his world-view was out of step with the times. And when Dogin made his monthly trips to St. Petersburg, it seemed that the Minister's memories of the Soviet years became more and more idealized.

Then there were men like Rossky, who didn't appear to have any worldview. They simply enjoyed power and control. Orlov had been alarmed by Assistant Security Director Glinka's surreptitious call to the apartment. Glinka knew how to play both sides of the fence, but Orlov believed him when he said that Rossky's activities over the past twenty-four hours had been unusually secretive. It started when Rossky insisted on handling, himself, the trivial investigation of an intrusion alert the day before. It was followed by unlogged and coded computer communications to an operative in the field, not telling anyone where he was going, and mysterious dealings with a local coroner.

I've been ordered to work with Rossky, Orlov told himself, *but I won't let him run rogue operations.* Whether Rossky liked it or not, he would toe the line or he would be restricted to a desk job. As long as Rossky had Interior Minister Dogin's support, threatening him would be difficult. But Orlov had overcome difficulties before. He bore the scars to prove it, and was willing to bear more if need be. He had learned English so that he could travel as a goodwill ambassador when, in fact, he was busy acquiring and sneaking home books just so he could see what the rest of the world was thinking and reading.

Orlov raised the collar of his off-white trench coat against the knifing wind and tucked his black-rimmed glasses into his pocket. They always fogged when he came back outside from the over- or underheated bus, and he didn't have time to fuss with them. As if it weren't frustrating enough to need them at all, these eyes that had once been keen enough to pick out the Great Wall of China from nearly three hundred miles in space.

Despite the problem with Rossky, Orlov's full-lipped mouth was relaxed, his high forehead unwrinkled beneath the brim of his gray fedora. His striking brown eyes, high cheekbones, and dark complexion were, like his adventurous spirit, a part of his Asiatic heritage — Manchu. His great-grandfather had once told him that his family was part of the first wave of warriors that had poured through China and Russia in the seventeenth century. Orlov didn't know *how* the old man could place them so precisely. But it suited him to think that he was descended from a pioneering people, benevolent despite having been conquerors.

Standing just under five-foot-seven, Orlov had the narrow shoulders and slender build that had made him an ideal, resilient cosmonaut. Though his record as a fighter pilot had been flawless, Orlov carried physical and mental mementoes from his years in space. He walked with a permanent limp, due to a left leg and hip badly broken when his parachute failed to deploy in what turned out to be his last mission. His right arm was severely scarred when he pulled a cosmonaut-in-training from the wreck of a MiG-27 Flogger-D. He had pegs inserted in his hip to enable him to walk, but declined to undergo plastic surgery on the arm. He liked the way his wife *oooohed* and *ohhhhhed* whenever she saw her poor singed bird.

Orlov smiled as he thought of his precious Masha. Though today's breakfast had been cut short by Glinka's call, the afterglow of being with her still warmed him. More so because it would have to hold him until tomorrow, which was the earliest he'd be seeing her again. As always before he left on a mission, the two of them went through a ritual they'd begun nearly twenty years ago, before he rode his first flaming rocket into space: they held each other tightly and made sure they parted with no unspoken thoughts or anger, nothing they would regret if he failed to return. Masha had come to believe that the day they broke the tradition, he wouldn't come back.

Those days with the Mir and Salyut space stations, he thought, smiling. Years of working with Kizim, Solovyev, Titov, Manarov, and the other cosmonauts who spent weeks and months in space. Enjoying the sterile beauty of the Vostok and Voskhod spacecraft, of the Kvant astronomy module that allowed them to explore the universe. Experiencing the sound and fury of the mighty Energia rockets sending payloads skyward. He missed it all. But eleven months before, the space program was broke and in near collapse, and the forty-nine-year-old officer had agreed to command this place, a hi-tech operations center that was being designed to spy on friends and foes abroad and at home. Ministry of Security Chief Cherkassov had told him he had the calm but detail-oriented nature that was perfect for running a high-pressure intelligence facility like this — though Orlov couldn't help but feel he was being demoted. He'd gone from touching the vault of heaven to being cast underground into hell, and he'd been spoiled by the many humanitarian scientists he had worked with at the Yuri Gagarin Space Center outside Moscow. As the Manchu had understood, progress and power should be used to ennoble people, encourage them to make sacrifices, not control and herd them.

But Masha agreed with Cherkassov. She told her husband it was better for someone with his temperament to run the Operations Center instead of someone like Rossky, and she was right about that. Neither the Colonel nor his new best friend, Interior Minister Dogin, seemed to know where the interests of Russia ended and their personal ambitions began.

As Orlov walked briskly along the broad boulevard, the bag lunch and bag dinner his wife had prepared tucked under his arm, he gazed across the river at the Frunze Naval College that housed the dozen soldiers of the Center's special operations force *Molot,* Hammer.

Masha had been right about Rossky as well. After he told her who his second-in-command was to be — the man who had been involved with their son, Nikita, in the incident in Moscow — Masha told him not to allow Dogin to force Rossky on him. She knew they would clash, while he thought that working on a common project, in such close quarters, would force them to trust and maybe respect one another.

Now reckoning seemed inevitable. What made his wife so smart . . . and him so naive?

His eyes moved along the structures on the opposite side of the Neva as the slanting sunlight put yellow faces on the stately Academy of Sciences and Museum of Anthropology directly across from him, and threw long, brown shadows behind them. He took a long moment to drink in their beauty before entering the museum and the complex below. Though he was no longer able to see the earth from space, there was still much to savor down here. It bothered him that Rossky and the Minister never stopped to look at the river, the buildings, and especially the art. To them, beauty was merely something to hide under.

Upon entering the museum, Orlov walked toward the Jordan Staircase and the entrance to the secret new arm of the Kremlin, a facility at once practical and idiosyncratic.

The practical side was the Hermitage site itself. It had been chosen over potential locations in Moscow and Volgograd because operatives could be moved in and out inconspicuously with tour groups; because agents could travel easily from here to Scandinavia and Europe; because the Neva would hide and disperse most of the radio waves coming from equipment at the Center; because the working TV studio they'd built gave them access to satellite communications; and most important, because no one would attack the Hermitage.

The idiosyncrasy came from Minister Dogin's devotion to history. The Minister collected old maps, and in his collection were the blueprints of Stalin's wartime headquarters under the Kremlin — rooms that were not only bombproof but led to a private subway tunnel that would have been used to shuttle Stalin from Moscow in the event of an attack. The Minister revered Stalin, and when he, now-President Zhanin, and the head of the Ministry of Security first planned this communications and spy facility for Boris Yeltsin, Dogin insisted on using the layout that worked for Stalin. The design actually worked out well, Orlov felt. As in a submarine, the tight, somewhat claustrophobic quarters helped to keep workers focused on the tasks at hand.

Orlov acknowledged the guard as he passed. The General used the keypad to enter;

once inside, he showed the receptionist his ID, despite the fact that she was Masha's cousin and knew him well. Then he made his way through the reception area and down the stairs to the TV studio. At the far end, he punched the day's four-digit code on a keypad and the door popped open. When Orlov shut it behind him, the dark stairwell's single overhead bulb snapped on automatically. He walked down the stairs where another keypad gained him access to the Center. Entering the dimly lit central corridor, he turned to the right and strode toward the office of Colonel Rossky.

THIRTEEN

Sunday, 9:40 P.M., Washington, D.C.

Rodgers was ushered quickly through the outer and inner gates, and was met at the White House by Assistant National Security Director Grumet. The fifty-year-old woman stood nearly six feet tall, had long, straight blond hair, and wore very little makeup. Rodgers had a great deal of respect for the Vietnam veteran, who had lost her left arm in a helicopter crash during the war.

"You're waiting for me," said Rodgers. "Am I late?"

"Not at all, sir," Grumet said, saluting the General. "The rest of us happen to be old married people who were sitting home watching TV when the blast happened. We had a little head start. I swear, just when you think the world can't get any sicker — "

"Oh, I read history," Rodgers said. "I *never* think that."

As Rodgers entered the doorway, he took off the jacket of his uniform and handed it to the armed Marine standing outside. Otherwise, the brass buttons would have set off the metal detector hidden in the jamb. The detector didn't *ping*. After running a portable detector over the jacket, the Marine returned it to Rodgers and saluted.

"What's been happening?" Rodgers asked Grumet as they walked down the short corridor to the Oval Office.

"We responded by the book," she said. "We closed down immigration and rounded up the usual suspects. The FBI put various bureaus and agencies on alert, dropped divers into the wreckage. Director Rachlin complained that the CIA spends too much money on political sensitivity training and not enough on keeping track of sociopaths, mad scientists, and ideological foes."

"That's Larry," said Rodgers. "More outspoken than Mr. Kidd. What the hell do these people want, Tobey?"

"Until we know more, we're treating it as a standard terrorist attack. It's possible that this was simply a criminal act, and that there will be a ransom demand. It's also possible that the bombing was the work of a psychotic individual or a domestic group."

"Like the bombing in Oklahoma City."

"Exactly. A group acting out their own deep anger and alienation from society."

"But you don't think so?"

"No, Mike, we don't. We think this was the work of a foreign terrorist group."

"Terrorists."

"Exactly. If so, they could simply want publicity for their cause. Generally, though, terrorist acts are used instrumentally — that is, they are part of a plan to achieve larger ends."

"The question is, what is the goal of these people?"

"We'll know soon enough," Tobey said. "Five minutes ago, the FBI got a call in New York saying that the President would be contacted by the terrorist. The caller provided the FBI with information about the size of the blast, its location, the kind of explosives used. It checked out exactly."

"Is he going to take the call?" Rodgers asked.

"Technically, no," Tobey said, "but he'll be in the room. We think that will satisfy — shoot!" she said as her pager buzzed. "They want us in there right now."

The two ran down the corridor. They were waved ahead by an assistant in the antechamber of the Oval Office, and were buzzed through the inner door.

President Mike Lawrence was standing behind his desk. He was drawn to his full six-foot-four-inch height, his hands on his hips, his shirtsleeves neatly rolled back a turn. Facing him was Secretary of State Av Lincoln. Lincoln was a former major league pitcher with a round face and thinning widow's peak.

Four other officials were also present: FBI Director Griffen Egenes, CIA director Larry Rachlin, Chairman of the Joint Chiefs of Staff Melvin Parker, and National Security Chief Steve Burkow.

All of the men looked grim as they listened to a voice coming from the President's speakerphone.

". . . save you the trouble of tracing this call," the thinly accented Russian voice was saying. "My name is Eival Ekdol. I am at 1016 Forest Road in Valley Stream on Long Island. It is a *Grozny* safe house, and you can have it, and me. I will also stand trial and denounce the officials who brought me down. It will be a good show."

Grozny, thought Rodgers as he took a seat beside the dashing young National Security Chief. *Oh, Christ.*

Ascetic FBI Director Egenes wrote on a yellow pad, *"Let me get people over there,"* and held it up.

The President nodded and Egenes left the room.

"Once you have me," Ekdol concluded,

"there will be no further acts of terrorism."

"Why blow up the tunnel and then surrender yourself?" Burkow asked. "What do you want in return?"

"Nothing. What I mean is, we want the United States to do nothing."

"Where, when, and why?" Burkow asked.

"In Eastern Europe," said Ekdol. "A situation will soon develop militarily and we want neither the U.S. nor its allies to become involved."

Chairman Parker picked up a phone near him. He turned his body so his voice couldn't be heard.

Burkow said, "We can't promise that. The United States has interests in Poland, Hungary — "

"You have interests in the United States as well, Mr. Burkow."

Burkow appeared to be taken by surprise. Rodgers just sat still, listening carefully.

"Are you threatening other American interests?" Burkow asked.

"Yes, I am," said Ekdol. "In fact, at a quarter past ten, a major suspension bridge in another American city will be blown up. Unless, of course, we've reached an agreement by that time."

All in the room looked at their watches.

"As you no doubt realize," said Ekdol,

"you have just under four minutes."

The President said, "Mr. Ekdol, this is President Lawrence. We need more time."

"Take all the time you want, Mr. President," said Ekdol. "But you'll pay for it with lives. You can't reach me in time, even if you dispatched personnel when I gave you the address. And though you'll have me, you won't stop *Grozny*."

The President slashed his hand from side to side and Burkow muted the phone.

"Hit me," Lawrence said. "Fast."

"We don't deal with terrorists," Burkow said. "Period."

"Sure we do," said Lincoln. "Just not in public. We have no *choice* but to deal with this man."

"What about the next Tojo wannabe with a bomb?" Burkow asked. "What if Saddam does it next? Or some neo-Nazi right here in the States?"

"We don't *let* it happen again," said CIA Director Rachlin. "We learn from this. We prepare. Right now, we don't want another New York. Defuse the bomb, nail the peckers later."

"But it could be a bluff," said Burkow. "He may be a nutcase who blew his wad under the East River."

"Mr. President," said Rodgers, "let the

119

bastard have this one. I know a little something about these *Grozny* fanatics. They don't bluff, and you see how hard they strike. Give them the win and we'll catch them with an end run."

"You have an idea?"

"I do," he said.

"At least that's something," the President said.

"Right now, a spitball in a slingshot would be *some*thing," Burkow said. "But is it the *right* something?"

Lawrence rubbed his face with his open hands while Burkow scowled at Rodgers. The National Security Chief was not big on capitulation, and he obviously had thought he'd an ally in Rodgers. Ordinarily, he would have. But this was much bigger than what was happening here, and they needed time and clearer heads to deal with it.

"Sorry, Steve," said the President. "I agree with you in principle. God, how I do. But I've got to give this monster what he wants. Put him back on the line."

With a jab of his finger, Burkow unmuted the telephone.

"Are you there?" the President asked.

"I am."

"If we accept your terms, there will be no blast?"

"Only if you do so at once," said Ekdol. "You have less than a minute."

"Then we agree," said the President. "Damn you, we agree."

"Very well," said Ekdol.

The phone was silent for a moment.

"Where are the explosives?" Burkow asked.

"They are in the back of just another truck crossing just another bridge," said Ekdol. "I just phoned the driver not to deliver them. Now, as I promised, you can come and get me. I'll say nothing of our agreement. But go back on your word, Mr. President, and you will be unable to stop my people in other cities and towns. Do you understand?"

"I understand," said the President.

And then the line went dead.

FOURTEEN

Monday, 6:45 A.M., St. Petersburg

Orlov touched the button on the speaker outside Rossky's door.

"Yes?" said the Colonel in a strident voice.

"Colonel, it's General Orlov."

The door buzzed and Orlov entered. Rossky sat behind a small desk to the left. There were a computer, telephone, coffee mug, fax machine, and flag on its gunmetal surface. To the right was the cluttered desk of his assistant and secretary, Corporal Valentina Belyev. Both of them stood and saluted when the General entered, Belyev smartly, Rossky more slowly.

Orlov returned the salute and asked Valentina to excuse them. When the door clicked shut Orlov regarded the Colonel.

"Has anything happened in the last day that I should know about?" Orlov asked.

Rossky sat slowly. "A great deal has happened. As to whether you should know — General, our nation's satellites, field agents, cryptography, and radio surveillance all become our responsibility later today. You have a lot to attend to."

"I'm a general," Orlov said. "My subordinates do all the work. What I'm asking, Colonel, is whether you've been doing more work than you should."

"Specifically what, sir?"

"What business had you with the coroner?" Orlov asked.

"We had a body to dispose of," Rossky said. "A British agent. Brave fellow — we'd been watching him for days. He took his life when our operative closed in."

"When was this?" Orlov asked.

"Yesterday."

"Why didn't you log it?"

"I did," Rossky said. "With Minister Dogin."

Orlov's features darkened. "All reports are supposed to go to the computer file with a copy to my office — "

"That's true, sir," Rossky said, "in an operational facility. But we are not that yet. We won't be securing the link from your office to the Minister's desk for another four hours. Mine *has* been checked and secured, and I used it."

"And the link from your office to mine?" Orlov demanded. "Is that secure?"

"You did not receive a report?"

"You know I didn't — "

"An oversight," Rossky smiled. "I'll discipline Corporal Belyev. You'll have a full report — if I may call Belyev back — in just a few minutes."

Orlov regarded the Colonel for a long moment. "You joined the Society for Cooperation with Army, Air Force, and Fleet when you were just fourteen, didn't you?" Orlov asked.

"That's right," Rossky said.

"You were an expert sniper at sixteen, and while other young men chose to leap Devil's Ditch from a running jump with a track suit and running shoes, you elected to leap the spikes at the widest point with heavy boots and a rucksack on your back. Colonel General Odinstev personally trained you and a select group in the art of terrorism and assassination. As I recall, you once executed a spy in Afghanistan with a spade thrown from fifty meters away."

"It was fifty-two." Rossky's eyes shifted toward his superior. "A record for a kill in the spetsnaz."

Orlov came around the desk and sat on the edge. "You spent three years in Afghanistan, until a member of your group was wounded on a mission to capture an Afghan leader. Your platoon commander decided to take the wounded man with you rather than administer the Blessed Death. As assistant commander, you reminded your superior that it was his duty to order the lethal injection, and when he refused you killed the commander — a hand over his mouth, a knife thrust to the throat. Then you took the wounded man's life."

"Had I done otherwise," Rossky said, "high command would have ordered the entire group executed as traitors."

"Of course," Orlov said. "But there was an inquiry afterward, a question as to whether the soldier's wound was sufficient to require death."

"It was a leg wound," Rossky said, "and he was slowing us down. The regulations are quite specific on that count. The inquiry was merely a formality."

"Nonetheless," Orlov continued, "some of your men were not happy with what you'd done. Ambition, a desire for promotion — those were some of the charges they made, I believe. There was concern for your safety, so you were recalled and became part of the special faculty at the Military-Diplomatic Academy. You taught my son and got to know Minister Dogin when he was still the Mayor of Moscow. Is that all correct?"

"Yes, sir."

Orlov moved even closer, his voice barely above a whisper. "You've served your country and the military vigorously for just over twenty years, risked your life and reputation. With all of this experience, Colonel, tell me: didn't you learn *not* to sit down in the presence of a superior officer unless given leave to do so?"

Rossky's face flushed. He rose at once, slowly, his posture rigid. "Yes, sir."

Orlov remained seated on the desk. "My career has been different than yours, Colonel. My father saw firsthand what the Luftwaffe did to the Red Army during the War. He passed his respect for airpower to me. I spent eight years in the Air Defense Forces, flying reconnaissance for four years, then helping to train other pilots in ambushes — drawing enemy aircraft into killing grounds of antiaircraft fire." Orlov stood and looked into Rossky's angry eyes. "Did you know all of this, Colonel? Did you study my dossier?"

"I did, sir."

"Then you know I've never had to formally discipline any of my subordinates. Most men are decent, even the conscripts. They only want to do their jobs and be rewarded for the work they do. Some make honest mistakes, and there's no reason to spoil their records because of that. I will always give a soldier, a patriot, the benefit of the doubt. Including you, Colonel." Orlov came closer until their faces were inches apart. "But if you try and go around me again," he said, "I'll catch you and have you returned to the academy — *with* a notation of insubordination on your record. Are we clear on that, Colonel?"

"We are — sir," Rossky said, nearly spitting out the word.

"Good."

The men exchanged salutes as the General turned and headed toward the door.

"Sir?" Rossky said.

Orlov looked back. The Colonel was still standing at attention. "Yes?" Orlov asked.

"What your son did in Moscow — was that an honest mistake?"

"It was stupid and irresponsible," Orlov said. "You and the Minister were more than fair with him."

"It was out of respect for your accomplishments that we were, sir," Rossky said. "And he has a great career ahead of him. Did you ever read the file on the incident?"

Orlov's eyes narrowed. "I've never had any interest in it, no."

"I have a copy," Rossky said. "It was removed from the records in general staff headquarters. There was a recommendation attached to it. Did you know that?"

Orlov said nothing.

"Nikita's company Senior Sergeant recommended expulsion for *guliganstvo*. Not for defacing the Greek Orthodox church on Ulitsa Arkhipova or beating up the priest, but for breaking into the academy supply depot to get the paint, and for striking the guard when he tried to stop him." Rossky smiled. "I think your boy was frustrated after my lecture about how the Greek armed forces sold weapons to Afghanistan."

"What's your point?" Orlov asked. "That you were able to teach Nikita to attack helpless citizens?"

"Civilians are the soft underbelly of the same machine that runs the military, sir," Rossky said, "a perfectly valid target in the eyes of the spetsnaz. But you don't want to debate established military policy with me."

"I don't care to debate anything with you, Colonel," Orlov said. "We have an operations center to launch." He started toward the door, but Rossky's voice stopped him.

"Of course, sir. However, since you've asked to be kept aware of everything pertaining to my official activities, I will log the details of this conversation — which now include the following. The charges against your son were not dismissed. The Senior Sergeant's report was simply not acted upon, which isn't the same thing. If it were ever called to the attention of the personnel directorate, it would have to be acted upon."

Orlov had his hand on the doorknob, his back to the Colonel. "My son will have to bear the consequences of his own deeds, though I'm certain a military judge would take into account his intervening years of service, as well as the way in which the records were suppressed and then released."

"Files sometimes show up on desks, sir."

Orlov opened the door. Corporal Belyev was standing there and saluted smartly. "Your impertinence will be noted in my own log, Colonel," Orlov said. He looked from Belyev to Rossky. "Would you care to add to the entry?"

Rossky stood stiffly beside his desk. "No, sir. Not at present, sir."

General Orlov walked into the hall and Belyev entered the Colonel's office. She shut the door behind her, and the General could only imagine what was taking place behind the soundproof door.

Not that it mattered. Rossky had been put on notice and would have to follow the rules to the letter . . . though Orlov had a feeling that rules might begin to change once the Colonel got Interior Minister Dogin on the phone.

FIFTEEN

Sunday, 10:15 P.M., Washington, D.C.

Griff Egenes returned to the Oval Office.

"State troopers are on the way to Forest Road," he said, "and one of my teams is choppering in from New York. They'll have this lunatic before the half hour."

"He won't fight them," said Burkow.

Egenes sat heavily. "What do you mean?"

"I mean, we've given him what he wants. He'll spout some radical crap and let himself be taken."

"Shit," said Egenes. "I really wanted to squeeze him."

"Me too," said Burkow.

The National Security Chief turned to Mike Rodgers. Though the mood in the Oval Office was grim, Burkow owned the gravest face of the group.

"So, Mike?" Burkow asked. "Who are these creatures and how do we squash the rest of them?"

"Before you answer," said the President,

"can someone tell me if the Russians have anything going militarily that can snowball into an invasion? Aren't we supposed to *watch* for these things?"

Mel Parker, the Chairman of the Joint Chiefs of Staff and the administration's silent man, said, "While Ekdol was busy dictating terms of unconditional surrender, I rang Defense Secretary Colon. He called the Pentagon. I'm told that several Russian divisions are on maneuvers right at the Ukrainian border. Pretty big numbers compared to what they usually do in the region, but nothing that would have sent up a warning signal."

"No troop movements anywhere else?" Rodgers asked.

"NRO is putting all their resources into finding out," Parker replied.

"But the border could be a staging area," the President said.

"It could very well be," said Parker.

"There's the goddamn problem," said FBI chief Egenes. "All this downsizing. We have too few HUMINT resources. A satellite can't tell us about foot soldiers bitching about tomorrow's march or what it says on a map inside a field tent. That's where the real intelligence is."

"That's a problem," Rodgers agreed, "but it has very little to do with this situation."

"How so?" asked Rachlin.

"The truth is," said Rodgers, "this Grozny-ite didn't buy himself a thing."

"What do you mean?" asked Tobey, who had been silent as she took notes for Burkow.

"Assume there's an invasion," Rodgers said, "say Russia goes into the Ukraine. We wouldn't intervene."

"Why not?" she asked.

"Because then we'd be at war with Russia," Rodgers said, "and what do we do next? We don't have the capacity to wage an effective conventional war. We proved that in Haiti and Somalia. If we tried, casualties would be heavy and they'd be all over TV. The public and Congress would shut us down faster than a crap game in church. And we can't go in with missiles, bombers, and big-scale attacks because of the collateral damage and civilian casualties."

"I'm crying big, fat, Betty Boop tears," Burkow said. "It's a war. People are going to get hurt. And if I'm not mistaken, the Russians fired the first salvo against a bunch of civilians in New York City."

"We don't know that the Russian government authorized that," Egenes pointed out.

"Exactly," said Secretary Lincoln. "And frankly, as unpopular as this might be, I'm not sure I'd want to see us fight a war for Eastern Europe, even a just one. Germany and France wouldn't join us. They might not even support us. NATO could conceivably turn on us. The expense of repelling Russia *and* rebuilding those nations after a war would be horrendous."

"No," Burkow said with an edge of disgust. "Better to build another Maginot Line to keep the enemy out, like the Three Little Pigs and their house of straw. I don't buy that. I believe you go to the den of the Big Bad Wolf, napalm the bejesus out of him, and make a coat from what's left. I know that isn't the politically sensitive thing to do, but we're not the ones who started this."

"Tell me," Lincoln asked Rodgers, "did the Japanese send you a box of chocolates and a thank-you note when you stopped Tokyo from being evaporated by those North Korean nodong missiles?"

"I didn't do it for a pat on the back," said Rodgers. "I did it because it was right."

"And we were all very proud of you," Lincoln said. "But I still count two Americans dead versus zero Japanese."

The President said, "I'm in Mel's camp on this one, but we're losing sight of our immediate problem: who's behind this and why." He looked at his watch. "I'm scheduled to go on the air at ten past eleven to talk about the bombing. Tobey, will you have the speech updated to talk about the capture of the bomber thanks to the fast work of the FBI, CIA, and others?"

The National Security Assistant nodded and walked to the nearest phone.

The President regarded Rodgers. "General, is this why you advised me to capitulate to the bomber? Because we were going to do what he wanted anyway?"

"No, sir," said Rodgers. "The truth is, we didn't capitulate to him. We distracted him."

Lawrence leaned back, his hands behind his head. "From what?"

"Our counterattack," Rodgers said.

"Against whom?" Burkow asked. "The prick told us who he was with and turned himself in."

"But follow the thread backward," Rodgers said.

"We're listening," said the President.

Rodgers leaned forward, elbows on his knees. "Sir, *Grozny* takes its name from Ivan Grozny, Ivan the Terrible — "

"Why am I not surprised?" muttered Rachlin.

"As far back as the Revolution, they've worked for political gain, not money," Rod-

135

gers said. "They were fifth columnists in Germany during the War and caused some minor trouble here during the Cold War. We traced some of the early, unmanned Redstone rocket failures to them."

"Who finances them?" asked Parker.

"Until recently," said Rodgers, "they were underwritten by extreme nationalistic political forces that needed terrorist enforcers. Gorbachev disbanded them in the mid-1980s, at which point they hunkered down overseas, especially in the U.S. and South America, and joined with the increasingly powerful Russian mafia in an effort to overthrow their westernized leaders."

"So they must really hate Zhanin," said Lincoln.

"You've got it," said Rodgers.

"But if they're not tied to the government," the President said, "what can they be planning in Eastern Europe? A military operation of any size can't be run without the approval of the Kremlin. This isn't Chechnya, with a handful of generals in the field dictating military policy to President Yeltsin."

"Hell," Rachlin observed, "I never believed he wasn't calling the shots behind his hand the whole time."

"That's just it," Rodgers said. "Something big just *might* be run without the Kremlin.

What we saw in Chechnya in 1994 was the beginning of a trend toward decentralization in Russia. It's a big country with eight time zones. Suppose someone finally woke up there and said, 'This is like a dinosaur. It needs a couple of brains to make the whole work'?"

The President regarded Rodgers. "Has someone, in fact, done this?"

Rodgers said, "Before the blast, Mr. President, we intercepted a bagel order sent from St. Petersburg to a shop in New York."

"A *bagel* order?" said Burkow. "Get real."

"That was my reaction," said Rodgers. "We noodled around with it, but it didn't make any sense until *after* the blast. Using the Midtown Tunnel as a point on a grid, one of our cryptologists figured out that it was a map of New York, with the tunnel as one of the highlights."

"Were the other points secondary targets?" asked Egenes. "After all, the World Trade Center bombers had alternate targets, including the Lincoln Tunnel."

"I don't think so," said Rodgers. "It looked to our analyst like stops in the bomb-making process. Now, Larry — you'll bear me out on this. For a couple of months now, we've been picking up microwave radiation from the Neva in St. Petersburg."

"It's really been cooking over there," Rachlin agreed.

"We thought the radiation was coming from a TV studio being built in the Hermitage," said Rodgers. "We now believe that the studio is a front for some kind of top-secret operation."

"A second 'brain' for the dinosaur," said Lincoln.

"Exactly," said Rodgers. "It was financed, apparently, using funds approved by Interior Minister Nikolai Dogin."

"The loser in the elections," said the President.

"The same," Rodgers said. "And there's one thing more. A British agent was killed trying to have a look at the place. So something *is* going on there. And whatever it is, whether it's a command center or military base, it's probably connected to the attack in New York through that bagel order."

"So," said Av Lincoln, "we have the Russian government, or some faction thereof, in league with an outlawed terrorist group and, quite possibly, with the Russian mafia. And they apparently control enough of the military so that they can make something major happen in Eastern Europe."

"That's right," said Rodgers.

Rachlin said, "God, how I'd love to grill

that arrogant little *Grozny* rat personally when we have him."

"I guarantee we won't get a thing from him," Egenes said. "They wouldn't have told him anything, then let him hand himself over to us."

"That would be kind of dumb," Rachlin agreed. "They gave him to us just so we could look good, like we wielded a swift and terrible sword of justice."

"Let's not spit on that," the President said. "We all know that JFK had to compromise the U.S. military in Turkey to get Khrushchev's missiles out of Cuba. The fact that only half the deal came out made him look like a hero and Khrushchev a chump. So," he said, "let's assume that, through St. Petersburg, a government official ordered the attack in New York. Could it have been President Zhanin?"

"I doubt it," said Secretary Lincoln. "He wants a relationship with the West, not war."

"Do we know that for sure?" Burkow said. "Speaking of Boris Yeltsin, we've been snowed before."

"Zhanin has nothing to gain," said Lincoln. "He ran against military expenditures. Besides, he and *Grozny* are natural-born enemies."

"What about Dogin?" the President asked. "Can this be his doing?"

"He's a likelier candidate," said Rodgers. "He paid for the place in St. Petersburg and probably owns the people in it."

"Is there any way we can talk to Zhanin about it?" asked Tobey.

"I wouldn't risk it," said Rodgers. "Even if he's out of the loop, chances are good that not everyone around him is trustworthy."

"So then what's your plan, Mike?" Burkow said testily. "From where I sit, one bomb has effectively put the United States on the sidelines. Christ, I remember when things like that used to galvanize people and get us *into* wars."

Rodgers said, "Steve, the bomb hasn't stopped us. From a strategic point of view, it may have helped."

"How?" asked Burkow.

"Whoever is behind this probably feels they don't have to watch us closely," Rodgers said. "Just like the Russians felt about Hitler after signing the Nonaggression Pact."

"They were wrong," said Lincoln. "He attacked them anyway."

"Exactly," said Rodgers. He looked at the President. "Sir, let's do the same. Let me send Striker to St. Petersburg. As promised, we don't do anything in Eastern Europe. In

140

fact, we let Europe tremble a little at our isolationism."

"That'll certainly tie in with American sentiments these days," said Lincoln.

"Meanwhile," said Rodgers, "we let Striker take these people apart from the brain down."

The President looked at each man's face in turn. Rodgers felt the mood in the room shift.

"I like it," said Burkow. "A lot."

The President stopped at Rodgers's face. "Do it," he said. "Bring me the head of the Big Bad Wolf."

SIXTEEN

Sunday, 8:00 P.M., Los Angeles

Paul Hood was sitting in a lounge beside the hotel pool. He had his pager and cellular phone by his side, and his Panama hat pulled low so that he wouldn't be recognized. He didn't feel like chewing the fat with old constituents just now. Except for the conspicuously absent tan, he probably looked the part of the modern, self-absorbed, independent film producer.

The truth was, even with Sharon and the kids frolicking a few yards away, in the deep end of the pool, he felt melancholy and strangely alone. He had his Walkman on, listening to an all-news channel as he waited for the President's address to the nation. It had been a long time since he'd followed a breaking news story as a citizen and not a public official, and he didn't like it. He didn't like the sense of helplessness, at not being able to share his grief with the press, with other officials. He wanted to contribute to the healing or the sense of outrage or even the vengeance.

He was just a man on a rubber chair waiting for news like everyone else.

No, not quite like everyone else, he knew. He was waiting for Mike Rodgers to call. Even though the line wasn't secure, Rodgers would find a way to tell him something. Assuming there was something to be told.

As he waited, his thoughts returned to the bombing. The target didn't have to be the tunnel. It could just as well have been this hotel's lobby, with its Asian tourists and businesspeople, filmmakers from Italy, Spain, South America, and even Russia. Scare them away and damage the local economy, from limousine services to restaurants. When Hood was the Mayor of Los Angeles, he had participated in a number of seminars about terrorists. Though they'd all had their own methods and reasons for doing what they did, they also had one thing in common. They struck at places people had to use, whether it was a military command center or a means of transportation or an office building. That was how they brought governments to the bargaining table, despite public posturing to the contrary.

He also thought about Bob Herbert, who had lost his legs and his wife in a terrorist bombing. He couldn't imagine how this was affecting him.

A bleached-blond young waiter stopped by Hood's chair and asked him if he wanted a beverage. He ordered a club soda. When the waiter returned, he looked at Hood for a moment.

"You're him, aren't you?"

Hood unhooked his Walkman. "Excuse me?"

"You're Mayor Hood."

"Yes," he smiled up, and nodded.

"Cool," said the young man. "I had Boris Karloff's daughter here yesterday." He set the glass on a wobbly metal table. "Pretty unbelievable about New York, isn't it? It's the kind of thing you don't want to think about, yet you can't *not* think about."

"True," said Hood.

The waiter leaned closer as he poured the sparkling water. "You'll appreciate this. Or maybe you won't. I heard Manager Mosura tell the house detective that our insurance company wants us to offer daily evacuation drills, like they do on luxury liners. Just so people can't sue the chain if we get blown up."

"Protect your guests and your assets," Hood said.

"Exactamundo," said the waiter.

144

Hood signed the bill and thanked the waiter as his phone chirped. He answered quickly.

"How are you, Mike?" he asked. He picked up the phone and began walking toward a shady corner, where there were no other guests.

"Same as everyone," Rodgers said. "Sick and mad."

"What can you tell me?" Hood asked.

"I'm heading to the office after meeting with the boss," he said. "A lot's happened. For one thing, the perpetrator called. Gave up. We've got him."

"Just like that?" Hood asked.

"There were some strings attached," Rodgers said. "We have to stay out of some business he says is going down overseas. Old Red zone. Otherwise, we get more of the same."

"Is this big business?" Hood asked.

"We're not sure. Army business, it appears."

"From the new President?" Hood asked.

"We don't think so," Rodgers said. "It appears to be a reaction to him and not necessarily his doing."

"I see," said Hood.

"In fact, we think the okay for all this came from that TV studio we've been tuned in to. Got a pretty solid paper trail. The boss has authorized us to have a look-see, pending all the paperwork. I've put Lowell on it."

Hood stopped walking under a palm tree. The President had authorized a Striker excursion into St. Petersburg, and Op-Center attorney Lowell Coffey II was going to seek approval from the Congressional Oversight Intelligence Committee. *That* was heavy-duty.

Hood looked at his watch. "Mike, I'm going to try and catch a red-eye back there."

"Don't," said Rodgers. "We've got some time on this. When things start to hop, I can chopper you up to Sacramento and you can hitch a ride from March."

Hood looked back at the kids. They were all supposed to take the Magna Studio tour in the morning. And Rodgers had a point. It would be a half-hour hop up to the Air Force base, then less than a five-hour ride back to D.C. But he had taken an oath to do a job, and it was a job — more accurately, a burden, a responsibility, which he didn't want to put on anyone else's shoulders.

His heart was beating fast. Hood knew what *it* wanted to do. It was already getting the blood to his legs so he could make the plane.

"Let me talk to Sharon," he said to Rodgers.

"She's going to kill you," Rodgers said. "Take a deep breath and a jog around the parking lot. We can *handle* this."

"Thanks," Hood said, "but I'll let you know what I'm doing. I appreciate the update. I'll talk to you later."

"Sure," Rodgers said glumly.

Hood clicked off and folded up the phone. He swatted it gently in his open palm.

Sharon *would* kill him, and the kids would be crushed. Alexander had been looking forward to doing the virtual reality Teknophage attraction with him.

Jesus, why can't anything ever be simple? he asked himself as he walked toward the pool. "Because then there would be no dynamics between people," he said under his breath, "and life would be boring."

Though he had to admit that a little boredom would be good right now. It was what he'd come back to Los Angeles in the hopes of finding.

"Dad, you comin' in?" his daughter, Harleigh, yelled as he approached.

"No, cheesehead," said Alexander. "Can't you see he's got his phone?"

"I can't see that far without my glasses, dorko," she replied.

147

Sharon had stopped squirt-gunning their son and was swimming in place. From her expression, he could tell that she knew what was coming.

"Gather round," Sharon said as her husband squatted by the side of the pool. "I think Dad's got something to tell us."

Hood said simply, "I have to go back. What happened today — we have to respond."

"They need Dad to kick ass," Alexander said.

"Hush," Hood said. "Remember, loose lips — "

"Sink ships," said the ten-year-old. "Exsqueeze me," he said as he went under.

His twelve-year-old sister went to hold him there, but Alexander darted away.

Sharon just glared at her husband. "This response," she asked quietly. "It can't possibly be made without you?"

"It can."

"Then let it."

"I can't," Hood said. He looked down, then off to the side. Anywhere but in her eyes. "I'm sorry. I'll call you later."

Hood got up and called out to the kids, who interrupted their chase long enough to wave. "Get me a T-shirt at Teknophage," he said.

"We will!" Alexander said.

He turned to walk away.

"Paul?" Sharon said.

He stopped and looked back.

"I know this is difficult," she said, "and I'm not making it any easier. But we need you too. Especially Alexander. He's going to be, 'Oh, Dad would have loved this' and 'Dad would have loved that' all day tomorrow. Sometime real soon, you're going to have to start 'responding' to not being around enough."

"You don't think this kills me?" Hood asked.

"Not enough," Sharon said as she pushed off the side. "Not as much as being away from your electric trains in D.C. Think about it, Paul."

He would, he promised himself.

In the meantime, he had a plane to catch.

SEVENTEEN

Monday, 3:35 A.M., Washington D.C.

Lieutenant Colonel W. Charles Squires stood on the dark airstrip at Quantico. He was dressed in civilian clothes and a leather jacket, his laptop computer standing on the tarmac between his legs as he hustled the six other members of the Striker team into the two Bell JetRangers that would shuttle them to Andrews Air Force Base. There, they would transfer to Striker's private C-141B StarLifter for the eleven-hour flight to Helsinki.

The night was crisp and invigorating, though, as always, it was the work itself that exhilarated him the most. When he was a kid growing up in Jamaica, he had never experienced anything more exciting than running onto the soccer field before a game, especially when the odds were against his team; that was how he felt each time Striker kicked into action. It was because of Squires's passion for soccer that Hood allowed him to name the team after the position he had played.

Squires had been sleeping in his small home on the base when Rodgers called, giving him his orders for the trip to Finland. Rodgers apologized that they were only able to get congressional approval for a seven-person team, rather than the usual twelve. Congress had to mess with everything they were given, and this time it was the roster that was pared. The thinking was, if caught, they could always explain to the Russians that they hadn't sent over a *full* force. In the world of international politics, distinctions like that apparently meant something. Fortunately, after the last mission, Squires had adapted Strikers' playbook to work with almost any number of team members.

Squires didn't kiss his wife goodbye: farewells were easier if she stayed asleep through them. Instead, he took the secure phone into the bathroom and talked to Rodgers while he dressed. The tentative plan was for them to pose as tourists once they arrived. Once the team was airborne, Rodgers would be in contact with Squires with additions or embellishments to the plan. As it stood, three operatives would go into St. Petersburg, four would wait in Helsinki as backup.

The Striker members who stayed behind would be disappointed, and they wouldn't be alone. Striker didn't go into action often,

151

but Squires kept them ready and finely tuned with drills, sports, and simulations; the four who remained in Helsinki would be especially frustrated to get so close and not be part of the action. But like any good, experienced military man, Rodgers insisted on having people ready to help with a retreat if one was necessary.

After the team had boarded the JetRangers, Squires climbed into the second chopper. Even before it was airborne, he pulled the portable computer onto his lap, plugged in a diskette handed to him by the pilot, and began checking the equipment that was already on the StarLifter, from the weapons to clothing and uniforms of what were considered powder-keg foreign nations, countries where on-site intelligence might be necessary on short notice: China, Russia, and several Middle Eastern and Latin American nations. There was also enough underwater and cold-weather gear for the entire team, though the inventory did not yet contain the still and video cameras, guidebooks, dictionaries, and commercial airline tickets they'd need if they were to pose as tourists. But Mike Rodgers prided himself on his attention to detail, and Squires knew that the items would be waiting for him at Andrews.

He glanced around the cabin at the Strikers

who had come with him. He looked from blond, beaming David George, who had gotten bumped from their last mission when Mike Rodgers took his place, to new recruit Sondra DeVonne, who had begun SEAL training and was recently seconded to Striker to replace the man they'd lost in North Korea.

As always, he felt a rush of pride as he looked at their faces . . . and the keen sense of responsibility that came from knowing not all of them might be coming back. Though he worked hard at what he did, he was somewhat more fatalistic than Rodgers, whose motto was, *"My fate's not in God's hands as long as there's a weapon in mine."*

Squires shifted his gaze to the computer and smiled as he pictured his wife and their young son, Billy, blissfully asleep. And he felt that sense of pride again as he thought of them secure in their beds because of more than two hundred years of men and women who had wrestled with the same thoughts as he did, experienced the same fears as they galloped or sailed, drove or flew off to protect the democracy in which they all passionately believed. . . .

EIGHTEEN

Monday, 8:20 A.M., Washington, D.C.

The small executive cafeteria was located on the ground floor of Op-Center, a secure room located behind the employees' cafeteria. The walls were soundproof, the blinds were perpetually drawn, and a microwave transmitter just outside, on an unused landing strip, kept up a drone that would sound deafening to an eavesdropper.

When he came aboard, Paul Hood had insisted that both cafeterias offer full, fast-food-style menus, from dry eggs on a muffin to personal pizzas. This wasn't just for the convenience of Op-Center employees, it was a matter of national security: during Desert Storm, the enemy had been tipped off that something was brewing by spies who kept track of the amount of take-out pizza and Chinese food that suddenly went into the Pentagon. If Op-Center was put on alert for any reason, Hood didn't want a spy or journalist or anyone else finding out from a kid who delivered Big Macs on a motorbike.

The executive cafeteria was always busiest between eight and nine in the morning. The day shift took over from the night shift at six, and day staff spent the next two hours reviewing intelligence that had come in from around the world. By eight, when the data had been assimilated and filed or discarded, and barring a crisis, the Directors of each division came to have breakfast and compare notes. Today, Rodgers had posted E-mail about a full staff meeting at nine, so the room would empty a few minutes before the hour to give everyone time to make it to the Tank.

When Press Officer Ann Farris walked into the room, her smartly tailored red pant-suit drew an admiring nod from Lowell Coffey II. She could tell right then that he'd had an exhausting night. When Lowell was alert, he had constructive criticism about everything from fashion to literature.

"Busy night?" she asked.

"I was with the Congressional Intelligence Oversight Committee," he said, turning back to a crisply folded copy of the *Washington Post*.

"Ah," she said. "*Long* night. What happened?"

Coffey said, "Mike thinks he's got a bead

155

on the Russians who were really behind the tunnel bombing. He sent Striker in to get them."

"So that little Eival Ekdol man they picked up wasn't working alone."

"Not at all," said Lowell.

Ann stopped by the coffee vending machine. She fed in a dollar bill. "Does Paul know?"

"Paul's back," he said.

Ann brightened. "Really?"

"Really and truly," said Lowell. "Caught the red-eye out of L.A., said he'll be in this morning. Mike's going to brief the entire team in the Tank at nine."

Poor Paul, Ann thought as she picked up her double espresso and collected her change. *Out and back in less than twenty-four hours.* How Sharon must have loved that.

The seats around the six round tables were occupied by executives doing surprisingly little. Psychologist Liz Gordon was chewing nicotine gum in the smoke-free room, nervously twirling a lock of short brown hair, sipping her dark coffee with three sugars and reading the new week's supermarket tabloids.

Operations Support Officer Matt Stoll was playing poker with Environmental Officer Phil Katzen. There was a small mound of quarters between the men and, instead of cards, both of them were using laptops linked by a cable. As she walked past them, Ann could tell Stoll was losing. He freely admitted that he had the worst poker face on the planet. Whenever things weren't going well, whether he was playing cards or trying to fix a computer responsible for the defense of the free world, sweat collected on every pore of his round, cherubic face.

Stoll surrendered a six of spades and a four of clubs. Phil dealt him a five of spades and a seven of hearts in return.

"Well, at least I've got a higher card now," Matt said, folding. "One more hand," he said. "Too bad this isn't like quantum computing. You confine ions in webs of magnetic and electric fields, hit a trapped particle with a burst of laser light to send it into an excited energy state, then hit it again to ground it. That's your switch. Rows of ions in a quantum logical gate, giving you the smallest, fastest computer on earth. Neat, clean, perfect."

"Yeah," Phil said, "too bad this isn't like that."

"Don't be sarcastic," Stoll said as he popped the last of a chocolate-covered doughnut in his mouth, then washed it down with black coffee. "Next time we'll play baccarat and things will be different."

"No they won't," Katzen said, sitting back as he raked in the pot. "You always lose at that too."

"I know," Stoll said, "but I always feel bad when I get beat playing poker. I don't know what it is."

"Loss of manhood," Liz Gordon piped in without looking up from her *National Enquirer*.

Stoll glanced over. "Come again?"

"Consider the elements," Liz said. "Strong hands, stone-faced bluffs, the size of the ante . . . the whole cigar-smoking, Wild West, backroom, night-with-the-boys thing."

Stoll and Katzen both looked at her.

"Trust me," she said, turning the page. "I know what I'm talking about."

"Trust someone who gets their news from the tabloids?" Katzen said.

"Not news," Liz said. "Fruitcakes. Celebrities live in a rarefied atmosphere that makes them fascinating to study. As for gamblers, I used to treat chronic cases in Atlantic City. Poker and pool are two games men hate to lose. Try Go Fish or Ping-Pong — they're much less damaging to the ego."

Ann sat at Liz's table. "What about intellectual games like chess or Scrabble?" she asked.

"They're macho in a different way," Liz said. "Men don't like losing those either, but they can accept losing to a man much easier than they can to a woman."

Lowell Coffey snickered. "Which is just what I'd expect a woman to say. You know, Senator Barbara Fox busted my chops harder last night than any man has *ever* done."

"Maybe she was just doing her job better than any man has ever done," Liz observed.

"No," said Coffey. "I couldn't use the kind of shorthand with her that I used with the men on the committee. Ask Martha, she was there."

Ann said, "Senator Fox has been a rabid isolationist since her daughter was murdered in France years ago."

"Look," Liz said, "all this isn't my opinion. Countless papers have been written on the subject."

"Countless papers have been written about UFOs," Coffey said, "and I still think it's all a sack of horsefeathers. People respond to people, not sexes."

Liz smiled sweetly. "Carol Laning, Lowell."

"Excuse me?" Coffey said.

"I'm not allowed to talk about it," Liz said, "but *you* are — if you've got the *cajones*."

"You mean Prosecutor Laning? *Fraser v. Maryland?* Is that in my psych profile?"

Liz said nothing.

Coffey flushed. He turned the page, creased and recreased the fold, and looked at the newspaper. "You're barking up the wrong tree, Elizabeth. I crashed into her car by accident after the trial. It was my first case and I was distracted. Losing to a woman had *nothing* to do with it."

"Of course not," Liz said.

"It's true," Coffey said as his pager beeped. He glanced at the number, then dropped the newspaper on the table and stood. "Sorry, kiddies, but you'll have to hear my closing argument some other time. I've got a world leader to call."

"Male or female?" Phil asked.

Coffey made a face as he left the room.

When he was gone, Ann said, "Don't you think you were a little rough on him, Liz?"

Liz finished with the *National Enquirer*, collected the *Star* and *Globe*, and stood. She looked down at the rosy-cheeked brunette. "A bit, Ann. But it's good for him. Despite the bluster, Lowell listens to what people say and some of it sinks in. Unlike some people."

"Thank you very much," Stoll said as he shut his computer and disconnected the computers. "Before you got here, Ann, Liz and

160

I were 'debating' about whether her ineptitude with hardware was actually a physical limitation or a subconscious antimale bias."

"It's the former," Liz said. "It would be the same as saying that your skills with hardware ipso facto make you a man."

"Thank you again," Stoll said.

"My God," Ann said, "I move that we all cut back on the morning caffeine and sugar intake."

"It's not that," Stoll said as Liz left. "It's just the Monday after an international blow. We decided we're all a little testy because nobody thought to preprogram their VCRs for the week we're going to be living here."

Katzen tucked his laptop under his arm and rose. "I've got some material to get for the meeting," he said. "See you folks in fifteen."

"And then every quarter hour after that," Stoll said, following him out, "until we're all old and gray."

Alone now, the Press Officer sipped her espresso and contemplated the primary Op-Center team. They were a bunch of characters, with Matt Stoll the biggest kid and Liz Gordon the biggest bully. But the best people in any field usually were eccentric. And getting them to work together in close quarters like this was a thankless job. The best Paul Hood could ever hope for among his eclectic officers was peaceful coexistence, shared purpose, and some degree of mutual, professional respect. He got that through high-maintenance, hands-on management — though she knew the toll that took on his private life.

Leaving the cafeteria to go to the meeting, Ann ran into Martha Mackall. The forty-nine-year-old Political Officer and linguistics expert was also hurrying to the meeting, though she never *seemed* to be in a hurry. The daughter of the late soul singer Mack Mackall, she had his cheek-splitting smile, smoky voice, and easy manner — layered atop her own core of steel. She always appeared cool, the result of having grown up on the road with her father, where she learned that drunks, rednecks, and bigots were more intimidated by a sharp mind and wit than by a sharp knife. When Mack was killed in a car crash, Martha went to live with an aunt who made her study hard, put her through college, and lived to see her make the move from her father's "Soul to Go" days to the State Department.

"Morning, glory," Martha said as Ann increased her speed to keep up with the taller woman.

"Morning, Martha," Ann said. "I understand you had a busy night."

"Lowell and I did the Dance of the Seven Veils up on the Hill," she said. "Those Congresspeople take a bit of persuading."

The two walked the rest of the way in silence. Martha was not one for small talk in any language, unless it was with the high and mighty. Increasingly, Ann had the feeling that if there was anyone who coveted Hood's job, it wasn't Mike Rodgers.

Mike Rodgers, Bob Herbert, Matt Stoll, Phil Katzen, and Liz Gordon were already sitting around the large, oval conference table in the Tank when Ann and Martha arrived. Ann noted that Bob Herbert appeared drawn. She assumed that he and his old friend Rodgers had spent the night working on the Striker mission — and dealing with some of the emotions the bombing had to have brought out in the wheelchair-bound Intelligence Officer.

The women were followed in by Paul Hood and a hustling Lowell Coffey. Even before the attorney was in, Rodgers had pressed a button in the side of the table and the heavy door had begun to shut.

The small room was lit by fluorescent lights; on the wall across from where Rodgers was sitting, the large, digital countdown clock was frozen at zero. Whenever there was a crisis with a timetable, the clock was set and a similar read-out appeared in every office — just so there was no mistake about when things had to be done.

The walls, floor, door, and ceiling of the Tank were all covered with mottled gray and black, sound-absorbing Acoustix. Behind this were several layers of cork, a foot of concrete, and more Acoustix. Buried in the concrete, on all six sides of the room, were wire grids that generated vascillating audio waves; no electronic information could enter or leave the room without being completely and irreparably distorted.

Hood sat at the head of the table. To his right, on a small extension, were a monitor and computer keyboard and telephone hookup. A tiny fiber-optic camera was attached to the top of the monitor and allowed him to see anyone on-screen who had a similar setup.

When the door was shut, Paul said, "I know we all feel sick about what happened yesterday, so there's no need to comment further about that. I want to thank Mike for the incredible job he did. He'll be telling you about that. In case you haven't already heard, there's more to this story than has been on the news. I've come straight from a plane flight and a quick shower, so I'm as eager to hear what he has to say as you are. I'd like to point out, though, that everything you'll be hearing is Priority One clearance. When we leave here, both Mike and I or Mike and Martha have to sign off on anyone less than that who needs to be told." Hood looked at Rodgers. "Mike?"

Rodgers thanked Hood, then briefed the team on what had happened in the Oval Office. He told them that Striker had departed from Andrews at 4:47 A.M. and would arrive in Helsinki around 8:50 P.M., local time.

"Lowell," he said, "where are we on the Finnish Ambassador?"

"He's given me a temporary okay," the attorney said. "He just needs a rubber stamp from the President."

"When will we have that?"

"This morning," Coffey replied.

Rodgers looked at his watch. "It's already four in the afternoon over there. Are you *sure?*"

"I'm sure. They start late and work late over there. No one makes any high-level decisions until after lunch."

Rodgers looked from Coffey to Darrell McCaskey. "Assuming that we get what we want from the Finnish government, is there any way Interpol can help us with intelligence from St. Petersburg?"

"That depends. You mean the Hermitage?"
Rodgers nodded.

"Do I tell them about the English agent who was killed there the other day?"

Rodgers looked at Hood. "DI6 lost a man there trying to eavesdrop on the TV studio."

"Are we asking Interpol to do essentially the same kind of reconnaissance?" Hood asked.

Rodgers nodded again.

"Then tell them about the Englishman," Hood said. "I'm sure there's a hotdog who'll be willing to take them on."

"What about at the border?" Rodgers asked. "If we have to go by land, is there any way the Finns can sneak our team across?"

"I know someone in the Ministry of Defense," McCaskey said, "and I'll see what I can wangle. Just understand, Mike, there are less than four thousand effectives in the border guard. They don't exactly want to go pissing-off the Russians."

"Understood," the Deputy Director said, then turned to Matt Stoll. The portly computer expert was tapping his steepled fingers together.

"Matt," Rodgers said, "I want you to use your computer contacts to find out if the Russians have been ordering or stockpiling anything out of the ordinary. Or if any of their top tech people have relocated to St. Petersburg in the last year."

"Those guys are pretty tight-lipped," Stoll said. "I mean, it's not like they have a lot of options in private industry if the government stops trusting them. But I'll try."

"Don't try — *do*," Rodgers snapped. Almost at once, he looked down and rolled his lips together. "Sorry," he said after a moment. "It's been a long night. Matt, I may have to send my team into Russia, and that won't be a day at the beach. I want them to know everything they can about their target and who they might encounter. Knowing something about the electronics will help a great deal."

"I understand," Stoll said stiffly. "I'll do some hacking, internetting, see what I can find."

"Thank you," Rodgers said.

Ann watched as the Deputy Director turned to Liz Gordon. She reacted with surprise when he spoke. Unlike Hood, who put little faith in psychological profiles of foreign leaders, Rodgers trusted their validity.

"Liz," he said, "I want you to put Russian Interior Minister Dogin through the computer. Factor in his loss of the presidency to Zhanin, as well as the influence of General

Mikhail Kosigan. Bob has information on the General if you need it."

"His name rings a bell," Martha says. "I'm sure he's in my file."

Rodgers turned to Environmental Officer Phil Katzen, who had his laptop open and ready. "Phil, I need a workup on the Gulf of Finland into the Neva, and the Neva where it passes the Hermitage. Temperature, speed, wind factor — "

The computer to Hood's right beeped. He hit F6 to answer, then pushed Control to hold the call.

Rodgers continued, "And I want whatever you've got on the composition of the soil under the museum. I want to know how deep the Russians may have dug there."

Katzen nodded as he finished typing.

Hood hit Control again. The face of his Executive Assistant, Stephen "Bugs" Benet, appeared on the screen.

"Sir," said Bugs, "there's an urgent call from Commander Hubbard at DI6. It pertains to this matter, so I thought — "

"Thanks," said Hood. "Put it through."

Hood snapped on the phone's speaker button, then waited. The bloodhound face appeared on the monitor a moment later.

"Good morning, Commander," Hood said. "I'm with the rest of my team, so I took the liberty of putting you on the speaker-phone."

"Fine," Hubbard said, his thickly accented voice deep and raspy, "I'll do the same. Mr. Hood, let me get straight to the matter. We have an operative here who would like to be part of the team you've sent to Helsinki."

Rodgers's expression soured. He shook his head.

Hood said, "Commander, ours is a carefully balanced unit — "

"I understand," Hubbard said, "but hear me out. I've lost two agents and a third is hiding. My staff wants me to send our own Bengal unit in, but it wouldn't do to have our two groups stumbling one over the other."

"Could your Bengal unit put me on the phone with the head of this new operation in St. Petersburg?"

"Pardon me?" said Hubbard.

"What I'm saying," said Hood, "is that you're not offering me anything I can't get myself. We'll share what we find out, as always."

"Of course," said Hubbard. "But I disagree. We can offer you one thing. Miss Peggy James."

Hood quickly input Control/F5 on his keyboard to access agent files. He hit DI6, typed *James*, and her dossier appeared.

Rodgers got up and stood behind Hood as he scanned the file, which was filled with data from DI6 as well as independent information collected by Op-Center, the CIA, and other U.S. agencies.

"She has quite a record," Hood said. "The granddaughter of a lord, three years in the field in South Africa, two in Syria, seven at headquarters. Special forces training, speaks six languages, holds four commendations. Rebuilds and races vintage motorcycles."

He stopped when Mike Rodgers pointed to a cross-reference to another file.

"Commander Hubbard, this is Mike Rodgers," he said. "I see that Ms. James also recruited Mr. Fields-Hutton."

"Yes, General," Hubbard admitted. "They were very close."

"Watch out for grudge matches," Liz muttered, shaking her head.

"Did you hear, Commander?" Hood asked. "That was our staff psychologist."

"We heard," a sharp female voice replied, "and I assure you, I'm not in this for revenge. I simply want to see that the job Keith started is finished."

"No one was questioning your abilities, Agent James," Liz said in a strong, unapologetic voice that left no room for debate. "But emotional detachment and objectivity fuel caution, and that's what we want in our — "

"Balls," snapped Peggy. "Either I go with you or I go in alone. But I *am* going."

"That will be quite enough," Hubbard said firmly.

Coffey cleared his throat and folded his hands on the table. "Commander Hubbard, Agent James — I'm Lowell Coffey II, Op-Center's attorney." He looked at Hood. "Paul, you're probably going to have my head for this, but I think you should consider their offer."

Hood's expression was unchanged, but Rodgers's eyes were wide and angry. Coffey avoided them.

"Martha and I still have a few points to work out with the CIC," Coffey said, "and if I can tell them that this is an international team, there's a much better chance we'll be able to bargain for things like more time, a larger geographical area, that sort of thing."

"You'll want me to fall on my sword too, Mike," McCaskey said, "but having Agent James on the team will help me too. The Finnish Minister of Defense is very close to Admiral Marrow of the Royal Marines. If we need other favors as this unfolds, he's the man we'll have to ask for them."

The General said nothing for a long moment, and the silence from London was provocative. Hood finally looked at Bob Herbert. The Intelligence Chief's lips were pursed and he was drumming the leather armrests of his wheelchair.

"Bob," Hood asked, "what do you say?"

His soft voice tinged with remnants of his Mississippi youth, Herbert said, "I say that we can get the job done just fine, all by ourselves. If the lady wants to go in alone, that's Commander Hubbard's business. I don't see why we need to toss an extra gear into a finely tuned machine."

Martha Mackall said, "I think we're getting dangerously territorial here. Agent James is a professional. She'll fit into your finely tuned machine."

"Thank you," Peggy said, "whoever you are."

"Martha Mackall," she said, "Political Officer. And you're welcome. I know what it's like to be kept out of the boys' club."

"That's bull," Herbert waved dismissively. "This isn't about black, white, male, female, or hands-across-the-goddamn-water. We've already got one first-timer on this mission: Sondra DeVonne, the *lady* who took Bass

172

Moore's place. All I'm saying is that we'd have to be crazy to take on another."

"Another lady, you mean," Martha said.

"Another rookie," Herbert shot back. "My God, when did every command decision become a mandate against *some*body?"

Hood said, "Thanks for the suggestions, all of you. Commander, I hope you'll forgive us for talking about your person in front of her back."

"I appreciate it," Peggy said. "I've always liked to know where I stand."

Hood said, "I have my reservations, but Lowell's right. A binational group makes sense, and Peggy seems to have the right stuff."

Herbert drove his palms into the edge of the table and whistled the first few measures of "It's a Small World." Rodgers returned to his seat. His neck was flushed above the collar of his uniform, and his dark brow seemed even darker.

"I'll make sure you get the specifics as we do," Hood said, "so that your agent can link up with Striker. Needless to say, Commander, Striker's leader, Lieutenant Colonel Squires, has our complete trust. I expect Agent James to follow his orders."

"Of course, General," Commander Hubbard said, "and thank you."

Hood looked at Rodgers as the monitor winked off.

"Mike," Hood said, "he was going to send her anyway. At least now we'll know where she is."

"It was your call," Rodgers replied. "It's just not the one I would've made." He looked at Hood. "This isn't D-Day or Desert Storm. We didn't need an international consensus. The United States was attacked, and the United States military was responding. Period."

"Semicolon," Hood corrected. "DI6 suffered casualties as well. The information they gave us reinforced our suspicions about the target. They deserve a shot at that target."

"As I told you, we don't agree on that," Rodgers said. "Ms. James had to be disciplined by her own superior. She's certainly not going to listen to Squires. But you're back, and you're in command." He looked around the table. "I've finished everything on my agenda. Thank you, everyone, for your attention."

Hood also looked around. "Any other business?"

"Yes," said Herbert. "I think Mike Rodgers and Lynne Dominick and Karen Wong deserve friggin' medals for the silk purse they made from a sow's ear last night. While everyone else in the country was runnin' around wringing their hands about the explosion, those three figured out who did it and probably why. Instead of a Purple Heart, though, we just kicked Mike in the pants. I'm sorry, but I just don't get it."

"Because we disagree with him," said Lowell Coffey, "that doesn't mean we think any less of what he did."

"You're tired and p.o.'d, Bob," said Liz Gordon. "This wasn't about Mike. It was about living in the world of today."

Herbert grumbled his disapproval of the world of today as he rolled away from the table.

Hood rose. "I'll contact you all individually during the morning to check on your progress," he said. Then he looked at Mike Rodgers. "Once again, in case anyone missed it, no one in this room could've done the job that Mike did last night."

Rodgers gave him a little nod, then buzzed open the door and followed Bob Herbert from the Tank.

NINETEEN

Monday, 8:00 P.M., St. Petersburg

As the digital clock in the corner of the computer monitor rolled over from 7:59:59, a change came over the Operations Center. The blue hue that had filled the room from the more than two dozen computer screens was replaced by a flood of changing colors which were reflected on the faces and clothes of everyone in the room. The mood changed too. Though no one applauded, the release of tension was palpable as the Center came alive.

Operations Support Officer Fyodor Buriba looked at Orlov from his lone console on a table tucked into the front right corner. A smile broke through the young man's neatly trimmed black beard and his dark eyes gleamed. "We have one hundred percent go, sir," he said.

Sergei Orlov was standing in the middle of the large, low-ceilinged room, his hands locked behind his back as his eyes ranged from screen to screen. "Thank you, Mr. Buriba," Orlov said, "and well done, everyone. All stations, double-check your data before we inform Moscow that the countdown to operations has begun."

Orlov began walking slowly from side to side, looking over the shoulders of his staff. The twenty-four computers and monitors were arranged in a semicircle on a tightly curved, nearly horseshoe-shaped tabletop. Each monitor was manned by an operator, and he relaxed a little at 8 P.M. exactly, as the blue of each screen was replaced by a stream of data, photographs, maps, or charts. Ten of the monitors were dedicated to satellite surveillance, four were tapped into a worldwide intelligence database that included reports legal as well as "hacked" from police departments, embassies, and government agencies, nine others were hooked to radios and cellular telephones and received reports from operatives around the world, and one was linked directly to the office of the Ministers in the Kremlin, including Dogin. This link was manned by Corporal Ivashin, who was handpicked by Colonel Rossky and reported directly to him. All but the map screens were filled with phrases in code. The words meant nothing to Orlov, to the person at the next monitor, or to anyone else in the Center. Each station had its own code so that the damage a mole might cause would be minimized. In the event that an operative was sick, a code-breaker program could be activated by both Orlov and Rossky, each of whom knew half of the two-part password.

When the screens came to life after weeks of checking and debugging, Orlov felt the same he had each time one of the huge rockets roared to life beneath him: relief that everything came on, as scheduled. Though his life wasn't at risk the way it was every time he rode a rocket, the truth was he had never contemplated life or death as he rode into space. That wasn't what exploration or being a fighter pilot or even living from day to day was about. His reputation was more important than his life, and Orlov's only thought, ever, was that he do his best and not screw up.

The front wall of the room was covered with a world map. Images from any of the screens could be superimposed on it using a projector set in the ceiling. On the side walls were shelves of diskettes and backups, top-secret data, files, and records about governments, the military, and agencies from around the world. In the center of the back wall was a door that led to the hallway and the cryptanalysis center, security room, mess, lavatory, and exit. Doors to Orlov's and Rossky's offices were on the right and left respectively.

Standing in the heart of the Center, Orlov felt as if he were commanding a ship of the future — one that went nowhere, yet had the ability to look down from the heavens or peer under rocks on the earth, one that could know nearly anything about almost anyone in a moment. Even when he was in outer space, with the earth turning slowly beneath him, he had never felt this omniscient. And because every government required accurate, timely intelligence, his funding and the operation of the Center had been unaffected by the chaos in many quarters of Russia. He almost understood how Czar Nicholas II must have felt, living in splendid isolation until the end came. It was easy to be in a place like this and feel cut off from the day-to-day problems of others, and Orlov made sure to pick up three or four different newspapers every day so as not to lose touch with reality.

Corporal Ivashin suddenly stood, faced the General, and snapped off a salute. He removed his headset and held it out. "General, sir," he said, "the radio room reports a private communication for you."

"Thank you," Orlov said, waving away the headset. "I'll take it in my office." He turned and headed toward the door on the far right.

Entering his personal code on the keypad to the left of the door, Orlov entered. His assistant, Nina Terova, poked her head from behind a divider in a back corner of the room. A stately, broad-shouldered woman of thirty-five, she was dressed in a tight-fitting navy-blue jacket and skirt. She had chestnut hair worn in a bun, large eyes, a handsomely arched nose, and a deep, diagonal furrow along her forehead where a bullet had creased her skull. A former officer on the St. Petersburg police force, she also carried scars on her chest and right arm, the result of having stood her ground to bring down two men during an attempted bank robbery.

"Congratulations, General," she said.

"Thanks," Orlov replied as he shut the door, "but we've still got several hundred checkpoints to go — "

"I know," Nina said. "And when we pass those, you won't be happy until we've put a successful day behind us, and then a week, and then a year."

"What's life without new goals?" the General asked as he sat behind his desk, a black acrylic surface on four thin, white legs made from the remains of one of the Vostok boosters that had carried him into space. The rest of the room was decorated with photographs, models, awards, and mementoes of his years in space, including a display case with his prize possession, a switch panel from the crude capsule that had carried Yuri Gagarin on the first manned flight into outer space.

He sat in a leather-upholstered bucket chair, swung it in front of the computer, and typed in his access code. The screen quickly filled with the back of Interior Minister Dogin's head.

"Minister," Orlov said into a condenser microphone built into the lower left corner of the monitor.

It was several seconds before Dogin turned around. Orlov wasn't sure whether the Minister liked making people wait for him, or whether he didn't like to appear to be waiting for others. In either case it was a game, and Orlov didn't like it.

The Minister smiled. "Corporal Ivashin tells me that everything went on as planned."

"The Corporal was out of line, not to mention premature," Orlov said. "We haven't reviewed the data as yet."

"I'm sure it will check out," Dogin said.

"And don't be hard on the Corporal for his enthusiasm, General. This is a great day for the entire team."

The entire team, Orlov rolled the phrase over in his mind. When he was working in the space program, a team was a group of dedicated people working toward a single goal: expanding human capabilities in space. There was a political agenda, but the importance of the work itself made that seem almost trivial. Orlov didn't have a team here. He had several of them, all pulling in opposite directions. There was a group working to get the Center on-line, another group sneaking information to Dogin, and even a team of paranoid in-betweeners headed by Security Director Glinka, desperate to determine which of the other teams they should be supporting. It might very well cost him his command, but Orlov promised himself that this place *would* work as a team.

"As it happens," Dogin said, "we couldn't have timed the countdown better. There's a Gulfstream jet moving through the South Pacific toward Japan. After refueling in Tokyo, the jet will fly on to Vladivostok. I'll have my assistant send the flight path through to you. I want the Center to monitor the plane's progress. The pilot has instructions to contact you after he lands in Vladivostok, which will be at approximately five o'clock in the morning, local time. When he does, let me know and I'll give you further instructions to radio to him."

"Is this a test of our system?" Orlov asked.

"No, General. The cargo on the Gulfstream is of vital importance to this office."

"In that case, sir," Orlov said, "until everything here has been thoroughly checked, why not let Air Defense handle it? Their Radio and Electronic Technical Forces would be — "

"Extraneous and obtrusive," Dogin said. He smiled. "I want you to follow the plane, General. I'm confident that the Center can handle it. Any and all communications from the aircraft will come to your radio room in code, of course, and any problems or delays will be reported to me directly by you or by Colonel Rossky. Do you have any questions?"

"Several, sir," Orlov admitted, "but I'll log the order and do as you ask." He entered a command, which automatically recorded the date and time, and a window opened in the bottom of the screen. He typed, *Minister Dogin orders monitoring of Gulfstream jet bound for Vladivostok.* He reread it and hit the Save button. It beeped to show that the save had been successful.

"Thank you, General," said Dogin. "All your questions will be answered in time. Now, good luck with the countdown: I look forward to hearing that the jewel in our intelligence crown is fully operational in less than three hours."

"Yes, sir," Orlov said, "though I wonder. Who's wearing that crown?"

Dogin was still smiling. "I'm disappointed, General. Impertinence doesn't suit you."

"My apologies," Orlov said. "I find it disturbing myself. But I've never been asked to run a mission with incomplete information or untested equipment, nor have I been in a situation where subordinates feel free to break the chain of command."

"We must all grow and change," Dogin said. "Let me remind you of something Stalin said in his speech to the Russian people in July 1941: 'There must be no room in our ranks for whimperers and cowards, for panic-mongers and deserters; our people must know no fear.' You are a courageous and reasonable man, General. Trust me and, I assure you, your faith will be rewarded."

Dogin pressed a button and his image winked out. Staring at the dark screen, Orlov was not surprised by the rebuke — though Dogin's answer hardly put him at ease. If anything, it caused him to wonder if he had trusted too much in Dogin. He found himself contemplating the World War that had prompted Stalin's speech and to wonder, with alarm he tried hard to suppress, if Minister Dogin somehow imagined Russia to be at war . . . and if so, with whom.

TWENTY

Tuesday, 3:05 A.M., Tokyo

Simon "Jet" Lee, Honolulu-born and -raised, resolved to devote his life to police work on August 24, 1967. On that day, at the age of seven, he watched as his father — who was a hulking movie extra — acted in a scene with Jack Lord and James MacArthur on their TV series *Hawaii Five-O*. He wasn't sure whether it was Lord's intensity or the fact that he was able to manhandle his father that gave him the police bug — though it was the habit of dyeing his hair jet-black, like Lord's, that gave him his nickname.

Whatever the reason, Lee joined the FBI in 1983, graduated third in his class at the Academy, and returned to Honolulu as a fully fledged agent. Twice he'd turned down promotions so he could stay in the field and do what he loved: hunt down bad guys and make the world a cleaner place.

Which was why he was in Tokyo, working undercover as an airline mechanic with the blessings of the Japanese Self-Defense Forces. Raw drugs were going from South America to Hawaii to Japan and, with his partner in Honolulu, Lee was tracking the private planes as they came and went, looking for likely suspects.

The Gulfstream III was a very likely suspect. Lee's partner in Hawaii had tracked the Gulfstream from Colombia and it was registered to a company that was owned by a baked-goods distributor in New York. Ostensibly, it was carrying ingredients used to make the distributor's specialty, exotic bagels. Awakened in his room at the inn just a five-minute drive from the airport, Lee had called his partner, JSDF Sergeant Ken Sawara, and hurried over.

Lee listened to the tower through his headset as he played around with a JT3D-7 turbofan in a corner of the hangar at the airfield. After two weeks of tinkering with the same engine, he felt he knew it better than anyone at Pratt & Whitney. The Gulfstream touched down and was due for a quick turnaround before heading to Vladivostok.

That made it even more suspicious, Lee thought, since the baked-goods distributor was thought to be tied to the Russian mafia.

Feeling a bit constricted in the bulletproof

vest he wore under his white jumpsuit, Lee set down his wrench and walked to the phone on the hangar wall. He felt the lopsided weight of the holstered .38 Smith & Wesson press against his left shoulder as he punched Ken's mobile number into the green phone.

"Ken," he said, "the Gulfstream just landed and is pulling up to hangar two. Meet me there."

Ken Sawara said, "Let me check it out."

"No — "

"But your Japanese is terrible, Jet — "

"Your Colombian is worse," said Lee. "See you there."

It was well before sunrise, and though the airport was not as busy as the one in Honolulu had been over six hours before, at 2:35 P.M. local time, it was busy enough as air traffic converged from the west and the east. Lee knew that many mobsters, men like Aram Vonyev and Dmitri Shovich, liked having their planes land at big public airports rather than at the small strips that government agents found easier to watch. Those two criminals especially liked having their planes come and go during the day, out in the open, where law officers and rival gangsters didn't expect to see them. In Honolulu, as in Mexico City and in Bogotá, Colombia, before that, this plane had landed and taken off in bright daylight.

The Gulfstream taxied quickly to the Yaswee Oil truck waiting near the hangar nearest to the runway. Here, as at the other fields, the Gulfstream had its own fuel trucks waiting. Though mobsters had their own reasons for moving goods somewhat out in the open like this, none was so brazen that he wanted to stay on the ground any longer than absolutely necessary.

If the plane followed the pattern — and there was no reason it shouldn't, Lee knew — then after less than fifty minutes on the ground in Tokyo it would be airborne again, its twin Rolls-Royce Spey Mk 511-8 turbofans carrying it to the northwest, into the dark, overcast skies. Soon it would be in Russia, just across the Sea of Japan.

Brushing the longish black hair from his forehead, Lee pulled a purchase order from his pocket and pretended to read it. He whistled as he walked onto the dark tarmac. He saw the winking lights of the small jet as it rolled toward the hangar for refueling, its tanks nearly empty after the 4,500-mile journey. He watched as the ground crew rolled the hose from the tank, and Lee knew then that the plane was carrying contraband. The crew was working faster, with more serious efficiency than usual. They'd been paid off.

189

From the corner of his eye he saw car headlights. That would be Sawara. As planned, he'd pull off to the side and wait — just in case Lee needed backup. The FBI agent intended to walk up to the plane, tell the crew foreman he was told to check for a faulty fuel switch, and while they took up the issue with the pilot he'd swing inside and have a poke around the cargo.

The Toyota pulled up beside Lee, pacing him. Lee stopped, confused, as he looked down at the driver's-side window. Then the window rolled down, showing Sawara's expressionless face.

"Can I help you?" Lee said to Sawara in Japanese, though with his wide eyes and a severely pinched brow he was actually asking, *What the hell are you doing?*

In response, Sawara lifted the .38 Special Model 60 revolver from his lap and pointed it at Lee. With speed and instincts that were uncanny, the agent dropped flat to his back on the tarmac an instant before the gun flashed.

Yanking his own .38 from its holster, Lee swung it across his chest and shot out the passenger's side front tire, then rolled to his right as Sawara tried to back away for another shot. The bare rim sparked and screamed as he slammed the car into reverse, one hand on the steering wheel, the other still holding the gun out the window. His second shot caught Lee in the right thigh.

The turncoat bastard! Lee thought as he put three bullets through the car door. Each shell entered with a dull *clung* and Sawara's third and fourth shots flew wild as Lee's bullets struck him. With a moan, the Japanese soldier arched to the left, toward the window, then his forehead drooped against the steering wheel. The car sped up, turning at crazy angles, as the wounded man's foot sat heavily on the pedal. At least it was moving away from him, and Lee watched as it collided with an empty luggage cart. The Toyota rode up on the side of the cart, crunching it down and going nowhere as the tires were lifted off the ground.

Lee's wound felt like a hellish muscle cramp, sunburn-hot to the bone and brutally tight from his thigh to his knee. It was impossible to move his leg without sending a sheet of pain from his heel to his neck. Craning his head around, Lee looked at the plane some two hundred yards away. The underbelly of the fuselage was flashing white and dark from the lights and the ground crew continued their work, though now two men had appeared in the open doorway. Both were dressed in dungarees and sweatshirts and neither man carried a gun. Either they weren't stupid, Lee thought . . . or they were.

The two men ducked back into the plane, shouting at one another.

Lee knew that they'd be returning soon, and mustering his will, he flopped onto his belly, got onto his left knee, and climbed to his feet. He winced with pain as he began hopping forward, unable to put weight on his right leg without causing a burst of white light to erupt behind his eyes. As Lee approached, he looked at the ground crew as they watched him. They were working quickly without wanting to appear as though they were hurrying, as if to say they'd taken the money and would do the job, but this wasn't their fight.

It was Lee's fight, however. One he'd been trained for, one from which he wouldn't run. Not when he had his quarry pinned in a plane that was suckling on a fuel tank, unable to go anywhere.

When he was nearly at the nose of the plane, one of the two men reemerged in the cabin door. He was holding a German Walther MP-K submachine gun, and he wasted no time firing a burst at Lee. Having expected that, the FBI agent pushed off on his good leg and dove toward the opposite side of the plane, putting the nose of the aircraft between himself and the gunman. He wondered where airport security was: they had to have heard the gunfire, and he didn't want to believe that they were all on the take like the ground crew and that son of a bitch Sawara.

The shells picked a jagged line in the tarmac to his right, but they were several feet away from where Lee hit the ground. Crawling forward on his elbow, he stretched his arm out to shoot at the nosewheel; that would keep the plane on the ground long enough for someone to look into what was going on. Unless everyone at the airfield, including the security forces, had been paid off.

An instant before Lee fired, a burst erupted from behind him, chewing into his armpit and shoulder.

He hadn't expected that. His arm jerked up and he missed the tire, sending four shots into the wing and fuselage. Then another burst hit him in the right thigh.

He turned and saw the bloodied form of Ken Sawara standing above him.

"You couldn't . . . just *leave* it," Sawara gasped as he dropped to his knees. "You couldn't let *me* go!"

Putting all his strength into his arm, Lee swung his .38 toward the soldier. "You want to go?" he said, sending a bullet into his forehead. "Go."

As Sawara dropped to his side, Lee turned his face toward the plane. He was struggling for air as he watched the men continue fueling the aircraft. *This couldn't be it,* he told himself. The crimefighter is betrayed by his partner and dies on oil-slick tarmac? No one to see, no sirens in the distance, no one to book the criminals or lend him a hand . . . not even a conscience-stricken worker?

Simon Lee died feeling like he'd failed, utterly.

A half hour later, the plane took off, bound for Russia. Because of the darkness, no one on the ground or in the aircraft saw the thin stream of black smoke curling from the port engine as the Gulfstream pushed skyward.

TWENTY-ONE

Monday, 12:30 A.M., Washington, D.C.

Over lunch ordered from the commissary, Lowell Coffey, Martha Mackall, and their aides worked in the attorney's wood-paneled office, picking through the legal minefield that was a part of every Striker mission.

Finland's President had approved a multinational Striker landing to examine radiation readings in the gulf, and Coffey's deputy, Andrea Stempel, was on the phone with the Interpol office in Helsinki arranging to get a car and fake visas for three team members to enter Russia. Nearby, on a leather couch, Stempel's assistant, paralegal Jeffrey Dryfoos, went over the wills of the Striker commandos. If the paperwork was not in order, reflecting up-to-date changes in marital status, children, and assets, documents would be faxed to the aircraft for signing and witnessing en route.

Coffey and Mackall themselves were looking at a computer monitor on the desk, drafting the "finding," the lengthy final-draft document that Coffey would need to present to the joint eight-person Senate and Congressional Intelligence Committee before Striker landed. They had already negotiated the kinds of weapons that could be used, exactly what type of operation would be run, the duration, and other constraints. Coffey had been involved with some findings that had gone so far as to specify which radio frequencies could be used and what time, to the minute, the team would exit and enter. After all was said and much was done, approval from the committee to enter Russia did not actually give them the right to do so under international law. But without it, if captured, the Striker team would be disavowed without approval and left to twist in the wind. With it, the U.S. would work quietly through diplomatic channels to arrange for their release.

Down the hall, past the offices of Mike Rodgers and Ann Farris, was Bob Herbert's tidy command center. The narrow, rectangular room consisted of several banks of computers on a small table, with detailed world maps on three walls and a dozen television monitors on the far wall. Most of the time the screens were dark. Now, however, five of them were aglow with satellite images of Russia, Ukraine, and Poland. Old pictures morphed into new ones every .89 seconds.

There was a long-standing debate in intelligence circles about the value of ELINT/SIGINT spies in space as opposed to reliable data gathered from HUMINT personnel on the ground. Ideally, agencies wanted both. They wanted the ability to read the odometer on a jeep from a satellite fifty miles in space, and ears on the ground to report on conversations or meetings held behind closed doors. Satellite spying was clean. There was no chance of getting captured or interrogated, no risk of double agents feeding false information. But it also didn't have the capacity of an intelligence officer on the ground to distinguish between real and false targets.

Satellite surveillance for the Pentagon, the CIA, the FBI, and Op-Center was managed by the highly secretive National Reconnaissance Office in the Pentagon. Run by the meticulous Stephen Viens, a college buddy of Matt Stoll, it consisted of banks of television monitors set in ten rows of ten. All of them watched different sectors of the earth, each generating an image every .89 seconds providing a total of sixty-seven live black-and-white images a minute at various levels of magnification. The NRO was also responsible for testing the new AIM-Satellite,

197

first in a series of orbiting audio-imaging monitors designed to provide detailed pictures of submarine and aircraft interiors by reading the sounds and echoes of sounds produced by people and instruments therein.

Three of the NRO's satellites were watching troop movements on the border of Russia and Ukraine, while two kept an eye on forces in Poland. Through a source at the United Nations, Bob Herbert had heard that the Poles were getting antsy with the Russian buildup. Though Warsaw had not yet authorized the mobilization of troops, leaves had been canceled and the activities of Ukrainians living and working in Poland, near the border, were being monitored by Warsaw. Viens agreed with Herbert that Poland deserved watching, and had the photos sent directly to his office, where Op-Center's surveillance analysis team was studying them as they appeared.

The printout of the day's activities of the soldiers in Belgorod indicated nothing unusual to Bob Herbert and his team of analysts. For nearly two days, the routine had been the same:

Time	Activity
0550	First Call
0600	Reveille formation

0610-0710	Physical training
0710-0715	Make beds
0715-0720	Inspection
0720-0740	Orders of the day given
0740-0745	Wash
0745-0815	Breakfast
0815-0830	Cleanup
0830-0900	Preparation for duty
0900-1450	Training
1400-1500	Prepare for lunch
1500-1530	Lunch
1530-1540	Tea
1540-1610	Personal time
1610-1650	Care and cleaning of weapons and equipment
1650-1840	Cleaning camp and general sanitation
1840-1920	Secure perimeter
1920-1930	Wash hands
1930-2000	Dinner
2000-2030	Watch TV news
2030-2130	Personal time
2130-2145	Evening formation
2145-2155	Evening inspection
2200	Retreat

While Herbert and his people stayed on top of the military developments, they also tried to collect information for Charlie Squires and his Striker commandos about the situation at the Hermitage. Satellite reconnaissance turned up no unusual traffic, and Matt Stoll and his technical staff weren't having much luck working up programs to enable the AIM-Satellite to filter out the noise in the museum itself. The lack of personnel on the ground compounded their frustration. Egypt, Japan, and Colombia had agents in Moscow, but none in St. Petersburg — and, in any case, Herbert didn't want to tell them that something was brewing at the Hermitage, lest they side with Russia. Old loyalties weren't necessarily changing in the post-Cold War world, but new ones were constantly being forged. Herbert didn't intend to help any of those along, even if it meant allowing extra time so Striker could study the site firsthand before defining their mission.

Then, at ten minutes after noon — 8:00 P.M. in Moscow — the situation changed.

Bob Herbert was called to Op-Center's radio room in the northwest corner of the basement. Wheeling over, he headed toward Radio Reconnaissance Director John Quirk, a taciturn giant of a man with a beatific face, a soft voice, and the patience of a monk. Quirk was seated by a radio/computer unit, UTHER — Universal Translation and Heuristic Enharmonic Reporter — which was

200

capable of producing a virtually simultaneous written translation of everything that was being said by over five hundred different voice types, in over two hundred languages and dialects.

Quirk removed his headset as Herbert arrived. The three other people in the room continued working at their monitors, which were trained on Moscow and St. Petersburg.

"Bob," Quirk said, "we've intercepted transmissions indicating that equipment is being collected at air bases from Ryazan to Vladivostok for shipment to Belgorod."

"Belgorod?" Herbert said. "That's where the Russians have been holding maneuvers. What kind of equipment are they sending over?"

Quirk turned his blue eyes toward the screen. "You name it. Automated communications trucks, vehicle-mounted radio relay stations, a helicopter-mounted retransmission station, Petroleum, Oil, and Lubricants trucks and trailers, along with full maintenance companies and field kitchen trucks."

"They're setting up a communications and supply route," Herbert said. "Could be a drill of some kind."

"I've never seen one this sudden."

"What do you mean?" Herbert asked.

"Well," Quirk said, "this is clearly an engagement build-up, but before the Russians engage there's always a great deal of communication about the expected time of the encounter and the anticipated size of enemy forces. We'll pick up their calculations on speed-of-movement scales, and there'll be conversations between frontline forces and headquarters about tactics — envelopment, turning movement, combined, that sort of thing."

"But you didn't get any of that," Herbert said.

"Zero. This is as sudden as anything I've ever seen."

"Yet when everything's in place," Herbert said, "they'll be ready for something big . . . like a move into the Ukraine."

"Correct."

"Yet the Ukrainians are doing nothing," Herbert said.

"They may not know anything's up," Quirk said.

"Or they may not be taking it seriously," Herbert said. "NRO photos show that they've got reconnaissance personnel close to the border — but not deep reconnaissance companies. Obviously, they don't expect to have to operate from behind enemy lines." Herbert drummed his leather armrests. "How soon before the Russians are ready to move?"

"They'll be in position by tonight," Quirk said. "By aircraft, it's just a short hop to Belgorod."

"And there's no chance that these are bogeys?" Herbert asked.

Quirk shook his head. "These communications are real, all right. The Russians use a combination of Latin and Cyrillic characters when they want to confuse us. The letters shared by the alphabets are supposed to throw us off because it's tough to know which alphabet they mean." He patted the computer. "But Uther manages to sniff them out."

Herbert squeezed Quirk's shoulder. "Good work. Let me know if you pick up anything else."

TWENTY-TWO

Monday, 9:30 P.M., St. Petersburg

"Sir," said red-cheeked Yuri Marev, "the radio room says they've received a coded communication via Pacific Fleet headquarters in Vladivostok. It's from the plane you've had me follow on the Hawk satellite."

General Orlov stopped his slow pacing behind the computer bank and walked to the young man, who was seated at the far left of the bank.

"Are you certain?" Orlov asked.

"There's no doubt, sir. It's the Gulfstream."

Orlov glanced at the clock on the computer screen. The plane wasn't due to land for another half hour, and he knew that region well: if anything, at this time of year the winds would work against them and the plane would be late.

"Tell Zilash I'm coming," Orlov said, walking quickly to the door that opened into the corridor. He entered that day's code on the keypad beside a door across the hall, then went into the cramped, smoke-filled radio room which was located next to Glinka's security operations center.

Arkady Zilash and his two assistants were sitting in a tiny room filled to the ceiling with radio equipment. Orlov couldn't even open the door completely, since one of the assistants was using a unit tucked behind it. The men were all wearing headsets, and Zilash didn't see Orlov until the General tapped him on the left earphone.

Startled, the gaunt radio chief removed his headset and stuck his cigarette in an ashtray.

"I'm sorry, sir," Zilash said in his low, raspy voice.

As if suddenly realizing he should stand, Zilash began to rise. Orlov motioned with his fingers for him to sit back down. Without meaning to, Zilash had always managed to test the boundaries of military protocol. But he was a radio genius and, more important, a trusted aide from Orlov's Cosmodrome days. The General wished he had more men like Zilash on his staff.

"It's all right," Orlov said.

"Thank you, sir."

"What did the Gulfstream have to say?"

Zilash turned on a digital audiotape recorder. "I've unscrambled it and cleaned it up a bit," he said. "The transmission had a great deal of static — the weather is terrible over the sea right now."

The voice on the tape was faint but clear. "Vladivostok: we have lost power in our port engine. We do not know how serious the damage is, but some electrical systems are out. We expect to land a half hour late, but can go no further. Will await instructions."

Zilash's big, hound-dog eyes peered up through the smoke. "Any reply, sir?"

Orlov thought for a moment. "Not yet. Get me Rear Admiral Pasenko at Pacific Fleet headquarters."

Zilash glanced at his computer clock. "It's four in the morning there, sir — "

"I know," Orlov said patiently. "Just do it."

"Yes, sir," Zilash said as he typed the name into his computer keyboard, accessed and input the scramble code, then radioed the base. When the Rear Admiral came on, Zilash handed the headset to Orlov.

"Sergei Orlov?" said Pasenko. "Cosmonaut, fighter pilot, and reclusive homebody? One of the few men I would get out of bed to talk to."

"I'm sorry about the hour, Ilya," Orlov

said. "How have you been?"

"I've been well!" said Pasenko. "Where have you been hiding these past two years? I haven't seen you since the all-service senior officers' retreat in Odessa."

"I've been well — "

"Of course," Pasenko said. "You cosmonauts exude well-being. And Masha? How is your long-suffering wife?"

"Also well," Orlov said. "Perhaps we can catch up later. I have a favor to ask, Ilya."

"Anything," said Pasenko. "The man who kept Brezhnev waiting to sign my daughter's autograph book has my undying friendship."

"Thanks," Orlov said as he thought back to how irate the leader of the Soviet Union had been. But children are the future, the dreamers, and there was never any hesitation on Orlov's part. "Ilya, there's a crippled aircraft that will be landing at the airport in Vladivostok — "

"The Gulfstream? I see it here on the computer."

"That's right," said Orlov. "I've got to get the cargo to Moscow. Can you give me a plane?"

"I may have spoken too soon," Pasenko said. "Every plane I can spare is being used to transport matériel to the west."

Orlov was caught off guard. *What can be*

happening in the west?

"I'd be happy to piggyback your shipment in my aircraft," Pasenko continued, "space permitting, but I don't know when that will be. Part of the rush is we're expecting several days of severe weather from the Bering Sea. Anything still on the ground tonight is expected to remain there for at least ninety-six hours."

"Then there isn't even time to send a plane from Moscow," Orlov said.

"Probably not," Pasenko said. "What is so urgent?"

"I don't know myself," Orlov said. "Kremlin business."

"I understand," Pasenko said. "You know, rather than have your goods sit here, Sergei, I can help arrange for a train. You can run your shipment north from Vladivostok and meet it when the weather clears."

"The Trans-Siberian Railroad," Orlov said. "How many cars can you get me?"

"Enough to carry whatever is in your little jet," Pasenko said. "The only thing I couldn't give you is personnel to man it. That would have to be approved by Admiral Varchuk, and he's in the Kremlin meeting with the new President. If it isn't a matter of national security, he can get thorny about interruptions."

"That's all right," Orlov said. "If you can get me the train, I can get a crew to run her. Will you let me know as soon as possible?"

"Stay where you are," Pasenko said. "I'll radio back within the half hour."

Signing off, Orlov handed the headset to Zalish. "Radio the military base on Sakhalin Island," he said. "Tell the operator I'd like to speak to a member of the spetsnaz detachment — I'll stay on the line."

"Yes, sir. Which member, General?"

"Junior Lieutenant Nikita Orlov," he said. "My son."

TWENTY-THREE

Monday, 1:45 P.M., Washington, D.C.

Paul Hood and Mike Rodgers were sitting behind Hood's desk studying the psychological profiles which Liz Gordon had just sent over.

If there was any strain between the men over what had happened in the Tank, it had been put aside. Rodgers had a strong independent streak, but he was also a twenty-year man. He knew how to take orders, including the ones he didn't like. For his part, Hood rarely overruled his deputy, and almost never in military matters. When he did, it was with the backing of most of his senior staff.

The Peggy James call had been a tough one, but the bottom line was simple. The intelligence community was small, much *too* small for grudges. The risk of sending a seasoned agent with Striker was acceptable, compared to the risk of alienating DI6 and Commander Hubbard.

Hood was careful not to be too solicitous with Rodgers after their little showdown. The General would have resented that. But Hood made himself more open to Rodgers's ideas, especially his enthusiasm for Liz Gordon's psychological profiles. Op-Center's Director put as much validity in psychoanalysis as he did in astrology and phrenology. Childhood dreams about his mother were as useful to understanding his adult mind as the gravitational pull of Saturn and bumps on the head were to predicting the future.

But Mike Rodgers believed and, if nothing else, it was useful to review the personal histories of their potential adversaries.

The concise biography of the new Russian President was on the screen, along with access to file photographs, newspaper clips, and video footage. Hood scanned through details of Zhanin's birth in Makhachkala on the Caspian Sea, his education in Moscow and rise from the Politburo to an attaché in the Soviet Embassy in London and then as Deputy Ambassador in Washington.

Hood stopped scrolling when he reached Liz's profile:

" 'He sees himself as a potential modern-day Peter the Great,' " Hood read Liz's summary, " 'who favors open trade with the West and a cultural influx from the U.S. to make sure his people continue to want what we have to sell.' "

Rodgers said, "That makes sense. If they want American movies, they'll have to buy Russian VCRs. If they want enough Chicago Bulls jackets or Janet Jackson T-shirts, companies will begin to open factories in Russia."

"But Liz says here, 'I don't think he has the same aesthetic sense as Peter the Great.' "

"No," Rodgers agreed. "The Czar was genuinely interested in Western culture. Zhanin is interested in building the economy and remaining in power. The question, which we also discussed with the President last night, is how sure are we of his devotion to this course of action as opposed to militarism."

"He has no military background whatsoever," Hood said, looking back over the biography.

"Right," said Rodgers. "And historically, that kind of leader is quick to try and use force to get his way. Anyone who's been in a combat zone knows firsthand the price you pay there. As a rule, they're the most reluctant to use force."

Hood continued reading. " 'Given the military warning General Rodgers heard at the White House meeting last night,' Liz wrote,

'I do not believe that Zhanin would pick a fight somewhere to prove himself or to appease the military. He prides himself on rhetoric and ideas, not on force or the use of arms. In these early days of his new government, his overriding concern will be not to alienate the West.' "

Hood sat back, shut his eyes, and pinched the bridge of his nose.

"You want some coffee?" Rodgers asked as he continued to scan the report.

"No, thanks. I swam in the stuff on the flight back."

"Why didn't you try and sleep?"

Hood laughed. "Because I got the last seat in coach, stuffed between the loudest-snoring humans on earth. Both of whom took off their shoes and passed right out. I can't watch those cropped and edited movies on airplanes, so I just sat there and wrote a thirty-page letter of apology to my family."

"Was Sharon mad or disappointed?" Rodgers asked.

"Both and more," said Hood. He sat back up. "Hell, let's get back to the Russians. I've got a better chance of understanding them, I think."

Rodgers gave him a light swat on the back as they looked at the screen.

"Liz says here that Zhanin isn't an impulsive man," Hood said. " 'He always sticks to his plans, guided by what he feels is moral or right, whether or not it's at odds with prevailing wisdom. See extracts Z-17A and Z-27C from *Pravda.*' "

Hood brought up the cited newspaper clippings and saw how, in 1986, Zhanin strongly backed the plan of Deputy Interior Minister Abalya to crack down on mobsters who were abducting foreign businessmen in Georgia, even after Abalya was assassinated, and how he earned the enmity of hard-liners by refusing to support a law in 1987 that would have banned the use of Lenin look-alikes for what were referred to as 'evenings of mockery.'

" 'A man of integrity,' " Hood read Liz's closing comments, " 'who has been shown to err on the side of risk-taking rather than caution.' "

Rodgers said, "Part of me wonders if that risk-taking would include a military adventure."

"Part of me wonders that too," Hood admitted. "He didn't hesitate to recommend using the militia against gangsters in Georgia."

"True," Rodgers said, "though you can argue that that isn't the same thing."

"How so?"

"Using force to maintain the peace is different from using force to assert one's will," Rodgers said. "There's a point of legality there that, psychologically, would make a big difference to someone like Zhanin."

"Well," Hood said, "this pretty well agrees with what you decided in the Oval Office last night. Zhanin's not the problem. Let's see who else might be, then."

Hood went to the next section of Liz's report. She had playfully titled it *Loose Cannons*. He began scrolling through the names.

" 'General Viktor Mavik,' " he read, " 'Marshal of Artillery in the Army.' "

"He was one of the officers who planned the attack on the Ostankino television center in 1993," Rodgers said, "defied Yeltsin, and still survived. He's still got powerful friends in and out of government."

" 'But he doesn't like acting alone,' " Hood read. "Then there's our friend General Mikhail Kosigan, whom she describes here rather colorfully as 'a real nutburger.' He was Chief Marshal of Artillery and openly defended a pair of officers who had been rebuked and reprimanded by Gorbachev for ordering suicide missions in Afghanistan."

" 'Gorbachev gave him the ultimate punishment short of a court-martial,' " Rodgers read, " 'a demotion, after which he went to

Afghanistan and personally commanded re-
peats of those same missions. This time,
however, they turned out differently. He
threw men and arms at the rebel hideout
until it was taken.' "

"He definitely sounds like someone to
watch," Hood said as he inched the text
ahead.

The next name on the screen was the
most recent addition.

"Interior Minister Nikolai Dogin," Hood
said, then read, " 'This man never met a
capitalist he didn't despise. If you look at
picture Z/D-1, you'll see that the CIA photo-
graphed him secretly visiting Beijing when
Gorbachev came to power. Dogin was Mayor
of Moscow at the time, and he was secretly
trying to rally the support of international
Communists against the new President.' "

"There's something about you former Mayors that worries me," Rodgers said as Hood
accessed up the photograph.

His deadpan remark drew a smile from
Hood.

The men leaned close to the monitor and
read the "Eyes Only" notation on the photograph. It indicated that the picture had been
turned over to Gorbachev by the U.S. Ambassador.

Rodgers sat back. "Dogin must have had

a hell of a lot of support to stay in power after Gorby found out about that."

"Absolutely," said Hood. "The kind of support you nurture over the years and build into a network. The kind of support that lets you slip a government right out from under a duly elected president."

The intercom outside the door beeped. "Chief, it's Bob Herbert."

Hood pressed a button on the side of his desk and the lock clicked open. The door swung in and an agitated Bob Herbert wheeled over. He dropped a diskette on the desk. Whenever Herbert was upset or puzzled, his Mississippi accent thickened. It was very thick now.

"Somethin' happened at eight P.M., local time," Herbert said. "Somethin' big."

Hood glanced down at Herbert's diskette. "What happened?"

"All of a sudden, Russians are every-god-damn-where." He pointed at the disk. "Run it. G'wan."

Hood downloaded the data and saw that Herbert wasn't exaggerating. Pilots and planes from Orenburg were being transferred to the Ukrainian border. The Baltic Fleet was on a low-level alert, ostensibly as a drill. And the battery of four Hawk satellites usually used to monitor the West had been

217

diverted to potential Russian targets in Poland.

"Moscow's paying special attention to Kiev and Warsaw," Rodgers said as he studied the satellite coordinates.

Herbert said, "What's interestin' about the Hawks is that the downlink station in Baikonur went silent at eight P.M., local time."

"Just the station?" Rodgers asked. "Not the satellite dishes?"

"Not the dishes," Herbert said.

"Then where's the data going?" Hood asked.

Herbert said, "We're not sure — though here's where it gets real curious. We detected increased electrical activity in St. Petersburg at exactly eight P.M., local time. Now, that happens to have been when the TV station in the Hermitage began broadcasting, so it could have been coincidental."

"But you wouldn't bet the Ponderosa on it," Hood said.

Herbert shook his head.

"This is what Eival Ekdol promised us," Rodgers said, still studying the deployment. "Something military. And it's being done very cleverly. If you take each of these events individually, they're all pretty routine except for the change in the Hawk targets. Matériel is moved from the port at Vladivostok on a regular basis. Maneuvers are held on the Ukrainian border twice a year, and it's time for that now. The Baltic Fleet frequently drills close to shore so that isn't unexpected."

"What you're saying," Hood said, "is that unless somebody had the big picture, it would seem as though nothing were amiss."

"Right," Rodgers said.

"But what I don't understand," said Hood, "is if Zhanin isn't behind whatever's going on, how could an operation of this magnitude be kept from him? He'd have to be aware that something's going on."

"You know better than anyone that a leader's only as good as his intelligence," Rodgers said.

"I also know that if you tell two people something in Washington, it's no longer a secret," Hood said. "That's got to be true in the Kremlin as well."

"It isn't," said Herbert. "If only *one* person knows something over there, it's no longer a secret."

"You're forgetting something," said Rodgers. "Shovich. A man like that can use threats and money to shut down the information pipeline pretty effectively. Besides, though he may not have the big picture, Zhanin probably knows about some of what's going on. Dogin or Kosigan may have gone to him right after the election and convinced him to authorize a few of the maneuvers and troop transfers to keep the military happy and busy."

"Dogin would benefit from that as well," Herbert pointed out. "If at some point any of this goes wrong, Zhanin's autograph is on several of the orders. There's mud on everyone."

Hood nodded, then cleared the screen. "So Dogin's the probable architect, and St. Petersburg is his sandbox."

"Yes," said Herbert. "And Striker's gone to play with him."

Hood continued to stare at the black screen. "The Interpol report is due at three," he said. "That's when you guys sit down with the Hermitage plans and updates and figure out how to get inside."

"Right," said Rodgers.

Herbert said, "I've got the Tactics and Strategy team putting together plans for getting our team across the Neva, using an airdrop, power rafts, or a midget submarine. Dom Limbos is overseeing it. He's worked river crossings before. And Georgia Mosley in supplies knows what gear she may have to dig up in Helsinki."

"Then you've ruled out the idea of Striker

going in as tourists?" Hood asked.

"Pretty much," said Herbert. "The Russians are still watching tour groups and photographing suspicious individuals in hotels, on buses, and at the museum and other sites. Even if our people never go back, we don't want their photos on file."

Rodgers looked at his watch. "Paul, I'm going to go sit in on the TAS session. I've told Squires he can expect a game plan before he lands at around four P.M., our time."

Hood nodded. "Thanks for everything, Mike."

"Sure," Rodgers said. As he rose, he looked at an antique globe paperweight on the desk. "They never change," he said.

"Who?" asked Hood.

"Tyrants," said Rodgers. "Russia may have been a riddle wrapped in a mystery inside an enigma to Winston Churchill, but what I see here is a story as old as history — a band of power-hungry individuals who think they know better than the electorate what's best for them."

Hood said, "That's why we're here. To tell them they can't do this without a fight."

Rodgers looked down at Hood. "Mr. Director" — he smiled — "I like your style. Me and General Gordon."

Rodgers left with Bob Herbert, leaving

Hood perplexed and feeling as though he'd bonded with his General — though if his life depended on it, he couldn't figure out how or why.

TWENTY-FOUR

Tuesday, 5:51 A.M., Sakhalin Island

Sakhalin Island in the Sea of Okhotsk is a rugged, six-hundred-mile-long stretch of fishing villages on the coasts and majestic pine forests and coal mines in the interior, of rutted roads and a few new highways, of ruins of Romanov prison camps and of ancient graves where the most common surname is *Nepomnyashchy* — "Unremembered." Situated one time zone west of the International Date Line, it is closer to the Golden Gate Bridge than it is to the Kremlin. When it is noon in Moscow, it is already 8:00 P.M. on Sakhalin. The island has long been a retreat for leaders, many of whom have had dachas, comfortable cottages in the hills, and for eremites who lose themselves in Sakhalin's untouched wilderness to seek God and peace.

The Russians have long maintained a military presence in Korsakov, on the island's southeastern tip near the Kuril Islands, which stretch from the northern tip of Hokkaido to the southern tip of Kamchatka. The islands were occupied by the Soviet Union in 1945, though Japan still claims the seven-hundred-mile-long string of islands and the nations have argued over them ever since.

The Russian base in Korsakov is spartan, consisting of an airstrip, a small harbor, and four barracks. Five hundred naval troops and two regiments of spetsnaz frogmen and naval soldiers are stationed here, daily air and sea patrols keeping an eye and electronic ear on the activities of Japanese salmon boats.

Twenty-three-year-old Junior Lieutenant Nikita Orlov sat at his desk in the command post, high on a peak overlooking the sea and the base. His black hair was close-cropped, save for the longish waves that hung down over his forehead, and his full, ruddy lips were set in a square jaw. His brown eyes were alert and gleaming as he reviewed local intelligence and faxed news reports from the previous night — and stole frequent glances out the open window.

The young officer loved getting up before dawn, learning what had happened while he slept, and then watching the sun peek over the horizon and burn across the sea toward the base. He loved the waking of the world, even though each day no longer held the promise it did when he was a boy and then a cadet: that the Soviet Union would stand as the most enduring empire in the history of the world.

As keen as his disappointment was, Nikita loved his country as passionately as ever, and he loved Sakhalin. He had been sent here straight out of the spetsnaz academy, in large part to get him out of Moscow after the incident with the Greek Orthodox church — but also, he had always felt, to keep him from sullying his father's good name. Sergei Orlov was a hero, valuable as a flight instructor to impressionable young pilots, useful as propaganda at international symposia and conventions. Nikita Orlov was a radical, a reactionary who yearned for the days before Afghanistan destroyed the morale of the world's greatest military, before Chernobyl damaged the nation's pride, before *glasnost* and *perestroika* caused the economy and then the union to come apart.

But that was the past. And here, at least, there was still a sense of purpose, still an enemy. Captain Leshev — perhaps suffering from a touch of cabin fever after three years in command of the spetsnaz troops on Sakhalin — spent a great deal of time organizing shooting competitions, which were his passion. That left Orlov in charge of most military matters, and he felt that someday

Russia would once again face Japan militarily, that they would try to establish a presence on the island and he might have the honor of leading the shock troops against them.

He also felt, in his heart, that Russia was not yet finished with the United States. The Soviets had beaten Japan in a war, and ownership of the islands was the prize. But there was a sense that Russia had lost a war with the United States, and the Russian spirit — certainly Orlov's spirit — bridled at that. Spetsnaz training had strengthened his belief that enemies must be destroyed, not accommodated, and that he and his soldiers should be unencumbered by any ethical, diplomatic, or moral considerations. He was convinced that Zhanin's efforts to turn Russia into a nation of consumers would fail just as Gorbachev's had, and that would lead to a final reckoning with the bankers and their puppets in Washington, London, and Berlin.

Fresh tobacco had arrived the day before, and Orlov rolled a cigarette as the rim of the sun rose above the dark sea. He felt so much a part of this land, of each sunrise, that it seemed possible to touch the tobacco to the sun itself to light it. Instead, he used the lighter his father had given him when he entered the academy, the orange glow of the flame illuminating the inscription on the side: *To Nikki, with love and pride — your father.* Nikita drew on the cigarette and slipped the lighter back into the vest pocket of his crisply pressed shirt.

With love and pride. What would the inscription have read after he received his commission? he wondered. *With shame and embarrassment?* Or when Nikita requested this outpost upon graduation, away from his father and nearer a very real enemy of Moscow. *With disappointment and confusion?*

The telephone rang, a relay from the communications shed at the foot of the hill. Orlov's aide had not yet arrived, so he picked up the trim, black receiver himself.

"Sakhalin post one, Orlov speaking."

"Good morning," said the caller.

Nikita was silent for several seconds. "Father?"

"Yes, Nikki," said the General. "How are you?"

"I'm fine, though surprised," Nikita said, his expression suddenly alarmed. "Is it Mother — ?"

"She's well," said the General. "We're both well."

"I'm glad," Nikita said flatly. "To hear from you after all these months — well, you can understand my concern."

There was another short silence. Nikita's

eyes were no longer joyous as he watched the sun rise. They grew hard and bitter as he pulled a long drag from his cigarette, thought back to his increasingly tense conversations with his father, then further back to his arrest four years before. He remembered how ashamed and angry the General had been about what he had done to that church, how the famous cosmonaut who couldn't go anywhere without being recognized was embarrassed to go out. How finally, on the night Colonel Rossky — not his influential father — had smoothed the matter over with the academy and gotten Nikita reinstated with just a week of double turns on the extra-duty post, his father had come to the academy barracks and lectured him about the infamy of hate and how great nations and great citizens have been destroyed by it. The other cadets had been silent, and when the great man left, someone came up with the Nikita and Sergei game, which the soldiers-in-training played for days: "Sergei" had to guess where in Moscow his son was painting hate slogans, while "Nikita" gave him hot-cold clues.

Nikita could still hear their voices, their laughter.

"The U.S. Embassy?"

"Cold — "

"*The Japan Air Lines terminal at Sheremet'yevo Airport?*"

"*Very cold —* "

"*The men's dressing room at the Kirov?*"

"*Warmer!*"

"Nikki," said the elder Orlov, "I've wanted to call, but I only seem to make you angry. I'd hoped that time would rid you of some of your bitterness — "

"Has it rid you of your arrogance," Nikita asked, "this celestial idiocy that what we ants do down here on the hill is petty or dirty or wrong?"

"Going into space didn't teach me that a nation can be destroyed from within as well as from without," Orlov said. "Ambitious men taught me that."

"Still full of piety and naïveté," said Nikita.

"And you're still brash and disrespectful," the General said evenly.

"So now you've called," Nikita said, "and we've discovered that nothing has changed."

"I didn't call to argue."

"No? What then?" Nikita asked. "Are you trying to see how far the transmitter at your new television station can reach?"

"Neither, Nikki. I'm calling because I need a good officer to lead his unit on a mission."

Nikita sat up straight.

"Are you interested?" the General asked.

229

"If it's for Russia and not for your conscience, I am."

"I called because you're the right officer for this job," the General said. "That's all."

"Then I'm interested," Nikita said.

"Your orders will come through Captain Leshev within the hour. You'll be seconded to me for three days. You and your unit are to be in Vladivostok by eleven hundred."

"We'll be there," he said, rising. "Does this mean that you're back on active duty?"

"You know everything that you need to know for now," the General replied.

"Very good," Nikita said, puffing quickly on his cigarette.

"And Nikki — take care of yourself. When this is over, perhaps you'll come to Moscow and we can try again."

"That's a thought," said Nikita. "And perhaps I can invite my former comrades from the academy. Seeing you just wouldn't be the same without them."

"Nikki — you wouldn't have heard me out in private."

"And you couldn't have cleared the Orlov name unless it was public," Nikita said.

"I did that so others might avoid making a similar mistake," the General said.

"At my expense. Thank you, Father." Nikita ground out his cigarette. "You'll excuse me, but I must get ready if I'm to be on the mainland by eleven hundred. Please give my regards to Mother and to Colonel Rossky."

"I will," the General said. "Goodbye."

Nikita hung up the phone, then took a moment to look at the half-risen sun. It annoyed him that so many others understood what his father did not: that the greatness of Russia was in its unity, not its diversity; that, as Colonel Rossky had taught, the surgeon who cuts out diseased tissue does so to cure the body, not to hurt the patient. His father had been selected as a cosmonaut because, among other things, he was even-tempered, brave, charitable, and an ideal figure to present to schools and international journalists and young fliers who wanted to be heroes. But it remained for trench fighters such as himself to do the real work of the new Russia, the rebuilding, purging, and undoing the mistakes of the past decade.

After informing the duty officer where he was going, Nikita grabbed his hat and left the outpost, feeling sad for his father . . . but curious what the General planned for his son.

TWENTY-FIVE

Monday, 2:53 P.M., over the Atlantic, northwest of Madrid

The inside of the C-141B StarLifter wasn't designed for comfort. It was custom-designed to weigh as little as possible to give the craft as much range as possible. The canvas-covered walls did nothing to buffer the mighty drone of the engines, and the bare ribs of the fuselage were dark under the bare bulbs. The troops sat on padded cushions on wooden benches. In turbulence, though the shoulder harnesses held the soldiers in place, it wasn't uncommon for the cushions to slide out from under them.

Though the benches could accommodate only ninety troops in relative comfort, the StarLifter was able to hold up to three hundred troops. With only eight people in the cabin and a pilot, copilot, and navigator on the flight deck, Lieutenant Colonel Squires felt as though he were flying first-class. His long legs were stretched in front of him, he had two of the thin cushions beneath him and one between his back and the hard metal, and best of all the cabin wasn't stuffy. On those occasions when the prime members of Striker traveled with backup troops from the other services, and the five German shepherds of the K-9 Corps, the cabin tended to fill quickly with the heat of the huddled, perspiring warriors.

After several hours in the air, Squires appreciated the comfort. He had spent the first hour with Sergeant Chick Grey and Private David George, taking inventory of the gear they might need for Helsinki, spent the next two hours with Private Sondra DeVonne reviewing maps of Helsinki and St. Petersburg on his laptop, and then he slept for four hours.

When Squires woke, George handed him a microwaved meal and a cup of black coffee. The rest of the team had eaten an hour before.

"I've *got* to talk to General Rodgers about getting us better food," Squires said as he flipped open the hinged Styrofoam lid of the tray and surveyed the turkey slices, mashed potatoes, string beans, and corn muffin. "We've got missiles that can fly around trees and over mountains and slip down someone's chimney, but they're serving us the kind of crap you get on commercial airplanes."

"It's still better than the rations my dad says they served in Vietnam, sir," George said.

"Yeah, maybe," said Squires. "But it wouldn't kill them to give us a decent coffeemaker. Hell, I'd pay for it myself. Doesn't take up any extra space, and they're idiotproof. Not even the Army could screw that up."

"You never tasted my coffee, sir," said Sondra, without looking up from her copy of *Wuthering Heights*. "When I'm home, my mom and dad keep the percolator under tight security."

Squires cut a piece of turkey. "What kind of coffee do you use?"

Sondra looked over. Her large brown eyes were perfectly framed by her round face, and her voice bore the lilting trace of a youth spent in her native Algeria. "Kind, sir? I don't know. Whatever's on sale."

"That's your problem," said Squires. "My wife buys whole beans. We keep them in the freezer, then grind them that morning. Usually something festive, like southern pecan or chocolate raspberry."

"Chocolate raspberry *coffee?*" said Sondra.

"That's right. We use a drip coffeemaker, not a pot that burns the coffee, and we take it off the heat and put it in a butler as soon as it's brewed. When we drink, we never use milk or sugar. Those are the great equalizers — they make all coffee taste the same."

"Sounds to me like a lot to do before roll call, sir," Sondra said.

Squires pointed his knife toward her book. "You're reading Brontë. Why not something off the romance racks?"

"This is literature," she said. "The rest is paint-by-numbers."

"That's how I feel about coffee," Squires said as he speared more turkey with his plastic fork. "If it isn't the real thing, if it's touch football, why bother?"

Sondra said, "I can answer that in one word, sir: caffeine. When I'd read Thomas Mann or James Joyce till four in the morning, I'd need something to get me to class by nine."

Squires nodded, then said, "I've got a better way."

"What's that?"

"Push-ups," he said. "A hundred of 'em, right out of bed, wakes you faster than caffeine. Besides, if you can make yourself do that first thing in the morning, the rest of the day'll seem like a piece of cake."

As they spoke, radio operator Ishi Honda made his way from the rear of the fuselage. A veteran Striker and judo black belt born

235

of a Hawaiian mother and Japanese father, the short, boyish Honda was handling communications during the recovery of Private Johnny Puckett, who was wounded in North Korea.

Honda saluted and handed Squires the receiver of the secure TAC-Sat communications radio he carried in his backpack. "Sir, General Rodgers is calling."

"Thank you," Squires said, swallowing the mouthful of turkey and taking the line. "Colonel Squires here, General."

"Lieutenant Colonel," said Rodgers, "it looks like your team will be going to the target, and *not* as tourists."

"Understood."

"You'll have the specifics before you land," Rodgers said, "regarding point of departure, transportation, landing, and timing — though we won't be able to tell you much about exactly what it is you're looking for. Everything we know will be in the report, including where the DI6 agent investigating the site was murdered. The Russians also got one of his informants, and another's on the run."

"Take no prisoners," Squires said.

"Right. Now, I've got mixed feelings about this, but you'll also have a new teammate — a British agent with a pair that clang."

"Do I know him?" Squires asked.

"It's a her," Rodgers said, "and no. But she's got the credentials. I'll have Bob Herbert send her file through along with the TAS data. In the meantime, get McCaskey an inventory of the wet gear you have on board. If there's anything else we think you'll need, he'll have it waiting in Helsinki. And Charlie?"

"Yes, sir?"

"Tell everyone good luck and Godspeed."

"Roger," Squires said, then signed off.

TWENTY-SIX

Monday, 11:00 P.M., St. Petersburg

"Three . . . two . . . one. We're . . . *on.*"

There were no cheers as Yuri Marev spoke, no smiles as General Orlov, pacing slowly behind the arc of computers, acknowledged with a nod the functional status of the Russian Operations Center. The countdown had proceeded without a hitch, and while the long day was coming to an end for most of the workers, Orlov felt as though his day was just beginning. He had asked to see all the data that came in over the next hour, which he would review with the Directors of satellite surveillance and weather, cellular and radio communication, on-site operations, cryptography, and computer analysis, imaging, and interception. These included the four-to-midnight shift heads of each department — the prime team, which covered the heavy data flow when it was eight in the morning to four in the afternoon in Washington — as well as the Deputy Directors, who worked the midnight-to-eight and eight-to-four shifts. Rossky would also be present, not only as Orlov's second-in-command but as the liaison officer with the military. Rossky was not only in charge of analyzing shared military intelligence and feeding it to other branches of the armed forces and government, but of commanding the spetsnaz strike team that was at the Center's disposal for special missions.

Orlov looked over at Rossky, who was standing behind Corporal Ivashin. The Colonel's hands were clasped behind his back, clearly enjoying all the quiet activity. He reminded Orlov of Nikita the first time he took him to see the boosters and spacecraft at Star City: the boy was so excited, he didn't know where to look first. Orlov knew that would change very soon, though.

As soon as the Center was declared operational, Orlov walked over to Rossky. The Colonel took a moment before turning and saluting slowly.

"Colonel Rossky," Orlov said, "I would like you to tell me exactly where my son is. Everything in code, no need to log the order."

Rossky hesitated a moment, apparently having tried and failed to ascertain Orlov's motive. "Yes, sir," he said.

Rossky told Ivashin to have the radio room contact the base at Sakhalin Island and ask Sergeant Nogovin for the information. All communications were in Pencil Code Two/Five/Three: letters had to be erased before it could be decoded. In this case, every second letter of every word in the code was false, as was every fifth word — save for the third letter of each false word, which was the first letter of the word that followed.

Ivashin had his answer in less than two minutes, and his computer quickly decoded it for him.

His hands still locked behind his back, Rossky leaned over the screen and read, "Junior Lieutenant Orlov and his unit of nine spetsnaz soldiers have arrived in Vladivostok and are awaiting further instructions." Rossky fired Orlov a look. "General," he said tensely, "is this a maneuver of some kind?"

"No, Colonel, it isn't."

Rossky's jaw tightened and unclenched several times. Orlov waited several long seconds to make sure that Rossky was smart enough not to be insubordinate, not to complain that he had been excluded from a military maneuver. Rossky had to feel humiliated in front of the staff, but he remained silent.

"Come to my office, Colonel," Orlov said, turning, "and I'll brief you on the disposition of the Sakhalin spetsnaz unit."

The General heard Rossky's heels click smartly behind him. Once the door was closed behind them, Orlov sat at his desk and looked at Rossky, who stood before it.

"You're aware of Minister Dogin's shipment on board a private aircraft?" Orlov asked.

"Yes, sir."

"There's a problem," Orlov said. "Engine trouble. It can't go on. Because of the severe weather and the shortage of aircraft, I've ordered the shipment to be transferred to a train which Rear Admiral Pasenko has informed me is at our disposal."

"A train from Vladivostok will take four or five days to reach Moscow," Rossky said.

"But that's not where it's going," Orlov said. "My plan is simply to get the shipment out of Vladivostok to a place where an aircraft will be able to rendezvous with it. I was thinking that we might be able to get a helicopter out of the Bada Aerodrome to meet the train in Bira. That's only six hundred miles from Vladivostok, and appears to be far enough to the west to remain clear of the path of the storm."

"You've done a great deal of work on this already, sir," said Rossky. "Is there anything I can do?"

"As a matter of fact, there is," said Orlov. "But first, Colonel, I'd like to know how you first heard about the shipment."

Rossky said matter-of-factly, "From the Minister."

"He communicated with you directly?"

"Yes, sir," said Rossky. "I believe you were at home at the time, having dinner."

The General swiveled over to his keyboard and opened the log file. "I see. But you logged a report for me to look at later."

"No, sir," said Rossky.

"Why not, Colonel? Were you too busy?"

"Sir," said Rossky, "the Minister did not want the matter to become part of Center records."

"The *Minister* did not want it," Orlov snapped. "Is it not a standing order that every duty assigned by a superior be logged?"

"Yes, sir."

"And are you accustomed to taking civilian commands over military ones?"

"I am not, sir," Rossky replied.

"I can speak for the Center," Orlov said. "We're an autonomous base serving all branches of government and the military. But what about you, Colonel? Do you have a special loyalty to the Ministry of the Interior?"

Rossky took a moment longer to answer.

"No, sir. I do not."

"Good," said Orlov, "because if there's another incident like this, I'll have you reassigned. Is that understood?"

Rossky's rock-rigid chin moved up and down slowly. "It is. Sir."

Orlov inhaled deeply and began scanning the day's log. He never thought that Rossky would rebel openly, and his restraint was to be expected. But he'd pushed the Colonel into a corner and he was about to push a little more. Rossky would have to do something.

"Did the Minister tell you anything else, Colonel, such as the contents of the shipment?"

"He did not," Rossky said.

"Would you withhold that information from me if Minister Dogin instructed you to do so?"

Rossky glared at his superior. "Not if the information is the business of this Center, sir."

Orlov fell silent as he failed to find the log of his own conversation with Dogin. He looked back at 8:11, which is when he remembered making the entry. The space was blank.

"Is something wrong, sir?" Rossky asked.

Orlov did a word-search of the entire file,

just to make sure he hadn't mislogged the entry. Outwardly calm, inwardly he was agitated when *Gulfstream* did not turn up anywhere.

The General regarded Rossky. The Colonel's expression was relaxed now, which in itself told him something: Rossky had removed the order.

"No," Orlov said, "nothing is wrong. I misplaced a log order. I'll reenter it when we're finished." He sat back, saw a satisfied twist tug on the sides of Rossky's mouth. "I've spent enough time on this matter, and I trust my wishes are clear."

"Quite, sir."

"I want you to inform Minister Dogin of my intentions, and to take over the operation personally. My son respects you, and I'm sure you'll work as well together now as you did in the past."

"Yes, sir," Rossky said. "He's a good officer."

The telephone beeped, and Orlov dismissed the Colonel as he picked up the receiver. Rossky shut the door without a backward glance.

"Yes?" Orlov said.

"Sir, it's Zilash. Would you please come to the radio room?"

"What's wrong?"

"The dish is picking up densely coded communications," Zilash said. "We've sent them over to cryptography, but we've started to wonder if something might be happening before we're able to translate the messages."

"I'm on my way," Orlov said.

He left without bothering to relog the Gulfstream entry, certain that it would only be erased again . . . and angry that a meeting designed to put Rossky in his place merely underscored his growing concern that Dogin and the spetsnaz planned to run the Center with him as a figurehead.

Rossky's words echoed in his mind. *"Not if the information is the business of this Center, sir."* In the space of just a few hours, the death of an enemy agent and information about the Gulfstream had been kept from him. The Center was one of the most powerful reconnaissance bases in the world: Orlov would not permit Rossky and Dogin to turn it into their own private resource, though he would not do anything just yet. He had learned from his days in space that it was most important to keep his head cool when his seat was heating up to five thousand degrees Fahrenheit — and the pair had not yet come close to raising the temperature that high.

In any case, he still had a facility to run,

and neither the Colonel nor a megalomaniac was going to keep him from doing his job.

Orlov sidled into the cramped radio room, which was even thicker with smoke than before. Zilash's narrow face was angled upward, his eyes staring at nothing in particular as he listened on his headset. He removed them after a moment and looked at Orlov.

"Sir," he said around his cigarette, "we've been following two series of coded communications, and we assume they're connected. The first is from Washington to an aircraft over the Atlantic, and the second is to Helsinki." He took two quick puffs, then stubbed the cigarette in an ashtray. "We had the satellite team take a look at the aircraft: it's unmarked, though they make it out to be a C-141B StarLifter."

"Big troop carrier," Orlov said thoughtfully, "a modified version of the C-141A. I know the plane well."

"I thought you might." Zilash smiled, then lit a fresh cigarette. "The StarLifter is on a course toward Helsinki. We listened to communications between the pilot and the tower: he'll be arriving around eleven P.M., local time."

Orlov looked at his watch. "That's less than an hour from now. Any idea who's on board?"

Zilash shook his head. "We tried to listen in on the cockpit with the Svetlana in the North Atlantic, but the captain says there's an electronic field in the plane."

"So it's definitely intelligence," Orlov said, though he wasn't surprised. He thought back to the British operative who had been spying on the Hermitage, and quietly damned Rossky for his handling of the matter. The man should have been watched, not driven to suicide — if indeed he took his own life. "Brief the Ministry of Security in Moscow," Orlov said. "Tell them I need someone in Helsinki to meet the plane and watch to see if the Americans are planning to cross over."

"Yes, sir," said Zilash.

Orlov thanked him, then went to his office and summoned Rossky and Security Director Glinka to talk about which plan to implement in case they had visitors.

TWENTY-SEVEN

Tuesday, 6:08 A.M., Vladivostok

Lenin once said of Vladivostok, "It's a long way away. But it's ours."

Through two World Wars, the port city located on the Muravyev Peninsula on the Sea of Japan was a major entry point for supplies and matériel from the United States and elsewhere. During the Cold War years, the military shut the city off from the world, yet Vladivostok prospered as the port and the Pacific Fleet grew, and both military and commercial shipbuilding brought workers and money into the city. Then, in 1986, Mikhail Gorbachev inaugurated the "Vladivostok Initiative," which reopened the city and made it what he called "a wide-open window on the East."

Successive Russian leaders have worked hard to make the city an integral part of trade in the Pacific Rim, but with the new openness have come gangsters from Russia and from around the globe, attracted by hard currency and goods that come into the port both legally and illegally.

The airport in Vladivostok is located nearly nineteen miles to the north of the city. It's an hour ride from the field to the train terminal, which is situated in the heart of Vladivostok, just east of the heavily traveled Ulitsa Oktyabra.

Upon arriving at the airport with his team, Lieutenant Orlov was met by a courier from the Rear Admiral's office. The young messenger handed the officer sealed instructions to call Colonel Rossky for his orders. As snow began to flutter from pale gray skies, Nikita ran to his unit, which was lined up by the bullet nose in front of the Mi-6, the largest helicopter in the world, capable of carrying seventy people up to 652 miles. The troops were dressed in camouflage whites, their hoods down, compact backpacks at their feet. Each man was armed with standard spetsnaz issue: submachine gun and four hundred rounds of ammunition, a knife, six hand grenades, and a P-6 silent pistol. Nikita himself carried an AKR with just 160 rounds of ammunition, the short-barreled submachine gun being standard among officers.

Nikita ordered his radio operator to unpack the parabolic dish. Less than a minute later, he was on a secure uplink to Colonel Rossky.

"Sir," Nikita said, "Lieutenant Orlov calling as ordered."

"Lieutenant," said Rossky, "it's good to hear from you after so many years. I'm looking forward to working with you."

"Thank you, sir. I feel the same way."

"Excellent," Rossky said. "What do you know about your mission, Orlov?"

"Nothing, sir."

"Very well. Do you see the Gulfstream on the landing strip?"

Nikita turned to the west, into the flurries, and saw the jet sitting on the tarmac. "Yes, sir."

"Markings?"

"N2692A," Nikita said.

"Correct," said Rossky. "I've asked Rear Admiral Pasenko to send a convoy. Is it there?"

"I see four trucks waiting behind the jet."

"Excellent," said Rossky. "You are to unload the cargo from the jet, put it on the trucks, and meet the train which is waiting at the station in the city. Only the engineer will remain on board: once the cargo has been loaded, you will move the train north. Your tentative destination is Bira, though confirmation will come once you are under way. You are in command of the train, and you are to take whatever measures you deem necessary to see that the cargo reaches its destination."

"I understand, sir, and thank you," Nikita said. He did not ask what the cargo was, nor did it matter. He would treat it as carefully as if it was nuclear warheads, which it could well be. He had heard that the Primorsky region of which the city was a part had designs on becoming politically or economically independent from Russia. This could be a preemptive move by newly elected President Zhanin to disarm the area before that happened.

"You will be in touch with me as you reach each station on the Trans-Siberian route," Rossky said, "but I repeat, Lieutenant: you are to take any and all measures to protect your cargo."

"Understood, sir," Nikita said.

Returning the telephone to the operator, the Lieutenant ordered his men into action. Snatching up their gear, they ran across the field to the Gulfstream, increasingly invisible in the thickening snows.

TWENTY-EIGHT

Tuesday, 11:09 P.M., Moscow

Andrei Volko had never felt so alone or frightened. In Afghanistan, even during the worst of it, there were fellow soldiers with whom to commiserate. When he was first approached by "P" to work for DI6, he felt sick to his stomach at the thought of betraying his country. But he took consolation from the fact that his country had abandoned him after the war, and that he had new friends in Britain and here in Russia — even though he didn't know who they were. No one would benefit, he knew, if he was captured and began rattling off the names of other spies. It was enough to know that he belonged to something, and that knowledge had sustained him in the bitter years when he was forced to deal with the aftermath of a back that had been broken in a dive into a trench.

But the tall, thick-waisted young man had none of that as he approached the terminal. He had been startled during dinner by a beep from the telephone Fields-Hutton had given him. It was hidden inside a Walkman, an item so desirable in Russia that he had an excuse to keep it with him always. His nameless contact had informed him of the death of both Fields-Hutton and another agent, and told him to try and make his way to St. Petersburg within the next twenty-four hours, where he was to await further instructions. As he'd hurriedly dressed, leaving only with the clothes he was wearing, the Walkman, and the U.S. and German currency Fields-Hutton had given him for just such an emergency, Volko no longer felt like he had Britain behind him. Getting to St. Petersburg was going to be lonely and difficult, and even now he wasn't sure he'd be able to make it. He didn't own an automobile, and flying from even one of the smaller airports, like Bykovo, was risky. His name would already be at all the counters, and agents might ask for two pieces of identification instead of the fake one with which he'd been provided. His only chance was to take the train to St. Petersburg.

Fields-Hutton had once told him that if he ever had to leave the city, not to head for the airports or railroad at once. He wasn't as fast as a fax machine. Enthusiasm among clerks tended to wane as lunch or late evening neared. So he'd walked the streets until now, moving as though he had an immediate destination when he had none, mingling with the decreasing number of people heading home from work or from food lines, circuitously making his way from his apartment off Prospekt Vernadskovo through side streets where black market goods were being hawked from car trunks to the nearby Metro station. From there, he rode the crowded train to the Komsomol'skaya Metro stop, with its distinctive six-columned portico, ribbed dome, and majestic spire, in the city's northeast. He walked around for nearly an hour before strolling toward the St. Petersburg Station, which services St. Petersburg, Tallinn, and all points in northern Russia.

The four-hundred-mile railroad that connected Moscow and St. Petersburg was designed by American engineer Lieutenant George Washington Whistler, the father of painter James McNeill Whistler, and constructed by peasants and prisoners who were flogged by railroad personnel and forced to work long hours under often unendurable conditions. Shortly thereafter, in 1851, the Nikolayevskiy Station was constructed. Now known as the St. Petersburg Station, it was the oldest terminal in Moscow and one of three stations situated off busy Komsomol'skaya Square.

On the left side of the square was the art nouveau Yaroslavl Station, built in 1904, which is the final stop of the Trans-Siberian Railway. To the right is the Kazan Station, a baroque collection of buildings completed in 1926 from which trains to the Urals, western Siberia, and central Asia departed.

The St. Petersburg Station stood beside the Komsomol'skaya pavilion, just northwest of the Yaroslavl Station. As Volko approached, he used his sleeve to dab perspiration from his high forehead and pushed his longish, dirty-blond hair from his head. *Calm,* he thought. *You have to act calm.* He put a big smile on his large, friendly mouth, like a man going off to meet his lover — though he knew the smile wasn't reflected in his eyes. He only hoped no one looked closely enough to notice.

Volko turned his large, sad brown eyes up at the tall, lighted clock tower. It was just after eleven. Trains departed four times a day, starting at eight in the morning and ending at midnight, and Volko's plan was to purchase a ticket for the last train and watch to see if passengers were being stopped by the police. If so, he had two options. One was to engage another passenger in conversation as he headed toward the train, since the police would be watching for someone traveling alone. The other option was to boldly walk up to one of them and ask directions. Fields-Hutton had told him that operatives who skulk in a fast-moving environment only call attention to themselves, and that it was human nature to ignore people who seemed to have nothing to hide

The lines at the ticket windows were long, even at this hour, and Volko stood in one in the center. He had bought a newspaper and looked at it as he waited without really assimilating anything he read. The line crept along, though Volko, usually an impatient man, did not mind. Every minute he was free gave him more confidence, and also meant that he would have to spend less time as a captive in the train before it departed.

He purchased his ticket without incident, and though police officers were watching people who came and went, and questioned a few men traveling alone, Volko was not stopped.

You're going to make it, he told himself. He passed beneath the ornate arch that led to the track, where the Red Arrow Express was waiting. The ten cars dated back to before the First World War; three were freshly painted a bright red, one green, though that didn't detract from their antique charm. A tour group was standing beside the second car from the rear. Porters had tossed their luggage in a disorderly pile, and militiamen were looking at their passports.

Searching for me, no doubt, Volko thought as he walked right past them. He entered the train one car forward of the tourists and sat in one of the thinly cushioned seats. He realized that he should have brought a suitcase. It would look suspicious for someone to be going to a distant city without at least a change of clothes. He looked around as the car filled up and saw someone pushing several bags into the overhead rack. He sat under one of them, by the window.

Settling in with his newspaper in his lap and his Walkman in his jacket pocket, Volko finally allowed himself to relax. That was when the cabin went quiet behind him and he felt the cold mouth of a Makarov pistol against the back of his neck.

TWENTY-NINE

Monday, 3:10 P.M., Washington, D.C.

Bob Herbert loved being busy. But not so busy that he felt like wheeling his chair out of Op-Center and not stopping until he hit his hometown — "No, not *that* Philadelphia" — in Neshoba County not far from the Alabama border. Philadelphia hadn't changed much since he was a kid. He loved going back and reflecting on happier times. They weren't necessarily more innocent times, because he remembered well the chaos that everyone from the Communists to Elvis Presley caused when he was a boy. But they were problems that, for him, went away when he buried himself in a comic book or squirrel gun or behind a fishing pole at the pond.

Now his pager told him that Stephen Viens at the National Reconnaissance Office had something for him to look at, and after cutting short a briefing for Ann Farris, he swung his wheelchair into his office, shut the door, and called NRO.

"Please tell me you've got photos of the nude swimmin' hole back in Renova," he said into the speakerphone.

"I'm sure the foliage is still covering it up," Viens said. "What I've got is a plane whose heat signature we've been following for DEA. It went from Colombia to Mexico City to Honolulu, then on to Japan and Vladivostok."

"The drug cartels are dealing in Russia," Herbert said. "That isn't news."

"No," said Viens, "but when it landed in Vladivostok, we had a satellite in position to eyeball it. This is the first time I've ever seen a plane being unloaded by spetsnaz troops."

Herbert sat up straight. "How many?"

"Less than a dozen, all in camouflage whites," Viens said. "What's more, the crates were quickly loaded onto trucks from the Pacific Fleet. We may be looking at multi-service drug dealing."

Herbert thought back to the meeting between Shovich, General Kosigan, and Minister Dogin. "It could be more than just the military consortin' with gangsters," he said. "Are the trucks still there?"

"Yes," said Viens. "They're off-loading crates by the dozens. One truck is almost completely full."

"Do the crates look like they're evenly balanced?"

"Perfectly," said Viens. "They're oblong. But both ends seem equally heavy."

"Give a listen with the AIM," Herbert said. "Let me know if there's anything rattling around in there."

"Will do," Viens said.

"And Steve, let me know where the trucks go," Herbert said, signing off and buzzing Mike Rodgers.

Rodgers was out of his office and stopped by when he got the page.

When Herbert was finished briefing him, Rodgers said, "So the Russians are openly consorting with the drug lords. Well, they have to get hard currency from somewhere. I'm just wondering — "

"Excuse me," Herbert said as his phone beeped. He punched the speaker button set in his wheelchair armrest. "Yes?"

"Bob, it's Darrell. The FBI lost their guy in Tokyo."

"What happened?"

"Gunned down by the crew of the Gulfstream," McCaskey said grimly. "The Japanese lost their Self-Defense Force guy in the cross fire."

"Darrell, it's Mike," said Rodgers. "Anyone hurt on the plane?"

"Not that we can tell, though the ground crew didn't say much. They're scared."

"Or bribed," Herbert said. "Sorry about this, Dar. Did he have any family?"

"A father," McCaskey said. "I'll see if there's anything we can do for him."

"Right," said Herbert.

"I guess that cements the link between the plane and the Russian drug dealers," said McCaskey. "Even the Colombians aren't insane enough to have a firefight at an international airport."

"No," Herbert said. "They shoot the guys who are supposed to try the cases. They all stink deeply, and I'd love to turn Striker loose on the lot of them."

Herbert hung up and took a second to collect himself. These things always made the Intelligence Officer queasy, the more so when there was any kind of family involved.

He looked at Rodgers. "What was it that you were wondering a minute ago, General?"

Rodgers was more somber than before. "If this connects with what Matt found out. Our boy genius just conferenced with Paul and me," Rodgers said. "He hacked the Kremlin payroll through the bank in Riyadh that holds about ten billion dollars in IOUs. He found out they've been employing some very expensive executives at the new TV studio in the Hermitage and in the Ministry of the Interior — people with no prior records anywhere."

"Meaning that someone may have created names and identities for payroll purposes," Herbert said, "to pay people who are working secretly in St. Petersburg."

"Correct," Rodgers said, "as well as to buy a lot of hi-tech stuff from Japan, Germany, and the U.S. — components which were sent to the Ministry of the Interior. It's beginning to smell a lot like Dogin put together a very sophisticated intelligence operation up there. Maybe Orlov is there to help with any orbital hardware they're using."

Herbert tapped his forehead. "So assuming Dogin is the bossman, and is tight with the Russian mafia, there's a good chance he's planning a coup. He doesn't need arms. Kosigan has those."

"No," said Rodgers. "It's what I was telling Paul earlier. What he needs is money to buy politicians, journalists, and support from abroad. And that money might very well come from Shovich in exchange for future considerations."

"Could be," Herbert agreed. "Or Dogin may be planning to raise money by selling drugs provided by Shovich. He wouldn't be the first world leader to do that. Just the biggest. He could have the crap carried around the world in diplomatic pouches by officials sympathetic to his cause."

"Makes sense," Rodgers said. "The diplomats take out drugs, come back with hard currency."

"So those crates up in Vladivostok are probably a part of all this," Herbert said. "Either drugs, money, or both."

"You know what's a real kick in the head?" Rodgers said. "Even if Zhanin found out about all this, he couldn't do a damn thing. If he acted, one of two things would happen.

"One," Rodgers said, "he defeats Dogin, but his subsequent purge is so far-reaching and debilitating that it scares off the foreign investors he needs to rebuild the country. Result: Russia ends up in worse shape than it is.

"Two," Rodgers continued, "Zhanin forces his enemies to attack before they're ready, causing a long and bloody revolt with nuclear weapons in God knows whose hands. Our main concern has got to be what it was in Panama under Noriega or Iran under the Shah. Stability, not legality."

"Good point," Herbert said. "So what do you think the President will do?"

"Just what he did last night," Rodgers

said. "Nothing. He can't inform Zhanin for fear of leaks. And he can't offer any military help. We bargained that option away. In any case, there's a danger in any kind of preemptive strike. You don't want to force Dogin and his cronies underground, where they would still be a tremendous threat."

"And how will the President explain to NATO that he's doing nothing?" Herbert said. "They're a bunch of chickenhearts, but they'll want to rattle their sabers."

"He may rattle along with them," Rodgers said, "or, if I know Lawrence, he may cloak himself in neo-isolationism and tell NATO to take a swim. That'll play well with the mood of the American public. Especially in the wake of the tunnel bombing."

As Herbert sat there, tapping his leather armrest, the desk phone beeped. He glanced at the ID number on the base. It was the NRO. He put it on speaker so Rodgers could hear.

"Bob," said Stephen Viens, "we haven't got your AIM reading yet, but we watched the first truck as it left the airport. It went straight to the railroad station in Vladivostok."

"What's the weather like at the site?" Herbert asked.

"Awful," said Viens, "which is probably

why they did it. Real heavy snows. It's storming all over the region, in fact, and it's supposed to stay that way for at least forty-eight hours."

"So Dogin or Kosigan decided to transfer the goods from a grounded airplane to the railroad," Herbert said. "Can you see anything at the station?"

"No," Viens said. "The train is inside the terminal. But we have the scheduled departures and we'll watch any one that leaves when it isn't supposed to."

"Thanks," Herbert said. "Keep me up-to-date."

When Viens clicked off, the Intelligence Officer contemplated the cargo being placed in an ITS target — identifiable, trackable, strikable.

"And important," he said under his breath.

"What was that?" Rodgers asked.

"I said, obviously the cargo is important," Herbert said. "Otherwise, they'd have sat out the storm."

"I agree," Rodgers said. "And not only is it vitally important, it's also out there in the open."

It took a moment before Herbert really heard what Rodgers had said. He frowned. "No, Mike, it's not out in the open. It's heading deep *into* Russia, thousands of miles from any friendly border. This is not a short hop and you're back in Finland."

"You're right," said Rodgers. "But it's also the quickest way to hamstring Dogin. No bucks, no buckshot."

"Jesus, Mike," Herbert said, "think this through. Paul believes in diplomacy, not warfare. He'll never agree — "

"Hold on," said Rodgers.

Herbert sat there while Rodgers went to the desk phone and buzzed Hood's executive assistant.

"Bugs?" he said. "Is Paul still sitting in on the TAS session?"

"I believe so," Bugs Benet responded.

"Ask him if he can come to Bob Herbert's office. Something has come up."

"Will do," Benet said.

When Benet clicked off, Rodgers said, "We'll find out right now if he agrees."

"Even if you can convince him," Herbert said, "the CIC will *never* in a million years go along with this."

"They already okayed a Striker incursion into Russia," Rodgers said. "Darrell and Martha will have to get them to approve another."

"And if they can't?"

Rodgers said, "What would you do, Bob?"

Herbert was silent for a long moment.

"Jesus, Mike," he said, "you know what I'd do."

"You'd send them in because it's the right mission and they're the right team, and you *know* it. Look," Rodgers said, "we both shoveled dirt on Bass Moore's coffin after North Korea — I was in on that incursion. I've been on other missions where troops have been killed. But that can't immobilize us. This is what we created Striker *for*."

Herbert's door beeped and he let Hood in.

The Director's tired eyes showed concern as they settled on Herbert. "You don't look very happy, Bob. What's up?"

Rodgers told him. Hood sat on the edge of Herbert's desk, listening without comment as the General informed him about the situation in Russia and his thoughts on Striker.

When he was finished, Hood asked, "How do you think our terrorists would react to this? Would it be a breach of our deal with them?"

"No," said Rodgers. "They specifically told us to stay out of Eastern Europe, not central Russia. In any case, we'd be in and out before they knew it."

"Fair enough," said Hood. "On to the larger question, then. You know how I feel about force as opposed to negotiation."

"Same as I do," said Rodgers. "Better to shoot off your mouth than a gun. But we won't be able to talk this train back to Vladivostok."

"Probably not," Hood agreed, "which raises another issue entirely. Let's assume you get an okay to send Striker to reconnoiter and you find out what's on the train. Say it's heroin. What then? Do you seize it, destroy it, or call Zhanin to send Russian troops to fight Russian troops?"

Rodgers said, "When you've got a fox in your gunsight, you don't put down the rifle and call for the hounds. That's how you end up with Nazis in Poland, Castro in Cuba, and a Communist Vietnam."

Hood shook his head. "You're talking about attacking Russia."

"Yes, I am," Rodgers said. "Didn't they just attack us?"

"That was different."

"Tell that to the families of the dead," Rodgers said. He walked toward Hood. "Paul, we aren't another fat, pass-the-buck government agency. Op-Center was chartered to get things done, things the CIA and the State Department and the military can't do. We've got a chance to do that. Charlie Squires put Striker together with the full knowledge that they would be called upon to play with fire, no different than any other elite military team, from the spetsnaz to Oman's Royal Guard to Equatorial Guinea's Guardia Civil. What we have to work toward — what we have to *believe* — is that if we all do our jobs and keep our wits, this thing can be kept under wraps and dealt with."

Hood looked at Herbert. "What do you think?"

Herbert shut his eyes and rubbed the lids. "As I get older, the thought of kids dying for political expediency is increasingly nauseating to me. But the Dogin-Shovich-Kosigan team *is* a nightmare, and like it or not, Op-Center is in the front line."

"What about St. Petersburg?" Hood asked. "We decided that cutting the brain from the body would be enough."

"This dragon is bigger than we thought," Rodgers said. "You take off the head, the body may still be alive long enough to do some serious damage. Those drugs or money or whatever is on the train can make that happen."

Herbert rolled over to Hood. He clapped a hand on his knee. "You look as unhappy as I did, Chief."

Hood said, "And now I know why." He looked at Rodgers. "I know you wouldn't risk your team unless you thought it was worth it. If Darrell can swing this with the CIC, do what needs to be done."

Rodgers turned to Herbert. "Head over to TAS. Have them draw up a plan leaving as small a Striker contingent as possible in Helsinki, then figure out the cleanest, fastest way of getting Striker to the train. Bounce it off Charlie each step of the way, and make sure he's comfortable with it."

"Oh, you know Charlie," Herbert said as he swung his wheelchair toward the door. "If it involves putting his ass on the line, he'll be for it."

"I know," Rodgers said. "He's the best of us."

"Mike," Hood said, "I'll brief the President on this one. Just so you know, I'm still not behind this one hundred percent. But I'm behind you."

"Thanks," Rodgers said. "That's all I want or expect."

The men followed Herbert out.

As he rolled alone toward the TAS command center, the Intelligence Officer found himself wondering why nothing in human affairs — whether it was the conquest of a nation or the changing of a single mind or the pursuit of a lover — could be accomplished without struggle.

It was said that trials were what made the

victory so sweet, but Herbert never bought that. From where he sat, he'd settle for having the victories come a little easier now and then. . . .

THIRTY

The room was small and dark with concrete walls and a fluorescent light overhead. There was a wooden table, a single stool, and a metal door. There were no windows. The black tile floor was faded and badly scuffed.

Andrei Volko sat beneath the flickering lights in the small, windowless room. He knew why he was here, and he had a good idea what was going to happen to him. The militiaman with the gun had led him from the train without a word, to two waiting armed guards and, together, the four of them had climbed into a police car and come to the station on Dzerzhinsky Street, not far from the old KGB headquarters. Volko had been handcuffed at the station. As he sat on the stool feeling utterly helpless, he wondered how they had found out about him. He assumed it was through something Fields-Hutton had left behind. Not that it mattered. He tried not to think how long and hard he would be beaten until his captors believed he knew absolutely nothing about any operatives apart from the ones they'd already taken. More important, he wondered how many days it would be before he was tried, imprisoned, and finally awakened one morning and shot in the head. What lay ahead seemed surrealistic.

He could only hear his thumping heart as it beat loudly in his ears. Every now and then a wave of terror rolled through him, a mix of fear and despair that caused him to ask himself, *How have I come to this point in my life?* A decorated soldier, a good son, a man who had only wanted what was due to him —

A key turned and the door swung open. Three guards entered the room. Two men wore uniforms and carried clubs. The third man was young, short, and dressed in crisply pressed brown trousers and a white shirt without any tie. He had a round face with gentle eyes and smoked a strong-smelling cigarette. The two guards positioned themselves alongside the open door, legs spread wide apart, blocking it.

"My name is Pogodin," the young man said firmly as he approached him, "and you are in quite a bit of trouble. We found the telephone in your cassette machine. Your fellow traitor in St. Petersburg had one also. However, unlike you, he had the misfortune of falling into the hands of a spetsnaz officer who dealt with him rather harshly. We also have the labels from the English tea bags you served the British spy. Very clever. I imagine you passed information inside them, then cleared the table so no one would ever notice the missing labels. There were fibers from one of the labels in his wallet. We wouldn't have found you if not for that. Do you deny any of this?"

Volko said nothing. He wasn't feeling especially brave, but all he had left was his self-respect. He wasn't about to lose it.

Pogodin was standing right beside Volko, looking down at him. "Commendable. Most people in your position screech like birds. Perhaps you don't know of our reputation for obtaining information?"

"I know," Volko said.

Pogodin regarded him for a moment. He looked as though he was trying to decide whether Volko was brave or stupid. "Would you care for a cigarette?"

The waiter shook his head.

"Would you care to save your life and repay some of the debt you owe to your country?"

Volko looked up at his youthful captor.

"I see that you would," Pogodin said. He used his cigarette to point to the men behind him. "Shall I send them away so we can talk?"

Volko thought for a moment, then nodded.

Pogodin told them to go and they shut the door behind them as they left. The young man walked around Volko to the table and perched on the edge.

"You were expecting somewhat different treatment, weren't you?" Pogodin asked.

"When?" Volko said. "Today, or when I returned from Afghanistan with a broken back and a pension that wouldn't support a dog?"

"Ah, bitterness," Pogodin said. "A greater motivator than anger because it doesn't pass. So you betrayed Russia because your pension was too small?"

"No," Volko said. "Because *I* felt betrayed. I was in pain every moment I worked, every time I stood."

Pogodin poked his chest with a thumb. "And I'm in pain each day I think of my grandfather being crushed by a tank in Stalingrad, or my two elder brothers killed by snipers in Afghanistan — and men like you betraying what they died for because you felt *uncomfortable*. Is that all the affection you can muster for Russia?"

Volko looked straight ahead. "A man has to eat, and in order to eat he must work. I would have been fired from the hotel if the Englishman hadn't insisted they keep me. He spent a great deal of money there."

Pogodin shook his head. "I should tell my superiors at the Ministry of Security that you are unapologetic and would sell your country again for a price."

"That wasn't what I wanted," Volko said. "It never was, and it isn't now."

"No," said Pogodin, drawing on his cigarette, "because now your friends are dead and you're facing death." He leaned toward the waiter, blowing smoke from both nostrils. "Here's how it can be different, Andrei Volko. Why were you heading to St. Petersburg?"

"To meet someone. I didn't know that he was already dead."

Pogodin slapped the waiter hard across the cheek. "You weren't going to meet the Englishman or the Russian. You wouldn't have been told who the latter was, and besides — they were already dead and DI6 knew it. When the spetsnaz officer tried to use their concealed telephones, the lines were inactive. He was too impatient. You have an ID to enter first, correct?"

Volko remained silent.

"Of course, correct," Pogodin said. "So you were headed to St. Petersburg to meet someone else. Who?"

Volko continued to stare ahead, his terror supplanted by shame. He knew what was coming, what Pogodin had in mind, and he knew he would have a terrible choice to make.

"I don't know," Volko said. "I was — "

"Go on."

Volko took a long, tremulous breath. "I was to go there, contact London, and await further instructions."

"Were they going to try and get you into Finland?" Pogodin asked.

"That — was my impression," Volko said.

Pogodin smoked while he thought, then rose and looked down at the waiter. "I'll be frank, Andrei. The only way you can save yourself is to help us learn more about the British operation. Are you willing to go to St. Petersburg as planned and work with us instead of with the enemy?"

"Willing?" Volko said. "In a relationship that began with a gun at my neck?"

Pogodin said coldly, "And it will end with one there if you don't cooperate."

Volko looked into the tester of smoke hanging under the lights. He tried to tell himself that he would be acting patriotically, but he knew that wasn't the case. He was just afraid.

"Yes," Volko said sullenly. "I'll go to St. Petersburg" — he looked into Pogodin's eyes — "willingly."

Pogodin glanced at his wristwatch. "There's a cabin reserved for us. It won't even be necessary to hold the train." He looked at Volko and smiled now. "I'm going with you, of course. And though I don't carry a gun, I trust you'll still be willing to cooperate."

There was menace in his tone, and Volko was still too shaken to answer. He didn't want other people to die on his account, but he also knew that everyone who played in this field knew the risks . . . himself included.

As his captor led him from the interrogation room back to the car, he told himself that he had two choices. One was to accept Pogodin's terms and earn himself a quick death. The other was to fight back and try to regain the honor he had somehow lost. . . .

THIRTY-ONE

Monday, 10:05 P.M., Berlin

The fat, heavy Ilyushin Il-76T was a high-performance Russian transport just over 165 feet long with a wingspan of over 165 feet. First introduced in prototype in 1971, and first flown in service with the Soviet Air Force in 1974, it could take off from short, unpaved airstrips, making it ideal for environments like those found in Siberia. It was also modified as a flight-refueling tanker for Russian supersonic strategic bombers. Il-76Ts had been sold to Iraq, Czechoslovakia, and Poland. Powered by four mighty Soloviev D-30KP turbofans, the jet had a normal cruising speed of nearly five hundred miles an hour and a range of over four thousand miles. The Il-76T could transport forty tons of cargo. If it were flying nearly empty, and if relatively lightweight rubber fuel bladders were installed in the cargo bay with extra fuel, the range could be increased by over seventy percent.

After contacting the Pentagon and explaining that Striker needed a ride into Russia, Bob Herbert was put in touch with General David "Divebomb" Perel in Berlin, who had the husky jet hauled from secret storage. It had been kept at the U.S. air base there since 1976, when it had been bought by the Shah of Iran and then clandestinely sold to the U.S. After studying the aircraft, the Air Force had gutted it for use as a spy plane. To date, the Il-76T had been used in only a handful of missions, measuring exact distances between landmarks to help calibrate spy satellites and taking radar and heat readings of underground installations to get a picture of their layout. On all of these flights, it had managed to fool the Russians as to its legitimacy by filing a flight plan through a mole in the Air Force. The mole was informed, by radio, to do it again for this flight.

This was the first time the Il-76T was going to be used to carry American troops, and the first time it would spend this much time over Russian airspace — eight hours, as it flew from Helsinki to the drop-off point and then on to Japan. In the past, it was never in the air long enough to be spotted, discovered to be unregistered, and investigated.

Both Herbert and Perel were keenly aware of the danger the crew and the Striker team faced, and both of them expressed their deep reservations to Mike Rodgers in a conference call.

Rodgers shared their concerns and asked for alternative suggestions. Perel agreed with Herbert that while the operation was within Op-Center's jurisdiction, the political issue was a matter for the State Department and the White House to decide. Rodgers reminded Herbert and pointed out to the General that until they knew for a fact what was on that train, this was strictly a reconnaissance matter. Until that situation changed, he had no choice but to pursue this course of action — regardless of the danger. On-site intelligence gathering, he said, was never risk free . . . and there were times, like now, when it was indispensable.

And so the Il-76T was prepped and loaded with paratroop and cold-weather gear and took off, headed to Helsinki with special clearance from Defense Minister Kalle Niskanen — though he was told that the flight was only to reconnoiter, not that troops would almost certainly be jumping into Russia. That was a problem Lowell Coffey would have to smooth over once the plane was airborne, though the fiercely anti-Russian Minister probably wouldn't have a problem with anything they wanted to do there. Meanwhile, Herbert contacted the Op-Center radio room and asked to be patched through to Lieutenant Colonel Squires.

THIRTY-TWO

Tuesday, 11:27 P.M., south of Finland

"It isn't hypocritical," Squires told Sondra as the StarLifter began its final approach to Helsinki airport. The Strikers had changed into civilian clothes and looked like any other tourists. "Yes, coffee is a stimulant, and it might be bad for your stomach if consumed by the barrel. But wine is bad for your liver and your mind."

"Not in moderation," Sondra said as she checked her gear again. "And wine tasters have as much right to fuss over vintage and flavor and body as someone does over coffee."

"I don't *fuss* over coffee," Squires said. "I don't swirl it around my Redskins mug and savor the aroma. I drink it, period. I also don't pretend that getting high sip by sip in an elegant setting *is* elegant." He chopped down with his hand. "End of debate."

Sondra scowled as she zipped up the nondescript backpack that contained a compass,

283

nine-inch hunting knife, M9 .45-caliber pistol, one thousand dollars in cash, and maps of the region that had been printed out by Squires's computer during the flight. It wasn't fair for him to pull rank like that, but she reminded herself that no one ever said the military was fair, that rank had its privileges, and all the other clichés her parents had thrown at her when she'd told them she wanted to join the military straight out of Columbia.

"If you want to travel, travel!" her father had said. *"We can afford it, take a year."*

But that wasn't it. Carl "Custard" DeVonne had been a self-starter who made a fortune in soft ice cream in New England, and he didn't understand why an only daughter who had everything would want to take her B.A. in literature and join the Navy. Not just the Navy, but fight her way into the SEALs. Maybe it was because she had had everything as a kid and wanted to test herself. Or maybe she needed to do something her overachieving father hadn't. And the SEALs, and now Striker, were certainly a test.

While she wondered how a man as bright as Squires could be so stubborn, a call came in from Op-Center. He took it, listened — intently as always, mostly without speaking — and then handed the phone back to Ishi Honda.

"Okay, lady and gentlemen, gather 'round," he said, hunching toward his troops like a quarterback in a huddle. "Here's the latest. Private George, when we reach Helsinki, you'll be remaining behind. Darrell McCaskey has arranged for you to link up with a Major Aho of the Finnish Ministry of Defense. The Major will take you to your partner, DI6 operative Peggy James, and the two of you will take on the Hermitage by your lonesomes. Sorry, but the rest of us have business elsewhere. You'll hitch a midget sub ride from the Gulf of Finland into the Neva. The Finns've got a butt-kick Defense Minister who's been running surveillance trips right into the mouth of the river. The Russians don't monitor closely because manpower is stretched thin and Moscow doesn't worry a whole lot about being attacked by Finland."

"Sloppy," Sondra observed.

"You and James will raft into St. Petersburg in daylight," Squires continued. "General Rodgers would have preferred for you to wait for nightfall, but that's when they make the mini-sub trips, so in you go. Fortunately, the Russian Navy maintains a mini-sub base in Koporskiy Zaliv Bay not far from the city. You'll be given Russian naval uniforms when you reach Helsinki. If you're stopped for any reason, Ms. James speaks fluent Russian and you'll have the appropriate documents. The Finns are turning out Russian papers in the Security Ministry's forgery division. Major Aho will give you your cover story as well as visas and papers so you can get out of the country as Russian soldiers on leave. Once you reach the Hermitage, find out anything you can about the communications center they appear to have down there. If you can cripple it without terminating anyone, do so. Any questions?"

"Yes, sir. I assume Major Aho's in charge of the mission while we're in Finland. Who runs it in Russia?"

Squires's jaw shifted to the side. "I was getting to that. Op-Center's come up with a new one for us. James was going to be a subordinate as long as an officer was present. Since there isn't going to be one — me — she's along as an observer. In other words, she's not obliged to take orders from you."

"Sir?"

"I know it's an odd one, Private. All I can tell you is, do your job. If she has ideas, listen to them. If she doesn't like yours, negotiate. She's a sharp player, so it should be okay. Any other questions?"

George saluted. "No, sir." If he was concerned or excited, it didn't show in his rosy, youthful face.

"Okay." Squires looked around. "The rest of us will be taking a little trip. We'll be transferring to a Russian transport we've had in cold storage, and flying to parts unknown. The rest of our mission will be communicated en route."

"Any idea what it is, sir?" Sondra asked.

Squires's steely eyes were on her. "If I did," said the Lieutenant Colonel, "I'd've told you. The minute *I* know anything, *you'll* know it."

Sondra managed to hold his gaze with her own, though her exuberance dissolved like the sugar she dared to use in her coffee. Their conversations earlier, and now this rebuke, had shown her a side of Squires she hadn't seen during her month with Striker: not the driving, blistering, "try-harder, move-your-ass, can't-you-hit-a-damn-bull's-eye?" side, but the imperious commander. The change from taskmaster to leader was subtle, but demanding. It was also, she had to admit, impressive.

As Squires dismissed the troops and Sondra sat back down, she shut her eyes and did what they'd taught her in SEAL training, worked on whipping up her enthusiasm again, reminding herself that she wasn't here for Squires but for herself and for her country.

"Private."

Sondra opened her eyes. The Lieutenant Colonel was leaning close so he could be heard over the drone of the engines, his expression less forbidding than it had been moments before.

"Yes, sir?"

"A bit of advice," he said. "Back at the base, you had one of the greatest go-get-'em attitudes I've ever seen. I don't know who you were mad at, or who you were trying to impress up here — " He touched his temple. "You sure impressed me, though. You also have skill and smarts or you wouldn't be here. But what the rest of my team knows, Private DeVonne, is that on a mission, the cardinal virtues *are* the cardinal virtues: prudence, temperance, fortitude, and justice. You understand?"

"I think so, sir."

"I'll put it another way," Squires said as he sat up and buckled up for the landing. "Keep everything open except your mouth and you'll do just fine."

Sondra slipped on her own shoulder harness and leaned back. She was still a little deflated and somewhat annoyed that the Lieutenant Colonel had chosen this time and this way to share his philosophy, but feeling more confident than ever that here was a man she could follow into battle. . . .

THIRTY-THREE

Monday, 4:30 P.M., Washington, D.C.

While Rodgers sat in his office, reviewing the latest Striker plans from TAS, Stephen Viens E-mailed the AIM-Satellite report on the crates:

> CONTENTS OF EACH CRATE APPEARS TO BE A SOLID MASS. PROBABLY NOT MACHINERY. EASY FOR TWO MEN TO LIFT. SENT PHOTO RECON TO MATT STOLL FOR ANALYSIS.

Rodgers muttered to himself, "Bricks of cocaine or packets of heroin would fill the bill. And I'd love to make the bastards eat each and every one of them."

There was a knock on the door. Rodgers buzzed Lowell Coffey in.

"You wanted to see me?" Coffey asked.

Rodgers waved him to a chair. Coffey removed his black trench coat and planted himself in the leather armchair. The attorney had bags under his eyes, and his hair wasn't as carefully combed as usual. This had been a long, tough day for him.

"How did it go with the Congressional Intelligence Oversight Committee?" Rodgers asked.

Coffey tugged his *LC* cuff links out from under the sleeve of his jacket. "I went over our revised outline with Senators Fox and Karlin, and was told we're crazy. Senator Fox said it twice. The answer was no change in the original Striker mandate. I think they have a problem with the prospect of engaging the Russian Army, Mike."

"I can't worry about the problems they have," Rodgers said. "I need my team in there. Go back and tell them we're not talking about an engagement, Lowell. We're just reconnoitering."

"Just reconnoitering," Coffey said dubiously. "They'll never buy that. *I* don't buy it. I mean, reconnoitering to find out what?"

"Where the soldiers are headed and exactly what they're guarding."

"You'll have to get on the train for that," Coffey said. "That's some pretty close reconnoitering. And if Striker is found out? What do I tell the Senators? Do we surrender or fight?"

Rodgers said bluntly, "Striker doesn't surrender."

"Then forget my even going back," he said.

"All right," Rodgers said. "Tell them we won't fight. Tell them we won't use anything stronger than flash/bang grenades and tear gas. We'll put everyone to sleep, no one gets hurt."

"I still can't do it," Coffey said. "I can't take that to the committee."

"Then screw 'em," Rodgers said. "Hell, we're still breaking international law even if we *get* their approval."

"True," Coffey said, "but if we get caught then, it's Congress in the hot seat and we don't get crucified. Do you have any idea how many national and international laws and treaties you can conceivably break with this one action you're proposing? The good news is, you'll never go to jail. You'll spend forty years in court fighting each of the charges."

Rodgers thought for a moment. "What if you tell the committee that it isn't the Russian government we'll be going up against?"

"In Russia? Who else would we be fighting?"

"We believe a rogue official, very high up, is in bed with drug lords," Rodgers said.

"Then why haven't we told the Russian leaders?" Coffey asked. "If he were to invite us in — "

"He can't," said Rodgers. "The election didn't leave President Zhanin strong enough to deal with the rebel faction."

Coffey considered the new information. "Rogue officials. Elected ones?"

Rodgers shook his head. "Appointed by the last President and sure to be gone when Zhanin finds the broom."

Coffey chewed the inside of his cheek. "That plus the drug angle could work. Congress likes tackling bad guys the constituents can hate. What about the President? Is he behind us on this, or are we on our own?"

"Paul told him what we're proposing to do," Rodgers said. "He doesn't like the downside, but he's itching to hit someone for what happened in New York."

"And Paul's behind you, I assume?"

"He is," said Rodgers, "as long as you can get me CIC approval."

Coffey crossed his leg. He shook a foot nervously on his knee. "I assume you're going to use something other than the StarLifter to get Striker in?"

"We've taken an Il-76T from mothballs in Berlin and sent it to Helsinki — "

"Wait a minute," Coffey said. "Ambassador

Filminor got the government to okay a Russian incursion?"

"No," Rodgers said. "Bob went to the Minister of Defense."

"Niskanen?" Coffey shouted. "I told you this morning he's crazy! That's why the Finns keep him in office. He actually scares Moscow. But he can't give the final okay for something like this. You need approvals from President Jarva *and* Prime Minister Lumirae."

Rodgers said, "All I needed from Niskanen was permission to get the plane in. Once my team is airborne, he or you or the Ambassador can deal with the President and Prime Minister."

Coffey shook his head. "Mike, you're all over the map on this one, and every inch of it's an earthquake zone."

There was a knock on the door and Darrell McCaskey entered. "Am I interrupting something?"

"Yes," said Coffey, "but that's okay."

Rodgers said, "I heard about the agent in Tokyo. Sorry."

The short FBI liaison and crisis management expert scratched his prematurely gray hair and handed papers to Rodgers. "He died with his boots on," McCaskey said. "I guess that's something."

Coffey shut his eyes as Rodgers turned his attention to the papers.

"These were faxed from Interpol," Mc-Caskey said. "Maps drawn up just after the fall of Poland showing the basement of the Hermitage. The Russians knew they'd be going to war, so they gutted the cellars, reinforced them to bunker strength, and drew up plans to move the local government and military command down there in the event of an attack. You've got eighteen-inch-thick cinder-block walls and ceilings, plumbing, vents — very little would have to have been done to turn it into a secure area for intelligence work."

Rodgers looked over the architectural plans. "That's what I would've done with it. I wonder why they waited so long."

"Interpol says the basement was, in fact, used on and off over the years for radio surveillance around the world," McCaskey said. "But you know the Russians. Wherever possible, they prefer on-site intelligence over electronic surveillance."

"The peasant mentality," Rodgers said. "A potato in the hand is worth a dozen in some rosy five-year plan."

"Basically, yes," said McCaskey. "But with moles being sniffed out and the collapse of the KGB, that may be changing now."

"Thanks," Rodgers said. "Get this over to Squires so he can review them with the man going into St. Petersburg." He looked at Coffey. "For people operating on fault lines, we appear to be doing some pretty good spy work. How about working on getting those clearances we'll need as soon as Striker is airborne again, which will be" — he looked at his computer clock — "in about an hour."

Coffey looked numb. He nodded as he rose, then tugged his cuff links again and looked at Rodgers. "One more thing, Mike. As an attorney and a friend, I should point out to you that according to our charter, section seven, 'Accountability of Military Personnel to Civilian Commanders,' subsection b, paragraph two, Striker reports to the ranking military officer. That's you. The Director can't countermand an order you've given."

"I know the charter almost as well as I know *Caesar's Commentaries on the Gallic War*. What's your point, Lowell?"

Coffey said, "If I fail to get congressional approval and Paul takes their thumbs-down seriously, the only way he can recall Striker is by dismissing you and appointing another Deputy Director. If he needed to do that quickly, he could go to the duty officers."

"I wouldn't put him in that position," Rodgers said. "I'd recall Striker if he asked me to. But in here" — he stood and touched his gut — "I don't think Paul will do that. We're a crisis management team, and as long as we do everything we can to ensure the safety of our Striker force, we're going to manage this crisis."

"You guys may end up out there all alone," Coffey told him.

"Only if it doesn't work out," Darrell McCaskey observed. "Our asses were supposed to be grass after North Korea, but we won that and no one complained."

Rodgers patted Coffey on the arm and returned to Hood's desk. "Don't go writing any epitaphs, Lowell. I've been reading Churchill lately, and something he told the Canadian Parliament in December 1941 seems appropriate. He said, 'When I warned them that Britain would fight on alone whatever they did, their Generals told their Prime Minister and his divided Cabinet: In three weeks England will have her neck wrung like a chicken.' " Rodgers smiled. "Churchill's answer, gentlemen, may just become Op-Center's new motto: 'Some chicken! Some neck.' "

THIRTY-FOUR

Monday, 11:44 P.M., Helsinki

The StarLifter landed on a remote runway at the corner of the Helsinki airport, and Major Aho was there to meet it. The tall weight lifter introduced himself in fluent English to Lieutenant Colonel Squires as "a token, black-haired Lapp" in the military. As the representative of Defense Minister Niskanen, he said he had specific instructions to give the Americans whatever they needed.

As they stood in the open door of the aircraft, the cold wind swirling in from the dark night, Squires told him the only thing he wanted was to close the door and wait for the Il-76T.

"I understand," said Aho, whose sonorous voice, like his carriage, had great dignity.

Leaving an aide behind to work as a liaison with the ground crew, Aho waited while Private George accepted and tendered a round of good-luck wishes, then escorted him to a waiting car. Both men sat in the back.

"Have you ever been to Finland, Private George?" Aho asked.

"Sir," said the soldier, "until I joined the Army, I'd never been out of Lubbock, Texas. After I joined, I never got out of Virginia till now. I wasn't around for the first mission. On the second mission, to Philadelphia, I was sick. On the third mission, to Korea, I got myself bumped by a General."

"In life as in chess, king takes pawn." Major Aho smiled. "At least you'll be making up for it this time out. You get to visit two countries."

George returned his smile. There was a priestly benevolence to the Major's expression and a softness in his fair eyes that George had never seen in a military officer. But beneath Aho's tight brown uniform, George also saw muscle definition he'd never seen, except in bodybuilding competitions on cable TV.

"But you're fortunate," said the Major. "The Viking men believed that a foreign warrior who came to Finland first, in peace, is invincible in battle."

"Only the men believed that, sir?"

Aho sighed. "It was a different world, Private. And — you haven't met your partner, is that correct?"

"That's correct, sir, though I'm looking

forward to it," George said diplomatically. In fact, she worried him. He had read the dossier that was faxed to the plane and wasn't at all sure he was ready for a civilian barnstormer.

"I wouldn't say this to her," Aho said, leaning toward him conspiratorially, "but Viking society was always about warrior men. Each man carried an axe, a dagger, and a sword on his person at all times, and wore garments of fox or beaver or even squirrel that left one arm free, his fighting arm. Each woman wore a box on either breast, made of iron, copper, silver, or gold, indicating the wealth of her husband. She also wore a neck ring to show her subservience to him. We had a bit of a row in the schools years ago about how to teach the history of these people." He settled back into his seat. "You can't offend women, you can't offend the British who were victims of the Vikings, you can't offend the Christians who were killed by the heathens — heathens who didn't want to see their cultures destroyed like those of the Visigoths, Ostrogoths, Burgundians, Lombards, and Alamanni. Fortunately, accuracy won over political expedience. Can you imagine being ashamed of a history such as ours?"

"No, sir," George said, then looked out

at the starry night sky. It was the same sky the Vikings had looked at — *in awe or fear?* George wondered. He couldn't imagine that the Vikings were afraid of anything but dishonor. His own training, like the training of Navy SEALs and the Army's Delta unit or the Russian spetsnaz, emphasized attitude as well as physical skills: not just twenty-hour marches with a fifty-five-pound rucksack to keep you in shape, but the belief that while death is fast, failure stays with you for a lifetime. And George believed that utterly.

Still, he couldn't deny that he felt a lot better when he "overdressed": wearing a hip pouch stuffed with flash grenades, a Kevlar bulletproof vest with lapel daggers for hand-to-hand combat, his Leyland and Birmingham respirator, and carrying a few spare 9mm magazines. Instead, in his rucksack, he had AN/PVS-7A night-vision goggles, an AN/PAS-7 thermal viewer to see hidden objects by the heat they generated, and his Heckler & Koch MP5SD3 with a collapsing stock and integral silencer — even the bolt noise was absorbed by rubber buffers — which, used with subsonic ammunition, couldn't be heard fifteen feet away. And his passport. He had that too. That was the exit strategy Darrell McCaskey had come up with.

"I don't think your ancestors did anything like what we're doing, though, sir," George said, trying not to let the details distract him. He turned away from the sprawling beauty of the Milky Way as the car entered the city proper and turned onto the main boulevard, the Pohjoesplanadi, the Northern Esplanade, which runs east and west through the center of the city. "I mean, it would've been kind of difficult to sneak a Viking with three weapons and a horned helmet into another country unnoticed."

"True," said Aho, "nor did they want to sneak in. They believed in panicking the countryside as they approached their target, forcing local officials to deal with domestic unrest as well as the invaders."

"And here we are, sir, coming by minisub," George said.

"We call them midget marauders," said Aho. "A little more gung-ho, don't you think?"

"Yes, sir," George said as they stopped in front of the majestic, sprawling Presidential Palace, which was built for the Russian Czars who ruled the city starting in 1812, after fires burned down the wooden buildings that Queen Christina of Sweden had built there over the previous two centuries. Aho led the private through a side entrance.

The Palace was quiet at this hour. After presenting his credentials to a guard, Aho greeted several members of the skeletal night staff, then took George to a small office at the far end of a narrow, dimly lighted corridor. Beside the six-panel door was a bronze plaque that said *Defense Minister*. Aho used two keys to let them in.

"Minister Niskanen has several offices in the city," said Aho. "He uses this one when he is on good terms with the President. He is not using it now." The Major grinned and said quietly, "There's something else that's changed. In the days of generals like Halfdan or Olaf Tryggvason, or monarchs like Knut or Svein Forkbeard, leaders didn't take disagreements to a parliament or congress or the press. They put a slave girl up against the wall, threw axes at her, and the man who hit her lost. Then everyone went back to drinking and the dispute was forgotten."

"I can see where that wouldn't work today, sir," George noted.

"Oh, it would work," Aho said. "It just wouldn't be very popular."

A light was on, and George saw a woman standing behind the desk, leaning on her rigid arms and looking down at a map. She was slight, with large, blue eyes framed by short-cropped dirty-blond hair. Her mouth was small and her lips naturally ruddy, her nose was strong and ended in a little upturn, and her skin was extremely pale with a faint smattering of freckles on her cheeks. She was dressed in a black jumpsuit.

"Ms. James," said Aho as he shut the door and doffed his hat, "Private George."

"Glad to meet you, ma'am," George said, smiling at her as he put down his rucksack.

Peggy looked up briefly, then resumed examining her map. "Good evening, Private," she said. "You look like you're about fifteen."

Her clipped accent and brusque manner reminded George of a young Bette Davis. "Fifteen and a half," he said, walking toward the desk. "If you mean neck size."

She looked up. "*And* you're a comedian."

"I have many talents, ma'am," he said. Still smiling, George leapt on the desk, his feet straddling the map; in the same quick move, he'd snatched up a letter opener and put the blade to Peggy's throat. "I've also been trained to kill, quickly and silently."

Their eyes locked, and almost at once George realized that that had been a mistake. She'd done it to distract him as she brought her rigid forearms together hard on either side of his wrist. The letter opener clattered to the desktop and, a moment later, she swung her stiff right leg across the map, kicking his legs out from under him. As he fell to his side, she grabbed the front of his shirt and pulled him to the floor, dropping him on his back and putting her foot on his neck.

"Just make sure," she said, "that if you plan to kill, you do so without the speech. All right?"

"All right," he said, kicking up with both feet so that he was momentarily resting on his shoulder blades. Locking his ankles around Peggy's neck, he pulled her down and flipped her onto her back. "Though I'll make an exception this time."

George kept the operative in a chokehold for several seconds to teach her a lesson, and then released her. As she sucked down air, he helped her to her feet.

"Impressive," she gasped, rubbing her throat with her left hand. "But you missed one thing."

"What, ma'am?"

She showed him the letter opener in her right hand. "I grabbed it when you brought me down. The way you were holding me, I could've stuck you anywhere."

Rubbing her throat, Peggy returned to the map while Private George looked at the letter opener and silently cursed himself. It didn't bother him that a woman had bested him; in training, Sondra and he had knocked each other around mercilessly. But on a mission, missing something like the letter opener would have meant the difference between living and dying.

Still standing by the closed door, Aho said, "Now that the introductions have been made, perhaps you'd care to go to work?"

Peggy nodded.

"When you reach the boat at the harbor," Aho said, "your password for the boat will be 'wonderful stem-post.' The response is 'handsome dragonhead.' Private George, I've already explained the process of gaining access to the midget submarine to Ms. James. I've also given her money and the Russian uniforms you're to wear." He grinned. "We have more Russian uniforms here, and better fitting, than the Russians do." He took a sealed packet from his inside jacket pocket and handed it to Private George. "Here are the papers identifying you as a Principal Shipboard Starshina Yevgeny Glebov and Senior Sailor Ada Lundver in the Russian Navy. You're the Sailor, Ms. James, assigned to coastal mapping and buoy refurbishing. This means that if anyone sees you, you'll have to look like you're following Private George's orders."

"He doesn't speak Russian," she said. "How will that work?"

"You've got a ninety-minute boat ride and a ten-hour submarine trip to teach him some basics," Aho said. He put his hat back on. "And that covers everything, I believe. Further questions?"

"None, sir," George said.

Peggy shook her head.

"Very well, then," said the Major. "Good luck."

George picked up the heavy rucksack containing his gear and jogged after Major Aho, who opened the door, walked into the hallway, and shut the door behind him.

George stopped short to avoid running into the door. "Officers!" he said with a disgusted sigh as he reached for the knob.

"Don't!" Peggy barked.

George turned around. "Excuse me?"

"Put your gear down," Peggy said. "You and I aren't going anywhere yet."

"What do you mean?"

She took an instant camera from atop a filing cabinet. "Smile," she said.

As Major Aho left the building, a woman and her dog were standing by the calm waters of the South Harbor, watching him. Valya had ridden her bicycle from the apartment

307

of their longtime Helsinki operative, a retired Finnish policeman, and had leaned it against a high lamppost while she walked away from the cone of light. When she was safely hidden in darkness, she let the dog rest from its short run — a cuddly, less energetic springer spaniel having replaced the wild Jack Russell terrier she'd used against the British agent in St. Petersburg. Valya didn't need to deactivate anyone here: she had come over simply to watch and report back to Colonel Rossky.

It had been easy for the Operations Center to track the jet from the United States, and even easier for her to follow the Major and his American friend when they left the airport. Now her driver was waiting out of sight on Kanavakatu, by the tall, majestic Uspensky Cathedral, and she was watching to see what the Finnish officer and his spy did.

His *two* spies, she noted as two companions joined Aho when he walked toward his car.

When she was sure they were going inside, Valya tugged on the dog's collar and it began to bark loudly, twice, twice again, and then two more times.

"Ruthie!" Valya shouted, tugging on the leash a second time. The well-trained dog fell silent.

Major Aho looked over, apparently failed to see anyone in the darkness, then slid into the passenger's side of his car, the other two climbing in the back. Beyond them, the Russian saw her partner's Volvo swing onto the Esplanade, alerted by the bark. They had agreed beforehand that he would follow the car to see where it went, then come back for her: she wanted to remain behind and make sure no one else popped out of this wing of the Palace. Having lost two agents, they might take unusual precautions to protect more. Some countries did that as a matter of course: five years before, when she first joined the spetsnaz intelligence bureau, her superior had been stung by a fake English operation covering the real one, and he took his life after being dismissed in disgrace. Valya Saparov had no intention of letting that happen to her.

She continued to stroll along the steps of the embankment, listening to the tranquil waters lap against the stone and into the drainpipes, watching the few cars and even fewer pedestrians that came and went along the thoroughfare.

And then she saw something that brought a smile to her lips: two people leaving the Presidential Palace, people who looked suspiciously like the ones who had departed with the officer shortly before. . . .

THIRTY-FIVE

Tuesday, 1:08 A.M., St. Petersburg

When he was making regular trips into space, General Orlov was accustomed to having his days and nights carefully regulated: when he would eat, sleep, work, shower, and exercise. When he began training others, he held to a tightly controlled regimen because it worked for him.

In the two years he'd been attached to the Operations Center, his regimen had deteriorated because of the demands on his time. He didn't exercise quite as much as he wanted, and that made him unhappy. In the last few weeks, as the on-line hour drew near, he hadn't slept as much either, and that made him even more cranky.

He had expected to be up late today, helping to iron out any problems with the various systems, though there were surprisingly few. And he had even been prepared, if necessary, to run an urgent counterintelligence operation using Rossky's spetsnaz intelligence operatives based in nearby Pushkin. Fortunately, word had reached Rossky that Ministry of Security agents had found and arrested the waiter who'd been working with the British spy, and were bringing him to St. Petersburg. No doubt he could be persuaded to help them ferret out other spies — a more effective tack than Rossky's ham-fisted handling of those two operatives. Orlov didn't believe for a moment that the British agent had taken his own life, and he was sorry they hadn't had the opportunity to interrogate him.

Disappointment and the ability to adapt were part of any job, and Orlov remained focused and alert. But he hated waiting for anything — especially missing pieces of a puzzle. In space, whenever he had to trouble-shoot, there was a checklist. Here, there was nothing to do but sit and keep busy while awaiting information.

The message came from Valya Saparov at 1:09 in the morning — just after midnight in Helsinki. Because she hadn't wanted to carry secure radio gear, she placed a straight-forward international call from a phone booth in Helsinki to a number at the St. Petersburg telephone exchange. There, an Operations Center employee routed the call to the intelligence base, where someone in the radio room picked up. In this way, telephone calls couldn't be traced to or from the Operations Center.

Calls from agents over unsecured lines were in the form of personal messages to friends, relatives, or roommates. If the operative didn't preface the message by asking to speak to someone in particular, the Center knew to disregard the contents. Messages were sometimes sent this way to confuse eavesdroppers who might be tracking a spy and trying to make sense of what they were reporting. When the operative said something about the weather, the listener knew that that was when the message proper began.

Valya asked for Uncle Boris, her name for Colonel Rossky, and he was notified by an operator at one of the nine computers linked to the phone and radio lines. He grabbed a headset and took the call. General Orlov took a duplicate pair from the operator and pressed one side to an ear, listening as a digital recorder taped the call.

"My little *ptitsa*," Rossky said, "my precious bird. How is your visit with your *karol?*" He used a nickname, "king," so a listener wouldn't be able to check on anyone's identity.

"Very well," she said. "Sorry to call so late, but I've been busy. The weather couldn't

312

be better for sight-seeing."

"Good," said Rossky.

"I'm out with the dog now, in fact. *Karol* went to the airport with two friends, but I didn't want to go. I decided to take a bicycle ride to the harbor instead."

"You thought you might end up there," Rossky said. "Is it nice?"

"Very," said Valya. "I watched two people getting ready for a trip on the gulf."

She'd said "on" the gulf and not "in" it, Orlov noted. That was significant. They were traveling on the surface and not by submarine.

"They're going to sea in the dark?" Rossky asked.

"Yes," said Valya. "A curious time to travel, but they are in a very fast boat and seem to know what they're doing. Besides, Uncle, I suspect they want to watch the sunrise from somewhere beautiful. A man and a woman — very romantic, don't you think?"

"Quite," Rossky said. "Precious, I don't want you out so late — why don't you go home and we'll talk tomorrow."

"I will," she said. "Have a good night."

A pensive Orlov handed the earphones back to the operator and thanked him while Rossky doffed his own set. The Colonel's expression was tense as he followed the General to his office. Though the message could be read by anyone in the command center, Orlov didn't want their options discussed openly. Moles could be anywhere.

"They *are* audacious," Rossky said angrily when the door was shut, "coming in by boat."

"It's our fault for not taking the Finns more seriously," Orlov said, sitting on the edge of his desk. "The question is, do we want these two to come in or stop them in the gulf?"

"Set foot on Russia?" Rossky said. "Never. We watch them by satellite and stop them the moment they enter Russian waters." He was staring past Orlov as though he were thinking aloud and not addressing a superior officer. "Standard operating procedure would be to drop mines from fishing boats, but I wouldn't want to tweak Minister Niskanen's nose so openly. No," he went on, "I'll have the Navy send the radio-controlled mini-sub from the Sea Terminal on Gogland Island. A collision . . . we report losses of our own, blame it on the Finns."

"Standard operating procedure," Orlov said. "But I repeat. What if we allow them to come in?"

Rossky's eyes returned to the General.

They were no longer enthusiastic, but glazed with anger. "General, may I ask you a question?"

"Of course."

"Is it your intention, sir, to stop me at every turn?"

"Yes," Orlov admitted, "where your tactics and ideas run counter to the mandate of this Center. Our mission is to gather intelligence. Killing these two operatives and crippling Niskanen's ability to send in other enemies doesn't do that. More agents will follow these two, if not from Finland then perhaps through Turkey or Poland. How thin can we spread our resources tracking them? Wouldn't it be better to know more about how they operate and to try and get them to work for us?"

While Orlov spoke, Rossky's expression had shaded from annoyance to anger. When the General was finished, his deputy hooked back a sleeve and looked at his watch. "The agents apparently hope to arrive before sunup, which will be in a little over four hours. You'd best give me your decision very soon."

"I need to know what resources you can spare to watch them," Orlov said as his phone beeped, "and whether the man Pogodin caught in Moscow can help us." He reached behind himself and put the phone on speaker in an effort to mollify Rossky. If the Colonel was grateful, he didn't show it. "Yes?" Orlov said.

"Sir, it's Zilash. Nearly ninety minutes ago, we picked up a rather odd communication from Washington."

"In what way odd?" Orlov asked.

"It was a heavily scrambled message to an aircraft flying from Berlin to Helsinki," said Zilash. "Corporal Ivashin ordered satellite reconnaissance of the aircraft. Though the flight path took it under heavy cloud cover — intentionally, it appears — we were able to get a couple of good looks at it through breaks. The aircraft is an Il-76T."

Orlov and Rossky exchanged glances. For the moment, their feud was forgotten.

"Where is the plane now?" Orlov asked.

"On the ground in Helsinki, sir."

Rossky leaned forward. "Zilash, were you able to see a number?"

"No, Colonel, but it's an Il-76T — we're sure of that."

"A lot of planes are being shifted around," Orlov said to Rossky. "Someone might be using the opportunity to defect."

"Two other possibilities come to mind," Rossky said. "The team Valya has been watching may be a feint to draw our attention

316

from some other mission, or the U.S. is running two entirely different operations from Finland."

Orlov agreed. "We'll know more when we see where the Il-76T is headed," he said. "Zilash — keep following the plane and let me know the instant you have anything else."

"Yes, sir."

As Orlov punched off the speaker, Rossky took a step toward him. "General — "

Orlov looked up. "Yes?"

"If the plane enters Russian airspace, the Air Force will want to bring it down, the way they did that Korean Airlines jet. They should be alerted."

"I agree," said Orlov, "though with a wall of radar and other early-warning devices, it would be suicidal to try."

"Under ordinary circumstances, yes," said Rossky. "But with the heavy increase in military air traffic over the past few days, it wouldn't surprise me if the plane simply tried to slip in and lose itself somewhere."

"Point well taken," Orlov said.

"And the boat?" Rossky asked. "We're obliged to inform the Navy — "

"I know what we're required to do," Orlov cut in. "But that one is mine, Colonel. Let them land, watch them, and tell me exactly what they're up to."

Rossky's jaw shifted. "Yes, sir," he said, saluting without enthusiasm.

"And Colonel?"

"Yes, sir?"

"Do your best to ensure that nothing happens to the crew. Your very best. I don't want to lose any more foreign agents."

"I always do my best, sir," Rossky said as he saluted again and left the office.

THIRTY-SIX

Tuesday, 12:26 A.M., Helsinki

The South Harbor district of Helsinki is famous not just for the crowded market square that adjoins the Presidential Palace, but for the boat rides which leave for Suomenlinna Island several times a day. Nestled at the entrance to the harbor, this imposing "Gibraltar of the North" is home to an open-air theater, a military museum, and an imposing eighteenth-century castle. Adjacent Seurasaari Island is connected to the mainland by bridge and is the site of the Olympic Stadium, which hosted the 1952 games.

At night, the landmarks are dark silhouettes against the darker skies. Had they been visible, Peggy James still would not have seen them. Major Aho had given her an automobile and explicit directions. Fifteen minutes after he'd gone to the airport with two decoys in his command, she'd driven herself and Private George to the harbor and the cruiser that would take them to Kotka and the mini-sub.

She had no time nor interest in sight-seeing. She had just one thing on her mind — getting into St. Petersburg. What mattered most was finishing the job Keith Fields-Hutton had started. Finding and killing the person or persons responsible for his death was not as high a priority, though she was prepared to do so if the opportunity presented itself.

The cruiser was a sleek Larson Cabrio 280, and after the password and response had been given the duo boarded the twenty-eight footer. Carefully placing her own backpack on the floor between her feet in the athwartship berth, Peggy sat beside George as the boat spun into the night. The operatives spent the bulk of the ninety-minute trip reviewing the maps of the Hermitage and the terrain between their landing point and the museum. The plan she had worked out with Major Aho before George's arrival was for the mini-sub to let them out in a rubber raft near the Southern Coastal Park, a short bus ride from their target. In a way, she preferred this masquerade to a wetsuit-type operation at night. Foreign authorities were more inclined to believe cover stories about daylight operations, since most operatives weren't reckless enough to try them.

The mini-sub was berthed in a windowless shed on the gulf. She would have preferred to fly, dropping rubber boats and parachuting just outside the target zone. But night dives into icy-cold waters were too risky. If she or Private George landed too far from the boat, they could die of hypothermia before it reached them. Besides, the jump might damage her delicate equipment, and it was imperative that that not happen.

After producing their photos, the agents were admitted by a young man dressed in a dark blue sweater and trousers. He had a square face and deeply cleft chin. His blond hair was cut almost to the scalp. He shut the door quickly behind them. A second man stepped from the shadows. He flicked on a flashlight and held a gun on the pair. Peggy shielded her eyes from the glare as the first man compared the photographs to the copies of the shots she'd faxed over bearing the Palace's ID number on top.

"That's us," Peggy said. "Who else would claim to look that awful?"

The man handed the photographs and faxes to his companion, who lowered the light to study the pictures. Peggy could see his face now, which was lean and hard and sharply chiseled as if it had been chipped from a two-by-four. He nodded.

"I'm Captain Rydman," he said to the newcomers, "and this is Helmsman Osipow.

If you'll follow me, we can get under way."

Turning, he led Peggy and Private George on a walkway that went around the sides of the dark shed. The other man followed close behind.

They passed several sleek, new patrol boats bobbing gently on the water and stopped by a slipway in a corner of the shed. There, rocking gently beside a short aluminum ladder, was the dark gray mini-sub. The hatch was open though no light came from within. Having read a file en route to Finland, Peggy had learned that the midgets were brought up every six months for maintenance, hauled from the water by ropes run through eyebolts welded to the hull, then literally cracked like an eggshell by unbolting the engine room from the forward bulkhead. Only fifteen meters long, the steel cylinders were capable of carrying four passengers at a top speed of nine knots. The trip to St. Petersburg would take until two o'clock, local time, which also included the vessel breaking surface after six hours to extend the induction mast and let the diesel engines run for a half hour to restock the batteries and air.

She was not claustrophobic. But peering into what looked like a large thermos bottle with its cap on the side, she knew that an uncomfortable ten hours lay before them.

Peggy saw three seats, and very little room aft to sit or even stand. She wondered where the captain was going to be.

Osipow climbed down the ladder into the darkness and threw a switch. The midget marauder's dim lighting came on and the helmsman took his seat at the steering controls — a short column with a joystick for maneuvering and an autopilot switch to maintain depth and azimuth. Beside it was a pump used to siphon off the condensation that collected inside the tight cabin, and a portside mine release handwheel. After Osipow had checked to make sure the controls, engine, and air were working, Rydman told George to enter.

"I feel like a monkey's fist," the Private said as he limboed to his seat, thrusting his chest up and twisting to the right, one arm behind him, steadying himself on the chair as he slid in.

"Ah, you've sailed," said Osipow, his voice nasal but strangely melodious.

"Back home, sir," said George, extending a hand to help Peggy in. "I once won a contest for who could tie the fastest fist at the end of a heavy line." He looked at Peggy when she'd squeezed into her chair. "A monkey's fist is a decorative knot you tie at the end of a line."

"Formed around a weight, though typically not on a lanyard. There isn't enough rope." She looked at George's face in the dull glow of the interior. It seemed slightly paler than her own. "You have a talent for underestimating me, Private. Or do you patronize all women?"

George settled back into the vinyl seat. He shrugged a shoulder, as though lightening the seriousness of the charge. "You're being a little touchy, Ms. James. If the Captain hadn't understood, I'd have explained it to him too."

Rydman said impatiently, "Let me explain to *both* of you that we're a little shorthanded. Ordinarily, I have an electrician who stays aft to monitor the engine and auxiliary electrics. But there wasn't room. So I would appreciate a minimum number of distractions."

"Sorry, sir," said George.

Instead of coming down, the Captain stood on a six-inch ring that girdled the squat tower and closed the hatch from inside. When Osipow told him that the lock signal had come on — a red light near the autopilot control — Rydman tested the periscope by turning it slowly, 360 degrees, and circling with it by stepping carefully on the narrow lip.

As he did, Captain Rydman said to his passengers, "We'll be snorkeling at eight knots for the initial part of our passage, which will take two hours. When we near Moshchnyy Island, which the Russians own, we'll submerge. Conversations will be held to a whisper. The Russians have mobile passive-sonar detectors there and also along the coast. Because they don't emit signals of their own like active sonar, but pick up radiated noise, we never know where they're listening or when. We've been able to slip through, but it helps to generate as little noise as possible."

"How will you know if they do spot us?" Peggy asked.

"The explosives dropped by the coast guard ships are difficult to ignore," Rydman said. "If that happens, we'll have to dive and abort."

"How often does that happen?" she asked, hating the fact that she didn't know. Intelligence operatives were supposed to know their equipment and target as well as they knew their own automobiles and homes. But DI6 had gotten into this so quickly there hadn't been time to prepare, other than to read the file dossier on the flight over. And there wasn't much on Finland's operations in the gulf. Agents usually went in with tour groups.

Rydman said, "It's happened three times in ten trips, though I never penetrated far into Russian waters. Obviously, this time will be different. But we won't be going in totally unprotected. Major Aho is sending out a helicopter to drop a pair of sonobuoys along our route. The signal will be monitored in Helsinki, and any incoming Russian vessels will show up as blips on Mr. Osipow's chart."

Osipow pointed toward a circular, computer-generated map roughly the diameter of a coffee saucer and located to the right of the control column.

When he finished turning the periscope, Rydman folded down a seat on the forward side of the tower and straddled it. Then he leaned toward the engine-induction mast that also served — with considerable echo — as a voice pipe to the helm.

"Ready, Mr. Osipow," the Captain said.

The helmsman switched on the engine, and it hummed with very little noise and vibration. As soon as it was on, he shut the light, leaving the vessel dark save for two shaded lights on the stern.

Peggy turned and peered out the small, circular porthole on her side of the mini-sub. Only a few small bubbles from the propeller in the stern drifted by as the submarine submerged to exit the shed. The darkness outside seemed to scowl at her and her eyes grew moist.

You've got to rein this in, she said to herself. The discontent. The frustration. The anger.

If only it were just Keith. She could mourn him and go on with her life, with difficulty but at least with a goal. But now that he was gone she realized that she *had* no goal, something that had been festering but sublimated for years. Suddenly, she was a thirty-six year-old woman who had chosen a lifestyle that had never permitted her to have much of a life, who had seen her country lose the fire and independence it had under Margaret Thatcher, lose its dignity because of a scurrilous monarchy. What had it all been for, all the years of toil and sacrifice, of losing her lover? She had been moving ahead because of momentum, because of the rapport and fun she had with Keith.

What is there now, she asked, *if England becomes just a satellite of the European community?* And not a respected one at that, unwilling to curry favor with the Germans the way the French had, unable to maintain élan and faith in the face of industrial collapse like the Spanish, or discard government after government the way the Italians had. *What the hell have I lived for — and what do I continue to live for?*

"Ms. James?"

Private George's whisper seemed to come from another world. It brought her back to the midget submarine.

"Yes?"

"We've got a ten-hour stretch ahead of us and it's too dark to study the maps," George said. "Could I impose on you to start me on that crash course in Russian?"

She looked at George's eager young face. *Where does his enthusiasm come from?* she wondered. Managing to smile at him for the first time, she said, "It's not an imposition. Why don't we start with some basic questions."

"Such as?"

She said slowly, *"Khak, shtaw,* and *puhchehmoo."*

"Which means?"

Peggy smiled. "How, what, and — perhaps most important — why?"

THIRTY-SEVEN

Tuesday, 2:30 A.M., Russian/Ukraine border

Operation Barbarossa was the largest military offensive in the history of warfare. On June 22, 1941, German troops invaded Russia, shattering the Nazi-Soviet Peace Pact. Their objective: to capture Moscow before winter. Hitler sent 3.2 million troops in 120 divisions against 170 Soviet divisions spread along 2,300 kilometers from the shores of the Baltic to the shores of the Black Sea.

As German panzer divisions pushed toward the Russian rear with incredible speed, the Luftwaffe blasted their inexperienced and badly trained Russian counterparts. As a result of this *Blitzkrieg,* the Baltic states were swiftly overrun. The damage inflicted by the Germans was catastrophic. By November, vital agricultural, industrial, transportation, and communications centers had been destroyed. More than 2 million Russian soldiers had been captured. Three hundred and fifty thousand Russian troops had been killed.

Three hundred and seventy-eight thousand were missing. And 1 million had been wounded. In Leningrad alone, 900,000 civilians were killed during the enemy siege. It wasn't until the last days of December that the battered but resilient Russians — helped by −20° temperatures that shattered German boot soles, froze their equipment, and destroyed morale — were able to mount their first successful counterattack. As a result of this counteroffensive, the Russians were just able to keep Moscow from enemy hands.

Ultimately, Operation Barbarossa was a disaster for the Germans. But it taught the Soviets an important lesson about the desirability of fighting an offensive rather than a defensive war. For the next forty years, their military grew with the almost fanatical goal of being able to launch and sustain an offensive war — as General Mikhail Kosigan had once put it in a speech to his troops, "to fight the next world war, if it comes, on everyone else's territory." To this end, missions for commanders of first-echelon tactical units were comprised of three components designed to destroy or capture enemy troops and equipment and seize and control key territory: the immediate mission, or *blizhaiashcha zadacha;* the subsequent mission, or *posledyushchaia zadacha;* and the follow-up

330

mission, or *napravlenie dal'neishego nastu-pleniia*. Within those broad missions, regiments were often assigned a key mission of the day, or *zadacha dnia,* which were goals that had to be completed within a specific time frame — no excuses accepted.

Whether it was in Hungary in 1956, Czechoslovakia in 1968, Afghanistan in 1979, or Chechnya in 1994, Moscow relied on its military and not on diplomacy to solve problems in its own backyard. Its guiding principles were *supriz, neozhadennost'* and *vnezapnost':* surprise, anticipation of the unexpected, and causing the unexpected. Often their efforts were successful, and sometimes they were not. But the mind-set remained, and Interior Minister Dogin knew it. He also knew that many Russian commanders yearned for the opportunity to redeem themselves after nine bloody years in Afghanistan and the lengthy and costly suppression of the rebels in Chechnya.

The time had come to give them a chance. Many of his men had been moved to Russia's border with Ukraine, where, unlike Afghanistan and Chechnya, they wouldn't be fighting rebel armies and partisan guerrillas. This war, this *aktivnost,* this initiative, would be different.

At 12:30 A.M., local time, in Przemysl,

331

Poland, less than ten miles from the Ukrainian border, a powerful pipe bomb exploded in the two-story brick building that served as the headquarters of the Polish Communist Party. Two editors working on the semi-weekly newspaper *Obywatel*, the *Citizen*, were blown into the surrounding trees, their blood and ink splashed on the two walls that remained standing, newsprint and flesh burned onto the chairs and file cabinets by the heat of the explosion. Within minutes, Communist sympathizers were in the streets, protesting the attack and storming the post office and police station. A local munitions depot was pelted with Molotov cocktails and exploded, killing a soldier. At 12:46 the local constable telephoned Warsaw to request military assistance to quell the uprising. The call was intercepted and simultaneously transcribed by a military intelligence station in Kiev and was passed to President Vesnik.

At exactly 2:49 A.M. President Vesnik telephoned General Kosigan to ask for his help in containing what looked like it might be a "situation" on the border between Poland and the Ukraine. At 2:50 A.M. 150,000 Russian troops entered Ukraine, from the ancient city of Novgorod in the north to the administrative center of Voroshilovgrad in the south. Infantry, motorized rifle regiments, tank divisions, artillery battalions, and air squadrons moved in frightening lockstep, showing none of the disorder or slovenly behavior that had marked the move against Chechnya, or the retreat from Afghanistan.

In Moscow, at precisely 2:50:30 A.M., the Kremlin received an urgent communication from President Vesnik in Kiev requesting troops to help the Ukrainian forces protect the nearly three hundred miles of border the Ukraine shared with Poland.

Russian President Kiril Zhanin was awakened with the news and was caught utterly off guard by the request. Even before he had reached his office in the Kremlin, Zhanin was telephoned in his car with another message from the Ukrainian President. As this one was read to him, it surprised him even more than the first:

"Thank you for your prompt action. The timely arrival of General Kosigan's forces will not only keep the population from panicking, but reaffirms the traditional ties between Russia and Ukraine. I have instructed Ambassador Rozevna to inform the United Nations and Secretary General Brophy that the incursion was by invitation and design."

Ordinarily, Zhanin's woolly mustache and shaggy eyebrows gave his oval face a paternal, even jovial look. But now his dark brown eyes were afire, his small mouth tight and trembling.

He turned to his secretary, Larisa Shachtur, a middle-aged brunette dressed smartly in a Western-style business suit, and told her to get General Kosigan on the telephone. She only got as far as General Leonid Sarik, senior liaison officer of the aviations operation group and combined tank army. Mavik informed her that General Kosigan had imposed a strict radio silence for the duration of the march itself, and that it would be lifted only when the troops were fully deployed.

"General Mavik," said the secretary, "it is the President calling."

The General replied, "Then he will understand the need for security as we honor our defense pact with a fellow republic of the Commonwealth."

The General excused himself to attend to his duties and hung up, leaving the President and his secretary listening to the gentle purr of the engine.

Zhanin looked through the tinted, bulletproof window as the dark spires of the Kremlin came into view against the night sky and deep gray clouds.

"As a young man," he said, breathing deeply to calm himself, "I managed to get a copy of Svetlana Stalin's book about her father. Do you remember it?"

"Yes," said Larisa. "It was banned for years."

"That's right. Even though she was critical of a man who had fallen from grace, a so-called nonperson. One thing she wrote about Stalin struck me. She said that toward the end of the 1930s, she felt he had reached the stage of what she called 'persecution mania.' Enemies were everywhere. He had fifty thousand of his own officers purged. He murdered more Russian officers at or above the rank of colonel than the Germans killed in the entire war." He filled his chest and exhaled slowly. "It frightens me, Larisa, to think that he may not have been as mad or paranoid as everyone thought."

The woman squeezed his hand reassuringly as the black BMW turned off Kalinina Prospekt and headed toward the northwest side of the Kremlin, Trinity Gate.

THIRTY-EIGHT

Tuesday, 3:05 A.M., over the Barents Sea

The Il-76T landed in Helsinki shortly before midnight, and the Striker crew, their cold-weather gear, and their arsenal were aboard ten minutes later. Their arsenal consisted of four trunks, each five by four by three feet, loaded with guns and explosives, ropes and pitons, gas masks and medical supplies. A half hour after they were aboard, the plane was refueled and airborne.

The initial phase of the flight had carried the craft northeast over Finland, then east across the Barents Sea and another time zone, flying just below the Arctic Ocean as it skirted the northern coast of Russia.

Lieutenant Colonel Squires's eyes were shut, but he wasn't sleeping. Nasty habit, he knew: he couldn't sleep unless he knew where he was going and why. He knew that further instructions from Op-Center would be forthcoming, since they were rapidly approaching the end of their flight plan, which

336

carried them to where the Barents met the Pechora Sea. Still, it was frustrating not to be able to focus on an objective and stay zeroed in. Crossing the Atlantic, he'd been able to concentrate on St. Petersburg and the mission there. Now that was in Private George's hands, and Squires had nothing. When he had nothing, the officer always played a little game to keep his mind from wandering to his wife and son and what they'd do if he didn't come back.

It was the What Am I Doing Here? game, in which he picked an appropriate word or two, reached deep into his guts, and tried to understand why he loved being a Striker so damn much.

The first time he'd played it, en route to Cape Canaveral to try and find out who put a bomb on board a space shuttle, he'd decided that he was here to defend *America*, not just because it was the best place to be but because our nation's energy and ideals were what motivated the whole world. If we were to go away, Squires was convinced that the planet would become a battleground for dictators who wanted to rule, not autonomous states that were competitive and vital.

In the second game, he'd asked himself how much he enjoyed leading this life because it made every inch of him feel *vital* and *challenged.* A lot, he had to admit. Much more than when he played soccer, because the stakes for himself and for his nation were so high. But there was no sensation like pitting his confidence, skills, and ability to self-start against circumstances that would cause most people to freeze or retreat or at the very least think twice about going ahead.

Today, while he wondered where the hell the call from Mike Rodgers or Bob Herbert was, he was thinking about something Op-Center's psychologist, Liz Gordon, had asked him when she first interviewed him for the command post.

"What are your thoughts on shared fear?" she had asked.

He'd answered that fear and strength were qualities that crested and troughed in any individual, and that a good team — and especially a good commander — had to be able to bring each member's levels to their peak.

"That's fear," Liz had said. *"I asked about shared fear. Think about it. Take your time."*

He had, and then he'd said, *"I guess we share fear because it's caused by something that threatens us all, as opposed to courage, which comes from the individual."*

He'd been naive and Liz had let it go. Now, after three missions, Squires had come to understand that *shared fear* wasn't something to overcome. It was a mutual support system that turned people of disparate backgrounds and intellects and interests into a single, bonded organism. It was what made the crew of a World War II bomber or a police squad car or an elite commando force closer than a husband and wife could ever be. It was what made a whole greater than the sum of its parts.

As much as patriotism and valor, shared fear was the glue that held Striker together.

Squires was about to tackle Seeing the World as a motivation when Mike Rodgers called on the secure TAC-Sat. Squires was instantly out of his reverie and, as his old soccer coach used to put it, "There with the goods."

"Charlie," Rodgers said, "sorry it's taken so long to get to you. We've been going over your game plan and we're really going to need World Cup performance on this one. In just over eleven hours, having stayed out of Russian airspace until the last possible moment, your team will parachute to a point in Russia just west of Khabarovsk. Bob is giving your pilot the flight plan and coordinates — and we hope that the Il-76T buys him enough time to get in and out before Russian air defenses realize it's not one of their own aircraft. Your target is a four-car-plus-engine train of the Trans-Siberian express. If the cargo is narcotics, currency, gold, or weapons, you're to eliminate them. If the weapons are nuclear, get us proof and disable them if you can. Sergeant Grey has the training for that. Any questions so far?"

"Yes, sir," Squires said. "If the Hermitage is involved, they could be shipping art. Do you want us blowing up Renoirs and Van Goghs?"

The line was silent for a moment. "No. Photograph and disengage."

"Yes, sir."

Rodgers continued, "Your target area is a one hundred-eleven-foot-tall cliff overlooking the track. The appropriate topographic maps will be sent to your computer. You'll rappel down and wait for the train. We chose that area because there are trees or rocks from the cliff face that you can use to block the track. We'd prefer that to using explosives that may cause casualties. If the train is running on time, you'll only have about an hour before it arrives. If it's running late, you'll have to wait. This one can't get away, though you're to make every effort not to hurt any Russian soldiers."

Squires wasn't surprised by the warning: ambassadors hated having to explain illegal incursions, let alone what the CIA called "maximal demotions." Though Squires was well trained to kill with everything from a shoelace to an Uzi, he had never had to do it — and he hoped he never did.

"The Il-76T will have gone to Hokkaido for refueling and then return," Rodgers said, "though it will *not* be your extraction vehicle. When you've completed your mission, you'll signal the Il-76T and go to the rendezvous point, the southern side of a bridge one-point-three miles west of the target."

Now, that *was intriguing,* Squires thought. The only reason Rodgers wouldn't tell him about the extraction craft was in case they were captured. He didn't want the Russians to know. As if the mission itself weren't stimulating enough, the mystery sent another part of Squires's motivation into overdrive. The part that, like almost every male he had ever known, loved flashy, secretive, state-of-the-art hardware.

"Charlie, this one isn't like North Korea," Rodgers said. There was more friend than general in his voice. Now that he'd had Squires's undivided attention while he laid out the specifics, he was ready to give him the overview. "We've reason to believe that elements in Russia are looking to rebuild the Soviet empire in a hurry. Though St.

Petersburg is probably involved, you're the key to stopping them."

"I understand, sir," Squires said.

"The plan's as complete as we can make it given the little we know," Rodgers said, "though I expect we'll have updates as H-Hour nears. I'm sorry we can't do more for you."

"That's okay, sir," Squires said. "It isn't Tacitus or any of those guys you quote, but I told Private George when we left him in Helsinki that the cartoon character Super Chicken had a perfect observation for tough situations like these: 'You knew the job was dangerous when you took it.' We knew it, General, and we're still glad to be here."

Rodgers laughed. "I'm trusting the fate of the world to a man who quotes Saturday morning cartoons. But I'll make a deal with you. Come back in one piece, and I'll bring the popcorn to your house next Saturday morning."

"You're on," Squires said, signing off and collecting his thoughts before briefing the team.

THIRTY-NINE

Tuesday, 3:08 A.M., St. Petersburg

For just over an hour, Sergei Orlov had been asleep in the chair at his desk — elbows on the armrests, hands folded on his abdomen, head slightly to the left. Though his wife didn't believe he'd actually disciplined himself to be able to fall asleep anywhere, at any time, Orlov insisted that it wasn't a talent he'd been born with. He said that when he first became an astronaut, he trained himself to snatch sleep in half-hour segments amid the long hours of training. More remarkable than that, he said he found what he called his "rest bits" nearly as refreshing over the course of a day as his normal six hours of sleep a night. And there was the added benefit that, instead of his energy and attention span flagging as the day went on, they remained high.

He could never work like Rossky, who needed to stay with his problems until he had wrestled them to the ground. Even now, with his night counterpart on duty, the Colonel was still at his post in the heart of the Center.

Orlov also found that daunting problems always seemed to make more sense after a short nap. During his last space flight, a joint mission with Bulgaria — and the first three-cosmonaut flight since the crew of *Soyuz 11* suffocated in their spacecraft — Orlov and his two comrades had tried to dock their *Soyuz* ship with the Salyut 6 space station. When engine failure left the ship and the station on a collision course, mission control ordered Orlov to fire his backup rocket to return to earth immediately. Instead, he fired a short burst to back a safe distance away, shut off his headset, and rested for fifteen minutes — to the dismay of his crew. Then he used the backup engine to effect the docking. Though there was no longer enough fuel in the backup rocket to return to earth, once inside the space station Orlov was able to troubleshoot the main engine, repair the faulty circuit, and salvage the mission . . . and the self-respect of the mission team at the Baikonur Cosmodrome. Later, back on earth, Orlov was told the on-board echocardiograph had showed that his cardiovascular activity slowed and remained down after his rest. Thereafter, cosmonaut training included "power naps," though they didn't seem to work as well for other cosmonauts as they did for Orlov.

He never slept to escape what was happening in his life, though when Orlov was finally able to shut his eyes at 1:45 A.M., it felt good to file away the concerns of the moment. He was awakened at 2:51 when his assistant, Nina, buzzed to tell him he had a call from the Ministry of Defense. When Orlov got on, Marshal of Communications General David Ergashev informed him about the troops moving into Ukraine and asked the new Operations Center for help monitoring European communiqués about their activities. Stunned by the news and wondering if this was just a high-level test of the Center's capabilities — why else wouldn't he have been told? — Orlov passed the order to Radio Officer Yuri Marev.

Through fiber-optic links with satellite dish stations outside of St. Petersburg, and through their own special lines in the city's own telephone center, the Operations Center was designed to monitor all electronic communications between the field and the Defense Ministry. It was also capable of monitoring all types of communications in and out of the office of the Chief Marshal of Artillery, the Chief Marshal of the Air Force, and the

Admiral of the Fleet. The Center's job was to make sure those lines of communication were not being monitored by outsiders. It could also be used as a centralized clearing-house to disseminate information among other government agencies.

Or they could simply listen in.

Before hanging up with Marev, Orlov asked him to tap into the data coming into the Ministry of Defense from General Kosigan and the Chief Marshals' offices. Marev's answer caught him off guard.

"We're already doing that," Marev said. "Colonel Rossky ordered us to follow the troop movements."

"Where is the information going?" Orlov asekd.

"To the central computer."

"Very good," Orlov said, recovering quickly. "See to it that the information comes directly to my screen as well."

"Yes, sir," Marev said.

Orlov turned to his computer monitor and waited. *Damn Rossky,* he thought. Either this was payback for their earlier dispute or Rossky was in this somehow — perhaps with his patron Dogin. But there was nothing he could do about it. As long as information was recorded in the Center's main computer, available for dispersal internally or among other agencies, Rossky was not obliged to report it to the General . . . even an event of this magnitude.

As he waited, Orlov tried to get a handle on the situation, starting with the stunning suddenness of Ukraine's request. Like many other officials, he had assumed the various maneuvers were President Zhanin's way of showing the world that he had not abandoned the military in favor of Western business. But now it was clear that the march into the former republic had been planned, and that that was the reason so many troops had been near the border or en route. But planned by whom? Dogin? And why? This wasn't a coup, and it wasn't a war.

The first data began coming in. Russian infantry was arranging to link up with Ukrainian forces in Kharkov and Voroshilovgrad, yet these weren't joint maneuvers. The appreciative communication from President Vesnik had made that very clear.

What was equally surprising was the unexpected silence from the Kremlin. In the eighteen minutes since the troops had crossed the border, Zhanin had made no public statement about the event. By now, every Western embassy in Moscow would be drafting and hand-delivering letters of concern.

Marev and his small team continued distilling raw data from the incoming communications. The numbers of people and machines being moved were staggering. But even more astonishing were some specifics of the deployment. To the west of Novgorod, near the Ukrainian Administrative Center of Chernigov, General Major Andrassy had set up a ten-kilometer line of artillery battalions in triangular support formation: two hundred meters of M-1973 and M-1974 howitzers with one kilometer between them and the next two-hundred-meter bank; nearly a kilometer behind them, in the center of the forward kilometer gap, was another two-hundred-meter spread of artillery. The guns were aimed at the White Russian border and were located close enough to be equipped with direct-fire optical sights.

This was no test. These were preparations for war. And if they were, he was wondering how much Rossky — and by association, himself — were involved in them.

Orlov asked Nina to get Ministry of Security Director Rolan Mikyan on the phone. Orlov knew the erudite Mikyan from his Cosmodrome days, when the Azerbaijani — who held a doctorate in political science — was seconded from the GRU, the military intelligence agency, to head up security at the space facility. The two had met several times over the past year to work out ways of sharing intelligence and prevent duplication of effort. Orlov had found that while the years hadn't dulled Mikyan's commitment to Russia, the upheavals had made him cynical — due, he suspected, to a late-blossoming fondness for his native republic.

Nina found the Director at home, though he hadn't been sleeping.

"Sergei," said Mikyan, "I was about to call you."

"Did you know about Ukraine?" Orlov asked.

"We're intelligence heads. We know everything that's going on."

"You didn't, did you?" Orlov asked.

"We seem to have had an information gap in that area," Mikyan said. "A blind spot that was contrived by elements in the military, it would seem."

"Do you know that we have a hundred and fifty howitzers pointed at Minsk?"

"The night Director just informed me," Mikyan said. "And aircraft from the carrier *Murometz* off Odessa have been flying along the Moldavian border, being very careful not to cross over."

"You've been at this longer than I have," Orlov said. "What's your reading?"

"Someone high up has masterminded a very

top-secret operation. But don't feel bad, Sergei. It's caught a lot of people by surprise including, it appears, our new President."

"Has anyone spoken to him?"

"He's locked away with his closest advisers now," Mikyan said. "Except for Interior Minister Dogin."

"Where is he?"

"Ill," Mikyan said, "at his dacha in the hills outside of Moscow."

"I spoke with him just a few hours ago," Orlov said disgustedly. "He was fine."

"I'm sure he was," Mikyan said. "Which should give you some idea about who masterminded this."

The phone beeped. "Excuse me," Orlov said to Mikyan.

"Wait," Mikyan said. "I've got to get to the Ministry, but first I was going to call because there's something you should consider. Dogin sponsored your facility in the Kremlin, and you went on-line shortly before the incursion. If the Minister is using the Operations Center to help run this thing, and he loses, you may be facing a firing squad. Crimes against the state, helping a foreign power — "

"I've just been thinking something like that myself," Orlov said. "Thanks, Rolan. We'll talk later."

When Mikyan hung up, Nina told Orlov that Zilash was on the line. The General switched to the interoffice line.

"Yes, Arkady?"

"General, Air Defense on Kolguyev Island reports that the Il-76T crossed over Finland to the Barents Sea and is now headed east."

"Do they have any idea where it's headed?"

"None, sir," said Zilash.

"A guess — anything?"

"Just east, sir. The plane is headed due east. But they said it could be a supply plane. We're using the 76Ts to ferry cargo from Germany, France, and Scandinavia."

"Did Air Defense try identifying it?" Orlov asked.

"Yes, sir. They're sending out the right signal."

That didn't mean anything, Orlov knew. The heat-emitting beacons placed in the noses of the planes were easy enough to build, buy, or steal.

"Has anyone talked to the 76T?" Orlov asked.

"No, sir," said Zilash. "Most of the transports are maintaining radio silence to keep the airwaves clear."

"Has Air Defense picked up outside communications with any other Russian aircraft?" Orlov asked.

"Not that we're aware of, sir."

"Thank you," Orlov said. "I'd like half-hour updates, even if nothing changes. And I want one thing more, Zilash."

"Yes, sir."

"Monitor and record any communications between General Kosigan and the Interior Ministry," Orlov said. "The regular phone lines as well as the General's private uplink."

The dead air lasted only a moment, though it seemed longer.

"You want me to spy on General Kosigan, sir?"

"I want you to follow my orders," Orlov replied. "I'll assume you were repeating them rather than questioning them."

"Yes, sir, I was, sir," said Zilash. "Thank you."

When Orlov hung up, he told himself he was wrong about the plane, that this was one of those drills the CIA occasionally ran to see how the Russians would react if they *thought* the crew of one of their planes or ships had become agents-in-place — operatives recruited to provide information about their own spheres of activity. There was nothing worse in any military confrontation than for commanders to start doubting the loyalty of their own troops.

But instinct argued against that, helped

along by caution. Assuming the plane was from the U.S. or NATO, he considered possible destinations. If it were headed for the U.S., it would have gone over the Arctic or across the Atlantic. To reach the Far East, it would have used the air lanes in the south. He thought back to his last conversation with Rossky, and to the question that seemed to have only one answer. Why use a Russian plane unless they were planning to go somewhere in Russia? And where in eastern Russia could they possibly want to go?

That question, too, seemed to have only one answer, and Orlov didn't like it.

He punched in 22. A deep voice rumbled from the phone.

"Operations Support Officer Fyodor Buriba."

"Fyodor, this is General Orlov. Please contact Dr. Sagdeev at the Russian Space Research Institute and get me a summary of U.S. and NATO satellite activity from nine P.M. until one A.M. this morning, covering the area of eastern Russia between the Sea of Okhotsk and the Aldan Plateau, as far south as the Sea of Japan."

"At once," said Buriba. "Do you want just the prime coverage — global positioning system reports and the times the data was downloaded, or do you also want the electro-optical sensor reports, isoelectric focus — "

"Prime coverage will be enough," Orlov said. "When you have that, correlate the data with the time the goods were transferred from the Gulfstream to the train in Vladivostok and see whether any of the satellites might have seen it."

"Yes, sir."

Buriba hung up, and Orlov sat back and gazed up at the black ceiling. Albert Sagdeev's Office of Space Debris Reconnaissance at the Russian Space Research Institute had been established to track the increasing numbers of discarded boosters, abandoned spacecraft, and dead satellites orbiting the earth and presenting real hazards for space travelers. But in 1982 its staff of five was doubled and it was also charged with clandestinely studying U.S., European, and Chinese spy satellites. Sagdeev's computers were tied to uplinks across the nation, and watched whenever the satellites transmitted data. Though most of it was digitally scrambled and couldn't be reconstructed, at least the Russians knew who was watching what and when.

It was conceivable — no, likely, the more Orlov thought about it — that the increase of Russian troop movements over the past few days would have caused the U.S. and Europe to keep a closer eye on military facilities like the naval base in Vladivostok.

And in so doing, they may have seen the transfer of the crates from the jet to the train.

But why should that attract enough attention to send a plane after it? he wondered. Especially when the train could be watched from space, if all the U.S. or Europe wanted to do was follow it.

If the plane intended to meet the train, it would probably want to spend as little time over Russian territory as possible. That meant an approach from the east, which gave his son anywhere from ten to fourteen hours to prepare.

Still, it was a dangerous undertaking for whoever was running the 76T, and the question remained. Why would anyone bother?

Despite all that was going on, Orlov knew he had to find out why the cargo was so important. He knew there was only one way to do that.

FORTY

Tuesday, 10:09 A.M., Ussurisk

The pre-War steam locomotive had a rusting boiler plate, dented cowcatcher, and a smokestack blackened with decades of soot. The coal tender was full. The cab was littered not only with coal dust but with souvenirs of previous trips across the breadth of Russia. There were pieces of dry, brittle leaves from the forests of Irkutsk, sand from the plains of Turkestan, smudges of oil from the fields in Usinsk.

Then there were ghosts. The shadows of the countless engineers who had worked the throttle or shoveled coal into the boiler. Junior Lieutenant Nikita Orlov could see them in the whistle's wood handle, dirty with age, on the iron floor whose studded surface had been worn smooth by the scuffing of shoes and boots. When he looked out the window, he could imagine the peasants who had looked at this engine in wonder and thought, *"At last, rail travel has come to Siberia!"* The long treks by ox or horse across the Great Post Road were a thing of the past. Now the hundreds of small communities had a lifeline of iron, not mud.

But history was one thing, and urgency was quite another. Orlov would have preferred a diesel engine to this relic, but it was all the transportation director in Vladivostok had been able to spare. If there was one thing Orlov had learned about government and the military, it was that a car or train or plane in hand, whatever the vintage, was more negotiable than nothing. You could always try to swap for something better.

Not that the engine was bad, he thought. Despite six decades of wear and tear it was in relatively good repair, Nikita concluded. The main rod, connecting rod, and driving wheels were strong, the cylinders solid. In addition to the coal tender, it was pulling two cars and a caboose. It traveled at a good speed, over forty miles an hour in the driving snow. At that speed, and with two soldiers stoking the boiler in shifts, Lieutenant Orlov expected to clear the storm within sixteen or seventeen hours. According to his aide and radio operator, Corporal Fodor, that would put them between Khabarovsk and Bira.

Nikita and the blond, baby-faced Fodor

sat on opposite ends of a wooden table in the first boxcar. One third of the wooden crates were stacked pyramid style, six rows deep in the far side of the car. The shutter on the right side of the train was open with a parabolic dish clamped to the ledge, facing out. Two cables ran from the dish to the briefcase-sized secure telephone sitting beneath it on a blanket on the floor. Fodor had tacked a canvas sheet over the open portion of the window to keep the wind and snow out. He had to get up every few minutes to brush the wet snow from the dish itself.

Both men were wearing heavy, white, fur-lined winter coats and boots. Their gloves and a lantern sat on the table between them. Nikita was smoking a hand-rolled cigarette and holding the backs of his bare hands next to the lantern. Fodor worked on a battery-powered laptop. They had to yell to each other in order to be heard over the screaming winds and rattling wheels.

"It would take, sir, three fifty-mile round-trips by an Mi-8 to carry the cargo to the nearest spot where a jet could land," Fodor said as he studied the green and black map on the screen. He turned the computer so it was facing the officer. "That's here, sir, just northwest of the Amur River."

Nikita looked at the screen, his thick, black brows pulled together in thought. "If we can get a plane, that is. I still don't understand the trouble in Vladivostok, why there was nothing available but this train."

"Maybe we're at war, sir," Fodor joked, "and no one bothered to tell us."

The phone beeped. Fodor leaned back and answered it, poking a finger in his other ear so he could hear. A moment later, he moved the lantern aside and handed the black receiver to Nikita.

"It's Korsakov, relaying a call from General Orlov," Fodor said, his eyes wide, a trace of awe in his voice.

His expression stony, Nikita got on and shouted, "Yes, sir."

"Can you hear me?" the General asked.

"Barely! If you'll speak up, sir — "

General Orlov said slowly, distinctly, "Nikita, we believe that an Il-76T controlled by a foreign government may try and intercept your train late tonight. We're trying to determine who or what is on board, but to do that I need to know what your cargo is."

Nikita's gaze shifted from his lap to the crates. He couldn't understand why his father didn't just ask the officer in charge of the operation. "Sir," he said, "Captain Leshev did not share that information with me."

"Then I'd like you to open one," General Orlov said. "I'm entering the order in my log and you won't be held responsible for inspecting the shipment."

Nikita was still looking at the crate. He had been curious about the contents and, acknowledging the order, asked his father to hold the line.

After handing the receiver to Fodor, Nikita pulled on his gloves and walked across the car to the crates. He slipped a shovel from a hook on the wall, wedged the blade under the lip of the wood, put his foot on the shoulder of the shovel, and pushed. The edge of the crate squealed and rose.

"Corporal, bring the lantern."

Fodor hurried over, and as the orange light fell on the crate they saw the bundles of American hundred-dollar bills, tied with white paper bands and stacked in neat piles.

Nikita pushed the lid back down with his boot. He told Fodor to open another crate, then walked across the rattling car to the table and picked up the phone.

"The crates contain money, Father," he shouted. "American currency."

"Here too, sir!" yelled Fodor. "American dollars."

"That's probably what all the crates contain," Nikita said.

"Money for a new revolution," General Orlov said.

Nikita covered his open ear with his palm. "Excuse me, sir?"

The General spoke up. "Has Korsakov informed you about Ukraine?"

"No, sir, they haven't."

As General Orlov briefed him on the movement of General Kosigan's armies, Nikita found himself growing irate. It wasn't just that he felt cut off from the real military action. Nikita didn't know if his father and General Kosigan had had any contact in the past, though he could tell they were on opposite sides of the incursion. And that presented a problem, for he would rather be working alongside the dynamic and ambitious General Kosigan than with a highly decorated test pilot . . . one who remembered he had a son only when Nikita embarrassed him.

When his father finished, the young officer said, "May I speak openly, sir?"

The request was extremely irregular. In the Russian Army, even speaking informally to a *komandir* or *nachal'nik* — a commander or chief — was unacceptable. The answer to any question was not *da* or *nyet,* yes or no, but *tak tochno* or *nikak nyet* — exactly so or in no way.

"Yes, of course," General Orlov replied.

"Is this why you sent me to chaperon this shipment?" Nikita asked. "To keep me from the front?"

"When I first contacted you, son, there was no front."

"But you knew it was coming," Nikita said, "you had to. At the base, we've heard that where you are now there can *be* no surprises."

"What you're hearing are the death throes of the propaganda machine," General Orlov said. "The operation took many high-ranking officials by surprise, myself included. And until I find out more about it, I don't want the money leaving the train."

"What if General Kosigan plans to use it to buy cooperation from local Ukrainian officials?" Nikita asked. "Delaying the money may cost Russian lives."

"Or save them," General Orlov pointed out. "It costs money to wage a war."

"But is it wise to second-guess him?" Nikita asked. "I've heard he's been a soldier since he was a boy — "

"And in many ways," General Orlov said sternly, "he is still a boy. You'll deploy your troops with round-the-clock watches in the train so that none of the cars can be approached, and admit no one without clearing it through me."

"Yes, sir," said Nikita. "When will I hear from you again?"

"I'll let you know more about the money or the Il-76T when I do," Orlov said. "Nikki, I have a feeling you're closer to the front than either of us realizes. Be careful."

"I will, sir," said Nikita.

The lieutenant pressed the button to the left of the mouthpiece and clicked off. He asked Fodor to clean the snow from the dish, then turned to the map on the computer. His eyes drifted along the route on the map, from Ippolitovka to Sibirchevo to Muchnaya and northward. Then checked his watch.

"Corporal Fodor," he said, "we should be arriving in Ozernaya Pad in approximately a half hour. Tell our engineer to stop when we do."

"Yes, sir," said Fodor, who went to the front of the car to use the intercom they'd rigged from the locomotive.

Nikita would see to it that the train was safe. This was for the future of Russia, and no one — not even his father, the General — was going to stop it.

FORTY-ONE

Monday, 7:10 P.M., Washington, D.C.

"Got it!"

Hood was napping on his couch, happy to turn over some of the routine duties to Curt Hardaway and the night crew, when Lowell Coffey entered his open office door with a flourish.

"Signed, sealed, and — ta-ta! — delivered."

Hood sat up and smiled. "CIC said yes?"

"They said yes," he said, "though it had nothing to do with me. It was the Russians themselves that got this for us by sending one hundred thousand soldiers into the Ukraine."

"I'll take it," Hood said. "Did you tell Mike?"

"I just saw him," Lowell said. "He'll be coming over."

Hood regarded the document with Senator Fox's signature right on top, where the good conservatives would see it. He was glad to see it too, though. Lying here, he had already resolved to back Rodgers on the Striker mission. Checks and balances were good, he had decided, but sometimes decisive action was better.

As Lowell left to inform Martha Mackall, Hood sat back down on the sofa, E-mailed Hardaway, then rubbed his eyes and remembered exactly why it was he wanted to run Op-Center at all.

Hood and everyone he knew — including the President, with whom he often disagreed — did what they were doing, first and foremost, because it wasn't enough to salute their flag with the hand and a pledge. They needed to give it their lives and their full commitment. Rodgers had given him the brass plaque that sat on his desk, something Thomas Jefferson had once written: "The tree of liberty must be refreshed from time to time with the blood of patriots and tyrants." From the time he was in college, he had wanted to be a part of that process.

That sacred process, he corrected himself.

Rodgers and Bob Herbert arrived then, and after shaking hands the men hugged each other.

"Thanks, Paul," Rodgers said. "Charlie's eager to do this."

Hood didn't say it, but he knew they were both thinking it: now that they had what they wanted, they both prayed it turned out right.

Hood fell into the chair behind his desk. "So they're free to go in," he said. "What're we going to do to get them out?"

Rodgers said, "However the CIC went, my friends at the Pentagon have given us the Mosquito."

"Which is?"

"A top-secret aircraft, Stealth variety. The Pentagon hasn't finished field tests, and brought it to Seoul because they thought it might be useful in a pinch during the crisis we had there. But it's the only way we can get into and out of Russia without being seen, heard, or smelled, so we really don't have a choice."

"Charlie's okay with it?" Hood asked.

"He's like a kid with a toy." Rodgers laughed. "Give him a big, new hunk of hardware and he's very happy."

"What's the timing on this?"

"The Mosquito should be on the ground in Japan around ten A.M., local time. The transfer to the 76T should take another forty-five minutes, and they'll wait there until we give them the go-ahead."

Hood asked quietly, "What if the Mosquito goes down?"

Rodgers took a deep breath. "It will have

366

to be destroyed as completely as possible. There's a self-destruct button for that, and it's pretty thorough. If the crew can't blow it up for some reason, Striker will have to. The Mosquito can't fall into Russian hands."

"What's the backup if the Mosquito fails?"

"Striker's got just over six hours of darkness to cross twelve miles to the 76T," Rodgers said. "The terrain's hilly but negotiable. Even in a worst-case scenario, with the temperature going down to five degrees above, they've got warm clothes and night-vision glasses. They'll be able to make it."

"How will the 76T hold up?" Hood asked.

"She's a cold-weather bird," said Herbert. "Nothing will freeze on her unless it gets to about ten below, which it shouldn't."

"And if it does?" Hood asked.

"If the temperature starts to drop," Herbert said, "we'll take off, notify Striker, and they'll have to hunker down until we can extract them. They've had the survival training. They'll be fine. According to Katzen's geographical studies, there's plenty of small game just west of the Sikhote-Alin' Range, and the hills are laced with caves for shelter or hiding."

"So we're okay if we get that far," Hood said. "What are our contingencies if the Russians ID the 76T and realize it isn't one of their own?"

"That's not likely," Rodgers said. "We managed to snatch an IFF beacon from one of the 76Ts they lost in Afghanistan. The Russians haven't changed their Identification Friend or Foe technology in years, so we're okay there. It's not like our planes, which broadcast millimeter-wave microwave signals to transponders on other crafts and at monitoring stations."

"What about communications with the 76T?"

"Our only contact with the plane has been in code," Rodgers said. "The Russians are used to us sending false communications to tie up their resources, and they tend to ignore outside communiqués to their own planes. Over the next few hours we'll talk to more of their planes to make sure they think that's what's going on — that we're harassing them on account of their troop buildup. Meanwhile, the 76T will maintain radio silence like most of the other Russian transports. If Russian Air Defense starts to get antsy, we'll talk to them. The cover story we've given the pilot is that he's bringing in ordnance machine shop spare parts from Berlin and rubber fuel bladders from Helsinki. Rubber's in especially short supply in Russia right now. If for some reason the Russians noticed the 76T earlier, this will explain why they were in Germany and Finland."

"I like it," Hood said, "very much. I assume they're taking the long way around Russia to stay out of the air lanes and out of the Russians' hair?"

Rodgers nodded. "Those skies are pretty crowded right now. If the 76T is forced to talk to the Russians, they'll buy that, since what we're allegedly carrying isn't as crucial as troops, rations, and weapons."

"And if their cover *is* blown for any reason?" Hood asked. "Which STOP do we use?"

"If we have to execute a Sudden Termination of Project over Russian airspace," Herbert said, "our radio goes dead and we get the hell out. Plus, there are a few tricks we can use as we retreat. They won't shoot us down unless they're absolutely sure we aren't one of theirs — and they won't be."

"Sounds good," said Hood. "Tell TAS and the rest of your team they've done an incredible job."

"Thanks, I will," said Rodgers. He picked up the globe paperweight and began turning it over in his hand. "Paul, there's something else that's been going on. It's another reason the Pentagon wanted to put on a little show with the Mosquito."

Hood looked up at Rodgers. "A show?"

Rodgers nodded. "Two of the four Russian motorized rifle divisions on the Turkestan front have been pulled off and sent to Ukraine," he said. "Kosigan took a tank division from the Ninth Army on the Transbaikal front and an airmobile brigade from the Far East front. If fighting breaks out with Poland and more forces are withdrawn from the Chinese border, there's a good chance Beijing will decide to make trouble. The Chinese recently put General Wu De in command of the Eleventh Group Army in Lanzhou. If you read Liz's report, you'll know that this guy is certifiable."

"I have read it," Hood said. "He was an astronaut in their aborted space program."

"Right," Rodgers said. "Now, we've run war simulations along these lines, so none of this is that far afield. In fact, the President has just asked the Pentagon to send them over. If the Chinese put their five Border Guard divisions on alert to threaten Russia with a second front, the Russians will not back down. Never have, never will. Skirmishes will break out, and war will follow unless a cool head — in this case, Zhanin — prevails. Our policy in that situation is to back the pacifist, but to do so we will have to align ourselves with Zhanin and perhaps even support him militarily — "

"Breaking our agreement with *Grozny*," Hood said. "Helluva situation. We help keep Beijing and Moscow apart and get peppered with terrorist strikes for our efforts."

"It's a real possibility," Rodgers said. "Which is why our aerial 'sneak attack' wing of other Stealth aircraft becomes real important. The longer we can be involved in the situation without *Grozny* finding out, the better off we'll be."

The phone beeped. Hood looked at the digital code on the LED band at the bottom. It was Stephen Viens at NRO.

Hood picked up the receiver. "What's doing, Stephen?"

"Paul? I thought you were on vacation."

"I'm back," Hood said. "What kind of intelligence organization are you running, anyway?"

"Funny," Viens said. "Bob wanted us to watch that Trans-Siberian train, and there's been a change."

"What kind?"

Viens said, "Not a good one. Have a look at your monitor. I'll send the image over."

FORTY-TWO

Tuesday, 9:13 A.M., Seoul

The windows of the hangar at the base outside of Seoul were bulletproof and painted black. The doors were locked, sentries were posted at each of them, and no one other than members of the Air Force's M-Team were allowed near the structure. The Mosquito unit was under the command of General Donald Robertson, a sixty-four-year-old dynamo who had discovered bungee jumping when he was sixty and did it once a day before breakfast.

Inside, the twenty-soldier team had run this drill dozens of times with a plastic and wood prototype. Now that the emergency and the cargo were real, they moved with even greater speed and precision, exhilarated by necessity, handling the surprisingly light, matte-black components confidently, silently. They had rehearsed loading it onto various aircraft, from the Sikorsky S-64 helicopter for missions under 250 miles to cargo planes ranging from the StarLifter to the RAF's old Short Belfast for runs of 5,000 miles or more. For the 750-mile trip to Hokkaido, General Milton A. Warden had okayed the use of a Lockheed C-130E. It had the largest cargo bay of any aircraft presently in South Korea, and the rear access to the main cargo hold, with its hydraulically operated ramp, made the process of getting in and out relatively easy. As Mike Rodgers had told Warden, speed would be desperately important once the Hercules landed in Japan.

While the M-Team loaded the cargo, the pilot, copilot, and navigator were reviewing the flight plan, checking the four Allison T-56-A-1A turboprop engines, and obtaining clearances from the tower at the secret U.S. air base midway between Otaru, on the coast, and the prefecture capital of Sapporo. The base had been established early in the Cold War as a staging area for missions into eastern Russia, and had been the home of between ten and fifteen U.S. spy planes until satellites rendered them relatively obsolete in the early 1980s. Now the troops stationed there called themselves "bird-watchers," keeping a radar eye and radio ear on Russian comings and goings.

But with two heavy transports on the way and the need for precise weather and geographical information, the bird-watchers were getting back into the flight game. And as the Hercules was rolled from the hangar in Seoul, the troops in Hokkaido were making preparations to help target, launch, and guide a vehicle that would leave the Russians wondering what had hit them.

FORTY-THREE

Tuesday, 4:05 A.M., the Gulf of Finland

The smell inside the midget submarine was terrible. The forced air was dry and stale. But for Peggy James, that wasn't the worst of it. She hated the total sense of disorientation. The submarine was constantly caught in currents, rocking from side to side or bobbing to and fro. The helmsman used the ship's rudders to adjust their course, which, for a moment, made the gentle hobbyhorse become a bucking bronco.

She was also having trouble seeing and hearing. To begin with, they were whispering. And the thickness of the hull and the surrounding water muted the sounds even more. Apart from the faint radiance given off by the control panel, the only light came from the small, hooded flashlight they were allowed to use. Its dull yellow light — not to mention the long hours she'd been awake, and the sleep-inducing warmth of the cabin — made it difficult to keep her eyes open.

After just two hours underwater, she was keenly anticipating surfacing at the halfway point some four hours from now.

The good news was, David George had picked up the Russian phrases fairly quickly, which reminded her never to judge a person by his drawl or to mistake wide-eyed eagerness for naïveté. George was smart and savvy, with a boyish enthusiasm that infused whatever he seemed to be doing. Even though he was no less a landlubber than she was, George didn't seem to mind the ride.

Peggy and George spent time reviewing maps of St. Petersburg and blueprints showing the layout of the Hermitage. She agreed with the DI6 analysts, who believed that any spy activities would be an adjunct to the new TV studio, and that Fields-Hutton was probably correct about the studio being located in the basement. Not only was the studio a perfect cover for the equipment the Russians would need and the kinds of signals they'd be sending, but the basement would put them far from the western side of the second floor. That was where the museum's numismatic collection was kept, and the metal in the coins might affect sensitive instruments.

Wherever it was located in the museum, the facility would need communications cables. And if they found those, she and Private George would be able to discover what was going on inside. Moreover, if the Center was underground, chances were good that the cables would be located in or near adjoining air ducts. Not only was it easier to run them through preexisting passageways, it was easier to get to them for repairs or upgrades. The question was, would they have to wait until dark to do their electronic search, or could they find someplace in the museum to use the equipment she'd brought?

Her eyes growing heavy in the dim light, Peggy asked George if they could finish later. He admitted he was getting tired also and could use a break. She shut her eyes and snuggled down in her seat, not thinking about the submarine but imagining that she was on a swing outside a cottage in Tregaron, Wales. It was where she had grown up and had vacationed so often with Keith, in a Cold War world that was strangely less dangerous and more predictable than the new, post-Communist order. . . .

FORTY-FOUR

Tuesday, 6:30 A.M., St. Petersburg

"General," Radio Officer Marev said over the telephone, "Zilash said you wanted to know about communications between General Kosigan and Minister Dogin. There is one taking place now, scrambled, Code Milky Way."

General Orlov shot upright in his office chair. "Thank you, Titev. Put it on the computer."

Milky Way was the most complex code employed by the Russian military. It was used on open lines and not only scrambled the communication electronically, but scattered it over numerous wavelengths — across the heavens, as it were — so that a listener without a descrambler would need literally dozens of receivers tuned to different channels to catch every piece of it. Both the Minister's office and Kosigan's command center had the proper descrambler. So did Titev.

As Orlov hung up and waited for the

descrambling and transcription, he ate the tuna sandwich Masha had made for him, and thought back over the past three hours. Rossky had retired to his office at 4:30. It was somehow reassuring to know that even the steel men of the spetsnaz had to rest. Orlov knew it was going to take a while for him to strike the right tone with Rossky, but he told himself that for all his flaws the Colonel was a fine soldier. The effort, however long it took, would be worth it.

Orlov had gone out to welcome the night crew to the fully operational facility, and had taken the opportunity to invite the Colonel's evening counterpart, Colonel Oleg Dal, to his office. Dal, who found Rossky even more abrasive than Orlov did, was a sixty-year-old Air Force veteran who had trained Orlov and was one of the many officers whose careers came to a virtual standstill after German teenager Mathias Rust penetrated Russian air defenses and landed his small plane in Red Square in 1987. Dal hated how Rossky refused to relinquish command of anything, even in areas where the Colonel was less experienced. He too understood that that was the spetsnaz way. But it didn't make him like it any better.

General Orlov informed Dal about the 76T and its eastward progress. It was southeast of Franz Josef Land in the Arctic Ocean. He also informed him about the efforts by United States intelligence to communicate with other Russian transports. Dal agreed that the 76T seemed to be suspicious, not only because it was flying to the east, away from the action, but because there was no record of any transfer of goods in Berlin or Helsinki. Though the records might be held up in red tape, Dal suggested a flyby to signal the pilot to break radio silence and explain his mission. Orlov agreed, and asked him to take the issue up with Air Force General-Major Petrov, who was in charge of the four air defense divisions that patrolled the Arctic Circle.

Orlov had decided to say nothing about the money on the Trans-Siberian train. He wanted to try and find out what Dogin and Kosigan were planning before taking action, and hoped that this call would be somewhat more informative.

Orlov quickly finished the last of his sandwich as the transcription began coming through. He pulled a cloth napkin from the paper bag and touched it to his lips. It bore a trace of Masha's perfume from when she'd packed it. He smiled.

As the voices began coming in, Titev had tagged them so the computer recognized which was Kosigan and which was Dogin. The text appeared in solid blocks, broken when someone else spoke and punctuated based on the inflection of the speaker. Orlov read with increasing concern. He was worried not only about the prospects for peace but about who was answering to whom in the relationship.

Dogin: General, we seem to have taken the Kremlin and the world by surprise.
Kosigan: That was my *zadacha dnia* . . . my mission of the day.
Dogin: Zhanin is still busy trying to figure out what's happening —
Kosigan: As I've said, force him to react rather than act and he's helpless.
Dogin: That's the only reason I let you move your troops this far before the money was in place.
Kosigan: Let?
Dogin: Agreed, let, what's the difference? You were right to want to put Zhanin on the defensive so soon.
Kosigan: Momentum we mustn't lose —
Dogin: We won't. Where are you?
Kosigan: Thirty-two miles west of Lvov, Poland. All the forward regiments are in place and I can see Poland from my command tent. All we await are the great acts of ter-

rorism Shovich's money is supposed to buy me. Where are they? I'm getting restless.

Dogin: You may have to wait a little longer than we'd planned.

Kosigan: Wait? What do you mean?

Dogin: The snow. General Orlov transferred the crates to a train.

Kosigan: Six billion dollars on a train! Do you think he suspects?

Dogin: No, no, it's nothing like that. He did it to get the cargo through the storm.

Kosigan: But on a train, Minister? So vulnerable —

Dogin: Orlov's son's unit is guarding it. Rossky assures me the boy's a real soldier, not a trained space monkey.

Kosigan: He could be in league with his father.

Dogin: I assure you, General, that is not the case. And no one will ever hear of the money afterward. When this is finished, we'll retire Orlov the Elder and return Orlov the Younger to his military hole where no one will ever hear of it. Don't worry. I'll have the cargo met west of Bira, clear of the storm, and flown to you.

Kosigan: Fifteen or sixteen hours wasted! The first of the major disturbances should have been happening by then! You risk giving Zhanin the time to take control of the situation.

Dogin: He won't. I've spoken with our allies in the government. They understand about the delay —

Kosigan: Allies? They're profiteers, not allies. If Zhanin traces this action to us and gets to them before some of the money lines their pockets —

Dogin: He won't. The President will do nothing for now. And our Polish hirelings will act the moment they are paid.

Kosigan: The government! The Poles! We don't need either of them! Let me send spetsnaz troops disguised as shipyard or factory workers to attack the police station and television station.

Dogin: I can't let you do that.

Kosigan: Let?

Dogin: They're professionals. We need amateurs. This has to look like a revolt that springs up across the nation, not like an invasion.

Kosigan: Why? Who do we have to mollify, the United Nations? Half the Army and Air Forces and two-thirds of the Navy of the Soviet Union belong to Russia. We control 520,000 Army troops, 30,000 Strategic Rocket Forces, 110,000 Air Defense forces, 200,000 Navy personnel — .

Dogin: We can't break faith with the entire world!

Kosigan: Why not? I can seize Poland and

then take the Kremlin. When we have power, what does it matter what Washington or anyone else thinks?

Dogin: And how will you control Poland when it's time to move on? Martial law? Even your troops would be spread too thin.

Kosigan: Hitler made object lessons of entire villages. It worked.

Dogin: A half century ago, yes. Not today. Satellite dishes, cellular telephones, and fax machines make it impossible to isolate a nation and break its spirit. I've told you before this must be a groundswell, and it must be guided by the officials and leaders who are already in place. People who can be bought but whom the Poles trust. We can't afford chaos.

Kosigan: What about the promise of broader powers when they win the elections there in two months? Isn't that enough to move the constables and mayors?

Dogin: It is. But they've also insisted on bank accounts if they lose.

Kosigan: Bastards.

Dogin: Don't fool yourself, General. We're all bastards. Just stay calm. I've alerted Shovich that the shipment will be late, and he's told his agents.

Kosigan: How did he take it?

Dogin: He said he used to mark time by

scratching lines on the wall of his cell. A few hash marks more won't bother him.

Kosigan: I hope so, for your sake.

Dogin: Everything is still on track — merely delayed. Instead of twenty-four hours from now, we'll be toasting our new revolution forty hours from now.

Kosigan: I hope you're right, Minister. One way or another, I promise you: I will go to Poland. Good evening, Minister.

Dogin: Good evening, General, and stay calm. I won't disappoint you.

When the transmission ended, Orlov felt the way he had the first time he was spun in a centrifuge during cosmonaut training: disoriented and sick.

The scheme was to take over Eastern Europe, oust Zhanin, and build a new Soviet empire, and it was ingenious in its evil way. A Communist newspaper in a small Polish town is blown up. The Communists in cities from Warsaw to the Ukrainian border counterattack hard, well out of proportion to the blast, and Dogin gets his groundswell as old-time Communists become encouraged — there were still a lot of them who respected the way Wladyslaw Gomulka tossed out the Stalinists in 1956 and formed Polish-style Communism with its odd hybrid of socialism and capitalism. Poland is torn in two as the old Solidarity alliances are revived and, with the Church, they begin railing against the Communists, just as they did when the Polish Pope urged Catholics to make Lech Walesa President. Closet Communists come out in the open, leading to a replay of the strikes, lack of food and other goods, as well as the disorder that Poland experienced in 1980. Refugees pour into the rich Ukrainian west so they can eat, old tensions between Catholics and the Ukrainian Orthodox Church are fired up, Polish troops and tanks are called in to stem the exodus, and Kosigan's troops are used to escort the refugees back to their homes in Poland. Those troops don't leave, and then the Czechs or Romanians become the next target.

Orlov felt as if he were dreaming, not only because of the events that were about to unfold but because of the position in which he'd placed his son. To stop Dogin, it would be necessary to order Nikita not to turn over the cargo that had been entrusted to him, and perhaps to take up arms against anyone trying to claim the crates. If Dogin were victorious, Nikita would be executed. If Dogin lost, Orlov knew his son: Nikita would feel as though he'd betrayed the military. Then there was also the possibility that

Nikita would disobey his father. If that happened, Orlov would have no choice but to arrest him after the train had stopped and the cargo had already been delivered. Insubordination or disobedience of orders carried a prison sentence of one to five years, and not only would it be the final break between them but Masha would take it much harder than the trouble Nikki had had back at the academy.

Since the transcript and even the broadcast could have been faked at the Center — digitally cobbled together from earlier recordings — there was nothing he could take to President Zhanin as evidence of treason. But the crates must not be delivered, and that was something he *could* tell the Kremlin. In the meantime, he hoped he could convince his son that Dogin, a man who had served his country selflessly and had helped to prevent the boy's expulsion from the Academy, was now an enemy of that country.

Colonel Rossky had not been resting.

Corporal Valentina Belyev had gone home, leaving Rossky alone in his office. He had been listening to communications between the offices at the Center, using a system that had been installed for him by the late Pavel Odina. It was because Pavel had put it in, and because no one else could ever know about it, that the communications expert had had to die on the bridge. Pavel was not a military man, but that didn't matter. Sometimes even the loyal service of civilians must result in death. It was like the tombs of ancient Egypt, the security of which was ensured by the death of their designers. There could be no room for sentiment where national security was concerned. Spetsnaz officers were expected to kill any man who was wounded or who hesitated. Deputy commanders were expected to murder commanders who failed to kill the wounded or cowardly. If necessary, Rossky would take his own life to protect a state secret.

The outside telephones and internal communications net at the Operations Center were both linked to Rossky's computer. But there were also electronic bugs, as fine as human hair, threaded through electrical outlets, inserted into air vents, and hidden beneath rugs. Each microphone had a keycode on his computer. That way, Rossky could listen to any of the conversations using headphones, or the conversations could be recorded digitally for playback or electronic transmittal directly to Minister Dogin.

Rossky had sat with his lips pressed tightly together as he played back the conversation between Orlov and his son. Then he listened as General Orlov ordered Titev to tap into the Minister's conversation with General Kosigan.

How dare he! Rossky thought.

Orlov was a popular man, a figurehead who had been hired because his fame and charisma were needed to get money from the Finance Minister for the Operations Center. Who was he to question the actions of Minister Dogin and General Kosigan?

And now Rossky listened as General Orlov, this much-decorated hero, told his son that upon receiving word of his destination, he was to proceed there and, upon arriving, to refrain from turning over the crates to Minister Dogin's representatives. General Orlov said he would send his own team from the naval college to confiscate the cargo.

Though Nikita acknowledged the order, Rossky could tell his heart wasn't in it. That was good. The boy would not be charged with treason and executed along with his father.

Rossky would gladly have committed the murder himself. But Minister Dogin did not allow lawless tactics among his lieutenants. Before the Center had become operational, the Minister had instructed Rossky to get in touch with him and he would contact

General Mavik, Marshal of Artillery, if it was necessary to have any of Orlov's orders countermanded.

When General Orlov radioed Major Levski, commander of the twelve-man *Molot* team, and ordered him to prepare for a flight to Bira, Colonel Rossky had heard enough. He entered a computer code that accessed a private line, a direct line to the Ministry of the Interior, and apprised Minister Dogin of the situation. Dogin said he would contact General Mavik to arrange for Orlov's departure, and instructed Rossky to begin making plans to assume control of the Operations Center.

FORTY-FIVE

Tuesday, 8:35 A.M., south of the Arctic Circle

Lieutenant Colonel Squires looked on absently as Ishi Honda checked the communications gear in his rucksack. While they were on the 76T, they used the airplane's uplink to talk to Op-Center. Once they were on the ground, however, they would be using the miniature black antenna tucked into the side of the ruck, next to the radio itself.

Honda knelt and unfolded the legs and arms of the seventeen-inch-diameter unit, checking to make sure that each prong was fully extended. He screwed the antenna's black, coaxial cable into the radio, slipped on his headset, and listened as the system went through a self-calibration check. Then he checked the microphone, counting backward from ten, and gave Squires an okay signal.

Next, he checked the global positioning system receiver, a remote-control-sized device with a luminous digital readout stored in a side pocket of the rucksack. He sent out a quarter-second signal which would enable him to make sure the device was working and yet wouldn't give the Russians time to fix their position. Private DeVonne was entrusted with the team's compass and altimeter, and would be responsible for getting them to the extraction point once the mission was completed.

Having woken from a nap, Sergeant Chick Grey checked his Tac III assault vest. Instead of containing a gas mask and 9mm submachine gun magazines, the pouches contained the C-4 they'd need for the mission. Before parachuting into Russia, all the Striker members would don their warm, rigid Nomex gloves, balaclavas, coveralls, goggles with shatterproof lenses, Kevlar vests, and assault boots. Then they would check the equipment in their Tac III overvests as well as the rappelling belts, the thigh pockets with flash/bang grenades, and their H&K 9mm MP5A2 submachine guns and Beretta 9mm pistols with extended magazines.

Only one thing was missing, Squires felt. He would have traded all the hot, hi-tech gear for a small fleet of fast-attack vehicles. Once they were on the ground in Russia, there wouldn't be much that Op-Center could do to help them with the train or extraction.

But a couple of FAVs to get them across the rocks and ice at eighty miles an hour, with maybe an M60E3 machine gun forward, a rear-seated gunner with a .50-caliber machine gun — now, *that* would be nice. Hell to parachute down and assemble, but nice.

Squires walked to the cabin to stretch his legs and get an update from the crew. Everyone was feeling good about not having been contacted by the Russians, pilot Matt Mazer noting that it wasn't a tribute to their stealth and cunning but to the massive amounts of air traffic. After checking the map and seeing how far they had left to go across the Arctic Ocean and then down the Bering Sea and southwest over Japan, Squires returned to the cabin — just in time to receive a call from Mike Rodgers. Now that the 76T was within range of the Russian receivers, the call was being relayed through a radio link Defense Minister Niskanen had set up in the tower at Helsinki so it couldn't be traced back to Washington.

"This is Squires, sir," he said when Honda handed him the receiver.

"Colonel," said Rodgers, "we have a new development with the train. The Russian unit has stopped and taken on passengers — civilians. There appear to be anywhere from five to ten men and women in each of the cars."

Squires took a moment to digest the information. He and his squad had practiced train-clearing exercises with terrorists and hostages, where the enemies were fewer in number and the civilians anxious to leave. But this was something different.

"Understood, sir," Squires said.

"There are soldiers in each car," Rodgers said. His voice sounded drawn, almost defeated. "I've gone over the photos of the train. You're going to have to get flash/bangs in through the window, then disarm the soldiers and off-load everyone. When you've done that, we'll contact Vladivostok and tell them exactly where to find the passengers. Leave them with whatever cold-weather supplies you can spare."

"I understand."

"Extraction time is at the bridge I told you about earlier," Rodgers said. "Pickup is exactly at midnight. You'll have eight minutes before the extraction craft leaves, so make sure you get there. The Congressional Intelligence Committee wouldn't give us any more time than that."

"We'll be there, sir."

Rodgers said, "I've got some serious reservations about this one, Charlie, but there doesn't seem to be any alternative. If it were up to me, I'd've hit the train from the air — but for some reason, Congress frowns on killing enemy soldiers. It's better to risk our own."

"It's the job we signed up for, sir," Squires said. "And you know me, General. It's the kind of job I *like*."

"I know," Rodgers said. "But the officer in charge of the train, a junior lieutenant named Nikita Orlov, isn't one of those kids who joined the Army for a regular meal. According to what little we have on file about him, he's a fighter. The son of a hero cosmonaut who has something to prove."

"Good," Squires said. "I'd hate coming all this way just to walk through a mission, sir."

"Colonel, it's me," Rodgers said sternly. "Save the bravura for the troops. More than wanting the train stopped, I want my Strikers back. Do you understand?"

"I understand, sir," Squires said.

After wishing him good luck, Rodgers hung up and Squires handed the phone back to Ishi Honda. The Radio Officer returned to his seat and Squires looked at his watch, which he hadn't bothered to reset as they zipped through the time zones.

Another eight hours, he thought. Folding

his hands on his belt, he extended his legs and shut his eyes. Before joining Striker just seven months before, he'd spent time at the Army's Natick Research and Development Center outside of Boston. There, he'd taken part in experiments designed to produce a uniform that instantly mimicked its surroundings like a chameleon. He'd worn uniforms with light-sensitive sensors that adjusted the light output of the cloth. He'd sat around while chemists toyed with the silk gene to create a synthetic fiber that changed color automatically. He'd tried to move in a comparatively bulky but remarkable EPS — electrophoresis suit — that had liquid dye poured between layers of plastic fabric, electrically charged particles coloring one or the other fabrics depending upon where and how strongly an electric field was applied. He remembered thinking at the time that before the century was out, camouflage suits, invisible Stealth tanks, and robot probes could make it possible for the United States to wage virtually bloodless wars. How the scientists would become the heroes, and not the soldiers.

He was surprised to find that that thought had saddened him, for while no soldier wanted to die, part of what drove all the fighters he ever knew was the desire to test themselves, to be willing to risk their lives for their country or their comrades. Without that danger, that price, that hard-fought victory, he wondered if anyone would cherish their freedoms as much.

With that thought on his mind, and Rodgers's voice still resonant in his ears, Squires drifted asleep thinking that at least there would always be chicken fights in the base pool, his son on his shoulders, and Private George falling backward, a look of surprise on his face. . . .

FORTY-SIX

Tuesday, 2:06 P.M., St. Petersburg

Several hours before reaching the coast of Russia, Peggy James and David George got twenty-seven minutes to taste the clean morning air of the Gulf of Finland. Then they reentered the mini-sub and undertook the second half of their journey. It was less than Peggy had wanted, but enough to keep her going.

An hour before reaching the coast of Russia, Captain Rydman lowered himself from his perch in the con and squatted in the narrow space between the hull and his passengers. Both Peggy and George had already checked their gear in the waterproof rucksacks and were struggling into their Russian uniforms. George looked away as Peggy wriggled into her blue skirt. Rydman did not.

After she finished, Rydman flipped open a twelve-by-fourteen-by-six-inch black metal box on the hull to the left of his head, then whispered, "When we surface, I'll give you sixty seconds to release the raft. You do that by tugging this pin." He hooked his finger through a ring attached to a nylon string, then pointed to the paddles on the top and bottom of the compressed raft. "These unfold in the middle. The raft has Russian markings that coincide with your documents," he said, "indicating that you're with the *Argus*-class submarine group operating out of Koporskiy Zaliv. I believe you've been briefed about this."

"Briefly," said George.

"How do you say that in Russian?" Peggy asked.

George squinted as he thought. *"Myed-lyenna,"* he said, triumphantly.

"That means *slowly*," she said, "but it's close enough. Captain," she looked at Rydman, "why just sixty seconds? Don't you have to replenish your air and batteries?"

"We can run another hour on them . . . enough time to get us out of Russian waters. Now then, I suggest you give your maps another look. Memorize the area nearest your drop-off point."

Peggy said, "Petergofskoye Shosse runs past the park. We follow it east to Prospekt Stachek, head north to the river, and the Hermitage is to the east."

"Very good," said Rydman. "And you

know about the workers, of course."

She looked at him. "No. What workers?"

"It was in the newspapers, for God's sake. Several thousand workers are scheduled to assemble in Palace Square tonight to mark the beginning of a twenty-four-hour nation-wide strike. It was announced yesterday, called by the Russian Federation of Free Trade Unions to obtain back wages and salary and pension increases for its workers. They're holding it at night so as not to frighten away tourists."

"No," she said. "We didn't know about it. Our myopic organizations can tell you what President Zhanin read in the loo, but they don't follow the news."

"Unless that's what he was reading," George pointed out.

"Thank you, Captain," Peggy said. "I appreciate all you've done for us."

Rydman nodded once, then shimmied back into the con to guide the midget submarine through the last leg of its journey.

Peggy and George were silent again as the submarine hummed through the deep. The English agent tried to decide whether having thousands of civilians and police gathered at the target site would help or hinder the process of getting inside. Help, she decided.

The police would be too busy keeping irate Russian workers in line to bother with a pair of Russian sailors.

The departure from the submarine was accomplished quickly. After using the periscope to ascertain that there were no boats nearby, the submarine broke the surface. Rydman quietly unscrewed the hatch, and Peggy climbed through. They were about a half mile from shore, and the air was thick with a dirty layer of smog. She doubted that anyone could see them, even if they'd been watching, as George handed her the surprisingly heavy rubber package. Still standing in the con, she hooked her finger through the ring and tossed the raft overboard. It was fully inflated when it hit the water. Her arms braced stiffly on the sides of the con, Peggy tucked her knees to her chest, brought her legs out, stood poised for a moment on the sloping side of the mini-sub, then stepped into the raft. George followed a moment later with the paddles. He passed them down to Peggy, then handed her their rucksacks and joined her in the raft.

"Good luck," Rydman said, poking his head from the con for a moment before shutting the hatch.

The midget submarine was gone less than two minutes after breaking the surface, leaving Peggy and George alone on the gentle waters.

They didn't speak as they paddled ashore, Peggy watching for the distinctive stiletto-like peninsula that marked the northern boundary of the large cove that bordered the park.

The current was with them and they paddled rapidly in order to stay warm. The icy winds slashed right through the jackets of their uniforms, with their plunging V-necks and thin, blue-and-white-striped T-shirts beneath them. Even the tight blue headbands of their white caps were barely strong enough to hold them on their heads.

The duo made it to shore in slightly over forty-five minutes. They arrived in a park that was relatively deserted where it met the chilly shore. Private George used the towline to secure the raft to one of several piles. While hitching on her backpack, Peggy complained loudly, in Russian, about having to check naval buoys when it was so chilly. As she did, she looked around. The nearest person was some two hundred yards away, an artist sitting in a collapsible lawn chair, beneath a tree, drawing a charcoal portrait of a blond-haired tourist while her boyfriend looked on approvingly. The woman was looking in their direction. But if she saw them she didn't react. A militiaman walked along a shaded footpath a few yards beyond them, while a bearded man napped on a bench, a Walkman on his chest and a St. Bernard resting on the grass beside him. A jogger ran past the artist. Peggy had never thought of runners or anyone else having leisure time in Russia. It seemed an odd sight.

Less than two miles to the south of the park, planes were landing regularly in the St. Petersburg airport. The roar of the engines disturbed the tranquility of the setting. But that was the paradox of Russia, the brutish rudeness of the modern day allowed to smother the beauty of the old. She looked north, toward the city itself. Through the filmy sky she saw the array of blue domes, gold domes, white cupolas, gothic spires, bronze statues, winding waterways and canals, and countless flat, brown roofs. It was more like Venice or Florence than like London or Paris. Keith must have loved coming here.

Private George completed his task and walked over after pulling on his backpack. "Ready," he said softly.

Peggy looked toward the broad Petergofskoye Shosse, less than half a mile away. According to the map, if they followed the road east, they would reach the Metro station. A change at the Technological Institute Station would bring them right to the Hermitage.

As they set out, Peggy chattered in Russian about the condition of the buoys and how the maps showing the currents required updating.

The man on the bench watched them go. Without moving his hands, which were folded on his belly, he spoke into the thin wire hidden in his shaggy beard.

"This is Ronash," he said. "Two sailors have just come ashore at the park and left their raft. Both are wearing backpacks and walking east."

Breathing deeply, Rossky's undercover operative turned his eyes back toward the beautiful Finnish girl and decided that on his next stakeout he would most definitely be an artist.

FORTY-SEVEN

Tuesday, 6:09 A.M., Washington, D.C.

It had been an uneventful night for Paul Hood.

He'd managed to locate Sharon and the kids at Bloopers the night before, and after hearing about the jelly bean burger and turkey ice cream soda, he'd stretched out on the couch in his office while Curt Hardaway ran the evening shift. A former CEO of SeanCorp, which provided navigation software to the military, Hardaway was an effective manager, a dynamic leader, and was familiar with the ins and outs of government. He had retired at sixty-five a millionaire, joking that he would have been a billionaire if he'd sold to private industry rather than the government. He once told Hood, *"I never skimp on quality, however little the government is paying. I don't want some kid sitting in the cockpit of a Tomcat thinking, 'All of this stuff was provided by the* lowest *bidder!'"*

Unofficially, both Paul Hood and Mike

Rodgers were off duty after 6:00 P.M. Officially, however, neither man was relieved until he left the premises. And while they were here, neither night Director Bill Abram nor Curt Hardaway ever attempted to "take the bones away from those two dogs," as Hardaway put it.

As he lay there through the night, his shoes off, feet on the padded armrest, he thought about his family — the people he didn't want to let down most, yet seemed to disappoint every which way he turned. Maybe that was inevitable. You let down the people closest to you because you know they'll be there when you get back. But boy, did it rip the conscience to ribbons. Ironically, the people he really seemed to have pleased yesterday were the people with whom he had the least in common, Liz Gordon and Charlie Squires. One because he'd acknowledged something she'd done by using it in a planning session, the other because he was letting him go ahead with a once-in-a-lifetime mission.

Between short snatches of sleep, Hood also stared at the countdown clock as it crept toward the extraction time they'd set for the tundra Striker mission.

Twenty-five hours, fifty minutes, and counting, he thought, looking at it now. *It had been thirty-seven-odd hours when Hardaway had first set it. How would we all feel when it cashed out at all zeroes?* Hood wondered. *Where would the world be then?*

It was at once depressing and strangely exhilarating. In any case, looking at the clock was better than watching CNN. The airwaves were full of the New York bombing and a possible relationship to the attack on the newspaper in Poland. Then there was Eival Ekdol ranting about his ties to the Ukrainian Opposition Force, soldiers who objected to the Russian incursion. That was smart, Hood had to admit. The miserable thug was swinging American opinion toward the Russian-Ukrainian union by speaking stridently against it.

Hood was awakened with word from the midget submarine, relayed via Helsinki, that Private George and Peggy James had been put ashore in St. Petersburg. Five minutes later, he was informed by Mike Rodgers — who hadn't slept much — that the 76T had crossed into Russian airspace and was speeding toward the drop point. It was expected to arrive in twenty minutes. Rodgers told him that the chaff the 76T dropped when it neared the coast disoriented the watching post at Nakhodka long enough for the plane to slip into the air lanes with the other transports. So far, no one had paid the plane any attention.

"Air Defense didn't react to the jamming?" Hood asked incredulously.

"We only did it to conceal where they were coming from," Rodgers said. "Once the 76T was in Russia, nothing appeared out of the ordinary. Our crew is maintaining radio silence, and on the way out they'll inform Nakhodka that they're going to Hokkaido to pick up replacement parts for decoy transmitters."

"I still can't believe we slipped through so easily," Hood said.

"For the last couple of years," Rodgers said, "the Russians have been more huff than puff. The soldiers manning the radar have been working longer shifts than we have. If nothing stands out as strange, it's unlikely they're going to catch it."

"Are you so sure it's that," he asked, "or could this be one of those traps that let a mouse in and don't let it out again?"

"We considered that possibility when we were planning the operation," Rodgers said. "There would have been no reason for the Russians to risk letting a strike force get on the ground. The truth is, Paul, the Russia you were worried about is no longer the Russia of reality."

Hood said, "They're still Russia enough to have us snacking on fingernails."

"*Touché*," said Rodgers.

Hood rose, phoned Bugs Benet, told him to send the department heads to the Tank, then went into his private washroom to scrub the sleep from his eyes. As he dried off, he couldn't stop thinking about Russia. Was Mike right about Russia or were they all just delusional, caught up in a false euphoria about the fall of Russian Communism and the Soviet Union?

Had it really fallen at all? Was this just a dream, smoke and mirrors, an interstitial period like the lulls between the great Ice Ages? Had the dark forces merely withdrawn from the spotlight to regroup and return, stronger than before?

Russians were not used to initiative and freedom. They had been ruled by dictators since the days of Ivan the Terrible.

Since Ivan Grozny, he thought with alarm.

As he headed for the Tank, Hood did not believe that however the next day's events turned out, the Evil Empire was dead at all.

FORTY-EIGHT

Tuesday, 2:29 P.M., St. Petersburg

During his first space mission, General Orlov had not been able to speak with Masha, and when he returned he found her emotionally taut. She pointed out to him that that was the first time since they'd known each other that a day, let alone three, had gone by without them talking to one another.

He'd thought, at the time, that it was a silly woman's emotion he couldn't understand. But then when Nikita was born and she bled profusely and was unable to speak, he realized what a solace just hearing the voice of your loved one could be. If she could only have told him, *"I love you,"* those long days of sitting by her bedside would have been easier.

He never again let a day pass without speaking to her, and was surprised to find how even the briefest talk anchored him as much as it did her. Although Masha was not supposed to know what he did at the

Hermitage, he had told her — though he did not tell her specifics or go into detail about personnel, other than Rossky: he had to have someone to complain to about him.

After calling Masha at 10:30 in the morning, and telling the disappointed woman that "business is so good" he wasn't sure when he'd be back, Orlov had gone to the command center. He'd wanted to be with his team to mark the passage of the first day's operational halfway point.

Rossky had come in at a few minutes past eleven, and both he and Orlov assumed what had quickly become their unofficial posts in the command center. Orlov walked slowly behind the bank of computer operators, each of whom was monitoring a section of the intelligence firmament. Rossky stood behind Corporal Ivashin monitoring the pipeline to Dogin and the other Ministers in the Kremlin. Rossky was even more intense and focused than usual as he followed military and political developments. Orlov didn't think the impending arrival of the two operatives from Finland would put him on such high personal alert like this, though he decided not to ask him about it. Questions to Colonel Rossky did not seem to elicit useful answers.

At 1:30 the Operations Center intercepted a report from the Air Defense station at

411

Nakhodka to the intelligence office of the Marshal of the Air Force that their radar had gone haywire for nearly four minutes but that everything seemed to be all right now. While Air Defense checked the electronic beacons of all the aircraft in the region against their radar blips to make sure there were no intruders, Orlov knew that it was the 76T from Berlin that had caused the disruption. It was now in Russian airspace and headed west — less than an hour from intercepting the train, if that was its intention.

He had immediately phoned Titev's afternoon counterpart in the radio room, Gregori Stenin, to contact the Marshal's office so he could speak with him. He was told the Marshal was in a conference.

"This is urgent," Orlov said.

Rossky asked Ivashin for his headphones. "Let me talk to them," he said.

While Orlov continued to listen on the telephone, Rossky was put through to Marshal Petrov. Orlov saw the glint of satisfaction in the Colonel's eyes.

"Sir," Rossky said, "I have a call for you from General Sergei Orlov at the Operations Center in St. Petersburg."

"Thank you, Colonel," Petrov said.

It was a moment before Orlov could speak.

For the head of an intelligence operation, he was suddenly feeling very ignorant . . . and very vulnerable.

Orlov told the Marshal about the 76T, and Petrov said that he had already scrambled a pair of MiGs to escort it to a landing or shoot it down. Orlov hung up and, his eyes still locked on Rossky's, he strode over.

"Thank you," the General said.

Rossky drew his shoulders back. "You're welcome, sir."

"I know the Marshal socially, Colonel."

"You are fortunate, sir."

"Do you know him?" Orlov asked.

"No, sir," Rossky said.

"Then explain." Though Orlov's voice was soft, he was commanding, not asking.

"I don't understand, sir."

Orlov knew now, for certain, that the conversation with Petrov and now with him was a game. But he wasn't about to get into a public power struggle in the command center, one he might well lose.

"I see," Orlov said. "Go about your duties, Colonel."

"Yes, sir," Rossky said.

Orlov returned to his post, beginning to suspect that even his appointment here had been part of a larger game. As he saw Delev, Spansky, and others snatch quick glances at him, the only question he had was who was loyal to him here, who might have been in on it from the beginning, and who — like Petrov — may have been brought in over the last few hours. The scope of the deception surprised him, but it didn't hurt as much as the thought that friends would desert him to preserve or advance their careers.

Orlov returned to his position behind the computer bank, though it was not the same position as when he had left it. The power base had shifted palpably to Rossky. Orlov knew he had to regain it. He'd never walked away from anything in his life, and he didn't intend to leave here defeated. But he knew he would have to undermine the Colonel quickly, and without being underhanded. He couldn't compete with Rossky on that level.

Orlov realized there was only one tack he could take just as Ivashin informed the Colonel that the local militia intelligence officer, Ronash, had called the St. Petersburg station house.

Rossky took the headphones, pressed one to his ear, and listened in silence as Sergeant Lizichev of the local militia told him what Ronash had seen.

The Colonel moved the attached microphone closer to his mouth. "Sergeant," he said, "tell Ronash to follow those two. They're the ones we want. They'll probably get on the Metro. If they do, tell him to go with them, and have plainclothesmen watching for them at the transfer point at the Technological Institute, and also at the Gostinyy Dvor and Nevsky Prospekt stops. They'll probably get off at Nevsky, and I'll meet your men there." He listened for a moment, then said, "Red-and-yellow-striped scarves — yes, I'll watch for them."

Rossky handed the earphones back to Ivashin, then walked over to Orlov. He stepped in close and spoke softly.

"You've been loyal to the Center and to Russia," Rossky said, "and have done nothing we would hold against you. For the sake of your pension and your son's career, you will continue to do so."

Orlov said in a strong voice, "Impertinence noted, Colonel. A rebuke will appear on your record. Was there anything else?"

Rossky glared at him.

"Good," said Orlov. He dipped his forehead toward the door. "Now come back prepared to follow orders — my orders — or report back to Minister Dogin in Moscow."

He knew that Rossky had to leave to catch the agents, although it would appear to the others as if he were obeying Orlov's command.

Rossky turned without saluting and hurried from the command center. Orlov knew that the Colonel wouldn't surrender the Operations Center during a coup. That's what it was, he realized now. And though he remained in the command center, his mind was on Rossky and what the Colonel's next step might be. . . .

FORTY-NINE

Tuesday, 9:30 P.M., Khabarovsk

"Rearview mirror says we've got company," pilot Matt Mazer told Squires.

The Striker had come to the cockpit three minutes before the jump to thank the Captain for his help. The radar screen clearly showed two MiG-like blips closing in at approximately seven hundred miles an hour.

"Be prepared to pop a gasket," Mazer said to copilot John Barylick.

"Yes, sir," said the rookie, who was cool but was working his chewing gum overtime.

The Air Force had cleverly equipped the 76T with an enlarged oil tank that was divided into two compartments: one that fed the plane, the other that could leak with the press of a button. The leaking oil was designed to give the plane a reason to turn around if they were spotted. They could go down at once, if necessary, to avoid being shot down or forced to a Russian airstrip — or, this close to the coast, they could break away from the pursuit craft and make a run for home.

In either case, Squires knew that the 76T would be unlikely to be ferrying them back.

"What do you want to do, sir?" the Captain asked Squires.

"We'll jump," he said. "I'll let Op-Center know what's happened and let them figure a way out for us."

The Captain took another look at the radar screen. "In about ninety seconds, the MiGs will be close enough to see you."

"Then we'll jump *fast*," said Squires.

"I like your style, sir," the Captain said, saluting.

Jumpmaster Squires hurried back to the cabin. He decided not to tell Striker what had happened. Not yet. He needed his team to be focused on the job. Though he would be happy to storm hell itself with any of these soldiers at his side, a stray concern at the wrong time by any one of them could cost lives.

At the FBI Academy in Quantico, the Striker team had practiced many kinds of aerial assault, from night jumps to Stabo assaults with the team hanging from helicopter lines and landing simultaneously on church steeples, cliffsides, and even the tops of moving buses. Each member had the poise, stamina, and smarts necessary for the job. But those in-depth examinations by the doctors, the "chancre mechanics," were easy: soldiers were either fit to serve or they weren't. Despite the best efforts of Liz Gordon and her team of psychologists, the real question mark was always how they would hold up under the stress of an actual mission — when there wasn't a fence made of two-by-fours to catch them in case they slid off the rooftop. When they knew that the rugged terrain wasn't the survival-training site at Camp Dawson, West Virginia, but the mountains of North Korea or the tundra of Siberia.

It wasn't for lack of respect or concern that Squires kept the information from them. It was to remove, as much as possible, another distraction from the successful execution of the mission.

The Strikers were lined up by the hatch, as they'd been for a half hour. Every five minutes, the navigator had provided Squires with their precise coordinates in case it had been necessary for them to jump early. While they stood there, the team prepared for "infil." Each member checked another's weapons and rucksacks, making certain they were tight against the chest, back, and sides, and that the ruck in back was firm against the bottom of the parachute where it wouldn't interfere with deployment. The rappelling equipment was stowed in rucks that three of the Strikers carried at the end of fifteen-foot tethers that would dangle beneath the soldiers as they fell. The teammates checked their padded-leather jump helmets, oxygen masks, and night-vision goggles. These were bug-eyed glasses so heavy that counterweights had to be attached to the backs of the helmet. After a few months of training with these goggles, most Strikers found that their neck sizes had gone up two sizes from the building of their neck muscles. At the last moment before the jump hatch was opened, they switched from the oxygen consoles to which they'd been hooked to the bailout bottles strapped to their sides.

The darkish, blood-red cabin lights had been turned on and icy winds slammed mercilessly through the cabin. It was impossible to hear anything but the air rushing by, and as soon as they were over their target and got the "go" signal, the lime-green jump light, Squires went out the door, pivoting on the ball of his right foot so that he was dropping facedown in the "frog" position. From the corner of his eye, he saw the second team member jump, Sergeant Grey, then looked at the big, round altimeter strapped to his left wrist.

The numbers rolled over quickly — thirty-five thousand feet, thirty-four thousand, thirty-three. Squires felt the frigid air push against his flesh even through the cold-weather clothing, chilling and then stinging him with the combination of cold and fist-hard pressure. He assumed the glide position as he fell, and when his altimeter read thirty thousand feet he tugged the silver rip cord. There was a mild jolt and his legs swung underneath him.

As he drifted down through the dark and cloudless sky, the air warmed perceptibly though it was still below zero. As team members above him lined themselves up with the luminescent strip on the helmet of the Striker beneath them, Squires searched the ground for landmarks: the train track, the bridge, the mountain peaks. They were all there, and that afforded Squires a measure of relief. One of the most important psychological aspects at the start of any mission was being able to hit the target. Not only did that make the soldiers feel capable, but the maps had made them familiar with the terrain in the target area. It was just one less thing to worry about.

Though it was dark, the night-vision goggles allowed Squires to pick out the target cliff, and he used the riser straps above him on either side to maneuver the shroud lines and guide himself as close to the edge as possible. He had told the Strikers that he would be landing in the forward position and that they were to come in behind him. The last thing he wanted was for one of his people to overshoot the cliff. If they were snagged on a projection, they'd have to be rescued, costing them time. If they landed on the ground, out in the open, they might be seen.

Gusts near the ground caught Squires by surprise. He landed just five yards from the edge of the cliff. Dropping to his side to reduce the surface he presented to the wind, the officer quickly released his parachute and bundled it in, standing as he watched Sergeant Grey land, then Private DeVonne and the others. He was proud of them as they landed with precision; within five minutes, the six Strikers had knotted their parachutes to a tree. Private DeVonne stayed behind to leave a small incendiary device beneath the bundle. It was set to go off at 12:18 A.M., after the Strikers had departed the area, destroying itself and the parachutes and leaving nothing for the Russians to present to the United Nations as "evidence" of a U.S. incursion.

As the Strikers huddled around Squires, they could hear distant engines that were more than just the 76T.

"Sounds like they've got company," said Private Eddie Medina.

"They knew about it and it's being handled," Squires said. "Private Honda, set up the TAC-Sat. Everyone else, get ready to move out."

While the five other Strikers moved out, using pitons and clamps to hook their heavy rappelling lines to the side of the cliff, Squires contacted Op-Center.

"Wake-up call," he said as Mike Rodgers got on the line. "What's the morning like there?"

"Sunny and mild," said Rodgers. "Charlie, you know about the MiGs — "

"Yes, sir."

"Okay. We're working on it. The 76T's going to make a run for Hokkaido, but it won't be coming back. We're working on a variation of the original plan. Be at the extraction point at the scheduled time. We'll have an aircraft there."

"Understood."

It was unspoken, but Charlie also understood that if there was a problem, the team would have to find a place to hide. Several sites had been marked on their maps, and the team would go to the closest one if the need arose.

"Good luck," Rodgers said before signing off.

Charlie handed the receiver back to Honda. While the radio operator packed up the TAC-Sat, Squires took a moment to look across the terrain. It didn't require the eerie green light of the night-vision goggles to look dead and desolate beneath the canopy of unnaturally bright stars. The track came toward them in a gentle curve from the plains to the east, passed through a natural path between the cliffs, and continued on across flat scrubland dotted with trees and patches of snow. To the south were mountains. The region was as quiet as anywhere he had ever been. The only sounds were the whistle of the wind in his helmet and the scuffling of the Strikers' boots against the dirt and loose rocks of the cliff.

Honda moved forward when he was finished. And with a final glance toward the eastern horizon from which their quarry would soon be coming, Squires moved to where the Strikers were just finishing with their preparations to descend from the ledge.

FIFTY

Tuesday, 9:32 P.M., Khabarovsk

Nikita had an uncanny sense about aircraft. Growing up at the Cosmodrome, he always heard the approach of helicopters before anyone else did. He could recognize jets by the sounds their engines made. His mother said that all those years his father had spent in cockpits had affected his genes, "filled them with aviation fuel," was how she'd put it. Nikita didn't believe that. He simply loved flying. But to have become a flier, to have been compared to the national hero Sergei Orlov, would have been impossible for him. And so he kept his love to himself, like a dream whose magic couldn't be communicated to another.

The train slowed as it came to a patch of track with thickly piled snow. Though the wind roared around the canvas flap over the open window, Nikita heard the distinctive drone of the MiG engines. Two of them, coming from the east toward a transport that was flying overhead. These weren't the first aircraft he'd heard, but there was something different about them.

He poked his head out the window and turned his left ear up. Though the falling snow made it impossible for him to see anything, the sound traveled clearly through it. He listened carefully. The MiGs weren't accompanying the 76T, they had caught up to it. And as he listened, he heard the 76T, and then the jets, head in the opposite direction, back toward the east.

That wasn't right. This might be the 76T his father had warned him about.

Nikita drew his head inside, oblivious to the snow caked on his hair and cheeks. "Get Colonel Rossky on the radio," he barked to Corporal Fodor, who was sitting at the table warming his hands above the lantern.

"At once," the Corporal replied as he hurried to the console.

While Fodor crouched beside the console, waiting to be patched through to the base on Sakhalin, Nikita's eyes ranged over the civilians they'd picked up as he considered other possible explanations for what he'd heard. A mechanical problem could have caused the transport to turn back, but it wouldn't have needed an escort. Was someone looking for the train, trying to pinpoint their location, attempting to help them? His father, perhaps? General Kosigan? Or could it be someone else?

"He isn't there," Fodor said.

"Ask for General Orlov," Nikita said impatiently.

Fodor made the request and then handed the phone to Nikita. "He's on, sir."

Nikita squatted. "General?"

"What is it, Nikki?"

"There's a transport overhead," said Nikita. "It was headed west until a pair of jets arrived, and then it turned."

"That's the 76T," Orlov said.

"What are my orders?" Nikita asked.

"I've asked the President for permission to send troops to meet you in Bira," he said. "I've not received an approval for my request. Until then, do whatever is necessary to protect your cargo."

"As war matériel or as evidence, sir?"

"That isn't your problem," Orlov snapped. "Your orders are to keep it safe."

"That I will do, sir," Nikita said.

Handing the receiver to Fodor, the young officer hurried to the rear of the car, making his way through the passengers. The five men and two women were sitting on mats playing cards or reading or knitting by lantern light. Nikita pulled open the door and crossed

427

the slippery coupling. Thickly packed snow fell on his shoulders as he pushed open the door.

Inside the car, the beefy Sergeant Versky was talking to one of his men as they kept watch at the window on the northern side. Another man was stationed at the window on the south. All of them snapped to attention as Lieutenant Orlov entered.

"Sergeant," Nikita said, saluting, "I want spotters on the tops of the train, two men on every car rotated in half-hour shifts."

"Yes, sir," said Versky.

"If there isn't time to request instructions," Nikita continued, "your men are to shoot anyone who approaches the train." Nikita looked at the civilians, four men and three women they'd placed in this car at the last station. One of the men was sitting against a crate, napping. "And don't leave the car unattended at any time, Sergeant. I won't have my cargo compromised."

"Of course not, sir."

Nikita left, wondering where Rossky had gone . . . and whether, absent the Colonel's orders, he could allow the crates to be turned over to his father.

FIFTY-ONE

"Another message from NRO," Bugs Benet said as Hood and the rest of the Op-Center officers sat around the conference table in the Tank.

"Thanks," Hood said to the video image of his assistant. "Put it through."

Viens's voice came on, but his picture did not. Instead, a black-and-white image was constructed on the screen at fifty lines a second.

"Paul," said Viens, "we picked this up just three minutes ago."

Hood swung the screen partly toward Rodgers, then watched as the white, hazy, moonlike terrain appeared, followed by the train, which occupied roughly one-third of the center of the image. The image was extremely hazy because of the falling snow, but what should have been an unbroken expanse of white on top of the cars was not. There were shadows.

"Sorry for the quality," said Viens. "It's snowing a hell of a lot. But we're certain those shapes on top are soldiers. They're in camouflage whites, so you can't see them per se — though you can make out the shadows."

"Those are soldiers, all right," Rodgers said tensely as he pointed a finger to the screen. "You can tell by the way they're arrayed. Last one facing forward toward the left, next one facing back to the right, next one forward right, and so on. These shapes here" — he traced a small line near one of the smudges — "appear to be a rifle."

Viens said, "That's how we figured it, Mike."

"Thank you, Stephen," Hood said, then switched the NRO chief off. The room was silent, save for the faint hum of the electronic grid surrounding it. "Can they know that Striker is on the ground?"

"Very possible," Bob Herbert said as the phone on the desk beeped.

"For you," Rodgers said as he glanced at the code number.

Because of the electronic field, Herbert couldn't be reached on the cellular phone attached to his wheelchair. He picked up the phone built into the side of the conference table, punched in his code number, and listened. When he hung up, his face looked waxen.

"The 76T is being escorted home by a pair of MiGs," Herbert said. "They'll start leaking oil and head for Hokkaido, but it won't be going back into Russia."

Rodgers looked at his watch, then reached for the phone near him. "I'm going to have the Mosquito go in from Hokkaido."

Herbert slapped the desktop. "No good, Mike. That's a round-trip of one thousand miles. The Mosquito's range is seven hundred — "

"I know what her range is," Rodgers shot back. "Seven hundred and ten-point-two miles. But we can get a cruiser up from the Sea of Japan. She can land on the deck — "

"We didn't get committee permission for the Mosquito to fly in solo," Martha Mackall said.

"We also didn't get approval for them to exchange fire with Russian soldiers," Lowell Coffey added. "This action was supposed to be reconnoitering only."

"I care about my soldiers," Rodgers replied, "not about those blowhards."

"Let's see how we can try to please everyone," Hood said, "and disappoint them all. Mike — "

"Yes, sir?" he said, breathing deeply.

"What do we do with Striker if we abort now?"

Rodgers took a long, deep breath. "The Mosquito goes in anyway," he said. "The nearest Agent-in-Place who could possibly sneak them out of Asia is in Hegang, Heilong-jiang, about two hundred miles away, and I won't have them make that trip."

"In China?" Coffey said. "No one in Russia?"

"Our people in Vladivostok became repatriated when the Iron Curtain came down," Rodgers said. "We haven't had the resources to recruit others."

"What about lying low until things quiet down," Phil Katzen asked. "The terrain is survivable — "

"The Russians know Striker's there, dammit!" Rodgers said. "They've got satellites too, and they'll *find* them!" He looked at Hood. "Paul, the best way out of this is straight ahead, as planned."

"Straight ahead," said Martha, "to a showdown with Russian soldiers at a time when the country's a tinderbox waiting for a match."

"The only way you'd keep that quiet," Coffey warned, "is to kill everyone on the train."

"Is it better to let a war happen," Rodgers

countered, "one that would suck in Europe and probably the Chinese? Why do I feel like I'm back in 1945, listening to all the arguments about why we shouldn't use the A-bomb to save American lives?"

Hood said, "Mike, the issue here *is* American lives. Striker lives — "

"Don't lecture me about Striker lives, Paul," Rodgers said through his teeth. "Please."

Hood sat quietly for a moment. "Fair enough."

Rodgers's hands were folded on the table. His thumbs were red and pressing down hard.

"You all right, Mike?" Liz asked.

He nodded and looked at Hood. "Sorry, Paul. I was out of line."

"Forget it," Hood said. "You and I could both use a movie and popcorn."

"Whew!" said Coffey. "Who's the family man here?"

Hood and Rodgers both smiled.

"All right," said Hood. "An R-rated movie."

"Hey, the guy's out of control," Coffey said. "Someone call the excitement police!"

Everyone but Ann was chuckling, and Hood tapped a finger on the table to bring them back. "What I was about to say a moment ago," he continued, "is that the diplomats haven't given up on solving this, and no one knows what President Zhanin will do. Do we jeopardize that by going ahead with the mission?"

"Whatever they do," Rodgers said evenly, "the crates on that train represent a lot of power for corrupt people. Even if it doesn't start a war, the cargo places influence in the hands of gangsters. Don't we have a responsibility to try and take that away?"

Coffey said, "Our first responsibility is to Striker and the laws we're all supposed to live by."

"Laws passed by your friends on the Hill," Rodgers said, "not moral law. You did what was necessary up there, but like Benjamin Franklin said, 'Necessity never made a good bargain.'" Rodgers looked at Hood. "You know me, Paul. Striker is dearer than my own life, but doing what's right is more important than both. And stopping that train is right."

Hood listened carefully. Rodgers and Coffey were coming at the problem from two directions, and neither of them was wrong. But the call was his, and he hated the fact that he was sitting here in comfort and security deciding the fate of seven people on a frozen cliff on the opposite side of the world.

He input Bugs's code on the computer, and his assistant's face appeared on the monitor.

"Yes, Paul?"

"Signal Striker on the TAC-Sat, see if Lieutenant Colonel Squires is free to come on. If not, when it's convenient."

"Will do," Bugs said, and his image winked off.

Rodgers didn't look happy. "What are you going to do, Paul?"

"Charlie's the commander in the field," Hood said. "I want his input."

"He's a professional soldier," Rodgers said. "What do you think he's going to say?"

"If he can take the call, let's find out."

"You don't do that to a soldier," Rodgers said. "That's not leadership, it's management. The only question we should be asking is, are we behind Striker or aren't we? Can we make this commitment and stick to it?"

"We can," Hood replied coolly. "But after your Korean mission, I went back and read the white papers you wrote as part of the ad hoc joint task force planning the rescue of our hostages from Khomeini's Revolutionary Guards. You were right about our forces being ready on paper and not in practice. And you were also right to be very concerned about extracting the advance party of Special Forces soldiers that would infiltrate Teheran a few days before the Eagle Claw mission. Without your prompting, the agents wouldn't have had a plan to get them out of the Mehrabad International Airport on Swiss Air if things went wrong. Why did you come up with that?"

"Because sneaking them out, one at a time, from the safe house would have given the Iranians more time to find them," Rodgers said. "It made more sense to buy commercial airline tickets and get them the hell out together."

"Who did you work that out with?" Hood asked.

"Ari Moreaux, who set up the safe house for us."

"Your man on the site," Hood said as Bugs's image reappeared. "Yes, Bugs?"

"I beeped Honda's helmet phones. We'll just have to wait."

"Thanks," said Hood. He looked at Rodgers again. "This isn't Vietnam, Mike. We're not withdrawing moral or tactical support from our personnel in the field. If Squires wants to go ahead, I'll back him and take the butt-whipping from Congress later."

"It's not your call," Rodgers quietly reminded him.

"Striker is yours to command," Hood

agreed, "but going outside the parameters established by the Intelligence Committee *is* my call."

Bugs came back on. "Lieutenant Colonel Squires is minding the headphones, Paul. I have him on the line."

Hood punched up the volume on the phone link. "Lieutenant Colonel?"

"Yes, sir!" said Squires, his voice clear despite the crackling caused by the snowfall.

"What's your disposition?" Hood asked.

"Five Strikers are nearly down the cliff. Private Newmeyer and I are about to descend."

"Lieutenant Colonel," Rodgers said, "there are Russian soldiers on top of the train. We make out ten or eleven, the all-NEWS network."

Facing north, east, west, and south, Hood knew. "We're concerned about letting you go ahead with the mission," Hood said. "What does it look like to you?"

"Well, sir," Squires said, "I've been standing here looking at the landscape — "

"The landscape?" Hood said.

"Yes, sir. This looks doable, and I'd like permission to proceed."

Hood caught the glint in Rodgers's eye. It was a flash of pride, not triumph.

"You understand the mission parameters," Hood said.

"We don't break any Russians," Squires said. "I think we can manage that. If not, we'll abort and head for the extraction point."

"Sounds like a plan," Hood said. "We'll keep an eye on the train and update you if necessary."

"Thank you, sir . . . General Rodgers. As they say in the foothills, '*Dosvedanya.*' See you later."

FIFTY-TWO

Tuesday, 2:52 P.M., St. Petersburg

Peggy stopped at the coin-operated telephone just above the Griboyedora Canal. After looking around, she pushed two kopeks into the coin slot. She answered George's mystified look by saying, "Volko. Cellular phone."

Right, he thought. *The spy.* With everything else that was going on, George had forgotten about him. One of the things Striker operatives had been trained to do was take in their surroundings in a seemingly casual glance, remembering details that most people would have missed. The ordinary person looked at the sky or the sea or a skyline — big, impressive sights. But that wasn't where "information" tended to be. It was in a glen under the sky or a cove beside the sea or a street running past a building. Those were the places Strikers looked. And at people, always people. A tree or mailbox wasn't a threat to a mission, but someone behind them could be.

And because he hadn't looked at the trees in the park or the busy thoroughfare when he'd arrived, Private George noticed that the man who had been napping on the bench was no longer asleep. He was walking slowly less than two hundred yards behind them and his St. Bernard was panting. He had been running to get there, not strolling.

Peggy said in Russian, "The Hermitage, Raphael's *Conestabile Madonna*, left side, every hour and half hour for one minute. After closing, go to Krasnyy Prospekt, Upper Park, lean on a tree, left arm."

The English operative had told him where to meet her and how to stand so she'd know him.

She hung up and they started walking again.

"We're being followed," George said in English.

"The man with the beard," Peggy said, "I know. This could make things a little easier."

"Easier?"

"Yes," she said. "The Russians know we're here, and the surveillance facility Keith was looking for could very well be involved. Anyway, if that man is wired we may be able to find it. Do you have a light?"

"Excuse me?"

"A match?" she said. "A lighter?"

"I don't smoke," George said.

"Neither do I," Peggy said impatiently, "but pat your pockets like you're looking for one."

"Oh. Sorry," George said as he slapped his shirt and pants pockets.

"Fine," Peggy said. "Now wait here."

Almost every soldier in Russia smoked, and though George didn't enjoy it, he, like Peggy, had mastered the art of inhaling the potent Turkish blend favored by Russian and Chinese militiamen — just in case Striker ever ended up in Asia. But George had no idea what she had in mind as he watched her pull a package of cigarettes from her breast pocket and walk toward the bearded man.

As George looked down at the ground, convincingly affecting boredom, the Russian pretended to be waiting for the dog to finish up with a tree, something the dog had no apparent inclination to do. The cigarette poking from her mouth, Peggy was about ten yards from the man when he turned to walk in the other direction.

"Sir!" she said in perfect Russian as she jogged after him. "Have you got a match?"

He shook his head as he strolled away.

Peggy came up behind him and, in one quick motion, grabbed the leash at the base

441

of the loop that was slung around his left hand. She twisted hard, and in the same motion stepped around so she was facing him. He groaned as the leash cut off the circulation in his fingers.

George saw her eyes drop to his beard. She nodded once when she spotted the wire. Peggy faced the Russian and put a rigid finger to her lips, indicating silence.

The Russian nodded.

"Thanks for the match," she said as she led the spy toward George. "That's a lovely dog you have."

She was talking, George knew, to keep the Russians from communicating with their agent. As long as someone was there, they wouldn't expect the Russian to answer their questions. He also realized she couldn't shut it off, or they'd know something was wrong.

Except for the fact that he was wincing slightly, it would have appeared to an observer that Peggy and the Russian were friends holding hands as they walked the dog. When they reached George's side, Peggy patted the Russian's left pants pocket with the back of her hand. She reached in, pulled out his car keys, and swept her free hand back and forth.

Still grimacing, the Russian pointed toward a row of cars on the far side of the park.

She looked at George, who nodded with understanding.

"I'm always surprised at how passive most large dogs are," Peggy said as they walked, the dog lumbering after them. "It's the little ones who cause trouble."

The three of them entered the park and headed toward a row of cars parked on the other side of the kidney-shaped green. When they had crossed it, the Russian led them to a black two-door sedan.

Upon reaching the passenger's side, Peggy faced the Russian and rapped on the car with a knuckle. "Does she bite?"

He shook his head.

She turned the leash and the pain brought the Russian up to the tips of his toes.

"Yes!" he said. "Be careful!"

She gave the Russian the keys and indicated for him to open the door. He did, then pointed to the glove compartment. Peggy knelt beside the car so that he could sit down and turn the knob with his right hand. One twist to the left, one to the right, then a full clockwise turn back to the right opened the compartment. Inside was a gas canister and a switch. George knew from a briefing on taking hostages-in-place — high-ranking persons, instead of ordinary people in the street — that wealthy people, military figures, and government officials often had booby traps in their cars that were triggered automatically in the event of kidnaping. In the case of the Russians, there was typically a noxious gas of some kind that went off after a short time. The abductee, of course, would know when to hold his or her breath.

After the Russian disarmed the device, Peggy tugged him out by the hand, took the keys, and handed them to George. She cocked her head toward the driver's side. George went around, climbed in, and started the car while Peggy slid into the backseat with the Russian. With her free hand, she released the dog from its collar and shut the door. The St. Bernard jumped up at the window, barking. Peggy ignored it as she turned down the volume on the Walkman microphone.

"Check for bugs," Peggy said to George as she settled in beside the Russian.

George removed the handheld bug transmitter locator from his ruck. He swept it around the car and toward the Russian. There was no loud screeching.

"We're clean," said George.

"Good."

George could hear the buzz of voices from the Russian's earphones. "But I think they're talking to him. Probably wondering why the mike has gone dead."

"I'm not surprised," said Peggy, "but they'll just have to wait." She looked at George in the rearview mirror. "What are your orders under these circumstances?"

"The manual says that if we're discovered, we disperse and get out."

"Safety first," she said. "Our manual says that too."

"It's more for security," said George. "We know things the Russians would love to — "

"I know," said Peggy. "But what do you *really* want to do?"

George replied, "Find out what's going on at the Hermitage."

"So do I," said Peggy. "So let's see if our friend and his beard can help." Peggy pulled a dagger from the sleeve behind her lapel and put it under the Russian's left ear. She released the leash and said in Russian, "What's your name?"

The Russian hesitated, and Peggy pressed the needle-sharp tip of the blade against his superficial temporal artery. "The longer you take, the more pressure I apply," she said.

The Russian replied, "Ronash."

"All right, Ronash," said Peggy. "We're going to make sure you don't tell your friends anything in code, so say exactly what I say. Understand?"

"*Da.*"

"Who is in charge of this operation?"

"I don't know," he said.

"Oh, come now," said Peggy.

"A spetsnaz officer," said Ronash. "I don't know him."

"All right," Peggy said, "Here's what you tell them: 'This is Ronash, and I wish to speak with the spetsnaz officer in charge.' When he gets on, give me the unit."

Ronash nodded tightly so as not to run the knife through his throat.

George glanced at her in the mirror. "What *are* we going to do?" he asked in English.

Peggy said, "Head for the Hermitage. We'll find a way in if we have to, but I have a better idea."

As George backed the car from the parking area, the dog stopped jumping. It just watched, its great tail wagging, as the car pulled away. Then it settled down on the grass, its big head flopping to the side and dragging the rest of its body with it.

So much for industry in the post-Cold War Russia, the Striker thought. *Even the dogs don't want to do any heavy lifting.*

As he swung the car toward the main thoroughfare, and then along the Obvodnyy

Canal toward the Moskovsky Prospekt, George couldn't help but marvel, by contrast, at the way Peggy had executed her duties, with cool efficiency. Though he didn't like having had his mission command posture usurped, he was impressed by her style and her ability to improvise. He was also damned curious and a little excited to see where all of this would lead — despite the fact that he was already up to his neck in waters that were definitely rising.

FIFTY-THREE

Tuesday, 10:07 P.M., Khabarovsk

With all the hi-tech wizardry the military had put at his disposal, Charlie Squires couldn't understand why they didn't have nonfog night-vision goggles instead of these "foggles," as the Strikers had nicknamed them. Sweat pooled on the inside bottom of the lenses, and if you covered your mouth with a muffler, as he'd tried to do, the perspiration warmed, turned to vapor, and you couldn't see. If you didn't use the muffler, your lips froze together and the tip of your nose went numb.

A warm face wouldn't matter much if he dropped off the hundred-foot-high cliff, so Squires chose to see — as much as one *could* see with thick snow swirling around. At least he could see the cliff.

Squires was descending, buddy style, with Private Terrence Newmeyer. One man started rappelling down the cliff, got a foothold, then extended a hand and steadied the other as he descended a little further. In the dark, on icy cliffs, Squires didn't want anyone rappelling without something for guidance — though he had to admit, these weren't the worst conditions he'd seen. Squires had once been invited to participate with Israel's Sayeret Giva'ati, the elite reconnaissance brigade, during their "hell week" training. The exercises included climbing down a twenty-four-meter-high cliff and then running an obstacle course. The olive fatigues of the soldiers were ripped to shreds by the end of the drill, though not from the cliff itself: throughout the descent, officers had been pelting the soldiers with both Arabic epithets and rocks. Compared to that climb, this one — foggles and all — was a day at the beach.

About fifteen yards from the bottom, five yards to their left, Squires heard Sondra yell at them to wait. Squires looked down and saw her huddled close to her climbing partner, Private Walter Pupshaw.

"What's wrong?" Squires shouted as he stole a quick look at the horizon. He was searching for smoke from the locomotive and didn't see it — yet.

"He's *frozen* to the cliff," Sondra yelled back. "He tore his pant leg on a rock. Looks like perspiration stuck the lining to the ice."

Squires shouted down, "Private Honda, get

449

me an ETA on the train!"

The radio operator quickly set up the TAC-Sat as Squires and Newmeyer made their way toward Pupshaw. The officer settled in slightly above and to the right of the Private.

"Sorry, sir," Pupshaw said. "I must've hit a real icy patch here."

Squires looked at the soldier, who resembled a big spider plastered to a wall.

"Private DeVonne," Squires said, "you get above him and dig in. I mean, hold on *real* tight. Private Newmeyer, we're going to use our rope to try and free him."

Squires grabbed the line that held him to Newmeyer and whipped it up, so it was resting on Pupshaw's arms, in front of his face.

"Pupshaw," Squires said, "let go with your left hand and let the rope fall to your waist. Then do the same thing with your right."

"Yes, sir," Pupshaw said.

Both Newmeyer and Squires lent him their hands for support as, cautiously, Pupshaw released his grip on the rock face with his left hand, then grabbed it again when the rope had slid down. He repeated with the right hand, and the rope was now level with his belt.

"Okay," Squires said. "Private Newmeyer and I are going to climb down together.

We'll put our weight on the rope so, hopefully, it'll slice through the ice. DeVonne, you be ready to take his weight when he comes free."

"Yes, sir," she said.

Slowly, Squires and Newmeyer descended in tandem, on either side of Private Pupshaw, the rope snagging on the ice where it had formed between the Striker and the cliff. It held for a moment, and the two men put more and more of their weight on the line until the ice shattered in a rain of fine particles. Squires had a firm grip on the cliff, DeVonne was able to hold onto Pupshaw, and after a tense moment when the rock beneath his right boot gave way, Newmeyer was able to regain his footing with a steadying hand from Pupshaw.

"Thank you," Pupshaw said as the four of them made their way to the bottom of the cliff.

When Squires reached the bottom, Sergeant Grey had the team gathered beside the track. There was a space of some ten yards between the base of the cliff and the track; to the west, roughly thirty yards away, was a clump of trees that appeared to have died sometime before the Russian Revolution. Private Honda was already on the TAC-Sat, and when he got off, he said that up-to-the-minute NRO reconnaissance put the train at twenty-one miles to the east, traveling at an average of thirty-five miles an hour.

"That will have them here in just over a half hour," Squires said. "Not a lot of time. Okay, Sergeant Grey. You and Newmeyer rig one of those trees to blow across the track."

Sergeant Grey was already unloading the C-4 from the pouches in his assault vest. "Yes, sir."

"DeVonne, Pupshaw, Honda — you three start for the extraction point and secure the route. I don't expect we'll find any disagreeable peasants out here, but you never know. There could be wolves."

"Sir," said Sondra, "I'd like — "

"Doesn't matter," Squires cut her off. "Sergeant Grey, Private Newmeyer, and myself are all that's needed for this part of the plan. I need the rest of you to cover our retreat, if it comes to that."

"Yes, sir," Private DeVonne saluted.

Squires turned to Private Honda, briefing him about the remainder of the mission. "You report to HQ as soon as the bridge is in view. Tell them what we're planning to do. If there's a message from them, you'll have to deal with it. We won't be in a position to use our radios."

"Understood," said Honda.

As the three Strikers started off through wind-gusted snows that ranged from ankle-deep to knee-deep, Squires joined Sergeant Grey and Private Newmeyer. Grey was already pressing small strips of C-4 to the trunk of a large tree near the tracks. Newmeyer was cutting the safety fuse, leaving the timer fuses they'd brought for Squires to use later. The safety fuses were marked in thirty-second lengths and he had measured out a piece ten lengths long.

"Make it four minutes," Squires said, looking over his shoulder. "I'm a little antsy about the train being so close that they hear it."

Newmeyer grinned. "We all did the fourteen-mile timed run in under a hundred and ten minutes, sir."

"Not in snow with full gear you didn't — "

"We should be okay," Newmeyer said.

"We also need to leave time to throw snow on the tree, so it looks like it's been there a while," Squires said. "And me 'n' Grey have another little job to do."

The Lieutenant Colonel looked ahead. In five minutes, they could reach a concave area of granite some three hundred yards ahead, one that would protect them from the blast — assuming the concussion didn't bring the cliff down on them. But Grey was experienced enough, and the explosives were small enough, that that wasn't likely to happen. That would still leave enough time for one of them to come back and clear away any traces of their tracks in the snow: it had to look as though the tree had cracked and come down by itself.

Grey rose when he was finished, and Squires squatted as Newmeyer lit the fuse.

"Let's go!" Squires said.

The Lieutenant Colonel helped Newmeyer up and the three men ran toward their little sanctuary, arriving with a minute to spare. They were still catching their breath when the sharp report of the low-explosive blast tore through the night, followed by the brittle cracking of the tree trunk and a dull thud as it hit the train tracks.

FIFTY-FOUR

Tuesday, 11:08 P.M., Hokkaido

The two-crewmen "glass cockpit" was low, flat, and dark behind a narrow, curved windshield. Three of the six flat color screens in the cockpit formed a single tactical panorama, while an extra-wide HUD — heads-up display — provided flight and target information that expanded upon the data contained on displays mounted inside the visor of the pilot's helmet. There were no dedicated gauges. The displays generated all of the information the pilot required, including input from the sophisticated sensors mounted to the exterior.

Behind the cockpit was a matte-black fuselage sixty-five feet, five inches long. There were no sharp angles on the flat-bellied craft, and the NOTAR tail system — no tail rotor — and advanced bearingless main rotor made the Mosquito virtually silent in flight. Ducted air forced, under pressure, through gill-like sections in the rear fuselage provided the craft with its anti-torque forces; a rotating directional control thruster on the tail boom enabled the pilot to steer. Already relatively lightweight because of the absence of drive-shafts and gearboxes, the craft had been stripped of all extraneous gear, including armaments, which cut the aircraft's empty weight from nine thousand to just six thousand, five hundred pounds. With an extra tank of fuel carried outside and burned off first — so the bladder could be jettisoned over the sea and recovered — and coming home from a mission fifteen hundred pounds heavier than it went in, the Mosquito had a range of seven hundred miles.

It was a breed of flying machine the press and lay public called "Stealth," but which the officers of the Mosquito program at Wright-Patterson Air Force Base preferred to call "low-observable." The point of such aircraft was not that they couldn't be seen. Enough radar energy directed at the F-117A or the B-2A or the Mosquito would enable an enemy to see it. However, there was hardly a weapons system in the world that could track and lock onto such an aircraft, and that was its advantage.

None of the low-observable aircraft currently in service would have been able to execute the mission at hand, which was why the Mosquito program had been inaugurated in 1991. Only a helicopter could fly in low over mountainous terrain at night, deposit or extract a team, turn around and get out again — and only a low-observable could hope to do that in the carefully monitored and cluttered skies of Russia.

Flying at two hundred miles an hour, the Mosquito would reach its target at just before midnight, local time. If the helicopter took more than eight minutes to complete its pickup in Khabarovsk, it wouldn't have enough fuel to reach the carrier that would be waiting for it in the Sea of Japan. But having run through every aspect of the mission on the cockpit computer simulator, pilot Steve Kahrs and copilot Anthony Iovino were confident in the prototype, and anxious for it to earn its wings. If the special forces team did their job, this would send them back to Wright-Patterson heroes and, more important, would deliver yet another body blow to the once-proud Russian military.

FIFTY-FIVE

Tuesday, 3:25 P.M., St. Petersburg

"General Orlov," Major Levski said, "I've had rather distressing news."

Only the Major's voice came in over the headphones plugged into the computer in Orlov's office. The naval base on the outskirts of the city was not yet equipped with video capabilities; nor, with the budget cuts in the military, was it ever likely to be.

"What is it, Major?" Orlov asked. He was tired, and his voice sounded it.

"Sir, General Mavik ordered me to recall the *Molot* team."

"When?"

"I've just gotten off the phone with him," said Levski. "Sir, I'm sorry but I must carry out — "

"I understand," Orlov interrupted. He took a sip of black coffee. "Be sure to thank Lieutenant Starik and his team for me."

"Yes, sir, I will," Levski said. "You understand, General, that whatever is happening, you're not alone. I'm with you. So is *Molot*."

Orlov's mouth perked at the edges. "Thank you, Major."

"I don't pretend to know what's going on," Levski continued. "There are all these rumors of an impending coup, of black marketeers being behind this. All I know is that I once tried to pull a vintage Kalinin K-4 out of a nosedive, sir. It had a bear of an engine — a BMW IV, very stubborn."

"I know the plane," Orlov said.

"I remember thinking as I burst through the clouds, looking straight down, 'This is a vintage beauty, and I've no right to give up on her, however temperamental she gets.' It wasn't just a duty, it was an honor. Instead of bailing out, I wrestled her to the ground. It wasn't pretty, but we both made it. And then I personally — *personally* — took that bastard Bavarian mechanism apart and fixed it."

"She flew?"

"Like a young sparrow," Levski said.

Orlov knew he was tired because that *Young Boy's Digest* story touched him. "Thank you, Major. I'll let you know when I get my hands on the damn engine cowl."

Orlov hung up and drained his coffee cup. It was nice to know he had an ally, other

459

than his devoted assistant, Nina, who was due back at four. And then there was his wife. She was with him always, of course, but like the dragon slayer who carried his lady's colors into battle, he still rode out alone. And at this moment the sense of isolation was stronger than any he'd experienced, even in the bleakness of outer space.

Using the keyboard, he switched back to the channel the militia used to monitor their field forces.

". . . want to be left alone," a female voice was saying in perfect Russian.

"Leave a surgical assault force free in Russia?" Rossky laughed. He was obviously communicating with his quarry on his cellular telephone, patched together either through the Operations Center or the local police station.

"We're not an assault force," said the woman.

"You were seen entering the Presidential Palace with Major Pentti Aho — "

"He arranged our transportation. We came to try and find out who killed a British businessman — "

"The official report and remains were turned over to the British Embassy," said Rossky.

"Cremated remains," said the woman. "The British don't accept that he died of a heart attack."

"And we don't accept that he was a businessman!" said Rossky. "You have another nine minutes to turn yourselves in or join your dead friend. It's that simple."

"Nothing is ever that simple," said Orlov.

Only the faint crackle of static filled the line for what seemed like a very long time.

"To whom am I speaking?" the woman said.

"To the highest-ranking military officer in St. Petersburg," said Orlov, more for Rossky's sake than the woman's. "Now who are you? And spare us the cover. We know how you came here and from where."

"Fair enough," said the woman. "We're COMINT officers who work with Defense Minister Niskanen in Helsinki."

"You are not!" Rossky bellowed. "Niskanen wouldn't risk his resources to disinter a corpse!"

"DI6 could not agree on a course of action," the woman explained, "so they consulted the CIA and the Defense Minister. They agreed that it would be less provocative for myself and my colleague to come in and try and find out why he was killed — and, once that was accomplished, to try and arrange

461

a dialogue to avoid retaliation."

"Cutouts?" Rossky sneered. "You would have taken a direct flight with cobbled passports, gotten in quickly to make your case. You came by midget submarine because you didn't want to be seen at the airport. You're *lying — !*"

"Which route crosses the Gulf of Bothnia?" Orlov asked.

"Route Two," the woman replied.

"How many provinces are there in Finland?"

"Twelve."

"This proves nothing!" said Rossky. "She was schooled!"

"That's right," she said. "In Turku, where I was raised."

"This is futile!" Rossky added. "She's in our country illegally, and in four minutes my forces will close in on her."

"If you can find me."

Rossky said, "The Kirov Theater is to your left, at the ten o'clock position. And there's a green Mercedes behind you. If you try to flee, you'll be shot."

There was another silence. While the woman may have swept the car for transmitters, Orlov knew that she probably hadn't noticed the cellular telephone in the trunk. The line was kept open when an agent was on the job. It didn't show up on transmitter detectors, but allowed them to triangulate the position of the car at all times.

The woman said calmly, "If anything happens to us, you'll lose an opportunity to communicate directly with your counterpart. Sir — I'm addressing the ranking officer, not the ruffian."

"Yes?" Orlov said. In spite of himself, he liked the way she'd said that.

"I believe, sir, that you are more than just the military head at St. Petersburg. I believe that you are General Sergei Orlov, and that you're in charge of an intelligence unit here in the city. I also believe that more can be accomplished by putting you in touch with your counterpart in Washington than by killing me and returning my ashes to Defense Minister Niskanen."

Over the past two years, Orlov and his staff had tried to find out more about their "doppelgänger" in Washington, their mirror image. An intelligence and crisis center that functioned much as theirs did. Moles at the CIA and FBI had been turned loose to discover whatever they could. But the Washington Op-Center was much newer, smaller, and tougher to penetrate. What this woman offered — because she was either very clever or very afraid — was the one thing he could not afford to let go.

"Perhaps," said Orlov. "How would you communicate with Washington?"

"Put me through to Major Aho at the Palace," she said. "I'll arrange it through him."

Orlov considered the offer for a moment. Part of him felt uneasy about cooperating with an invader, but a larger part felt comfortable trying diplomacy rather than giving an order that was certain to result in bloodshed. "Release the man you're holding," he said, "and I'll give you your chance."

The woman said without hesitation, "Agreed."

"Colonel?" said Orlov.

"Yes, sir?" Rossky replied, his voice taut.

"No one moves except by direct order from me. Is that understood?"

"It is understood."

Orlov heard rustling and the sounds of muffled conversation. He couldn't tell whether it was from the car or from the Technological Institute Metro stop, where Rossky had gone to catch his rats. In either case, he knew the Colonel wouldn't be idle, that he'd do something to save face . . . and to make sure that the two operatives did not get away.

FIFTY-SIX

Tuesday, 7:35 A.M., Washington, D.C.

Hood had learned that the paradox of crisis management was you invariably had to lop off the head of Medusa, face the heart of the situation, when you were most tired.

The last time his head had rested on a pillow, Hood was in a Los Angeles hotel room with his family. Now here he was, more than twenty-four hours later, sitting in his office with Mike Rodgers, Bob Herbert, Ann Farris, Lowell Coffey, and Liz Gordon, waiting for the first reports from a pair of Striker teams that had been sent to attack a foreign country. However they dressed up the language — which was what Ann would have to do in press releases if the teams were discovered or captured — that's exactly what Striker was doing. Attacking Russia.

Hood's staff was marking time as they waited to hear from either team, and he only half listened as he considered the ramifications of what they were doing. From

465

the out-of-sorts look on Mike Rodgers's face he was evidently doing the same.

Coffey hooked a finger under his sleeve and checked his watch.

Herbert scowled. "Checking Mickey's hands every minute isn't going to make the time go any faster," he said.

Liz sat up and jumped to his defense. "It's like chicken soup, Bob. It doesn't hurt."

Ann started to say something but stopped when the phone beeped. Hood rapped the speaker button.

"Mr. Hood," Bugs Benet said, "there's a call for you relayed through Major Pentti Aho's office from St. Petersburg."

"Put it through," Hood said. He felt like he did on hot summer mornings, when the air was still and silent and it was difficult to breathe. "Any guesses, Bob?" he asked, hitting mute on the phone.

"Our Striker man there may have been caught and forced to call," he said. "I can't think of any other — "

"This is Kris," said Peggy.

"Scratch that," said Herbert. "Kris is Peggy's code name if she's free. Kringle if she's stuck in the chimney, so to speak."

Hood unmuted the phone.

"Yes, Kris," he said.

"General Sergei Orlov would like to speak

466

with his counterpart," Peggy said.

"Are you with the General?" Hood asked.

"No. We've raised him by radio."

Hood touched mute and looked at Herbert. "Can this be on the level?"

"If it is," Herbert said, "Peg and George worked a Galilee-grade miracle."

Rodgers said, "That's what Striker's trained to do. And the lady was no slouch either."

Hood unmuted. "Kris, his counterpart agrees."

A strong voice said in thickly accented English, "And with whom have I the honor of speaking?"

"This is Paul Hood," he answered as his eyes took in the faces of his officers. He noticed that everyone in the room was leaning forward in their chairs.

Orlov said, "Mr. Hood, this is a pleasure."

"General Orlov," said Hood, "I've followed your career for many years. We all have. You've many admirers here."

"Thank you."

"Tell me, do you have video capabilities?"

Orlov said, "We do, through the Zontik-6 satellite."

Hood glanced at Herbert. "Can you hook me into it?"

The intelligence chief looked as though

someone had turned a cold hose on him. "He'll see the Tank. You can't be serious."

"I am."

With an oath, Herbert called his office on his cellular phone, swinging his wheelchair around and huddling over it so Orlov couldn't hear.

Hood said, "General, I would like to talk face-to-face. If we can arrange that, will you agree to it?"

"Gladly," Orlov said. "Our respective governments would shudder if they knew what we're doing."

"I'm shaking a little myself," said Hood. "This isn't exactly standard operating procedure."

"That is right," said Orlov. "But these aren't ordinary circumstances either."

"How true," said Hood.

Herbert turned around. "We can do it," he said, his eyes imploring. "But I urge you — "

"Thanks," Hood said. "General Orlov — "

"I heard," he said. "Our audio is very good here."

"What does he think ours is?" Herbert muttered. "CIA hand-me-downs?"

"Ask your man to access channel twenty-four," Orlov said, "on what is undoubtedly a state-of-the-art communications control systems satellite dish and transmitter, Model CB7."

Hood grinned at Herbert, who wasn't in the mood. "And ask him," said Herbert, "if cosmonauts still urinate on the bus tires before they head to the launch pad."

"We do," Orlov said, his voice wafting past Hood's critical expression. "Yuri Gagarin started the tradition after drinking too much tea. But women cosmonauts do it too. In matters of equality, we have always been ahead of you, I think."

Ann and Liz both looked at Herbert, who shifted uncomfortably in his wheelchair as he put in the call to the satellite room.

It took two minutes for the connection to be made, and then the General's face winked on — the thick-rimmed black glasses, strong cheekbones, swarthy complexion, and high, unworried forehead. Looking into those intelligent brown eyes, eyes that had seen the earth from a perspective granted very few people, Hood felt he could trust them.

"Well," said Orlov, smiling warmly, "there we are. Thank you again."

"Thank you," Hood said.

"Now let us be frank," said Orlov. "We're both concerned about the train and its cargo. It concerns you enough that you sent a strike force to intercept it. Perhaps to destroy it. It concerns me enough to have posted guards to stop them. Do you know what the cargo is?" Orlov asked.

"Why don't you tell us?" Hood replied. He figured that they might as well hear it from the horse's mouth.

Orlov said, "The train is carrying currency which will be used in Eastern Europe to bribe officials and finance anti-government activities."

"When?" Hood asked.

Herbert raised a finger to his lips. Hood touched mute.

"Don't let him try and tell you he's on our side," Herbert said. "He could stop the train if he wanted. Someone in his position has to have friends."

"Not necessarily, Bob," Rodgers pointed out. "No one knows what's going on in the Kremlin."

Hood unmuted the phone. "What do you propose, General Orlov?"

"I cannot confiscate the cargo," Orlov said. "I haven't the personnel."

"You're a general with a command," Hood said.

"I've had to have an ally here scan my own line and office for bugs," he said. "I am Leonidas at Thermopylae, betrayed by

Ephialtes. I am holding a very dangerous pass here."

Rodgers smiled. "I liked that one," he said under his breath.

Orlov said, "But though I can't get to the cargo, it mustn't be delivered. And you mustn't attack the train."

"General," Hood said, "that isn't a proposal. It's a Gordian knot."

"I'm sorry?" Orlov said.

"A puzzle, one that's very difficult to solve. How can we satisfy those criteria?"

"With a peaceful meeting in Siberia," Orlov said, "between your troops and mine."

Rodgers swept a finger across his throat. Reluctantly, Hood killed the speaker again.

"Be careful, Paul," Rodgers said. "You can't leave Striker out there defenseless."

Herbert added, "Especially with Orlov's son in charge of the train. The General's looking to protect his boy's butt. The Russians could gun Striker down, armed or not, and the U.N. would tell them they had every right."

Hood hushed them with his hand and got back on the phone. "What do you suggest, General Orlov?"

"I will order the officer in charge of the train to have the guards stand down and allow your team to approach."

"Your son is in charge of the train," said Hood.

"Yes," Orlov replied. "My son. But that changes nothing. This is a matter of international importance."

"Why don't you just order the train to turn back?" Hood asked.

"Because I would lose the cargo to the people who sent it," Orlov said. "They would simply find another way to transport it."

"I understand," said Hood. He thought for a moment. "General, what you propose would put my people at grave risk. You're asking them to approach the train in the open, in full view of your troops."

"Yes," said Orlov. "That's precisely what I'm asking."

"Don't do it," Rodgers whispered.

"What would you want our people to do when they reached the train?" Hood asked.

"Take as much of the cargo as they can carry out of the country. Hold it as evidence that what is going on is not the work of the legal government of Russia, but of a corrupt and powerful few," Orlov replied.

"Minister Dogin?" Hood asked.

"I'm not at liberty to remark," Orlov said.

"Why not?"

Orlov said, "I may not win this, and I have a wife."

Hood looked at Rodgers, whose resistance to Orlov showed no sign of softening. He wasn't sure he blamed Rodgers. Orlov was asking a lot and offering only his word in return.

"How long will it take to communicate with the train?" Hood asked, aware that the extraction of Striker could not be delayed.

"Four or five minutes," Orlov said.

Hood looked at the countdown clock on the wall. The Russian train was due to reach the Striker position in approximately seven minutes.

"You won't have any longer than that," Hood said. "Machinery is in motion — "

"I understand," said Orlov. "Please leave this line open and I will return to you as soon as possible."

"I will," Hood said, then hit mute.

Rodgers said, "Paul, whatever Striker was planning will already have been done, whether it's ripping up the track or planning to ambush the engine. Depending on the disposition of the TAC-Sat, we may not even be able to stop them."

"I know," said Hood, "but Charlie Squires is smart. If the Russians stop the train and come out with a white flag, he'll listen. Especially if we tell them what to say to him."

Herbert said bitterly, "I'm glad you're will-

473

ing to trust those vodka chuggers. I'm not. Lenin plotted against Kerensky, Stalin against Trotsky, Yeltsin against Gorbachev, Dogin against Zhanin. Cripes, Orlov is plotting against Dogin! They stab their own in the back, these guys. Think of what they'll do to us."

Lowell Coffey said, "Given the alternative of armed confrontation — "

"And Orlov's heroic nature," Liz said, "which seems very important to him."

"Right," Coffey agreed. "Given all that, the risk seems reasonable."

"Reasonable because it's not your two potatoes on the line," Herbert said. "Heroic reputations can be manufactured, as Ann will attest, and I'd rather have an armed confrontation than a massacre."

Rodgers nodded. "As Lord Macaulay put it back in 1831, 'Moderation in war is imbecility.' "

"Death in war is worse," Liz said.

"Let's see what Orlov delivers," Hood said. Though as he watched the small green numbers of the clock flick by, he knew that whatever it was he would only have seconds to make a decision that would affect lives and nations — all of it based on what his gut told him about a man's face on a computer screen.

FIFTY-SEVEN

Tuesday, 10:45 P.M., Khabarovsk

When Orlov raised the train, Corporal Fodor informed him that Nikita had gone to the engine to watch the track ahead. The Corporal said it would take a few minutes to bring him back.

"I don't have a few minutes," Orlov said. "Tell him to stop the train where it is and come to the phone."

"Yes, General," the Corporal said.

Fodor hurried to the front of the gently rocking car, lifted the receiver of the intercom, and pushed the buzzer on the box beneath it. After nearly a minute, Nikita picked up.

"What is it?" Nikita asked.

"Sir," said Fodor, "the General is on the line. He's said that we're to stop the train where we are and he'd like to speak with you."

"It's noisy up here," said Nikita. "Repeat?"

Fodor shouted, *"The General has ordered*

us to stop the train at once and — "

The Corporal bit off the rest of the sentence as he heard a cry from the engine, through the door and not over the intercom; a moment later he was flung forward as the wheels screeched, the couplings groaned, and the car was jolted hard against the coal tender. Fodor dropped the receiver as he jumped back to help steady the satellite dish, which one of the soldiers had been heads-up enough to hold, but the receiver itself was knocked on its side and one of the coaxial cables was ripped from the back of the dish. At least the bottom-heavy lantern hadn't fallen over, and when the train came to a rest and the soldiers and civilians helped each other to their feet amid the spilled boxes, Fodor was able to check the equipment. Though the connector had been torn off and was still attached to the dish, the cable itself was all right. He pulled off his gloves and began trying to repair it at once.

Because the large boiler sat in front of the cab, the engine's only windows were on the sides. Nikita had been looking out one of them when he saw the fallen tree through the thick, falling flakes. He had shouted to the engineer to stop, but when the poor young man didn't act fast enough Nikita

476

threw the brake for him.

The three men in the cab were flung roughly to the floor, and when the train stopped Nikita heard shouting from above and from the rear cars. He got to his feet quickly, his right hip numb where he'd landed on it, took a flashlight from the hook on the wall, and ran to the window. He searched the snow with the wide beam. One man had been thrown from the top of the first car, but he was already climbing from a snowbank.

"Are you all right?" Nikita yelled.

"I think so, sir." The young soldier stood unsteadily. "Do you need us up front?"

"No!" Nikita barked. "Get back on lookout."

"Yes, sir," the soldier replied, saluting sloppily with a snow-covered glove as a pair of hands was extended to pull him back to the top of the car.

Nikita told the two men in the cab to keep a careful watch at the windows, then he climbed to the top of the coal tender. The winds had stopped and the snow fell straight down. It was disturbingly quiet, like the cottony silence after a car crash, and the sound of his boots on the coal was crisp and brittle. He scuttled across, kicking up snow and coal dust, then dropped nimbly to the coupling of the first car. Wheezing from the cold, he used the flashlight to find the doorknob.

"Take six men out to the track," he hawked at the burly Sergeant Versky as he entered. "A tree has fallen across it and I want it cleared *now*. Have three men stand guard while the other three move it."

"At once, sir," said Versky.

"Watch out for possible sniper positions," Nikita added. "They may have night-vision capability."

"Understood, sir."

Nikita turned to Fodor. "How is the phone?"

"It will take several minutes to repair," Fodor said as he crouched beside the lantern.

"Do it quickly," snapped the Lieutenant, huffing out white clouds of vapor. "What else did the General say?"

"Just to stop the train and come on the line," Fodor said. "That's all."

"Damn this," Nikita said. "Damn it all."

As the Sergeant's crew pulled flares from a supply sack, Nikita ordered the civilians to restack the crates. A soldier came in from the next car, looking slightly rattled, and Nikita sent him back to secure the crates and make sure the soldiers there stayed alert.

"Tell the caboose to be on the lookout," Nikita added. "We may be approached from the rear."

The Lieutenant stood with his legs apart in the center of the car, bouncing impatiently on the balls of his feet. He tried to put himself in the place of his enemy.

The tree may have fallen or the tree may have been placed there. If the latter, then the ambush had failed. Had they struck the tree, they'd have been stopped beside a cliff — an ideal place from which to pick off the soldiers on top of the train. But here, hundreds of yards away, they could get maybe one or two soldiers before being spotted. And there was no way anyone could approach the train without being seen and, once seen, shot.

So what, then, is their game?

His father had called to tell him to stop the train. Had he known about the tree? Or had he learned something else, perhaps about explosives or ambushers ahead?

"Hurry!" Nikita said to Fodor.

"Almost ready, sir," the Corporal replied. Despite the cold, his forehead was flush and spotting with perspiration.

Nikita was becoming angrier with the helplessness he felt, and increasingly aware of a weight in the air around him. It was more than just the isolation and dampered sounds. It was a growing sense that whether he was predator or prey, the enemy he sought was very near.

FIFTY-EIGHT

Tuesday, 3:50 P.M., St. Petersburg

"I think they forgot all about us."

Private George was amused by the thought as he drove toward the Hermitage, negotiating the tricky turns he had to make after crossing the Moika River. He stayed to the right of the Bronze Horseman, then turned right on Gogolya Street and made his way toward the adjoining Palace Square.

Peggy had shut off the radio after Orlov and Paul Hood had switched satellites and it became clear that no one else was coming on the line. After leaving their shaken but grateful passenger off, she and George decided to continue on to the Hermitage, where they could leave the car, lose themselves in the crowd, and get their bearings before undertaking the second part of their mission.

"I mean, that's kinda rude, don't you think? We travel like watery walnuts a couple thousand miles, do the job, and no one bothers to get back on the line and say, 'By the way, guys — nice work.' "

"Did you come here for their approval?" Peggy asked.

"No. But it's nice to get it."

"Don't worry," Peggy said. "I have a feeling that before we're out of here, you'll crave anonymity."

As the white columns of the Hermitage came into view, growing amber in the late afternoon light, George could hear and then see the army of workers that Captain Rydman had warned them about.

He shook his head. "Who'd've ever thought it?"

Peggy said, "Probably the last time anyone protested here was when it was still called the Winter Palace and Nicholas II's itchy guards gunned the workers down."

"It's scary," George said, "that there are people who want to bring the iron heel back."

"Which is why I don't mind not getting thanked," Peggy said. "It's fear keeps us going, not a pat on the rump. Vigilance is its own reward. That's how Keith felt."

George looked at her in the rearview mirror. There wasn't a hint of nostalgia in her voice for her dead lover, nor did he see the loss in her eyes. Maybe she was one of those people who didn't cry in public, or perhaps not at all. He wondered how she would react when they reached the building where Keith had died.

There were at least three thousand people scattered across the large checkerboard of the Palace Square. They were facing a low stage and podium that had been erected in front of the General Staff Arch. Police were directing traffic away from the square, and Peggy told Private George to pull over before they reached them. He parked next to an outdoor café with brown umbrellas over every table, each umbrella advertising a different brand of beer or wine.

"The marketers didn't waste any time coming here," he grunted disapprovingly to Peggy as they stood side by side.

"They never do," she replied, then noticed that one of the police officers was looking at them.

George noticed him too. "They'll ID the car," he said.

"They won't expect us to stay in the area, though," Peggy said. "As far as they know, we've completed our mission."

"Don't you think our friend Ronash has already given them physical descriptions which are being faxed all over St. Petersburg?"

"Not quite yet," she said. "But we do have to get out of these uniforms anyway if we're going to leave as tourists." Peggy checked her watch. "We've got to meet Volko in an hour and ten minutes. I suggest we go inside. If we get stopped on the way I'll tell them we're from the Admiralty, which is a block to the east. I'll say we're just watching to make sure the crowd doesn't spill over. Once we're inside, we'll change, pose as a young couple in love, and make our way to the Raphael."

"Finally, a masquerade I can relate to," George said as they started toward the square.

"Don't like it *too* much," Peggy said. "We're going to have a little spat inside so I can stalk off and strike up a conversation with Volko."

George grinned. "I'm married. I can relate to that too." The grin broadened. "Strikers among strikers," he whispered. "I like the irony."

Peggy didn't return his smile as they went around the fringes of the crowd in the Palace Square. George wondered if she'd even heard him as she looked at the orderly mob, at the sculptural grouping over the General Staff Arch, at her feet — anywhere but the Hermitage itself and the river beyond, on whose banks Keith Fields-Hutton had died. He thought he saw dampness in the corners of her eyes and a heaviness in her step that

484

he had not seen before.

And he finally, happily, felt close to the person he had been sitting beside, hip-to-hip, for the better part of a day.

FIFTY-NINE

Tuesday, 10:51 P.M., Khabarovsk

Spetsnaz soldiers were trained to do many things with their chief weapon, the spade. They were left in a locked room with just the spade and a mad dog. They were ordered to chop down trees with them. On occasion, they had to dig ditches in frozen ground with them, ditches deep enough to lie in. At a specified time, tanks were rolled over the field. Soldiers who hadn't dug deep enough were crushed.

With the help of Liz Gordon, Lieutenant Colonel Squires had made a special study of spetsnaz techniques, searching for those that best accounted for the remarkable endurance and versatility of their soldiers. He couldn't adapt them all. Regular beatings to toughen the soldiers would never have been approved by the Pentagon, although he knew commanding officers who would have sanctioned them gladly. But he adapted many spetsnaz methods, including his favorites — their abil-

486

ity to create camouflage in a very short time and to hide in the unlikeliest places.

When he had learned about the soldiers posted on top of the train, he realized they'd be watching the treetops, cliffs, boulders, and snowbanks along the route. He knew that someone in the engine would be watching the tracks for explosives or debris. But he also knew that he had to get under the train unseen, and that the best place to hide would be on the tracks themselves.

The glow of an engine-mounted headlight would be diffused and dull, and the soldiers would be paying careful attention to the rails. So he felt safe using a small hatchet to hack through two of the dry, old crossties, chop a shallow ditch in the railbed, lie on his back, and have Grey cover him and his sack of C-4 with snow — leaving an arm-thick tunnel on the side so he could breathe. After interring Newmeyer nearby, Grey hid behind a boulder, far from the train; when Squires and Newmeyer tackled the two cars and the fireworks started, Grey would move on his target, the engine.

Squires had heard, then felt, the drumming approach of the train. He hadn't been nervous. He was below the surface of the rails where even the cowcatcher, if there was one, wouldn't touch the snow piled on top of him. His only concern was that the engineer see the tree too soon or not see it at all and collide with it. In the latter case, not only would the train be damaged but the wheels would kick the tree back and over him, in which case he would be, as he'd joked to Grey, "ground Chuck."

Neither of those had happened. But when the train did stop and Squires was able to burrow a little hole in front of his eyes, he saw that he was under the coal tender. That was one car ahead of where he had hoped he'd be.

At least the camouflage worked, he'd thought as he discreetly began to push the snow from himself. There was something very gratifying and historically right about Russian troops falling for a Russian scheme — like Rasputin being killed by Czarists and the Czar being killed by Revolutionaries.

As he'd finished brushing away the snow, Squires had heard shouting. Despite the fact that virtually every inch of skin was covered with Nomex garments, he was cold — a chill that seemed deeper, for some reason, because of the flat darkness surrounding him.

No sooner was he free than he heard boots crunch hard in the wet drifts. This was followed by the lighting of flares, which spread rosy circles of light in the snow and caused the dark underbelly of the train to glow devilishly.

Carefully placing his backpack on his belly, Squires began wriggling backward, out of the ditch and along the railbed toward the first car. Soldiers were moving to the right of him, and he stopped for a moment to unbutton the safety strap of the holster he wore low on his right hip. Though Squires didn't want to cause an international incident, he would rather read newspaper accounts of his crimes and misdeeds than have others read about his death on a frozen plain in Siberia.

Squires's backward crawl went quickly, and he was underneath the coupling between the coal tender and the first car just as the Russian soldiers reached the fallen tree. This, despite the fact that he was pushing up mounds of snow with his shoulders and had to limbo over them backward. Opening the ruck flap, the Striker removed the C-4 and gingerly pressed it against the metal as flakes of damp, rusted iron fell like snow. When the explosives were secure, he took out the three-inch-diameter timer and, with an insistent push from the heel of his hand, slipped the positive and negative ends into the plastique. There were two buttons above a numeric keypad, and he pressed the button on the left. That turned the unit on, and he used the numeric keypad to enter the countdown. He would give himself one hour. After punching in 60:00:00, he hit the button on the top right to lock it in. Then he hit the left-button, right-button sequence one more time to start the countdown.

Squires pushed his feet against the ruddy snow and wriggled to the middle of the first car. He heard thumping overhead, toward the upper right. The sudden stop must have dislodged the cargo and it was being restacked. Kicking backward another few feet, he stopped directly beneath the noise and put the C-4 there. He plugged in a timer and repeated the process that would cause this larger batch of plastique to explode. Moving under the second car, Squires rigged it to go off with a third slap of C-4 and a timer.

When he was finished, Squires allowed himself to enjoy a long, deep breath. He gazed across his chest toward the front of the train and saw that the men were nearly finished removing the tree. He didn't have much time.

Sliding out from under the ruck, Squires set it gingerly to his right as he sidled to the left. When he was out from under the train, he turned over on his belly and lay in the long, flare-cast shadow of the train. He looked at the luminous dial of his watch and was pleased at how quickly the operation had gone. He knew it was one of those things that, had he had time to rehearse it back at Andrews, would have taken ten or twenty percent longer to accomplish in the field. Why it worked that way, he had no idea. But it did.

He looked back toward the first car and, walking on his elbows, made his way to a drift near the coal tender. He began pushing the snow aside; that was Newmeyer's signal to start digging himself out. The Private was trembling and had bitten down on the mouth covering of his balaclava to keep his teeth from chattering. Squires gave him a reassuring pat on the shoulder as Newmeyer rolled onto his belly. He had been buried with his 9mm Beretta on his chest, and he holstered it now.

Newmeyer knew what to do, so Squires crawled back to the second car to get in position.

This was one action he wished he *had* been able to rehearse. But though a spetsnaz soldier might be able to function without sleep for seventy-two hours, and Israeli Sayeret Tzanhanim paratroop recon commandos could land on top of a running camel, and he had seen an Omani Royal Guard officer kill a man with a hatpin to the throat, Squires knew that no soldier in the world could *improvise* like a Striker. That was the beauty of the team, why they fit perfectly with Op-Center's mandate to bronco-bust unfolding crises.

Squires hooked the detonator to his belt, slipped on his compact respirator, then drew a flash/bang grenade from his left hip pouch. He slid the pull ring of the grenade over his right thumb, still holding the safety spoon. Then he pulled an M54 lachrymatory gas canister from its pouch and held it in his left hand, his thumb through the ring. When Newmeyer had done likewise, the two men rose slowly, in the shadows, and stood just to the right of the windows of the first and second cars.

SIXTY

Tuesday, 7:53 A.M., Washington, D.C.

"So where is he?"

Hood was thinking those exact words just as Herbert said them.

For several minutes now, everyone in his office had been silent and he'd been replaying the conversation with Orlov in his mind, trying to reassure himself that he hadn't given the Russian anything that could be used against the Strikers. Orlov already knew about both groups, and knew where they were. Hood was convinced, still, that the talk had been about how to defuse the crisis. Orlov could have used his status in Russia long before this to aggrandize himself, if that was what he wanted. He wanted to believe that the cosmonaut was a humanist as well as a patriot.

But his son is commanding the train, Hood reminded himself, *and that outweighs saintly intentions.*

Everyone jumped when Hood's phone

beeped. He punched the speaker button and answered.

"Relay from Striker Honda," said Bugs Benet.

"Let's have it," Hood said, "and please bring up the mission map on the computer. Cut in if General Orlov gets back to us."

As he spoke, the Director slid the phone to the edge of the desk, toward Mike Rodgers. The General seemed to appreciate the gesture.

Honda's voice came through on the secure line, strong and surprisingly clear. "This is Private Honda reporting as ordered."

"This is General Rodgers. Go ahead, Private."

"Sir, the target bridge is in sight and the snows are starting to let up. Three Strikers are present at coordinates 9518-828 to secure the route for retreat, three Strikers are at train, coordinates 6987-572. The Lieutenant Colonel plans to rig the train with C-4, get all the passengers off with flash/bang and tear gas, take the train, and let it blow up farther down the track. He was afraid shrapnel from the boiler might hurt someone. He'll join us at the extraction point when the target has been neutralized."

Hood looked at the grid on the computer screen. The distances involved were tight but manageable.

"Private," said Rodgers, "did the Russians show any sign of standing down?"

"Sir, we didn't see them. The Lieutenant Colonel blew a tree across the track. We heard that. Then we heard the train coming, we heard the brakes, and we heard it stop. But we can't see it from here."

"Any shooting?"

"No, sir," said Honda.

"If it's necessary to get an order to the beta team, can it be done?" Rodgers asked.

"Not without one of us going back," said Honda. "They won't be answering the radio. Sir, I've got to join the others but I'll try and report any new developments."

Rodgers thanked him and wished him well as Hood beeped Benet on the second line. He asked for up-to-the-minute surveillance photos of the site to be sent to his printer as soon as they were received by the NRO. Both Rodgers and Herbert went to the printer behind Hood's desk to wait for the hard copy to arrive.

A moment later, Orlov came back on the computer monitor. He looked more worried than before, and Hood clandestinely motioned for Liz to come over. She stood to the side, out of range of the fiber-optic camera on top, but was able to see Orlov's face.

"Forgive the delay," Orlov said. "I told the Radio Officer to have the train stopped and to get my son on the line, but then the link went dead. I honestly don't know what has happened."

"I've learned that my team put a tree across the track," said Hood, "but I don't believe there was a collision."

"Then perhaps my order was relayed in time," said Orlov.

Hood saw the General look down.

"Nikita is calling," said the General. "Gentlemen, I will be back."

The image winked off and Hood turned to Liz. "What's your impression?"

"Eyes steady, voice a little low, shoulders rounded," she said. "Looks like a man telling the truth and not happy with the weight of it."

"That's how I read him." Hood smiled. "Thanks, Liz."

She smiled back. "You're very welcome."

And then the printer began to hum and suddenly both Rodgers and Herbert looked to Hood much as Orlov had as they watched the first photograph roll from the slot of the digital imager.

SIXTY-ONE

Tuesday, 10:54 P.M., Khabarovsk

Repair of the uplink cable was hampered by the fact that the tips of Corporal Fodor's fingers were numb from the cold. Squatting beside the dish, he'd had to cut away an inch of casing with a pocketknife in order to expose enough wire to twist and poke into the contact. The fact that two of the civilians were watching him, discussing better ways of stripping wire, didn't help.

When Fodor finally finished, he handed the receiver to the Lieutenant, who was standing directly behind him. Fodor's movements were not triumphant, but quick and economical.

"Nikita," General Orlov said. "Are you all right?"

"Yes, General. We're clearing away a tree — "

"I want you to stop."

"Sir?" Nikita asked.

"I want you to call in your command.

497

You're not to engage the American soldiers, do you understand?"

Icy air blew through the window, against his back. But that wasn't what made Nikita cold. "General, don't ask me to surrender — "

"You won't have to," said Orlov. "But you *will* obey my orders. Is that clear?"

Nikita hesitated. "Completely," he replied.

"I'm in contact with the American commander," Orlov said. "Keep the line open and I'll give you further — "

Nikita didn't hear the rest. There was a dull *clunk* on the wooden floor of the train. He turned away from the phone and saw the grenade roll toward him slowly; an instant later it erupted in a flurry of intensely bright flashes and loud pops. The people in the car began to shout and he heard another thud, followed by the hiss of escaping gas.

Even as he drew his pistol and made his way to the door at the front of the car, Nikita couldn't help but think about how clever this was: a flash grenade to make them shut their eyes, followed by tear gas to make sure they kept them shut — but without the optic damage that might have resulted from taking the gas in open eyes in such a tight space.

No permanent disfigurement to take to the

United Nations, the Lieutenant thought angrily.

Nikita guessed that the Americans were attempting to smoke his soldiers out and capture them in order to make off with the money. No doubt the attackers had already scattered, to positions in the surrounding countryside, and it wouldn't pay to send troops after them into the dark. But the commandos wouldn't get him, and they wouldn't get his cargo. As he felt his way through the dark with his left hand, he cursed his father for believing the Americans could be trusted . . . that they, and not General Kosigan, had Russia's best interests at heart.

As he neared the door, Nikita shouted, "Sergeant Versky, cover us!"

"Yes, sir!" Versky yelled back.

When he reached the front of the car and emerged from the rolling clouds of tear gas, Nikita opened his eyes. He saw Versky's men splayed belly-down in the snow, ready to shoot at any sign of enemy fire. Behind him, Corporal Fodor and another soldier were helping the disoriented civilians from the train.

Nikita backed away from the car. He called to a soldier on top who was facing the other side of the train.

"Private Chiza, do you see anything?"

"No, sir."

"How can that be?" Nikita yelled. "The grenades came from that side!"

"No one approached, sir!"

This was impossible, Nikita thought. Those hand grenades were lobbed in, not fired from a rocket launcher. Someone had to have been close to the train, and then it occurred to him that if someone was, there would be footprints in the snow.

His frozen breath trailing behind him, Nikita trudged through the deep snow toward the engine to look on the other side.

SIXTY-TWO

Tuesday, 10:56 P.M., Khabarovsk

Crouched behind a boulder the size of his dad's vintage T-Bird, Sergeant Chick Grey didn't actually see Squires or Newmeyer toss their grenades through the windows of the train. But when the pride of Long Island, Valley Stream's South High School track and field team saw the snow turn from charcoal to magnesium-white, it was as if a starting gun had gone off. He'd already snatched a look at the engine, and now he spun around the boulder, legs churning, body bent low as he raced toward it through the snow. He saw Squires and Newmeyer pull themselves up through the respective windows of their boxcars. He listened for the distinctive sound of the Berettas, didn't hear it, then saw smoke pour from the back door of the second car, then caught a glimpse of Newmeyer bent over the coupling between it and the caboose. A moment later, the red car came free, leaving a soldier firing helplessly from the cupola.

501

Grey felt a rush of pride for what Squires had orchestrated: if no one was hurt, this would be an operation for the special forces time capsule.

Jerk-hole! he thought, and veered to the left, then to the right as he ran. He realized he'd courted doom by anticipating success, and atoned in crude but accepted Striker fashion.

When he was still several yards from the train, Grey saw a flare-cast shadow moving toward the front of the engine on the other side. Someone was coming around and, not wanting to stop, Grey leapt toward the injector pipe that ran perpendicular to the cab, just above the trailing truck. He grabbed it, swung his legs sideways into the window, let go of the pipe, and landed inside, squatting.

The engineer turned in surprise. Grey curled the fingers of his left hand tightly, hardening the outside of his hand, and drove it up under the soldier's nose. He followed that with a hatchet kick, driving the side of his left foot into the man's knee and dropping him to the floor.

The Sergeant didn't want the man unconscious, just cooperative, in case he couldn't figure out how to start the train. But the throttle and floor brake were easy enough to operate, and after kicking the latter so it was in the upward, *off* position, he pulled the vertical throttle toward him from the left. The train lurched forward.

"Out!" Grey barked at the soldier.

The peach-faced young Russian was fighting to get his legs under him but gave up, settling on his knees.

The Striker gestured roughly toward the window. "*Dah — dosvedahnya!*" he said, using the only Russian he knew. "Yes — so long!"

The Russian hesitated, then made a sudden grab for the Beretta in Grey's left hip holster. The Striker cocked his left elbow back hard, into the Russian's temple. The soldier hit the corner of the cab like a fighter caught by a ghost uppercut.

"You dog!" the Sergeant snarled. Pushing the throttle higher, Grey scooped the Russian onto his shoulder as if he were a sack of flour, hoisted him to the window, and dumped him back-first into a passing snowbank. He took a moment to look back and saw Russian soldiers running to try and catch the train. But gunfire from the two cars drove them back, and soon the Striker express was running into the night at three-quarters throttle.

When the train started up, Nikita was just

coming around the cowcatcher. Jumping back off the track, he grabbed the handrail of the ladder behind and above the cowcatcher and walked up the three steps to the platform. Crouching there, his back against the boiler plate, he held his AKR submachine gun tight against his side and watched, with rising anger, as Private Maximich was hurled from the window and the other Americans fired to send his men, the rightful owners of the train, rushing behind trees and rocks for cover.

These are the men my father courted! he seethed as the last of the tear gas curled from the windows and the locomotive picked up speed.

Still crouching, Nikita switched the short-barreled gun to his left hand and stepped two feet up from the platform onto the ledge above the air reservoir. The narrow walkway ran above the injector pipe midway up the boiler, and as he held onto the narrow hand-rail that ran along the top of the engine, the Junior Lieutenant held the short-barreled submachine gun toward the cab.

And as Nikita passed under the steam dome, just eight feet from the cab, the un-suspecting American soldier looked out.

504

SIXTY-THREE

Tuesday, 4:02 P.M., Moscow

Interior Minister Dogin was feeling good. Very good.

Sitting alone in his office for the first time that day, he savored his impending triumph. General Kosigan's troops were moving into Ukraine without incident. There were even reports of expatriate Russians and Ukrainians alike greeting them with Soviet flags.

Polish troops were being moved to the border with Ukraine. NATO and the United States shifted troops from England to Germany and in Germany toward Poland, and there was a blustery show of strength as NATO warplanes flew over Warsaw. But not a single non-Polish troop entered the country on the ground. Nor would they. Not with Russian operatives ready to raise hell in tinderboxes around the world. The United States would watch Russia recover its historic sphere of influence before allowing American soldiers to be spread out in rebellions and invasions from Latin America to the Middle East. Right now, Dogin's emissary in Washington, Deputy Chief of Mission Savitski, was discussing Russian objectives in a closed-door meeting at the State Department. Zhanin's new Ambassador had already had his meeting with Secretary of State Lincoln. By taking the second meeting, the U.S. had unofficially acknowledged that there was a second viable government in Russia, one that needed to be reckoned with. And *Grozny* didn't even have to bomb a city to get that acknowledgment.

Dogin's new political friends had agreed to wait for their money, and President Zhanin was finding roadblocks in the information and command conduits. He could not respond quickly or accurately, and Dogin took pride in how much more effective this was than the failed coup against Mikhail Gorbachev. It wasn't necessary to isolate the leader with guns and soldiers. All one had to do was hamstring his ability to see and hear and he was helpless.

Dogin chuckled contentedly. What could the idiot do, go on the air and tell the electorate that he didn't know what was going on in the government — could someone please tell him?

The Minister's one fear, that Shovich would

get restless with the unexpected delay, failed to materialize. No doubt he had already used one of his fake passports to leave the country, staying on the move like Patton during World War II to confuse his enemies and rivals. Not that it mattered to Dogin where Shovich was. He would be content if the worm remained beneath a rock somewhere.

Thus far, he thought, *the only disappointment has been Sergei Orlov.* The Minister and his allies were trying to make their sick country well, which required circumventing the laws. He had expected an orderly, traditional-minded man like the General to be unhappy with their unorthodoxy, but he hadn't expected him to challenge them by pulling rank on Colonel Rossky. Doing so, Dogin reflected confidently, Orlov had effectively ended his career. He'd quit the Russian line and joined the British 27th Lancers for their ride into the Valley of Death.

Dogin felt bad for him. But Orlov had done his job, helped get reluctant politicians to go along with Operations Center funding because he was a man of integrity and honor. And he would have been allowed to stay if only he'd joined the team.

The Minister looked at the antique maps on his walls, and felt a thrill as he contemplated adding a new-old one, the reborn Soviet Union.

He glanced at his watch, noted that the storm should have passed by now and the money train should be reaching Khabarovsk. He picked up the telephone and asked his assistant to get General Orlov on the line. Once the train's arrival had been confirmed, he would have an airplane sent to meet them in Birobidzhan, the capital of the Jewish region on the Bira River. The Dalselmash harvester factory had a landing strip that would accommodate a medium-sized military aircraft.

The man who got on the line was not the wary but composed officer he'd spoken to earlier. He was surprisingly aggressive.

"Your plan has gone sour," the General said bluntly.

The Minister was suspicious. "Which plan? Has something happened to the train?"

"You could say that," Orlov replied. "As we speak, American commandos are attacking it."

Dogin sat up very straight. "The train was your responsibility — your son's!"

"I'm sure Nikita is doing his best to hold them off," Orlov said. "And the Americans are at a disadvantage. They don't want to hurt our people."

"They would be insane to," Dogin replied.

"Where is Rossky?"

"Chasing spies," Orlov said. "But they eluded him. They caught the man who was tailing them and used his radio to put me in touch with an operations center in Washington. That's how I know about their plan. We tried to work things out."

"I don't want to hear about your failures," Dogin said. "I want Rossky found, and when he is you're relieved of your command."

"You forget," Orlov said. "Only the President can replace me."

"You will resign, General Orlov, or I'll have you removed from the Center."

"How will Rossky and his brownshirts get in?" Orlov asked. "As of now, the Center will be sealed off."

Dogin warned, "They will take it back!"

"Perhaps," Orlov said. "But not in time to help you save your train . . . or your cause."

"General!" Dogin yelled. "Think about what you're doing. Think about your son, your wife."

"I love them," Orlov said, "but I'm thinking about Russia now. I only wish I weren't alone. Goodbye, Minister."

Orlov hung up, and for nearly a minute Dogin sat squeezing the phone. It was impossible to imagine that he had come so far only to be undermined by Orlov's betrayal.

His brow flushed, hands shaking with rage, he set down the receiver and had his assistant call Air Force General Dhaka. The Americans had to have come in by air and no doubt were planning to get out the same way, fast and dirty. He would make that impossible, and if anything happened to his cargo the Americans would have to replace the money — or their soldiers would be returned to them through Shovich, a piece at a time.

SIXTY-FOUR

Tuesday, 11:10 P.M., Khabarovsk

Squires peered through the last, thin puffs of tear gas as they floated to the ceiling and then wound out the window and door. His eyes and mouth protected by gear that already seemed a part of him, his ears alert for danger, he ran to the cases stacked or strewn haphazardly in the rear of the car. He used his lapel knife to pry up the edge of one of the wooden crates.

It was money. Lots of it, the profits of suffering earmarked to cause more suffering.

Instead, he thought, looking at his watch, *in thirty-two minutes it will be confetti.* He and his mini-team would ride the rails another twenty minutes to where the Russians wouldn't be able to reach the train. Then they would hike toward the bridge as behind them, like Sodom and Gomorrah, the two cars of this rotten bank would blow cloud-high. He experienced the flush of righteousness that Americans from Thomas Jefferson to Rosa Parks must have felt, the satisfaction and pride of saying no to something wrong, to someone corrupt.

Squires started toward the rear door of the train. As he was about to enter the second car to check on Newmeyer, his head was wrenched around by the sound of gunfire.

From the engine? he thought. *How can that be?* Grey wouldn't be shooting at anyone now that they were under way.

Calling for Newmeyer, Squires ran toward the front of the car, stepped into the black clouds that fierce winds were pounding down from the smokestack, and felt his way cautiously around the coal tender.

There had only been time for a brief burst, but Nikita knew he'd tagged the American. He'd seen the way his shoulder had jerked back, saw the dark splash of blood on the camouflage whites.

Nikita moved rapidly along the side of the locomotive. It seemed cut off from the rest of the train, which was hidden behind clouds of coal smoke and glittering particles of windblown snow. Upon reaching the cab, he lowered his gun and edged along the injector pipe toward the window.

He looked in.

The cab was empty. His eyes darted from

corner to corner, which were lit by the dull orange coal fire —

He looked up as a dark forehead and then the barrel of a Beretta poked down from the roof of the cab. Nikita dove through the window, catching a bullet in the back of his right thigh as the American sprayed the side of the train with gunfire.

Grimacing, Nikita squeezed his leg with his left hand as blood dampened the back of his trousers. The wound ached as though his thigh were in a tight vise, but what bothered Nikita more was that he hadn't anticipated the American going out the window and over the top of the cab.

The question was, what would he do now?

Nikita got off his back, putting his weight on his left leg, and hobbled toward the throttle. The important thing was to stop the train and buy his troops time to catch them.

His eyes shifted from window to window as he crossed the cab, the barrel of his gun raised, his finger crooked around the trigger. The American would have to come back in to start the train up again, and the only way to enter was by one of the two windows.

And then there was another sickeningly familiar thud and the cab erupted with burning white light.

"*No!*" Nikita bellowed as he shut his eyes

and backed against the rear wall of the cab. The roar of the flash/bang grenades was amplifed by the close quarters and metal walls of the cabin. He pressed his hands to his ears to protect them, cursing his helplessness. He couldn't even fire blindly about the cab for fear of being struck by his own ricocheting bullet.

But it mustn't end this way, he told himself. Staggering toward the front of the cab, Nikita tried to use the side of his left leg to nudge the throttle back. But he was unable to stand on his right leg and, dropping to his knees, he put his left hand on the throttle. Screaming from the pain of the earsplitting blasts, he pulled the throttle toward him only to be pushed away by a hard boot heel. Nikita made a futile attempt to grab whoever was there, but clutched only air and light. He swung the gun to the left and right, hoping to strike flesh, to find his target.

"Fight me!" he screamed. "Coward!"

Then the brightness died and the explosions stopped and the only sound was the loud buzz in Nikita's ears and the banging of his heart.

Peering into the dark, the Lieutenant saw a figure slumped in a corner. The blood had crystallized from the cold, but he recognized the wound, saw that he had blasted several holes in the jacket but only one shell caught what appeared to be the outside edge of a bulletproof vest.

He raised his gun and aimed it at the man's forehead, just above the goggles.

"Don't!" a voice to Nikita's left said in English.

The Russian officer turned and saw a Beretta pointing at him from outside the window. Behind it was a tall, powerful figure dressed the same as the wounded man.

He would be damned if a lawless raider was going to dictate terms. Nikita swung his gun around quickly, intending to shoot whether the other man fired or not. But the man lying in the corner suddenly came to life, locking his legs around Nikita's torso, flopping him onto his back, and holding him there as the other man entered and disarmed him. Nikita grappled with the men, but the pain in his leg kept him from standing or putting up much of a fight. The newcomer knelt on Nikita's chest, pinning him, and used the bottom of his boot to kick the throttle forward, driving the speed of the train back up again. Still camped on Nikita's chest, he pulled off what looked like a rappelling belt and lashed the ankle of Nikita's good leg to a handle just below the window. The Russian could neither reach it nor escape, and for the second time that night he felt ashamed.

The two of them planned this together on the roof of the cab, he thought bitterly. *And I stumbled into it like a sports club novice.*

"Our apologies, Lieutenant," the man said in English as he stood and raised his goggles.

A third man reached the cabin and, after shouting in, was told to enter. He swung in through the window.

The new arrival tended to his companion's wound by the light of the coals, while the other man — obviously the group's leader — bent to look at Nikita's wound. While he did so, Nikita reached out with his left arm to try and push the throttle. The leader grabbed his wrist and the Russian tried to kick at him with his free foot, but the pain was too great.

"They don't give medals for suffering," the man said to Nikita.

As Nikita lay there panting, the leader pulled an empty rope bag from around his shin, used a small knife to cut off the strap, and slipped the band around the blood-soaked leg, just above the wound. He gave it a firm pull. He used another length of strap to bind his hands and tie them to an iron hook on the floor of the train.

"We'll be leaving the train in a few minutes," the man said. "We'll take you off and see that you get medical attention."

Nikita had no idea what he was saying, nor did he care. These men were the enemy, and one way or another he was going to stop them from doing whatever they planned.

His hands behind him, he used his thumb-nail to dig the glass stone from his regimental ring. It had been designed to come free like that. It had also been designed so that a half-inch blade would pop up from beneath the stone when it came out. And with no one watching his hands, he began to saw against the leather strap.

SIXTY-FIVE

Tuesday, 4:27 P.M., St. Petersburg

After making their way through the strikers, Peggy and George had gone to the rest rooms at the Hermitage and changed into the clothes they carried, the Western-style jeans, button-down shirts, and Nikes favored by Russian youth. They folded their uniforms into their backpacks, then walked hand in hand up the large State Staircase to the first floor of the Large Hermitage, the home of the museum's extensive collection of Western European art.

One of the gems of the collection, Raphael's *Conestabile Madonna*, painted in 1502, is named for the city in central Italy that had been its home for centuries. The round painting is seven inches tall by seven inches wide, nestled in an ornate gold frame as wide on each side as the art, and shows the Madonna, in a blue robe, sitting in front of rolling hills cradling the infant Jesus in her arms.

Peggy and George had arrived shortly before Volko was due. Peggy acted as though she was looking at art when she was actually keeping an eye on the Raphael. George, who had never even seen a photograph of the operative, was holding her hand lightly as his eyes ranged from painting to painting. Because it wasn't his wife's hand, he felt guilty enjoying Peggy's touch, the warmth of her fingers against his palm, the feathery lightness of her fingertips against the side of his hand. Thinking about how deadly that hand could be made her touch that much more electric.

At exactly 4:29 Peggy's hand tensed though she didn't break her stride. George glanced toward the Raphael. A man about six-two was walking slowly around the side of the room, toward the painting. He was dressed in loose white chinos, brown shoes, and a blue windbreaker that bulged around a spreading waist. As he neared the Raphael, Peggy squeezed George's hand harder. The Russian cut across the room and was headed toward the right side of the painting, not the left.

Peggy gently tugged George around, then led him slowly toward the door. She hugged his arm now with both of hers, letting him support her. All the while her eyes searched the room, moving slowly instead of darting so as not to attract attention. Everyone else in the room was moving or looking at paintings, all except for a short man in starched brown trousers. His round face seemed out of place here, a dark cloud amid the many sunny, adoring expressions —

Peggy stopped by Raphael's *Holy Family*. She pointed from the beardless Joseph to the Virgin as though discussing them.

"There's a man in brown pants who seems to be watching Volko," she whispered.

"I only saw a woman," George said.

"Where?"

"She's standing in the adjoining room," he said, "the one with the Michelangelo. She's reading her guidebook, facing this room."

Peggy pretended to sneeze so that she could turn away from the painting. She saw the woman, her eyes in her book, though she was holding her head very steady and definitely watching Volko with peripheral vision.

"Good catch," Peggy said. "They've got both exits covered. But that doesn't mean they know who we are."

"Maybe that's why they sent Volko," George said. "They're using him as bait. And he was letting you know that."

A minute had passed and, looking at his watch, Volko began walking away from the painting. The round-faced man began to turn away as Volko approached, but the woman only half turned. The way she was standing, she could still look into the room. The round-faced man stopped.

"Why did she keep watching?" Peggy wondered aloud as she and George wandered over to the next painting.

"Maybe our friend Ronash described us to him."

"It's possible," she said. "Let's split up and see what happens."

"That's crazy. Who'll watch our backs — "

"We'll have to watch our own backs," Peggy said. "You go out behind Volko and I'll go past the woman. We'll meet in the ground-floor main entrance. If one of us gets in trouble, the other gets out of here. Agreed?"

"No way," said George.

Peggy opened her own guidebook at random. "Look," she said quietly but firmly, "someone's got to get out and report on what's happened. Describe these people, break them. Don't you see that?"

George thought, *That's the difference between a Striker and an agent. One is a team player, the other a lone wolf.* In this case, however, the lone wolf had a point.

"All right," he said. "Agreed."

Peggy looked up from the book and pointed to the room with the Michelangelo. George nodded, glanced at his watch, then pecked her on the cheek.

"Good luck," he said, then set off in the direction Volko had headed.

As George approached the round-faced man, he felt a kind of undertow pulling them together. He kept his face averted, searching the crowd for Volko as he entered the Loggia of Raphael, a gallery copied from one of the same name in the Vatican. He didn't see the round-faced man as he walked beside the spectacular murals by Unterberger, nor could he find Volko —

"*Adnu minutu, pazhahlusta,*" someone said from behind him. "A moment, please."

George turned, his muscles tensing as the round-faced man approached. He understood "please," and gathered from the raised index finger that the man wanted him to wait. Where the conversation would go from here, though, he had no idea.

He was smiling pleasantly as, suddenly, Volko came rushing from behind the round-faced man. He'd doffed his windbreaker, which was why George had lost sight of him, and had it stretched tightly between his hands. In one quick motion, he wrapped it around the throat of the round-faced man while he was looking at George.

"Damn you, Pogodin!" he yelled, his own face turning crimson from the strength he put into the attack.

Two security guards from down the hall came running toward Volko, radios pressed to their mouths, calling for support.

"Go!" Volko gurgled at George.

The Striker backed toward the entrance to the Western European gallery. He glanced over his shoulder to see if Peggy would come back and saw that both his partner and the woman were gone. When he looked back at Volko, Pogodin had already drawn a small PSM pistol from inside his jacket. Before George could move, Pogodin had reached around his chest and fired backward at his assailant.

He shot just once and the Russian fell to a knee and then onto his back, blood pooling at his side. George turned away quickly and, resisting the urge to go after Peggy and make certain she was safe, he headed toward the magnificent Theater Staircase and made his way downstairs.

As he departed, George was unaware of another pair of eyes that had been watching from behind an archway at the southern end of the gallery, spetsnaz-trained eyes as sharp and carnivorous as those of a hawk. . . .

SIXTY-SIX

Tuesday, 11:47 P.M., Khabarovsk

It moved like Peter Pan's shadow, an ever-changing black shape barely seen against the dark objects below it and the dark sky around it.

The matte-black, swept-tip rotors and seamless, round-surfaced fuselage of the Mosquito threw off little reflected light and were RAM-coated — covered with radar-absorbing material. The engines made very little sound, and the armored crew seats, shoulder harnesses, lumbar support cushion, seat cushion, seat bucket, and helmets of the two crewmen were also flat black so they wouldn't be seen inside the cockpit.

The helicopter passed without notice over the concrete buildings of small cities and the wood or stone shacks of villages. Inside the cockpit, the radar and full-color topographical displays, working in conjunction with the CIRCE autopilot — computer-imaged route, correction-enabled — helped the pilot adjust to sudden changes, allowing him to avoid other aircraft that might spot them, or to change his course away from peaks that rose higher than the four thousand feet at which it was flying.

A British ship in the Arctic Ocean picked up radio communications from Moscow to Bira ordering aircraft sent to rendezvous with the train. Copilot Iovino's quick calculations using the on-board computer showed that the planes would be reaching the train just as the Mosquito was leaving. Unless the Russians picked up a decent tailwind or the Mosquito slammed into an unyielding headwind, they should get away without being seen.

Unless there was a delay, said pilot Kahrs. In that case, his orders were to abort the mission and head for the Sea of Japan. The commitment of the Air Force to recovering the strike force was not dictated by compassion, but by the size of the Mosquito's fuel tank.

"Coming up," said copilot Iovino.

Kahrs looked at the topographic display. The solid images moved and shifted on the twelve-inch screen, having been mapped by satellites and translated into point-of-view images by Pentagon computers. Objects as small as large tree branches showed up on the screen.

As the helicopter slashed low over a flat-topped hill and ducked down into a valley, the computer map showed the trackbed.

"Going to RAP," said Kahrs — real airspace profile, indicating that he'd be looking out the window instead of using the tactical displays.

Kahrs looked up from the screens and peered through the night-vision sensor, with its wide field-of-view forward-looking infrared scanner. Roughly a mile ahead, he saw a fire in the snow and people strung around it. That would be the off-loaded crew.

He touched a button beside the HUD. All the Strikers carried a locator signal in the heels of their shoes. He scanned for the pulse, which was superimposed on an overhead map. Three beeped red in one area, four in another.

Kahrs raised his eyes higher. Behind high hills in the distance he saw knots of smoke coiling toward the sky. Three of the signals were coming from there.

"Got the train," Kahrs said.

Iovino punched coordinates into a keyboard and looked at the topographic display. "The extraction site is one-point-five miles northwest of our current position. Obviously, the team split up."

"How are we on time?" the pilot asked.

"Fifty-three seconds ahead of schedule."

526

Kahrs began to descend, simultaneously swinging the Mosquito toward the northwest. The aircraft handled like the balsa-wood gliders Kahrs used to throw when he was a kid, slicing the air lightly and cleanly, the silence of the rotors enhancing the sensation.

Clearing the walls of the first of three roughly parallel gorges, the pilot leveled off at five hundred feet and flew due north.

"Trestle sighted," he said as he saw the old iron structure that crossed the three gorges. "Target located," he added when he saw the Strikers at the mouth of the trestle.

"Contact forty-six, forty-five, forty-four seconds," Iovino said after punching coordinates into his keypad.

Kahrs looked toward the southeast, saw the churning smoke of the train.

"I only see four of the six," Kahrs said. "Get the low-down ASAP."

"Roger," said Iovino.

While Kahrs sped toward the target, Iovino watched the digital numbers of the countdown clock on his screen. At seven seconds to contact, he pressed the button that caused the aft hatchway to slide forward into its pocket. That took one second. At five seconds to contact, the Mosquito slowed and he touched a second button that caused a roller arm to swing over and a twenty-five-foot-long black ladder to unroll. It deployed in four seconds, and the Mosquito glided to a halt twenty-seven feet above the ground.

Ishi Honda was the first one on board. Iovino turned toward him.

"Where are the others?" the copilot asked.

"On the train," Honda said as he snuggled into the tight space and helped pull Sondra aboard.

"What are they planning to do?"

"Get off and meet us," Honda said as he and Sondra both reached down to Pupshaw.

Iovino looked at Kahrs, who nodded to indicate that he'd heard.

"What do we gain by meeting them?" Kahrs asked Iovino.

Even before Pupshaw was inside, Iovino was using the computer to calculate the extra fuel it would take to fly to the train as opposed to hovering here and waiting. The one incalculable was when the three Strikers would get off the train, but he had to assume that would be before they arrived.

"We're better off meeting them," Iovino said as he pressed the buttons that caused the ladder to withdraw and the hatch to shut. Those were battery-controlled and didn't cost anything, fuel-wise; an extended ladder with the hatch opened added to the drag to the craft, which did eat into their fuel.

"Let's give 'em a lift," Kahrs said, keeping the Mosquito at twenty-seven feet as he pivoted to the southeast, smooth and delicate as a compass needle, and sped toward the oncoming train.

SIXTY-SEVEN

Tuesday, 8:49 A.M., Washington, D.C.

"What kind of Oil Can Harry operation are you guys running, Paul?"

Paul Hood looked at the puffy face of Larry Rachlin in his TV monitor. The thinning gray hair was plastered neatly to the side, and the light hazel eyes were angry behind the gold-framed glasses. An unlit cigar moved up and down as the CIA Director spoke.

"I have no idea what you're talking about," Hood replied. He looked at the clock on the bottom of the screen. Just another few minutes until Striker was safe, and then two hours after that until the Mosquito was tucked away on a carrier, all evidence of the incursion gone.

Rachlin removed the cigar and pointed with it. "Y'know, that's why you got that job instead of Mike Rodgers," he said. "You got a poker face like Clark Gable in *Gone with the Wind.* 'Who, me, Larry? Running a covert operation?' Well, Paul, despite Stephen Viens's noble attempts to try and tell me a satellite was off-line, we've got some photos from a Chinese sky-spy showing commandos attacking a train. Beijing asked me about it and, unlike you, I really didn't know a damn thing about it. Now, unless some other country has gotten hold of an Il-76T — which the Chinese put at the scene of the crime, and which I happen to know the Pentagon owns — this makes it your operation. The CIC tells my guys they didn't authorize any kind of shooting war over there. They, too, would like to know exactly what you're doing over there. So I repeat: what's going on?"

Hood said casually, "I'm as mystified as you are, Larry. I was on vacation, you know."

"I know. And you came back fast."

"I forgot how much I loathe L.A.," Hood replied.

"Oh, sure. That was it. Everybody hates L.A., so why do they keep going?"

"The well-marked freeways," said Hood.

"Well, how about I ask the President what's going on?" Rachlin said, poking the cigar back into his mouth. "He'll have all the information right there on his desk, right?"

"I wouldn't know," Hood said. "Give me a few minutes to talk to Mike and Bob and

531

I'll get back to you."

"Sure, Paul," Larry said. "Just remember something. You're new here. I've been at the Pentagon, the FBI, and now here. This isn't the City of Angels, friend. It's the City of Devils. And if you try and pull anyone's tail, you're gonna get burned or pitchforked. Understand?"

"Message received and appreciated, Larry," Hood said. "As I said, I'll get back to you."

"Do that," said the CIA Director, using the tapered tip of his cigar to punch off his image.

Hood looked over at Mike Rodgers. Everyone else had left to attend to departmental business, leaving the Director and his deputy to wait for word from the Mosquito.

"Sorry you had to hear that," Hood said.

"No sweat," said Rodgers. He was sitting in an armchair, his arms crossed, his brow creased. "You don't have to worry about him, though. We've got photos. That's why he has to bluster so damn much. He doesn't really carry a lot of weight."

"What kind of photos?" Hood asked.

"Of him on a boat with three women who weren't his wife," Rodgers said. "The only reason the President replaced Greg Kidd with him is that Larry had wiretaps of the President's sister trying to hold a Japanese company up for under-the-table campaign contributions."

"That lady's a piece of work." Hood smiled. "President Lawrence should have given the CIA to her instead of Larry. At least she'd have used it to spy on our enemies instead of on us."

"Like the man said," Rodgers told him, "this is Purgatory. Everyone's an enemy here."

The phone beeped. Hood thumbed the speaker button.

"Yes?"

"Incoming from Striker," said Bugs.

Rodgers jumped over.

"Private Honda reporting in," said a clear voice from a sea of quiet.

"I'm here, Private," said Rodgers.

"Sir, myself, Pups, and Sondra are on board the extraction craft — "

Rodgers felt his gut tighten.

" — the other three are still on the train. We don't know why they haven't stopped yet."

Rodgers relaxed slightly. "Any indication of resistance?"

"There doesn't appear to be," said Honda. "We can see them moving in the windows of the cab. I'll keep the line open. Contact in thirty-nine seconds."

Rodgers's hands were fists and he leaned on them as he stood beside the desk. Hood's hands were folded beside the phone, and he took the opportunity to pray for Striker.

Hood looked at Rodgers. The General raised his eyes to meet the Director's. Hood could see the pride and concern in those eyes, understood the strength of the union between these men, a union deeper than love, closer than marriage. Hood envied Rodgers that bond — even now, when it was causing him so much concern.

Especially now, Hood thought, for those fears made the bond even stronger.

And then Honda's voice came back on, with an edge that hadn't been there moments before.

SIXTY-EIGHT

Tuesday, 4:54 P.M., St. Petersburg

The distance between Peggy and the main entrance of the Hermitage couldn't have been greater if she were still in Helsinki. At least, that was how the English operative felt as she walked briskly toward the next gallery to the south, paintings of the School of Bologna. From there, if she could make it, the walk to the State Staircase was a short one.

Peggy knew the woman was following her and would also have backup, someone who would be watching and reporting back to a command center. Perhaps the one right here in the Hermitage, operating with or without Orlov's approval.

Peggy stopped to look at a painting by Tintoretto, just to see what her stalker would do. She watched her intently, as though she were a fingerprint under a magnifying glass.

The woman paused in front of a Veronese. There was no playacting. She stopped abruptly, obviously, wanting Peggy to know that she was being followed. Perhaps, Peggy thought, the woman was hoping she would panic.

Concentration put two little creases above her nose. Peggy considered and rejected a number of options, from taking a painting hostage to starting a fire. Counterattacks like those invariably brought more forces to the scene and made escape less likely. She even contemplated trying to reach the TV studio and surrender to General Orlov. But she quickly rejected that idea: even if he was willing to arrange a spy swap, Orlov wouldn't be able to ensure her safety. Besides, the first lesson fifth columnists learned was never to box themselves in, and that basement was more than just a box, it was an already-buried coffin.

Peggy knew, though, that she wouldn't be allowed to run for long: now that she and George had been spotted, exits would be closed to them, then corridors, and finally galleries. And then they would be boxed in. Peggy'd be damned if she was going to let the Russians control the time and place of their confrontation.

The thing to do was to blind them until she could get out of here, or at the very least draw their attention away from Private George. And the best way to do that was to start with the art connoisseur on her tail.

Peggy wondered what would happen if she offered herself to the woman in a way that was just too inviting to refuse — before the Russians were all in place and ready to receive her.

Turning suddenly from the Tintoretto, Peggy began walking briskly, nearly jogging, toward the State Staircase.

The woman followed, keeping pace with her quarry.

Peggy hurriedly rounded the corner of the gallery and reached the magnificent staircase, with its walls of yellow marble and two first-floor rows of ten columns each. Starting down the steps, the Englishwoman knit her way through the sparse late afternoon crowd, headed toward the ground floor.

And then, halfway down, she slipped and fell.

SIXTY-NINE

Tuesday, 11:55 P.M., Khabarovsk

It had been two minutes before Squires had planned to stop the train when the Russian officer said, *"Cigaryet?"*

The Strikers had been standing in the cab of the train, securing their gear, when Squires looked down.

"We don't smoke," the Striker commander had said. "It's the new army. You got any on you?"

The Russian didn't understand. *"Cigaryet?"* he said. He used his chin to point to his left breast.

Squires had looked back out the window as the train went into a gentle curve. He slipped down his night vision goggles. "Newmeyer," he'd said, "see if you can help the man."

"Yes, sir," the Private had replied.

Leaving the wounded Sergeant Grey in the corner, Newmeyer had bent over the Russian. He'd reached into the officer's jacket and withdrawn a worn leather packet of tobacco with a thick rubber band holding it closed. A steel lighter with Cyrillic initials and an engraved portrait of Stalin was tucked under the rubber band.

"Must be an heirloom," Newmeyer had said, glancing at the engraving in the ruddy light of the cab.

Newmeyer had then opened the pouch, found several rolled cigarettes inside, and removed one. Nikita had extended his tongue and Newmeyer placed it on the end. The Russian pulled the smoke between his lips and accepted a light.

Newmeyer had closed the top of the lighter and put everything back together with the rubber band.

Nikita blew twin clouds of smoke from his nostrils.

Newmeyer bent close to replace the tobacco pouch. As the Striker had leaned over their prisoner, Nikita suddenly bent forward at the waist, butting his forehead into Newmeyer's head.

With a moan, Newmeyer fell back and dropped the pouch. Sitting up and grabbing it, the Russian used the heel of his hand to cram the pouch and lighter into the gears of the throttle. Then, as Newmeyer made a belated lunge for him, Nikita quickly pushed the iron lever away from him.

The train had sped up as the gears chewed down on the pouch and on the lighter his father had given him. Strips of leather and chucks of steel infused the gears, bending the teeth, locking them in a disfigured embrace.

"Shit!" Squires had said as Newmeyer fell back, holding his hand.

The officer had gone to the throttle and tried to push it in the opposite direction, but it refused to yield.

"*Shit!*" he'd repeated.

Squires had glanced, then, from the Russian's untriumphant expression with eyes that seemed distant, out of focus, to Newmeyer. The Private wasn't even rubbing his head, which showed the beginnings of a nasty bruise. He was crouched with a knee on the Russian's chest and a look of self-loathing.

"I'm very sorry, sir," had been all he could think to say.

Well, hell, Squires had thought. *The sonuvabitch Russian was only doing what we'd have done, and he did it right.*

And now the train was a runaway, building speed as it cleared the curve and headed toward the trestle. There was no time to gather up Grey and the Russian and jump off before they reached the gorge. And they had just about two minutes before the locomotive ceased to exist.

Squires jumped back to the window and peered down the track. On the horizon, he saw what looked like a cloud of locusts in the green glow of the goggles. It was the extraction craft — though it wasn't like any chopper he'd ever seen. From the smooth lines and color he knew at once that it was a low-observable. He was flattered. Even Muammar Gadhafi hadn't rated the debut of a Stealth aircraft, though they'd all been on alert, when Reagan and Weinberger crossed his "line of death" in the Gulf of Sidra and blackened the eyes of Tripoli back in 1986.

The helicopter was coming at them fast and low. The snow had stopped completely, visibility was good, and it probably wouldn't take long for the pilot to figure out that the train couldn't be stopped. The question was, was there enough time for them to be extracted some other way?

"Newmeyer," Squires said, "help Grey to the roof. We're getting out of here."

"Yes, sir," the crestfallen Striker replied.

Rising from the Russian, Newmeyer avoided his oddly detached gaze as he went over to Grey, bent beside him, and carefully hefted the Sergeant onto his shoulder. The barely conscious noncom did his best to hold on as Newmeyer rose. Then the Private watched, more alert now, as Squires twisted the Russian onto his chest.

"Go!" Squires said to Newmeyer, pointing to the door with his forehead. "I'll be okay."

Reluctantly, Newmeyer kicked the door open, pulled himself up onto the bottom of the window, and gently eased Grey to the flat roof of the cab.

Grabbing a fistful of the Russian's hair, Squires reached back, undid the rappelling belt that had kept him on the floor, tied it tightly around his wrists, and walked him toward the door.

SEVENTY

Tuesday, 4:56 P.M., St. Petersburg

When she first saw the spy's surprising twist on the stairs, Valya thought that she intended to shoot her and her instinct was to duck. The Russian started to go down, but when she realized that the spy was falling, Valya checked herself and darted after her. It was always surprising what one could get from a wounded or dying individual. Often their guard was down or they were so dazed that they said things, sometimes important things.

Guests gasped but stood aside as the woman rode down the twenty or so steps on her shoulder, appearing not to hit her head, then reaching the landing with an awkward somersault over one shoulder onto her side. She lay moaning in a fetal position, her legs moving weakly, as visitors gathered around. One called to a guard for assistance, while two others knelt, one of them doffing his jacket and slipping it under her head.

"Don't touch her!" Valya yelled. "Get away!"

The Russian reached the bottom of the stairs and pulled a snub-nosed pistol from an ankle holster.

"This woman's a wanted criminal," she said. "Leave this matter in our hands."

The Russians backed away quickly. The foreigners saw the gun and did likewise.

Valya hopped over Peggy so that she was facing her. Then she looked up at the stragglers.

"I said *leave!*" Valya shrilled, and swept outward with the back of her hand. "Go!"

The last of the gawkers did, and Valya looked back at Peggy. The spy's eyes were shut and her right arm was under her chest, her hand against but under her chin. Her left arm was limp at her side.

Valya didn't care what might be broken or damaged inside of her. Holding the gun under the woman's chin, Valya rolled her onto her back.

Peggy winced, her mouth formed a pained little oval, and then she relaxed again.

"That was an unpleasant fall," Valya said in English. "Can you understand me?"

With apparent effort, Peggy nodded a little.

"You British are dropping like autumn leaves," Valya said. "First I terminated the comic book publisher and his team, now you." Valya pushed the mouth of the gun into the soft flesh under Peggy's throat. "I'll see that you get to a hospital," she said, "after we talk."

Peggy's lips moved. "Be . . . before — "

"No, no," said Valya with a wicked grin. "After. I want to know some things about your operation first. For instance, in Helsinki, what was the name of — "

Peggy moved so quickly that Valya didn't have time to react. She raised the closed fist that had been resting on her chin, the fist in which she held her lapel knife. The blade was pointing down, and Peggy jammed it into the depression above Valya's clavicle and tore inward, toward the larynx. At the same time, she used the elbow of her left hand to push Valya's other arm to the floor, in case the gun discharged.

It didn't. The Russian woman released the gun and grabbed desperately at Peggy's fist with both of her hands, scratching vainly to dislodge the knife.

"What I was going to say," Peggy sneered, "was, 'Before you worry about taking me to a hospital, make sure the fall was an accident!' " She pushed the knife harder and Valya gurgled and slumped to her side. "That agent you killed was *my* autumn leaf," she added, "and this is for him."

"Don't move!" a voice shouted in Russian from the top of the staircase.

Peggy looked up at a slender, ascetic-looking man in the uniform of a spetsnaz colonel. At the end of his outstretched, very steady arm was a P-6 silent pistol. Behind him, still gasping and rubbing his throat, was the man Volko had attacked.

"I'm going to get out from under your friend," Peggy replied in Russian. She turned to her side to throw Valya off. The woman's eyes were shut and her face was white as her life poured haphazardly onto the marble floor.

The Colonel was walking down the steps behind his firearm. Peggy dumped Valya onto her back and rose, her own back to the steps.

"Arms up," the officer said to her. If he felt any remorse about Peggy's victim, she didn't hear it in his voice.

"I know the drill," Peggy said, turning wearily as she started to raise her hands.

When they were chest-high she turned suddenly, holding the snub-nosed pistol she'd picked up when she threw Valya over. There were no tourists in the way as she fired at Colonel Rossky, who stopped where he was, seven steps up, and took her salvo as if he were in a duel. He met it with fire of his own.

Peggy didn't stay where she was. Immediately after firing her short burst, she threw herself to the left, onto the ground, and rolled until she hit the banister.

After several seconds, the echoing gunfire stopped and only a pungent, rising, rapidly thinning tester of smoke remained of the exchange — that, and the crawling red stains on the front of Colonel Rossky's uniform.

The officer's expression didn't change. His breed had been trained to suffer pain in silence. But after a moment the extended arm wavered, the P-6 fell to the floor, and then Rossky followed it, doing a delicate turn as he dropped to his back. His arms splayed, head facing down, the spetsnaz warrior slid to the landing, where he came to a stop beside Valya.

Peggy trained her pistol on Pogodin, who had been crouching at the top of the staircase, behind the ornate newel. She had seen him kill Volko and he deserved to die. But he seemed to read her thoughts, or perhaps saw the promise of death in her eyes, and broke suddenly from the staircase, running back toward the gallery. Peggy heard the distant clatter of running feet; whether it was security, panicked tourists, or even strikers itching for a fight, she had no idea. But as much as she wanted Volko's killer dead, there wasn't time to chase him.

Turning, Peggy tucked the gun inside her shirt and ran down the stairs screaming in Russian, "Help! The killer is up here! He's a madman!"

As security forces pushed past her, she hurried, still shrieking, through the main entrance. There, Peggy quieted as she lost herself among the strikers who had crowded inside, hoping that it wasn't one of their own — or a government plant pretending to be one of their own — who had gone berserk. . . .

SEVENTY-ONE

Tuesday, 8:57 A.M., Washington, D.C.

"They're climbing to the roof of the engine!" Honda said, his lazing-in-the-sun calmness gone, replaced by what sounded to Rodgers like fear or horror. "The thing's going like a torpedo — a runaway, it looks like."

"Can't they get off?" Rodgers asked.

"Negative, sir. The train's just starting over the bridge now, and there's nowhere to exit except straight down a couple hundred feet. I can see Grey — shit! Sorry, sir. Newmeyer just laid him on the top of the cab and followed him up. The sergeant is moving but he seems to be hurt."

"How hurt?" Rodgers asked urgently.

"I can't tell, sir. We're too low and he's lying down. Now I see — I don't know who it is. A Russian soldier, it looks like. He's definitely hurt. There's a great deal of blood on his leg."

"What's the Russian doing?" Rodgers asked.

"Not much. Lieutenant Colonel Squires is handing him out to Newmeyer, holding him by the hair. Newmeyer is trying to get his hands under the Russian's arms. Looks like he's struggling. Hold on, sir."

There was talk in the helicopter, and Private Honda was quiet for several seconds. Rodgers couldn't make any of the conversation out. Then, near the radio, Rodgers heard Sondra say, "Then we'll jettison our clothes or weapons. We'll make up the weight."

Obviously, Squires was planning to bring the Russian onboard and the pilot was justifiably concerned. Rodgers's undershirt began to dampen along his spine.

Honda came back on. "The pilot's concerned about two hundred added pounds and about how long it's going to take us to get them aboard. If he doesn't try to get them, he's going to have a revolt on his hands."

"Private," said Rodgers, "this is the pilot's mission now and he's got a crew to worry about too. Do you understand?"

"Yes, sir."

They were the toughest words Rodgers had ever had to utter, and Hood gave the General a reassuring squeeze on the forearm.

"The Russian's torso is out of the train,"

Honda continued, "but he looks like dead weight."

"But he's not dead?"

"No, sir. His hands and head are moving."

The line was silent again. Rodgers and Hood looked at one another, aborted vacations and who-answered-to-who forgotten as they suffered this wait together.

"I can see the Lieutenant Colonel now," said Honda. "He's leaning out the window and his hand's holding up the front of the Russian's coat. He's motioning — pointing into the cab, moving his finger across his throat."

"The controls are dead," Rodgers said. "Is that it?"

"We think that's what he's saying," said Honda. "Hold on, sir. We're about to make a pass over the train. And then I think . . . yes, sir."

"What, Private?"

With rising excitement Ishi Honda said, "Sir, the pilot told us to lower the ladder. We've got eighty seconds to reel our boys in."

Rodgers was finally able to breathe. And as he took each breath, he watched the numbers of the computer clock flick by inexorably. . . .

SEVENTY-TWO

Tuesday, 11:57 P.M., Khabarovsk

The Mosquito had slashed overhead like a time-lapse thundercloud, dark, powerful, and silent. Squires followed the helicopter with his eyes as it passed the engine and coal tender, then stopped, pivoted 180 degrees, and began inching back toward them.

The ladder dropped fast and straight and Sondra came down several rungs. Holding tightly to one, she leaned back, her arm stretched down, ready to help.

"Come on!" she cried.

"Newmeyer!" Squires yelled over the roar of the engine.

"Sir?"

"Let go of the Russian and get Grey out of here. You too."

Newmeyer obeyed without hesitation. Like any special forces team, the Strikers had been trained to take orders implicitly and immediately in a crisis situation, however those orders went against their instincts or emotions.

Later, when he thought about it over and over, Newmeyer would Monday-morning-quarterback the entire evacuation process, whether he was in bed, drilling, or talking to psychologist Liz Gordon. Now, though, he did what Lieutenant Colonel Squires had ordered.

Releasing the Russian, Newmeyer put his shoulder back under Grey. The helicopter arrived directly overhead as he stood, the pilot coming down a foot to bring the bottom of the ladder level with Newmeyer's knees.

The Private put his foot on the second rung and began to climb. As soon as he was within range, both Sondra and Private Pupshaw reached down to haul Grey in.

Even as she allowed Pupshaw to finish bringing the Sergeant inside, and extended her hand to Newmeyer, Sondra's eyes were on Lieutenant Colonel Squires.

"Thirty seconds!" copilot Iovino called back at them.

"Sir!" she shouted as he tried to get himself under Nikita. "Half-minute warning!"

"Twenty-five!" Iovino shouted.

Squires let go of the Russian's hair, hoisted him onto his shoulder, then sat on the edge of the window. As he struggled to get to his feet, Nikita pushed at him, trying to get back in the cab.

"Twenty!"

"*Damn* you!" Squires hissed, grabbing the back of the Russian's coat as Nikita slumped back into the cab.

Nikita hooked his arm around the handle beside the window and held on tight.

"Fifteen!"

Sondra's face and voice were beginning to show the strain. "Lieutenant Colonel — fifteen seconds!"

Still standing in the window, Squires motioned for the chopper to come over to the side.

The Mosquito edged east and the pilot descended slightly so the ladder was level with Squires. Squires gestured for him to come a little lower.

"Ten seconds!"

Releasing Nikita's coat, the Lieutenant Colonel held onto the top of the train with his left hand, while with his right he unholstered his Beretta, pointed it at the top of Nikita's arm, and fired. The Russian howled, lost his hold on the handle, and fell back into the cab.

Squires jumped in after him.

"No!" Sondra shouted, and scampered down the ladder. Newmeyer ran down after her.

"Five seconds!" Iovino yelled.

"Wait!" Sondra screamed up at him.

The ladder was hanging directly beside the window of the cab. Grunting and swearing, Squires pushed the limp Nikita out the window. Sondra and Newmeyer both got a hand on his coat and yanked him out.

The pilot waited as Pupshaw reached out and helped Newmeyer as the Russian was passed up the ladder.

The Lieutenant Colonel clambered back into the window. The instant her hands were free, Sondra reached toward him. His hand came out —

The first cargo car exploded, followed a heartbeat later by the second. The blasts caused the engine to hop violently, the back end rising higher than the nose, separating from the coal tender, which bucked up, coal flying, and pinwheeled to the west, snapping free of the engine. When it slammed down, the engine was slightly off the track.

"Lieutenant Colonel!" Sondra cried as Squires fell back into the cab and the pilot pushed the helicopter up and ahead to stay clear of the blast. "Captain, don't leave yet!"

The pilot raced north and climbed to keep clear of shrapnel.

"Get back in!" Newmeyer cried to her, his voice cracking.

Sondra's eyes reflected the raging red fireballs as she watched the engine skid forward on the tracks, racing ahead of the blast at an angle, the wheels kicking up sparks and smoke.

"He's still in there!" she said through her teeth. "We have to go back!"

And then the blast-weakened trestle folded under the engine and the stalled, helpless caboose. The collapse seemed surreal, occurring in slow motion and speeding up only when the fires of the explosion caused the boiler to explode. The blast sent pieces of the locomotive flying up, down, and sideways, dark shards riding the red and black fireball. And then all of it, the tracks and iron supports, the shattered train and trailing scarves of flame, tumbled into the gorge.

The fires shrank to flamelets as the Mosquito knifed away through the cold skies.

"No," Sondra was saying over and over as strong hands reached down and grasped her shoulders.

"We've got to bring the ladder in!" Iovino yelled back.

Newmeyer looked down at Sondra. "Come back in!" he cried over the howl of the wind. "Please!"

Sondra climbed into the helicopter, helped along by Newmeyer and Pupshaw. As soon as she was inside, Honda reeled in the ladder and the hatch slid shut.

His expression somewhere short of homicidal, Pupshaw used his first-aid kit to tend to Grey, then went over to the Russian. Except for Nikita's moans, the silence in the Mosquito was awful and absolute.

"He was right there," Sondra said at last. "Just a few more seconds, that's all I needed — "

"The pilot was giving them to you," Newmeyer said. "It was the explosion."

"No," she said. "I lost him."

"That's not true," said Newmeyer. "There was nothing you could have done."

She snapped, "I could have done what my guts told me to — shot the bastard he was trying to save! We made our flying weight," she said bitterly, then turned her glazed eyes toward the Russian. "And if it were up to me, we'd lose even more weight." Then, as though repulsed by her own inhumanity, she said, "Oh, God, *why?*" and turned away.

Beside her, Newmeyer wept into the sleeve of his coat as Pupshaw bound Nikita's arm and leg as carefully and gently as his sorely tested charity would allow.

SEVENTY-THREE

Tuesday, 9:10 A.M., Washington, D.C.

Ishi Honda's voice was thick and slow and weighed on Rodgers from his soul out.

"Newmeyer and Sergeant Grey were rescued from the train," he said, choking, "along with a Russian officer. We . . . we were not able to extract Lieutenant Colonel Squires. He remained — "

Honda stopped and Rodgers could hear him swallow.

"He remained on the train, which has been destroyed. Our mission has been accomplished."

Rodgers was unable to speak. His throat, his mouth, his arms were paralyzed. His spirit, accustomed to the suddenness with which battle could snatch away life, was still deadened by what he'd just heard.

Hood asked, "How is Sergeant Grey?"

"He took a bullet in the shoulder, sir," said Honda.

"And the Russian?"

"Hit in the thigh and grazed in the arm," Honda answered. "Because of the fuel situation, we can't put him down. He'll have to come with us to Hokkaido."

"Understood," Hood said. "We'll sort all that out with the Russian Embassy."

"Private," said Rodgers, his eyes damp, "tell the team that I gave them the impossible to do, and they did it. Tell them that."

"Yes, sir," said Honda. "Thank you, sir. I'll tell them. Over and out."

Hood shut the speaker and looked at Rodgers. "Is there anything I can do, Mike?"

After a moment, the General said, "Can you get them to give Charlie back and take me?"

Hood didn't answer. He just clasped Rodgers's wrist. The General didn't seem to feel it.

"He had a family," Rodgers said. "What do I have?"

"A responsibility," Hood replied softly but firmly. "You've got to hold yourself together so you can tell that family what happened and help them through this."

Rodgers turned toward Hood. "Yes," he said. "You're right."

"I'll call Liz," Hood said. "She can help. She'll also have Striker to deal with when they get back."

"Striker — " Rodgers started, choked. "I

559

have to see to that. If they have a mission tomorrow, someone's got to be ready to lead it."

"Get Major Shooter to start the process," Hood said.

Rodgers shook his head and rose. "No, sir. That's *my* job. I'll have recommendations to discuss with you by this afternoon."

"Very good," Hood said.

Bob Herbert rolled in then, braking his wheelchair and swinging toward the men. He was grinning broadly. "Just got word from the Pentagon this second," he said. "They listened to the Russian aircraft as they flew over the target area. The pilots spotted the off-loaded Russians, saw the wrecked train, and didn't catch so much as a glimpse of the extraction craft." He clapped once, as though his hands were cymbals. "How's *that* for 'low observability'?"

Rodgers looked at him. Herbert's smile froze as their eyes met.

"We lost Charlie," the General said.

Herbert's smile fluttered, then crashed. "Oh, man — man," he said. Lines appeared in his forehead and his ruddy cheeks paled. "Not Charlie."

"Bob," said Hood, "we need you to help us tie this up with the Russians. One of their officers is on the extraction craft. We'd prefer if he could be snuck out of — "

"Paul, are you effin' crazy?" Herbert yelled. He rolled forward menacingly. "Give me a second to swallow this shit!"

"No," Rodgers said in a firm voice. "Paul is absolutely right. We're not finished yet. Lowell has to inform Congress about what's happened, Martha has to work her charms on the Russians, the President has to be briefed, and if the press finds out about this — as I'm sure they will — Ann will have to deal with them. We can mourn later. Right now, we've all got work to do."

Herbert looked from Rodgers to Hood. The red from his face had pooled over his collar. "Yeah, right." He turned his chair around. "Gotta keep the wheels of government spinning, with blood for oil. Nobody did much for me either when I got half blown up. Why should Charlie be any different?"

"Because this is what would have made him feel like he hadn't died for nothing," Rodgers shouted at Herbert's back. "We'll honor Charlie Squires, I promise you."

Herbert stopped and his head slumped forward. "Yeah, I know," he said without turning. "It just hurts like a bitch, you know?"

"I know," Rodgers said quietly as tears finally spilled from his eyes. "I surely do know that."

SEVENTY-FOUR

Tuesday, 4:15 P.M., Moscow

Five minutes after the Pentagon intercepted the communication from the Russian jets to their base, Interior Minister Dogin received a call from Air Force General Dhaka's office.

"Mr. Minister," said the caller, "this is General Major Dragun. The intercept craft you requested found no sign of foreign aircraft. Only military and civilian passengers from the train."

"Then the team must still be down there," Dogin said.

"Moreover," Dragun persisted, "the General has asked me to inform you that a train you commandeered in Vladivostok has been spotted at the bottom of the Obernaya Gorge, east of Khabarovsk."

"In what condition?" Dogin asked, even though he knew the answer. Damn Orlov and his team, he knew.

Dragun replied, "The train has been destroyed, utterly."

Dogin's mouth opened as though he'd been punched. It was several moments before he could draw breath to speak. "Let me talk to the General," he croaked.

"Unfortunately," said Dragun, "General Dhaka is in a meeting with representatives of President Zhanin. It will be quite some time before they're finished. Would there be a message — Mr. Minister?"

Dogin shook his head slowly. "No, General Major. There will be no message."

"Very good," Dragun said. "Good afternoon, sir."

Dogin slashed the cradle with the side of his hand.

It's over, he thought, *all of it.* His plan, his dreams, his new Soviet Union. And when Shovich learned that his money had been lost, his life would be over as well.

Dogin lifted his hand. When he heard a dial tone, he buzzed his assistant and asked him to get Sergei Orlov on the phone.

Or will he avoid me too? Dogin wondered. Maybe the Soviet Union *had* returned, though not in the way he'd expected.

Orlov came on immediately. "I was about to phone you, Minister. There's been a shoot-out in the museum. Colonel Rossky is in very critical condition, and one of his operatives, Valya Saparov, has been slain."

"The perpetrator — ?"

"An agent who came in via Helsinki," said Orlov. "She escaped into a crowd of striking workers. The militia is looking for her now." He hesitated. "Do you know about the train, Minister?"

"I do," said Dogin. "Tell me, Sergei. Have you heard from your son?"

Orlov's voice was cosmonaut-professional. "There has been no communication with the people from the train. I know they were taken off — but I don't know about Nikita."

"I believe he's all right," Dogin said confidently. "There's been so much carnage, like in Stalingrad. Yet one or two flowers always survive."

"I hope you're right," said Orlov.

Dogin took a deep breath, trembled letting it out. "I appear to be one of the casualties. I, General Kosigan, perhaps General Mavik — the ones who didn't stay to the rear. The only question is who will get to us first, the government, Shovich, or the Colombians who gave the money to him."

"If you go to Zhanin, you can request protection."

"Against Shovich?" Dogin snickered. "In a country where one hundred American dollars can buy an assassin? No, Sergei. My fortunes burned with the train. It's ironic, though. I hated the gangster and everything he stood for."

"Then why, Minister, did you ever get involved with him? Why did so many people have to suffer?"

"I don't know," Dogin replied. "Honestly, I don't. General Kosigan convinced me we could move him aside later, and I wanted to believe that — though I never did, I suppose." His eyes ranged over the old maps on his walls. "I wanted this so very much . . . to bring back what we've lost. To return to the time when the Soviet Union acted and other nations reacted, when our science and culture and military might was the envy of the world. I suppose, in retrospect, this was not the way to do it."

"Minister Dogin," said Orlov, "it could not have been done. Had you built this new union, it would have fallen. When I returned to the space center in Kazakhstan last month, I saw the bird droppings and feathers on the staircases, and the boosters covered with plastic that was covered with dust. And I ached for a return to the past as well, to the era of Gagarin and the time when our space shuttles, the Burans, were going to allow us to colonize space. We cannot prevent evolution and extinction, Minister. And once it has occurred, we cannot reverse it."

"Perhaps," said Dogin. "But it is in our nature to fight. When a man is dying, you do not ask if a treatment is too expensive or too dangerous. You do what you feel must be done. Only when the patient has died, and reason has replaced emotion, do you see how impossible the task was." He smiled. "And yet, Sergei — yet I must admit that for a time I thought I was going to succeed."

"If not for the Americans — "

"No," said Dogin, "not the Americans. It was just one American, an FBI agent in Tokyo who fired at the jet and forced us to transfer the money. Think of it, Sergei. It's humbling to think that one unassuming soul changed the world where the mighty failed."

Dogin was breathing easier now. He felt oddly at peace as he reached to the right and opened his top desk drawer.

"I hope you will stay on at the Center, Sergei. Russia needs people like you. And your son, when you see him — don't be too rough with him. We wanted to recapture what we once had . . . and he wanted to see it for the first time, outside the history books. Though the methods may have been questionable, there was no shame in the dream."

Replacing the receiver, Dogin looked at

the map of the Soviet Union in 1945, and continued to look at it through clear eyes as he put the barrel of the Makarov against his temple and pulled the trigger.

SEVENTY-FIVE

Tuesday, 4:22 P.M., St. Petersburg

It seemed strange to General Orlov that the three men who had had such key roles in the day's events — Dogin, Paul Hood, and himself — had conducted their business from desks, had not seen daylight since the crisis began.

Devils in the dark we are, conducting the affairs of men. . . .

There was only one thing Orlov had to do, and he couldn't do it, not yet. Having called General Dhaka's office to request news of his son and the rest of Nikita's command, all he could do was sit and think and wait.

He let his body sink back into the chair, his arms on the rests, hands hanging over the front and seeming to weigh so very much. Orlov had been forced to fight his own countrymen, all of whom loved Russia in their own way, and now the tragedy of what had happened, and his part in it, began to weigh on him.

He bent his head toward his watch,

promptly forgot what time it was. *Why hasn't anyone called?* he wondered. Surely the pilots had been able to ascertain how many soldiers were on the ground.

The beep of the phone startled him, like the hiss of a coiled snake. But it brought him to life and he grabbed the receiver before the first beep had died.

"Yes?" His temple was beating against the earpiece.

His secretary said, "There's a video call for you."

"Send it," Orlov said urgently.

Orlov's eyes were on the monitor as Paul Hood's face came on. The American took a moment to ascertain that it was Orlov he was looking at.

"General," Hood said, "your son is all right."

Orlov's jaw trembled for a moment, then he smiled with relief. "Thank you. Thank you very much."

"He's in the extraction craft," Hood continued, "and we'll arrange for his safe return as soon as possible. That may take a day or two, since he was wounded slightly in the arm and leg."

"But he's all right — in no danger."

"We're taking good care of him," said Hood.

Orlov slumped forward slightly, his body relaxing with the good news. But there was something in the American's eyes, a hollowness in his voice, that suggested something else was wrong.

"Is there anything I can do for you?" Orlov asked.

"Yes," said Hood, "there is. I want you to tell your son something."

Orlov rose attentively on his elbows.

"Your son did his best to resist extraction. I'm sure he thought it was his duty to go down with the ship, or perhaps it was a point of honor not to leave on an enemy craft. But in so doing, he caused the death of my team commander."

"I'm deeply sorry," Orlov said. "Is there anything I can do to — "

"General," Hood interrupted, "I'm not selling guilt or asking for anything. We'll reclaim the remains through diplomatic channels. But my second-in-command was very close to the team leader, and he wanted you to relay something to your son."

"Of course," said Orlov.

"He says that in the Russian folktale 'Sadko,' the Czar of the Sea tells the hero that any warrior can take lives, but a truly great warrior struggles to spare them. Make sure your son understands that. Help him to be a great warrior."

"I've not had great success convincing my son of anything," Orlov said, "but I give you my word, great warriors will grow from the seeds that have been sown here."

Orlov thanked Hood again, and then the General signed off and thought in respectful silence about the nameless, faceless man but for whom his own life and the life of his wife would now be a shambles.

And then he got up from his desk and took his hat from the rack and went outside. Except for the dwindling crowd of protesting workers, the day looked exactly like it had when he arrived, and he was startled to realize that exactly twenty-four hours had passed since he'd arrived for the showdown with Rossky.

Twenty-four hours since the world nearly changed.

And twenty-four hours since he had hugged his wife.

SEVENTY-SIX

Tuesday, 10:00 P.M., Helsinki

It was easy for Peggy to get out of the Hermitage.

When the shots were fired on the staircase, rumors erupted among the striking workers that the Army was coming and the gathering was going to be broken up. The crowd quickly began to disperse, then rejoined almost as fast, like mercury, when police began to rush inside and leaders realized that the gunplay had nothing to do with them. The mass of workers then sloshed toward the Hermitage, clogging the main entrance where there were no longer any guards, walking and tripping inside, causing panic among tourists trying to get out, and drawing the guards back again. They used nightsticks and rigid forearms, hands pressed knuckle-to-knuckle, to protect the art and drive the strikers back.

Peggy left as a panicked tourist.

The day was growing dark, and once outside Peggy made her way to the Nevsky Metro stop. It was crowded with rush-hour commuters, but the trains came every two minutes and, paying her five kopeks, she was able to leave shortly after arriving. From there, it was a short run across the Neva to the Finland Station, which made stops in Razliv, Repino, Vyborg, and Finland.

Private George was already there, sitting on a wooden bench in the waiting room, reading an English-language newspaper, a plastic bag of souvenirs at his side. She watched him after showing her visa and passport at the ticket window and purchasing passage to Helsinki. He would read for a minute, look up and around for a few seconds, then read again.

Once, he looked up for several seconds longer than usual. Not at her, but she was certainly in his range of vision. Afterwards, he got up and walked away with his newspaper and postcards and Hermitage snow globe and other mementoes. That was to let her know he had seen her and wouldn't be watching anymore. Once he was gone, Peggy walked over to the central kiosk and bought English and Russian newspapers of her own, several magazines, and sat down to await the midnight departure of the train.

Security was no tighter than usual at the

train station, events in Moscow and Ukraine obviously consuming the resources and attention of the rank-and-file militia. Peggy boarded the train without incident after presenting her credentials and leave papers at the gate.

The train was a modern one, brightly lit with faux-plush seats in the coach which were narrow but soft, to make unsophisticated travelers think they're riding in high style. Though Peggy couldn't stand the ambience here or among the crushed red and yellow velvets of the lounge car, neither her aesthetic disapproval nor the pressure of the last few hours showed on her relaxed features. Only when she was in the airplane-style rest room, checking her clothes and flesh for spots of the dead woman's blood, did she allow herself a moment of release.

She leaned on her hands on the stainless-steel sink, shut her eyes, and said in a voice below a whisper, "I did not go to seek vengeance, but it's mine and I'm comforted by it." She smiled. "If there's parole in the afterlife, sweet love, I promise to be on my best behavior to get from where I'm going to where you've surely ended up. And thank Volko. What he did for us should put him at the feet of God himself."

Several times during the journey, Peggy

bumped into Private George, though the two of them didn't speak other than to say "Excuse me" when they passed in a snug corridor. Though they had been able to get out of Russia, that was not to say there weren't spies on the train who might not have a good description of them and would be looking at couples or watching men and women traveling separately. For that reason, Peggy spent as much time as possible hovering around a group of Russian soldiers in the lounge car, contributing comments now and then to suggest that she was one of them and even allowing one of them to come on to her to give her a guardian angel if she needed one. Upon reaching Finland shortly before dawn, she gave the soldier a false phone number and address as the two passed through customs. A verbal declaration was sufficient to get Peggy through, though the Russians were treated to a thorough hand-luggage search.

Peggy and Private George fell in side by side as they walked briskly into the street. The Englishwoman squinted into the sun as it poked its orange crown into the new day.

"What the hell happened back at the museum?" George asked.

Peggy smiled. "I forgot, you didn't know."

"No, I didn't. I kept imagining that scene

in *The Guns of Navarone* where the woman spy bought it."

"I pretended to trip down the stairs," Peggy said. "When the woman showed her hand by running after me, I had to cancel her. I used her gun on a spetsnaz officer who seemed to feel that he could take a few bullets and still wring my little neck. He couldn't. There was a lot of confusion after that, and I just slipped out."

"They'll never make a movie out of your life," George said. "No one'd believe this."

"Life is always more interesting than the movies," Peggy said. "That's why they have to make the damn things forty feet high."

The two chatted about possible departure plans, George deciding that he'd take the next flight he could get on, Peggy saying that she wasn't sure how or when she was going to leave Helsinki — that all she wanted to do right now was to walk and feel the sun bake her face and avoid any closed space that reminded her of a midget submarine, the backseat of a car, or a cramped train.

The two stopped walking in front of the Finnish National Theater. They looked at one another with warm smiles and soft eyes.

"I confess I was wrong," Peggy said. "I didn't think you'd be up to this."

"Thanks," George replied. "That's encouraging, coming from someone with so much more experience, someone so much older."

Peggy was tempted to throw him on his back the way she had when they first met. Instead, she offered him her hand.

"The face of an angel and the soul of an imp," she said. "It's a good combination, and you carry them well. I hope to see you again."

"Ditto," he said.

She half turned, stopped. "When you see him," she said, "the chap who grudgingly allowed me to join you, thank him."

"The team leader?" George asked.

"No," said Peggy. "Mike. He gave me a chance to take back some of what I lost."

"I'll tell him," George promised.

And turning to the sun like a moth to flame, Peggy walked down the empty street.

SEVENTY-SEVEN

Friday, 8:00 A.M., Washington, D.C.

An overnight rain had left the runway at Dover Air Force Base in Delaware damp and misty, reflecting the mood of the small group that had gathered to meet the C-141 transport. Standing beside an immaculate honor guard, Paul Hood, Mike Rodgers, Melissa Squires, and the Squires's son, Billy, were of one heart, and that heart was bleeding.

When they had arrived in the limousine following the hearse, Rodgers had thought that he should remain strong for Billy. But now he realized that apart from being unnatural, it was impossible. When the cargo hatch was opened and the flag-draped coffin was rolled out, tears warmed Rodgers's cheeks and he was as much a boy as Billy, anguished and in need of comfort and despairing that there was none to be had. The General stood at attention, enduring as best he could the sobs of Lieutenant Colonel

Squires's widow and son to his left. He was glad when Hood came from his right to stand behind the couple, the hem of his trench coat billowing slightly in the wind, his hands on their shoulders ready to offer words or support or strength or whatever was necessary.

And Rodgers thought, *How I have misjudged this man.*

The honor guard fired off their guns, and as the coffin was loaded onto the hearse for the ride to Arlington, and the four of them stood alongside it, the spindly five-year-old Billy suddenly turned to Rodgers.

"Do you think my daddy was afraid when he was on the train?" he asked in his pure, little-boy voice.

Rodgers had to roll his lips together to keep from losing it. As the boy's big eyes waited, it was Hood who squatted in front of him and answered.

"Your dad was like a police officer or a firefighter," Hood said. "Even though they're all afraid when they face a criminal or a fire, they want to help people and so they pull bravery out of here." He touched a finger to the lapel of Billy's blazer, right over his heart.

"How do they do that?" the boy asked, sniffling but attentive.

"I'm not sure," Hood replied. "They do it in a way that heroes do."

"Then my daddy was a hero?" asked the boy, obviously pleased with the idea.

"A great one," said Hood. "A superhero."

"Bigger than you, General Rodgers?"

"Very much bigger," Rodgers said.

Melissa put an arm around Billy's shoulder and, managing a grateful smile at Hood, ushered him into the limousine.

Rodgers watched Melissa as she climbed in. Then he looked at Hood.

"I have read — " he started, stopped, then swallowed hard before he began again. "I have read the greatest speeches and writings in human history. But nothing ever moved me the way you just did, Paul. I want you to know that I'm proud to know you. And what's more, I'm proud to be serving under you."

Rodgers saluted Hood and climbed into the car. Because his eyes were on Billy, the General didn't see Hood wipe away a tear as he followed him in.

SEVENTY-EIGHT

The following Tuesday, 11:30 A.M., St. Petersburg

Paul Hood, his wife, and their two children took a long walk in the park off the Nevsky Prospekt before separating — Sharon and the children to watch a group of schoolchildren play soccer, Hood to sit on a bench by an ancient tree, where a short man in a leather flight jacket was feeding breadcrumbs to the birds.

"It's odd to think," said the man in clear, comfortable English, "that creatures of the sky must come to earth to feed and build nests and raise families." He swept a hand across the sky. "You'd think there would be a place for them up there."

Hood smiled. "From up there, they get a special perspective on things down here. And that's quite a lot, I think." He looked at the man. "Don't you, General Orlov?"

The former cosmonaut scrunched up his lower lip and nodded. "It is, at that." He

581

looked at the new arrival. "How are you, my friend?"

"Very well," said Hood.

Orlov pointed across the park with a half-torn piece of bread. "You brought your family, I see."

"Well," said Hood, "I sort of owed them the rest of a vacation. This seemed like a very good place to take it."

Orlov nodded. "There is no place like St. Petersburg. Even when it was Leningrad, it was the jewel of the Soviet Union."

Hood's smile warmed. "I'm glad you agreed to see me. That makes this doubly rich."

Orlov looked down at the bread and finished tearing it up. He scattered the pieces and brushed off his hands. "We have both had quite an extraordinary week. We thwarted a coup, stopped a war, and we have each had a funeral — yours of a friend, mine an enemy, but both of them ends that came too soon."

Hood looked away and sniffed down still-fresh sorrow. "At least your son is well," he said. "That's helped to make this endurable. Perhaps all of it will have been for something."

"With luck, that will be so," Orlov agreed. "My son is recovering at our apartment here in the city, and we'll have several weeks to talk and mend old hurts. I think he'll be more receptive to me than in the past, what with the wounding of his spetsnaz mentor and the court-martial of Generals Kosigan and Mavik. I hope he'll see that it takes very little courage to run with vandals." Orlov reached into his jacket. "There's something else I hope," he said as he pulled out a slim, old book bound in leather and stamped on the cover and spine with gold lettering. He handed it to Hood.

"What is it?" Hood asked.

" 'Sadko,' " said Orlov. "It's an old copy — for your second-in-command. I've ordered fresh editions to be distributed among the troops here in St. Petersburg. I read it myself and found it quite stirring. It's odd that an American should be the one to point out to us the richness of our own culture."

"Perspective," Hood repeated. "Sometimes it's good to be a bird, sometimes it's good to be on the ground."

"Truly," said Orlov. "I've learned a great deal from all of this. When I accepted this post, I thought — perhaps you did the same — that I would spend my time the way a supply officer does, filling intelligence needs for others. But I realize now that it's our responsibility to put these resources to good use. Indeed, when my son returns to duty,

I'm going to assign him to a special force whose job will be to hunt down that monster Shovich. I'm hoping, in fact, that our two operations centers can collaborate on that."

Hood said, "It will be an honor, General."

Orlov looked at his watch. "Speaking of my son, I'm joining him and my wife, Masha, for lunch. We haven't done that since I was still flying rockets, and I'm looking forward to it very much."

He rose, and Hood did likewise.

"Just keep your expectations on the ground," Hood said. "Nikita, Zhanin, you and I — we're all just people, no more, no less."

Orlov clasped his hands warmly. "My expectations will always be up there." Orlov pointed by raising his brow. Then he looked past Hood and smiled. "And despite what you may feel, teach your son and daughter to do likewise. You may be surprised at how things work out."

Hood watched as Orlov left, then turned and glanced toward the corner of the park where Alexander and Harleigh had been. He saw Sharon standing alone, and he had to search for a moment before he spotted his children. They were playing soccer with the Russian youths.

"I may be at that," Hood said aloud.

Pushing his hands in his pockets, he took a last look at Orlov, then walked with a light step and lighter heart to his wife's side.

ABOUT
THE CREATORS

Tom Clancy is the author of *The Hunt for Red October, Red Storm Rising, Patriot Games, The Cardinal of the Kremlin, Clear and Present Danger, The Sum of All Fears, Without Remorse,* and *Debt of Honor.* He is also the author of the nonfiction books *Submarine, Armored Cav,* and *Fighter Wing.* He lives in Maryland.

Steve Pieczenik is a Harvard-trained psychiatrist with an M.D. from Cornell University Medical College. He has a Ph.D. in International Relations from M.I.T. and served as principal hostage negotiator and international crisis manager while Deputy Assistant Secretary of State under Henry Kissinger, Cyrus Vance, and James Baker. He is also the bestselling novelist of the psychopolitical thrillers *The Mind Palace, Blood Heat, Maximum Vigilance,* and *Pax Pacifica.*

We hope you have enjoyed this Large Print book. Other Thorndike Press or Chivers Press Large Print books are available at your library or directly from the publishers. For more information about current and upcoming titles, please call or write, without obligation, to:

Thorndike Press
P.O. Box 159
Thorndike, Maine 04986
USA
Tel. (800) 223-6121 (U.S. & Canada)
In Maine call collect: (207) 948-2962

OR

Chivers Press Limited
Windsor Bridge Road
Bath BA2 3AX
England
Tel. (0225) 335336

All our Large Print titles are designed for easy reading, and all our books are made to last.